THE
SCRAELING

Chronicles of The Scraeling.
The Second:

THE
SCRAELING

— a story of England after
the Conquest

M J Burr

Printed in the United States of America.

First Printing 2018

ISBN: 978-0-473-45055-7

Acknowledgements

Every effort has been made to trace ownership of the map entitled 'The Fens 1070-1086', but without success. Anyone who can assist with this is invited to contact the publisher at the above address.

Cover design by Fletcher Mancer of Mimic Technology, New Plymouth, New Zealand.

Layout by DIYPublishing.co.nz

This work of fiction draws heavily upon historical figures whose actions and philosophies were as I depict them. Any resemblance to any living person is coincidental.

For my son

Rob

who is much more like The Scraeling than he thinks.

Also by MJ Burr

An End of Honour – a novel of Titokowaru's War.

Look Away, Dixieland.

Chronicles of The Scraeling
The First: The Landwaster – a story of Harald Hardraada.

Prologue

Constantinople, 1080.

*I*t's only proper that the scriptorium of a monastery should lead a man to reflect upon the manner of God's design for His creatures, for the shelves around me are filled with the writings of the fathers of the Church on the ways of God as they have discovered them. Sometimes, though, I know surprise at His design for me.

Between the years of my youth and that in which I attained fifty years of age I dwelt as much in the future as in the present, and I took some pride in the reputation I had amongst men for foresight, for being hard to surprise, for deviousness and even for downright cunning. Those attributes, and I worked hard on acquiring them, were as important to me as my equally hard-won skills with sling, bow and throwing-knife.

My usefulness to Harald Sigurdsson, known to all the world as Hardraada the Landwaster, rested on my reputation in all these things, but in chief upon my knowledge of the ways of men and the world, and of how both could be bent, at need, to his will were sufficient thought only given to ways and means. That knowledge led the dread lord of the North to single me out as 'the most dangerous little bugger alive' in a company that, for thirty years, included some of the most unscrupulous, violent and fearsome pagans who ever walked the earth to the embarrassment of its Creator.

Hardraada may even have been right for, as my readers know, I spent those years secretly working, planning and scheming to bring an end, not only to the Landwaster, but to the world of violence and savagery that had made him what he was. I sought and purposed not only Hardraada's end, but the end of the Viking world itself. That came on a sunny September day, in a meadow outside the English city of York, when I delivered the greatest army ever to leave the ice-lands of the north to utter destruction on the axes of the terrible hus-carls of

Harold Godwinsson, king of England.[1]

In that way I fulfilled my vow to the memory of the holy women who had been mothers, aunts, teachers and guardians to me, the pitiful cripple once shut away by his family in the convent on which Hardraada's wolves had descended in my fifteenth year. Aye, in a night of pillage, rape and slaughter that haunted my nightmares for years after.

With the fulfilment of that vow, my vengeance was complete. I set myself then to offer my services to a new king of Norway; to build a world that would replace the one I had torn down, and I looked to do so in the company and love of Elisabeth, my golden woman who was once Hardraada's queen before the Landwaster flung her to me in disdain when her company no longer served his ends.

But then I watched my world collapse, even as I rejoiced in the end of the viking scourge as God had led me to wreak it. It was long before I could accept His design as it was revealed to me. But now, living high above the ancient waterway that sparkles in the distance and pondering the pathways of the life that has led me here, I say that truly are God's ways mysterious in bringing light from the darkness that often confounds our hopes and dreams. More, the slamming of one door may resound enough to open another.

For, from the ashes of my life in the convent came a world freed of the viking curse and blessed by the shining purity of the love that Elisabeth and I shared. And, from the ruins of my service to the new king of Norway the countries of Scandinavia did, indeed, gain a new beginning. Finally, from the long-past days of my servitude and deceit I gained a son of whom any man might be proud.

But, lest I outrun my story, let me tell it as I lived it; as it was told to me, as it has been written, and as my knowledge of men and the world they make persuade me that it occurred.

Read, then, the story of The Scraeling and marvel at the hand of God in it.

---

1 *See 'The Landwaster'.*

England
circa 1070

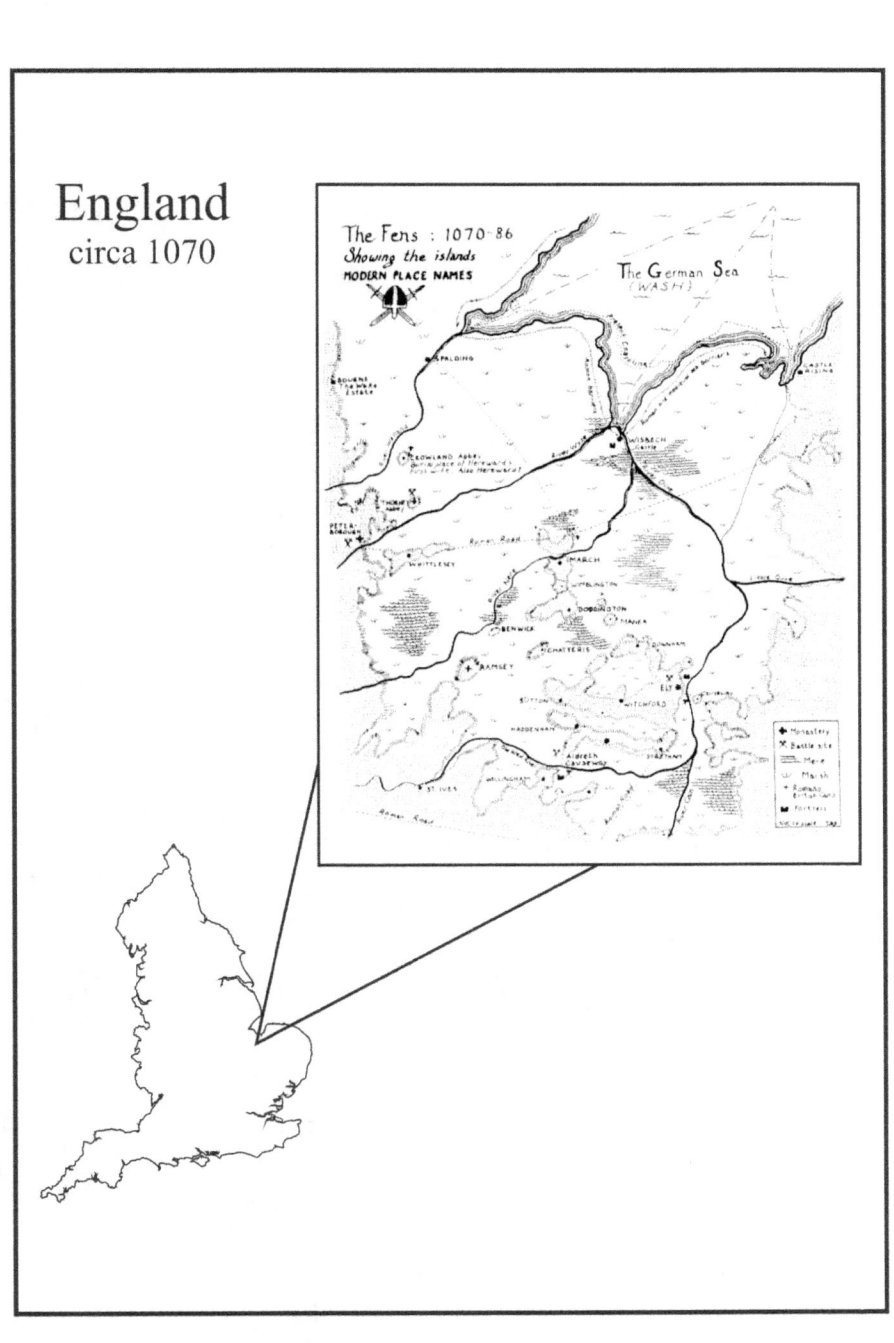

The Fens : 1070-86
Showing the islands
MODERN PLACE NAMES

The German Sea
(WASH)

Senlac Ridge, Hastings, East Sussex, 15 October 1066.

*M*instrels and poets might write of the thin drizzle of an October dawn being tears for yesterday's fallen, thought the young warrior as he picked his way among the mounds and heaps of the slain. As far as he was concerned, though, the misty rain was nothing but a nuisance – just another cross to bear on top of the stench of his days-old and soiled underclothes and the weariness that consumed him, flesh, bone and soul, after the short and fitful night's sleep in his mail at the edge of the Senlac battlefield.

"Jesu!" came a voice from his right, "I'd give half the land the duke's offering, for a couple of day's sleep. 'Slong's I can have it now."

The first warrior tried to spit from a mouth that was still dry from his awakening. "You've got to be alive to be tired, Odo" he said, "so look happy. None of these buggers do." and he fumbled at his belt for a water-jack. What a dreadful place a battlefield was the day after, he decided as he swirled the tepid water round inside his mouth before swallowing gratefully. Yesterday had been noise and fury, charge and retire, hack and slash, thrust and parry amid the screams of stricken men and gutted horses from early morning until the twilight, but at least there had been movement, purpose, life and comradeship among the men who had assaulted the ridge and those who awaited them at its summit. Most of all there had been blood hot with the determination to do it to the enemy before he did it to you, but now there was nothing.

And nothing disturbed the early morning where a near-vanquished army dozed, mortally weary and licking wounds that had nearly proved fatal, and nothing disturbed the heaps of the slain where the other army slept its last sleep in ruin and death. Across the field the only things moving were the half-dozen in helmet and hauberk stumbling out to search among the slain for the body of a king. "Find me Harold" had been the duke's command, "and mark the spot, for I will raise an abbey on it in thanksgiving."

"Shouldn't be so difficult, Leo. We all saw the Fighting Man banner yesterday. Some of us saw too bloody much of it" Odo's voice broke in, and the warrior fought back the waves of tiredness to answer him.

"Won't help, Odo" he said, "Ponthieu brought that in last night as a gift for the duke."

"Didn't help him explain why he cut into a dying man's crotch though. William's expelled him from the army. Fucking silly 'f you ask me. A dead Saxon's a good Saxon, an' the duke was glad enough t' send Ponthieu in after Harold in the first place rather than go himself, eh?"

"Jesu!" exclaimed Leo, darting a glance all around. "That mouth of yours Odo! Shut it, would you? No, no, I don't want to talk about it – just shut it! It's dangerous!" And he moved away as swiftly as his aching legs would allow, uphill to the ridge that ran across the top of the field; the ridge that had been held to the last the day before and the one along which he had himself ridden in charge after charge once his destrier had scrabbled its way to a toehold on the flat ground.

Here the dead lay in even thicker heaps, Saxon *hus-carl* and Norman knight indistinguishable in their helmets and hauberks, and he paused a moment while the roar of battle filled his head as it had filled his world the day before in this very place. Then his world had been the reach of the lance from his destrier's broad back until the sweep of an axe had lopped its darting head from the shaft so that he smashed the ash staff down upon a snarling face and reached ...

There – yes, there. Further along the ridge than he remembered. Had his *hus-carls* been trying to get him from the field? No matter. It was Harold all right – or all that was left of him, and Leo shook his head as he looked at the remains – mere meat, hacked worse than anything he had seen in the shambles stalls of Rouen. The headless torso gaped open in a tremendous chest wound and the slit in the hauberk that allowed a mailed man to mount a horse was lost in the welter of black and dried blood that had burst from the groin after the passage through cloth, flesh and muscle of the sword hard-swung from the high Norman saddle. *You wouldn't butcher a pig that way*, thought Leo, feeling his own groin contract involuntarily.

He shook his head again and reached for the water-jack to wet his lips before he took the horn from his sword-belt to send a note pealing through the drizzle. The searchers made their way to the horn as quickly as their own stiffness allowed and stood a moment silently looking down before

Leo's gruff suggestion that they get on with it brought the offer of the only cloak they had between them.

What was left of the last Saxon king of England was hefted onto the cloak, and as it was swung clear of the surrounding carnage one of the searchers whistled. "Look at him" he commented, nodding sideways. "Care to face that?"

'That' was a huge *hus-carl*, well over six feet in height and lying five yards from his king with a dead hand still fast around the haft of a four-foot double-headed axe. His face was clotted with his own blood, and a shaft standing from the right eye-socket revealed how he had died.

"I did" said Leo into the silence. "His name's – his name was – Penda. That blood on his leggings isn't his, either. When he took the head off my lance, he'd turned from over there – aye, that pile of our dead's due to him – to face me. He must've been wading in fucking blood. No jest. Wading in it."

"Jesu!" said Odo. "Some axeman, to take the head off a lance. You're a lucky man to be standing here then. How'd you manage it?"

"I hit him with the stump" said Leo, his eyes far away, "and threw his aim off. Still, the blow he struck took my horse's leg off clean as a whistle, right through the shoulder– and it screamed, threw me and bolted somewhere on three legs. All the while he was bellowing his name to rally his own kind, and all I could hear as I hit the ground, trying to get my sword out, was 'Penda! Penda! Penda!'" He shuddered at the memory.

"Thought I was done, and no error" he said. "When I stopped rolling – no shield, no sword, no helmet, no breath after I hit the ground – I saw him against the sky. And – believe this or not; I don't care – he held his hand, waiting for me to get up. Aye, he did."

One of his companions whistled. "Fuck – what then?"

"Then" said Leo slowly, "I got to my feet, clawing for my blade. Scared shitless too, and I don't mind who knows it. He was like a mountain standing there – a mountain who'd just cut the leg off a warhorse and made it look easy. He whirled up that axe, and took a step towards me, and . . . and I pissed myself. I'm not joking."

"But then his head snapped back and he screamed. And I saw why. The arrow was sticking out of his eye and he was swaying there like a tree in a gale, one hand to his face but the other still round that fucking axe. Then something hit me from behind and I fell over again. I think it was one of Count Eustace's four, 'cause then they were past us and into the group round Harold. I must've bounced off someone's leg, or his shield or ... whatever."

"So you saw Harold go down?" asked one of the group and Leo shook his head, his exhaustion coming in waves.

"Not really – couldn't tell one from another, and every fucking bell in the world was ringing inside my head by then. But I remember being glad I didn't have to face that monster. All I could think of last night, and what kept me from sleeping was, if he hadn't stopped; if he'd stepped forward to take me on the ground – Christ Jesus, I would have and no mistake – if he'd taken me on the ground, the arrow would've missed. And he'd be alive and I wouldn't. Aye, Penda. *Vale*, my friend."

He shook himself and stooped to the corner of the cloak. "Now come on. Let's go and see if new kings are more generous than old dukes used to be. Eh?"

The royal Court of Norway, Nidaros, January 1067.

"It's important to begin as you mean to go on, majesty' said the Scraeling doggedly. "Look – please excuse my presumption, but I'd be doing less than my duty to you and the throne if I didn't point out that you're a young king, and therefore vulnerable." He paused, aware that Magnus' brows had come down.

"And that" he said hastily, for this was Hardraada's son he faced after all, "that'll lessen over time. Of course. But at the moment – at the moment I say – everyone's waiting to see which way the Landwaster's successor will jump, and that's why things are dangerous."

"Who's 'everyone', lord Ranulf?" asked the king, his free hand scratching the ears of the huge wolfhound that had been his father's. "Who in particular?"

"The jarls of the north" said the Scraeling promptly. "Our Icelandic 'allies' for another. And outside your majesty's realm – Svein Estrithsson, King of Denmark. And he's perhaps the most dangerous of all."

"I think I see where you're going" said the young king, "but please talk me through your thinking, lord Secretary."

"Well" began the Scraeling, "Svein ended the wars between himself and your father profoundly lucky to have hung onto his throne. Only your father's decision to pursue . . . ah, other avenues of foreign policy, prevented . . ."

"You mean his idiotic pursuit of the English throne, don't you?" broke in Magnus, and the Scraeling spread his hands in deference.

"We must always remember, majesty," he said, "that things seem different viewed within their proper time and, ah . . . context. At the time, the Danish wars had served their purpose in uniting the land and providing practice for the army, and so . . ."

"Yes, yes, very well" said Magnus. "So, what's changed?"

"A great deal has changed" said the Scraeling, hoping that Magnus' question was a rhetorical one. *Jesu – he can't be serious. Can he?* he thought.

Aloud, though, he said "To begin with, the loss of your majesty's father, King Harald, and nine out of ten of Europe's most formidable army with him – that's changed many things. Now Svein's the most powerful man in Scandinavia. In fact, given that Scotland's in its usual state of turmoil and the Bastard of Normandy's hanging on to England by his fingernails and eyebrows, it's probably not stretching the case to suggest that at this moment, Svein commands the greatest military force between here and the kingdom of France. Even though the arse is still hanging out of his breeches."

That brought a snort of laughter from the others in the room and Magnus joined in. "And how d'you see Svein?" he asked, "Leaving his breeches out of it?"

The Scraeling pursed his lips. "He's had time enough to rebuild since your father let him off the hook" he said. "But I never saw him as an ambitious man, not in all the dealings I had with him on Norway's behalf. However – and this is important, majesty – things were very different then, and I'm sure those in this room who served King Harald then will agree with me." There was a buzz of agreement and the Scraeling continued,

"For a start, he was only a petty king then, and he knew it, for all his bluster. He was lucky to avoid death in battle several times, and nothing he did contributed to our king's decision to break off the war. Well, all that's changed too, majesty. As far as Svein's concerned, I'd say that what we need to do is offer him assurances of our neighbourly intentions towards him – show him he's no need to fear us, open trade negotiations – that sort of thing."

"If he's half as shrewd as he ought to be, lord Ranulf, he'll have worked out already that he's no need to fear us, surely?" returned the king, and the Scraeling nodded.

"A point well made, sire" he acknowledged. "I believe that, militarily, Norway hasn't been as low as this since King Harald returned from the Rus. Styrkar, here –" nodding towards the marshal of Norway "– can tell us about that in detail. But you see, that's just why we should bend every effort towards starting off a trading relationship. Trade is what the Danes're good at, and they're greedy buggers – pardon me – so especially if the terms of that trade were to favour them – oh, not obviously, but pitched in such a way that the potential was there for them to exploit us just a bit – they wouldn't miss the chance, and they'd enjoy it. And they'd want to keep *that* going as long as they could, so . . . I'm sure you can see the benefits. All of the benefits."

Styrkar shifted in his chair and eased the shoulder that had taken a sword-cut in the retreat from Stamford Bridge. "I'd agree" he said. "Scraeling's right. We'll come again, majesty, but we need a breathing-space, and Svein's turn to gloat a little – well, that'll give it to us. But Scrae— lord Ranulf, can you work out those terms of trade you mentioned? It'll take a bit of doing. I mean, we'll need to balance Svein's greed against our merchants' losses and that. I'd not know where to begin."

"But I do" said the Scraeling confidently. "Been thinking about it for a while. We'll work something out, never fear."

"Very good" said Magnus. "And do you have something worked out for the northern jarls and Iceland too?"

Again the Scraeling spread his hands. "Well majesty" he began, "now you mention it, why . . ." But the rest of his words were lost in the hoot of laughter that swept round the long table.

"Knew it" chuckled Styrkar to his neighbour, "Old One-Eyed Skallagrim was a good friend of mine. He c'd never make up his mind whether the Scraeling was more'f a cunning little bastard or a dangerous little bastard. But one thing he did know, he allus said, was he was glad the Scraeling was on his side."

If only you knew thought the Scraeling, who had heard the remark. *I was never on Skallagrim's side for one moment of one hour of one day of the thirty years I suffered him. But I won in the end, and if I have anything to do with the new Norway, it won't be long before I have you so bound about with restrictions, Styrkar, you'll take up fishing for a living and give up war-making forever. There's been altogether too much of that, and I'm just the man to put an end to it, so laugh while you can, marshal of Norway, laugh while you can. Fuck you and your warmongering both. Your day is over.*

"Well" came back Magnus, "since lord Ranulf's been giving the matter some thought, perhaps we can leave the matter of the jarls and our Icelandic friends until the next council meeting. Till then?" and as the table arose, he added, "Lord Ranulf, a word if you please . . ."

The Chronicle.

*I*n fact, I played up the menace of Svein, who was actually a man I admired and liked. All courtiers do, because proving their indispensability guarantees their employment. And it was the time to do so, for the lost battle of Stamford Bridge had decimated the biggest viking army that had ever left Scandinavia.

No, I'm wrong there – decimation takes away only a tenth, and Odin's ravens had called nine-tenths of the Landwaster's last host. Aye – three hundred ships had sailed to England, and thirty had sufficed to bring the survivors home. The ice-lands were stripped, purged and laid bare of warriors and leaders alike. Women farmed the land and boys fished the seas, and if there was a home in Norway, Orkney or Iceland that had escaped the loss of a father, son or husband – I didn't know of it. And I would have known of it, for among my other duties I had been Hardraada's secretary, a job whose functions were as loose as the word implies.

But I felt I could offer something to fill such a void for, though a man with only one sound leg might neither farm nor fish, I could do things much more valuable. Magnus, the Landwaster's elder son by Thora Thorbergsdotter was, I'd always felt, a disappointment to his warrior father for he was sickly and inclined to be studious. He had little idea of how to deal with the kingship that had been thrust upon him in the wake of his father's death, for his appointment as regent of Norway had been nothing but a formality in everyone's mind.

His brother Olaf was little more fitted to become king, as Hardraada's daughters by his first wife, Maria and Ingigerd, had been the apples of their father's eye even though their mother, Elisabeth, was regarded merely as another piece of treasure he had brought home from Kiev. In consequence the two boys had

little knowledge or experience of the craft of kingship, and it was there that I saw
the part I might play in making Norway the friend of all and the enemy of none.

But a sheepfold with a neglectful shepherd only invites the wolf. I could think
of several – both within and without – who would covet the throne of Norway if
they saw it weakly held, so my advice to King Magnus Haraldsson was designed
to alert him to that.

That night.

"All I have to do" said the Scraeling into the mass of golden hair that cascaded over his face, "is to play Magnus like a fish until he comes to depend on me and my advice, and we'll make a better Norway and a better world."

"Is it truly so easy, darling?" asked Elisabeth drowsily, "he can't be stupid. Neither of his parents was. Unspeakable perhaps – in fact, unspeakable definitely, and Thora still is – but both had quite a lot of animal cunning."

"True, my love," admitted the Scraeling, "but Magnus isn't his parents' son in all things. He's been frail physically all his life – quite remarkable when you consider the giant of a man his father was, and Thora – well, she's nothing if not possessed of hearty appetites."

"In every imaginable way" agreed Elisabeth. "But if she wasn't the rutting animal she is, darling, perhaps Hardraada would have held on to me and then . . ." her voice tailed away.

"And then" the Scraeling finished, pulling her towards him and his hands moving, "we wouldn't be able to do this . . ." but Elisabeth giggled and pulled away.

"Hold on, my man, hold on. First things first – what exactly is it you're trying to do with Magnus? And what's his frailty got to do with it? You know, there's lots I can do to help my man because I get on well with so many of the ladies of the Court. Not Thora, of course, but she spends so much of her time in drink that no-one respects her anyway. But – I need to know what the Scraeling's about, darling, so I can say the right things, and argue the right way, and suggest the right suggestions, and start conversations I want to go places and stop those that should be stopped. You know . . . that sort of thing, my love."

"You're amazing" said the Scraeling in genuine admiration. "I sometimes forget you grew up at your father's court. Didn't miss much, did you?"

"Being royal isn't an excuse for being stupid, dearest" said Elisabeth, lifting her face for his kiss. "So – tell me all about it."

So the Scraeling told her what he had sworn on the way home from the bloodiest repulse of northern arms in the history of Scandinavia, when he and Olaf, Magnus' brother, had brought home just one in ten of the huge northern fleet that Hardraada had led from Nidaros in the previous September to win the kingdom of England.

"Standing there facing a drizzling Scottish day with Orkney just a smudge ahead of us" he said, "I was mindful of the king I had left in Riccall. Not Hardraada, but Harold of England. I promised him, when I turned down his offer of becoming Chancellor of England, that I would use whatever influence I had in the new Norway for good rather than ill, for peace rather than war. I would turn *drakkars* into merchantmen and pirates into traders, and I would use what *drakkars* remained to us to guard, from Orkney, England's northern flank against Scots and Normans alike."

He paused, and a world of sadness was in his next words. "That was before Harold lost a battle he needn't have fought, of course. And now the Bastard rules in England – if he can hang onto it – and Harold's dead, and I'd wager my cousin Penda with him, because the big ox survived one lord on a battlefield, and that's one more –" and his voice caught a moment – "more than a Saxon *hus-carl* is sworn to do." Elisabeth stroked his face in a gesture more eloquent than any words could have been, and the Scraeling pressed her hand to his lips before continuing.

"But that needn't turn me from my purpose. We can still make a land here that honours truth and justice and fairness. A people who trade rather than take. A nation that fights only when it needs to, and not when it wants to. That was the way of Ulf and Haldor and Skallagrim, and the Landwaster. War was a matter of policy for them – the way to do things. Well, Elisabeth my love, not again. Not in my lifetime. Not by all I hold holy, and that starts with you my golden beauty. Never, never, never again."

Elisabeth leaned forward across the pillow and kissed his eyelids. "You've got beautiful eyes, my love" she said. "And such long curling eyelashes. Wasted on a man. But – what's your policy got to do with Magnus' frailty?"

The Scraeling chuckled. "Typical woman" he said. "Two conversations at once – but since you ask – the key to settling the northern jarls is face-to-face contact between them and Magnus. They have to see that he's their king. But not in the way Hardraada did – that was all about being on hand to crush dissent, to punish disobedience, to take from the disfavoured and give to the favoured. None of that; not any more."

"Magnus needs to show Norway he's about fairness, justice, truth. And he'll do that by visiting all parts of his realm, at least in the first instance. Then he'll insist that the outlying jarls come regularly to court in return, so he can 'consult' them. That way he'll control them physically and they'll stay out of mischief, because the royal court will be where the good things are to be had. Oh, he'll give them power all right. Just as much of it as he – or we – deems wise. But any amount of power, however little, will be two or three times what they got under your late husband, you see?"

"But as we agreed, he's not strong. The sheer burden of meetings, councils, travel – all of that – will take its toll of him. I, with those I'll nominate to the king, will need to do the bulk of that actual work and he'll need to content himself with opening and closing councils, distributing royal favours and appointments, charming nobles into seeing it his way – that sort of thing."

"And all the time he – and we – will be preaching the way of justice, fairness and truth. In the end, my love, we'll change the old ways. And in our lifetime. Promise . . ."

Elisabeth lifted a head still golden in her forty-fifth year and smiled at the man she had chosen eighteen years before in the depths of her misery as the unloved queen of a new and alien land. "I believe you, lord Secretary. It's clear we stand on the edge of new ways. But some things from the past are worth keeping and shouldn't be changed even in the strength of all your convictions. Had my lord thought of that?"

The Scraeling's brow furrowed. "Ah . . . not sure, dearest. What exactly d'you mean? What things?"

"Well" said Elisabeth, her hand moving smoothly between them to elicit a startled gasp, "there's this for a start. That shouldn't change, no matter what, and I'm glad to see it hasn't. And then" she said, sliding across his torso, "don't forget this one of the old ways either . . ."

"Oooohhh!" said the Scraeling faintly, "those things. All right then, quite right . . ."

London, January 1067.

"That's the way it's going to be" said William Fitz Osbern. "Because it's the way the king wants it. But more than that – it's the only way to hold a land where we're outnumbered by dozens to one."

"Oh come on" said Fitz Gilbert, holding out his cup to be filled, "We've killed the Englishmen who really matter. At Hastings we got three Godwinssons, all their *hus-carls*, the nobles, the thegns – the ones who matter, just as I say. Cut the head off a viper and it's not dangerous any more, surely."

"You're not quite right there, Richard" said Mortain, and the others fell silent. Robert of Mortain, like Fitz Gilbert a half-brother to William, Duke of Normandy who'd been the new king of England for the past three months, seldom spoke but when he did he was listened to. Tonight he was in an expansive mood.

"You're forgetting people like Morcar and Edwin, the northern earls – we'll need to put them away, my water tells me. Probably the sooner the better, too."

"You reckon they're a threat?" returned Fitz Gilbert. "And them not even turning up for the battle? They'd rather have us than the Godwinssons is what I've heard."

"Don't believe it" advised Fitz Osbern, picking up the wine flask in his turn. "The north's for the north, and most of 'em spit when you mention the word 'English', even if *all* of 'em spit at the word 'Godwin' though. No – scratch a Northumbrian and he'll bleed viking. Just like we used to in Rollo's day."

"Umm. Well, you're the scholar, William" conceded Fitz Gilbert. "But the Duke's crowned – the leading men of England've submitted, aye?"

"The leading men of *this* part of England've submitted, granted." said Mortain. "But as William said, those other bastards see things as they want to see them. Put it another way – they held back from what they call 'Senlac', aye. You were there – we all were. Would we've won if the northern earls – the Danelaw they call 'em – had turned out to support Harold? Hey?"

Fitz Gilbert frowned. "What're you saying?" he demanded.

"Just this" returned Mortain, "How much trust would you put in two of your vassals who turned their backs on your call? The northern earls weren't worth a pinch of shit to Godwinsson, perjured bastard though he was, mind you, and they'll be worth less to us. You mark my words – we'll need to go in there one day, and go in hard, too. No getting away from that."

"But for the rest" said Fitz Osbern, seeing the first signs of truculence in a Fitz Gilbert who'd had a cup too many, "the king's policy of intermarriage's the right one."

"Why?" said Mortain, who had caught Fitz Osbern's drift and Fitz Gilbert's mood.

"English see it as the right way to go" said Fitz Osbern. "Why they did it themselves in Wales – made widows then married them. Godwinsson himself cut the head off some Welsh rebel with a name I can't get my tongue around, then married his widow."

"That right?" muttered Fitz Gilbert. "Wonder what they talked about on their wedding night?"

"Doubt if they talked at all" returned Mortain. "You didn't meet Godwinsson when he came to Normandy, did you? No, you'd have been on the way back from the Holy Land then, I think."

" 'S right" said Fitz Gilbert, "what about him?"

"A real charmer" said the other. "Birds out of trees, horses from their stalls, women into bed. Or up against a wall, if there was one handy. Good-looking bugger too. But a real womanizer through and through."

"That why Ponthieu cut his nuts off on the field?" sniggered Fitz Gilbert, and Mortain's face closed.

"Some things're best left alone" he said shortly, "and that's one of them. No, brother Richard, just accept it – intermarriage is the king's way of settling us in among the Saxons with the least grief. We'll never hold this land by force 'cause there aren't enough of us to hold it and Normandy too, so we're going to do right by them as they see it. Then, if they cut up at any time – we've got an excuse" he said, drawing a thumb across his throat. "But we're going to be legal. We're going to be in the right. Get used to it."

"Fair enough" said Fitz Osbern soothingly. "But we're a bit ahead of ourselves. There's a long way to go before the king c'n carve up England on any basis. We've beaten Godwinsson, had the south acknowledge William as king, and had him crowned. Not bad for three months' work, but there's three *years'* work ahead of us, I reckon, before we can even get close to calling this place ours. Three years at least."

Reading, England, the same month.

The boy raised his voice to announce his arrival before ducking inside the hut and pulling the door shut behind him to keep out the biting winter wind that had pushed him the half-mile from the manor house.

The man who sat whittling by the fire jumped to his feet as the newcomer flung back the cloak and exclaimed, "Master Osmund! Does Lady Gytha want for something then?"

The boy smiled and brought a wicker basket from under his cloak. "No, Garth, my mother wants for nothing. But thank you. She's sent me with this for you and yours, in fact, so – here. With our gratitude, as always" and he held out the basket of bread, meat and eggs. "How's your shoulder today?"

"Well enough, master, well enough thank'ee. Got my grip back – well most of it, an' the rest day by day like enough. See" and he held out what he had been whittling.

The boy Osmund took the small piece of wood and turned so that the fire, the only light in the gloomy hut, fell upon it. "An axe" he said. "In fact, my father's axe by the knob at the end of the shaft, yes?"

Garth nodded. "Aye, master. Your father's axe. Can't seem to get him – or it – out of m' head these days. Not that I wants to, o' course. But seems every night I fall to sleep an' me head . . . m' head's full o' what it were like on that ridge. You know, in the afternoon what were gettin' so dark, an' the Normans gatherin' below the ridge – "

He paused as the door flew open again and a cloaked woman and two children entered as hastily as had the boy, to draw up short as they saw his presence. "Oh Master Osmund!" said the woman, "Master Osmund, we wasn't expectin' –" but the boy held up a hand.

"No, Aelfgifu, you couldn't have known. Mother sent me here with these –" and he waved towards the basket on the rough table that was the major piece of furniture in the room, "and I was just asking Garth how his shoulder is. Hello Algar, hello Annis" he smiled at the young twins, who shyly buried their faces in the stuff of their mother's long woollen skirt.

"Oh bless you, master Osmund, and bless Lady Gytha too!" exclaimed Garth's wife, "that's ever so generous! I'll say an extra prayer for her in her illness, so I will!"

Osmund smiled a smile that lit up a face grave for a thirteen-year-old. "Thank you for that, Aelfgifu. God knows, not much that's good has happened to any of us since my father went away in September, but my mother is improving at last. But Garth was telling me about . . . about his carving. Say on, Garth . . . if you would?"

Garth nodded and recounted the tale that Osmund had heard a hundred times already. And that he was prepared to recount a thousand times more, if need be, for the comfort it brought a boy whose world had collapsed at Senlac when his beloved father had honoured the oath of a *hus-carl* either to bring his lord safe home from the battlefield or to die upon it with him.

"'Twere the end o' the battle; we all knew that 'cause it were getting dark. And we all knew if we c'd get the king through to dark and off the field, well, we c'd fight another day 'cause northerners'd be coming down the London road, an' the London men with 'em. An' we were tired, lord Osmund, so tired you'd not believe it . . ."

He paused, and his eyes were on that field of desperation far away to the southeast. "Been all day, y'see, an' we shoulda been able to stand there in the shield-wall for all'f it, 'cause we held the top. The ridge, like. An' horses won't charge uphill – not an' into a wall'f spears. Too clever for that are horses, aye."

"But them fyrdmen . . . they ran downhill after some of the French who broke on the shield-wall, see, an' the Norman cavalry chopped 'em up and rode 'em into the ground. An' maybe that gave the Bastard the idea, 'cause he did it again. Twice more. An' the last time . . . the last time left us too thin to hold the wall. And once them Normans got onto the flat ground at the top've the ridge, master, well then 'twere mounted men against foot. Aye." Osmund saw the tears sparkle in Garth's eyes and the boy laid a hand on his arm.

"Can't blame the *fyrd*, Garth. They're farmers. Not trained men like you. Can't blame them."

"Can't I, lord Osmund? Can't I? Buggers never listened t'the trained men among them, did they? An' they did it three times, master. Three times! Why they . . ."

"Garth, Garth" came Aelfgifu in almost a whisper as she bustled around the table, and Garth drew a deep breath.

"Aye, love. Sorry, lord Osmund, but in me head I . . . I knows that, hadn't been for us losing the high ground . . . c'd've held until night right enough, an' then . . . then the king. . . an' your father, God rest him . . ."

"Tell me about my father, Garth. Please. Tell me how he fell."

Garth passed a large hand across his face and laid it across the boy's smaller one where it still lay on his forearm. He drew a ragged breath and said, "We wasn't the only ones thinkin' 'bout the dark. There was a . . . they stopped, like, jus' for a moment before they came again . . . an' lord Penda, he says 'Garth, look there.' An' where he pointed, master, there was the Bastard hisself an' four Normans – oh aye, I knew who he was, right enough, for he'd ridden up an' down in the morning with his helmet off to show hisself to his men. Anyway, 'twas him right enough an' I saw him stand in his stirrups an' point at us where we stood under the banners, the Fighting Man an' the Wessex Dragon."

"An' your father lifts his voice an' calls on all around to pick up a shield an' form a wall 'cross the ridge where the slope ran off downhill. An' 'cause he was Penda, and men loved him for what he was, all them who could – *fyrd*, *hus-carls* whose lords were down, anyone – picked up what they could find and went forward with him."

"'We hold this brow' called lord Penda, 'we hold this brow to keep the horsemen of the Bastard from our king, and we hold it till dark. Simple enough? Even for you farmers, hey?' But he smiled as he said it, an' they laughed back and said, 'Show us how the Emperor's *varangers* do it then, big Penda, an' we'll show you how the farmers of Wessex reap Normans!'"

"Then your father turned to me and said, 'Time for the axe, man of mine, for I need your shield and long spear on the end of this wall and not before me as it has ever been. God keep you, Garth, and send us both home after this day.' He held up his hand an' . . . an' I clasped it, and he turned away callin' some jest to the farmers, to take his place in the centre of their line.' And the tears were back now, running unchecked down his face.

"And the four Normans? What of them?" asked Osmund, not because he didn't know but because Garth needed a moment.

"Them? They held back" came the answer after that moment, "but they sent in as many's the ridge would hold ahead of 'em. Just as lord Penda foresaw – the four were for the king's banners, an' the others were to take us first an' blow us aside. An' they never had too much trouble, master, for a man on horseback's already five foot up in the air. But we did what we could before our line broke."

And he told of the desperate struggle to prevent the Normans getting a foothold on the level ground of Senlac Ridge. Of how the line had shuddered and bent five or six times, to straighten miraculously but each time a little more slowly, under Penda's urging and his desperate feats of valour with the hissing, whirling axe, until it eventually bent, bent . . . and splintered into a dozen confused and separate fights. Of how Garth had driven his eight-foot spear in under a lifted sword and through the Norman armpit under it. And of the crushing impact of the mace that had struck him on the helmet while he was doing it – "Helmet your father made me wear, master" – to slide down to cause first numbness in his shoulder and then such fire that he had lost consciousness.

"Rain woke me" he said, his eyes far away, "rain in m'face, lord Osmund. Couldn't see nothing. Thought I was blind, but m'helmet was driven down over me eyes. Didn't know about my shoulder till I tried lifting a hand to the helmet, like. Then I knew. Jesu did I know."

Daylight had long gone, but a watery moon that promised yet more rain had been sufficient for him to drag himself bit by bit to his knees, and his reward for that had been to retch helplessly at the pain coursing from his broken shoulder. Slowly and agonisingly he fumbled one-handed at the neck lacings of the viking *byrnie* that had been his lord's gift to him together with the helmet, until he had opened the shirt halfway down his chest, then he drew several deep breaths to nerve himself to lift his dangling left arm and lodge the wrist in the neck of the mail shirt. The effort was nearly too much for him, but he fought through the waves of dizziness that threatened to overcome him until, using his teeth and the fingers of his right hand, he had secured the useless limb in place with the leather byrnie laces.

"Then I scratched round, master, an' found a spear. Not mine – I c'd see mine, still where I'd left it, like. In that bloody Norman, an' him fuckin' stark—"

"Garth! The children!" came Aelfgifu's voice and Garth lifted a hand.

"Sorry m'dear. Sorry. Anyways, lord Osmund. I used spear to get to m'feet an' went looking for lord Penda. An' I found him at last – nearest man to King Harold, he was, lyin' there where the Dragon of Wessex'd been. Your father took an arrow in the eye, lord Osmund. No man bested him. Well, who could? He died a warrior's death, keepin' the Bastard from his king an' his land, an' it took some coward wi' a bow an' a lucky shot to fell him. But it . . . it would've been quick, master. Dead before he hit the ground."

And Garth had wrestled the ring from Penda's finger for his widow, fought to his feet again and stumbled away from that place of the dead and those who slept as the dead. At daybreak, chance had guided his footsteps to the advance scouts of the London contingent which had come up a day too late, and they had taken him, delirious by then, in a hastily-improvised horse-litter back along the London road.

"It's taken a long time to mend, Garth. Your shoulder." said Osmund, and Garth shook his head.

"Gett'n better day by day, young master. There's plenty worse off'n me. An' see – I'll have that finished by tomorrow" he said, holding up the carving.

"Garth, have you offered lord Osmund anything? Food? Drink?" asked Aelfgifu, and Garth looked stricken.

"For shame, Garth! Where are your manners?" cried his wife.

Osmund held up a hand. "Thank you, Aelfgifu, but I can't stay. I like to light the candles with my own hand. Father used to do that, and . . . and it'll be time to do it when I've run home. If I go now, that is. But thank you. Another time!"

"Perhaps day after t'morrow? When you come for this whittlin'? 'Less you want me to bring it up t'the house?" asked Garth, and the boy's face lit up.

"For me? Truly? Oh thank you, Garth! That's . . . that's . . ."

"That's no more'n the lord of this manor deserves, lord Osmund. Our thanks to you and your lady mother for the food. Ah, daylight's goin' fast, young master."

"Aye. Till the day beyond tomorrow, Garth. Thank you. Thank you . . . for all. Farewell." And he was gone.

"That boy's heart won't never mend" muttered Garth, half to himself, and Aelfgifu sighed.

"Aye. He loved lord Penda like no other, the poor love. Yet you were talking of his father, and he spoke only about your shoulder. He'll be as good a lord as Penda one day, you'll see."

"If he gets the chance" growled Garth. "Who's to know who'll rule in the big house by time he's of age?" And he stretched out his big arms to drag Algar and Annis to him in an embrace that was more about protection than love.

The royal apartments, Nidaros, Norway, February 1067.

"We've asked you here, lord Styrkar, as one of the few men left to us who were prominent in the land under our father, Harald III. We prize your opinion and value your counsel the more highly because of that."

Fuck me, thought Strykar, *is this really the Landwaster's pup talking? Kingship's got to him – he didn't sound as if he had a fire-iron up his arse even a month ago.* Aloud, he said, "I'm just a simple soldier, majesty, who served your father best he could and who'll serve you the same – if I have your confidence."

"Indeed you do, lord Styrkar, indeed you do. But soldiers as senior as you, we've noticed, are rarely simple. On the contrary – you didn't become marshal of Norway under our father by being simple in any wise, we think."

Granted thought Styrkar, *I became marshal of Norway by putting the skids under Haldor Snorreson when I let Hardraada know I thought he was a bloody forgiving king to put up with Haldor's criticisms and insults. I couldn't get past Haldor myself, so I had Hardraada move him over for me. Anyway – who's this fucking 'we'? Magnus an' the Holy Ghost?*

"Kind of you majesty, but any other talent I've got's only what I've picked up from your father's other servants – and your own, of course."

"Well, lord Styrkar, one of those servants of our father is whom we want to ask about. Tell us – what's your opinion – your candid opinion, that's why we're here tonight – of lord Ranulf?"

Styrkar puffed out his cheeks. "The Scraeling, majesty? Your father's secretary. His top planner, organiser, adviser and all-round cunning man. Worth his weight in gold to your father. Handy man on a battlefield too. He's not a warrior as we know warriors – his leg shows that. But with weapons of his choice, he's deadly. I've seen him in action, once with a bow at sea cleaning up pirates – no, twice with a bow – in, aye, Miklagaard too – and once with a sling somewhere in Greece, I think. Don't think anyone who saw him pick off the Bulgar leaders'll ever forget it. Aye, men follow him – why, majesty, may I ask?"

Magnus waved a hand. "Kings need to bear in mind not only counsel, but those who offer the counsel, Styrkar. We are not our father, and it may well be that the counsellors of our father may not . . . suit us in these very different times."

Odin's balls! Styrkar kept his face immobile with an effort. "Majesty, I advise you to think very carefully, and then again, before getting rid of the Scraeling. I soldiered with your majesty's father from Shepetovka to Stamford, an' I know how much the Scraeling was to him and to us all in those years. Your father relied on him – we all did – and never was he found wanting."

"Quite, quite, lord Styrkar. Nothing we have said either states or implies that we intend to rid ourself of lord Ranulf's services, but as we have said, we are not our father and different counsellors will doubtless serve different ends. You, now, are rather different – it would be foolish indeed to disturb the smooth working of our army, for it and it alone stands between us and he who was, only four years ago, our most dangerous enemy."

Magnus leaned forward, as if he wanted to take Styrkar into his confidence. "Lord Styrkar, we have no hesitation in telling you that Svein of Denmark disturbs our sleep of nights, and that the problem he poses may call for a solution which goes beyond the one suggested by lord Ranulf." He leaned back again and smiled.

"But your assessment of lord Ranulf is what we wanted, and you have given us that. We thank you, and bid you goodnight . . . servant and trusted friend."

Styrkar bowed and left, doing his best to look like a simple soldier, but his mind was whirling. *New times need new counsellors?* Right then, where'd that leave . . . *one of the few men left who'd served under his father*, eh? But again, his hint that it would be . . . *foolish to disturb the smooth working of the army* . . . was a plain enough statement that the trusted friend could count himself safe in the future.

And what was that future? *Buggered if I know* he thought, *'cept it probably doesn't involve the Scraeling*. Pity about that. The Scraeling was a good man, and Styrkar had genuine admiration for his cunning and his courage; two of the three virtues that Norsemen prized above all others. Still – virtues or no virtues, Styrkar didn't esteem the Scraeling enough to stand in front of him if Magnus wanted him removed.

Styrkar didn't esteem anyone enough for that.

At the same time in London.

"Look, I'll make it as simple as I can" said the new king of England, and he rose to his feet and began to pace with his head down and hands clasped behind him. Those who knew William recognised the signs of the volcano building within the former Duke of Normandy and lowered their eyes.

"Everything we know about the English tells us what stubborn people they are. They're convinced each one of 'em is as good as the next. They've got a form of vassalage, but nothing like ours. Very well. If we simply take them over – assuming for a moment that we had the men – we'll have to hold them down for your lifetime and mine because they'd nurse their grievance until Judgement Day, right?"

He paused to lift his bullet head and scowl at his chief vassals around the table. Four months short of his fortieth birthday, the Conqueror – as even his enemies were beginning to call him in preference to 'The Bastard' – was a commanding figure whether in council chamber or on a battlefield. He had grown up surviving intrigue, evading assassination, fighting revolt and betrayal to become the foremost horse-soldier of an age that knew little of the art. The force of his will was palpable and summed up in the powerful shoulders and the long-reaching cavalryman's arms that bulged with muscle, even in repose.

"Besides – and we shouldn't lose sight of this – His Holiness didn't license us to pillage this kingdom. Money's not, and never was, the point of what we've done. What we did was visit God's wrath on a usurper who'd spat on his honour and God's law. So God punished him, through our arms, and because we did that, we need to give this country leadership. And that's what we'll do – and because we haven't got the men to do it any other way, we'll do it theirs, and through their leading men. Such as . . ."

Oh very neat thought FitzGilbert, looking down at his hands where they lay clasped in front of him. *And I'd wager you even believe it too.* Like all of them he was only too well aware of his half-brother's strict morality and his propensity for telling himself that since he did God's work on a daily basis, all who challenged him not only mocked God but would surely pay a high price for it.

" . . . of Northumbria. The archbishops of Canterbury and York – "

Stigand? Good God, that bugger's in league with the Devil himself. Why,

Aldred of York crowned Harold, I hear, because not even a perjured bastard like Harold Godwinsson'd have Stigand touch him! thought FitzGilbert in disbelief.

" . . . in fact, any who didn't come against us in arms shall keep their lands and fortunes and be welcomed into our peace." FitzOsbern cleared his throat and William cocked an eye at him. "Yes my lord?"

"Majesty, how then will your earlier promises of land and wealth come about?" The question hung in the room like smoke over the fire of a summer day, but William waved dismissively.

"More of that later, my lord, later. When I return from Normandy, where I go at month's end. The earls Edwin and Morcar will accompany me, together with Waltheof – that's the leading men of the kingdom out of the way, so my governors, that's you, William, and you, Odo, can lie abed later in the morning, right?"

A rumble of laughter ran round the table at one of the king's rare quips, but died as William returned to his place and placed his fists on the tabletop. Leaning forward – and again those present were reminded of a bull – he said "We're going to rule by co-operation until we see if it's going to work. And if it doesn't, it'll be their fault. But for the safety of our vassals, all of you here will, within the month, begin work on the castleries I've given you. And they're mainly in the old earldom of Wessex, because Harold won't be needing them any more. They're smallholdings, true, but they're what we'll build this land on, so get on to them, get dug in, get building the strong places – and get busy with knowing the natives."

"Make no mistake – this is the richest, most civilised, most cultured country in Europe. Its scholars are famous and its wealth scarcely less. We're going to hold this land—"

Oh but money's not the point . . . is it? thought FitzGilbert with a wry smile, "So, remember that we've got a toehold in a land of a million and a half's what I'm told, and we've done it with seven and a half thousand men. Seven and a half thousand *lucky* men, because all of them'll be rich when we've sorted out the details. That'll be when we've nailed this place down, but there's a way to go yet. So keep it quiet in my absence, right?"

Bjørgvin, Norway, April 1067.

The Scraeling glanced round the table and cleared his throat, noting that the faces turned towards him showed emotions ranging from indifference to actual hostility, so he nodded at none in particular and offered what he hoped was an encouraging smile.

"It's been an interesting couple of days" he began. "And I'm taking back with me your concerns and your suggestions. Chief among . . ."

"Good of you" interrupted an elderly thickset man from halfway down the long table, "but will the king listen? And if he won't, haven't we wasted our time?" Those sitting nearest the speaker mumbled assent, and the man sitting next to him tapped the table in acclamation.

"We haven't" went on the speaker, "been accustomed to anything like that in the past, and no-one should know that better than you, Scraeling. You were Hardraada's eyes, ears and brains weren't you? Now you want us to believe that the Landwaster's son really wants to know what we think about things? I can't see it. So isn't this all wind and piss?" Another rumble of agreement, louder this time.

"Hang on, Jarl Anders" said the Scraeling. "Different king, different times. Magnus isn't like his father – not at all. And if I'm being honest – which I want to be, always, with you men, I can say that the reason for his difference ought to be obvious to you. He's his father's son by blood, not nature—"

"Thank the Christ for that, at least" from the end of the table, and the Scraeling nodded in agreement before continuing,

"And the reason for that is precisely because Hardraada couldn't see a king in him. Not the sort of king the Landwaster was. As I say – different king!"

"Same adviser, though" from Thorfinn of Orkney only three places from the Scraeling's right hand.

"That's true" shot back the Scraeling, "but have any of you suffered by that? I said I'd tell you the truth, and that's what I'm telling you now. I want to see Magnus rule as his father would never have ruled. I want to see Norway the friend of all and the enemy of none. I went to England with the Landwaster - and what happened there, and what I brought home, changed things completely. And that's what I want to discuss now, before I return to the Court."

He paused, seeking the right note. "We're here, right now, in a fishing village. You're not hearing this at Court after being summoned to attend it. That's the way Hardraada would have done it."

"Nah" from Anders. "Hardraada wouldn't have sent for us at all – not until he'd made up his mind what he wanted from us!" The Scraeling inclined his head in acknowledgement, recalling as he did so that Anders was – had been – related to Finn Thorkelsson, whom Hardraada had deposed as jarl of Jamtland and slaughtered so that his favourite, Eystein Orri, might have the title and lands.

"That's my point" said the Scraeling, looking swiftly around the table. "Here we all are, all of us having travelled to a place none of us own and that many of us have never heard of. We've come together to discuss the new Norway, and we've come together as equals. I came here to lay certain proposals before you and to get your opinions of them. Which I've done. I'm not here to tell you what Magnus has already decided. As I said – different king, different times, yes?"

Heads nodded, and the Scraeling pressed on. "Now – different times. As I've said to some of you already, and as everyone here knows, Norway's on its knees. The English adventure bled us white. Look around you and recall that, of us all around this table, I'm the only one who went to England with Hardraada. Look around the table again and reflect on who's *not* here because his bones are still lying under an English sky. We're what's left."

He paused to allow his words to sink in, and sipped at the cup of water by his right hand. "Who's working your lands, men of Norway? Who's fishing your waters? Women, old men and boys, that's who. And we all know it. Different times, see? It's also the king's view that we – all us Norse – are in this together, and that's why he wants your opinion of his proposals for the future. He's of a mind to share power, gentlemen, and for one, I'm keeping that idea constantly before him."

"So, Jarl Anders, Jarl Thorfinn – no it's not wind and piss. You – we – have the chance to use our wisdom and experience of life to send this country in a new direction, to where it'll be a menace to none but fish. Magnus will come – he's told me this – he'll come to places like this, aye, to meet with people like you, and you'll come to Court to offer advice and counsel. He can't do without you, and that's the plain truth. Some more truth, and this is from me, not the king – is that Magnus isn't a strong man,

33

so after a while you'll need to come to Nidaros more than he leaves it. But, after today at least you'll know why."

"When's all this going to start?" came a voice from up the table, and the Scraeling leaned forward.

"It's already started" he said. "What we've been doing these last two days is the beginning, Leif. Didn't hurt a bit, did it?"

Tonsberg, Norway, June 1067.

Knorre Knudsen wasn't very bright. But he was fairly shrewd, and he knew he had his Norwegian counterpart over a barrel with his pants round his ankles.

"Look, I'll say it again" he said, leaning forward. "We both know there's lotsa call for everything Danish right now – leather goods, woollens, cups and plates– everything. Now you've got some nice stuff here, these fancy plates, aye. But 'cause they came in from Denmark – an' I wouldn't mind knowing your supplier's name – no? Oh well, thought not . . . 'cause you brought 'em in, like, you've imported them. An' that makes you liable for Norway's import tax. An' once you've added that tax to your transport costs, added a little bit to keep body an' soul together, maybe a bit more to keep certain heads turned the other way here an' there, who'm I to know? Anyway – time you've done all that, your stuff's so expensive you'll not shift it with a horse an' cart." He paused to swig at his cup in the dark recesses of his back shop and nodded at the man who sat opposite.

"So" he continued, "best you sell it to me an' have done. I'm not liable for the import tax, 'cause it don't apply to Danish citizens – which I am. I c'n undersell you quicker'n falling over – believe me, my friend, it gives me no pleasure t'point it out – an' while I don't like to say it 'cause of my regard for you, well . . . I gotta live too. I'll give you a good price, 'course" he said, leaning forward with sincerity oozing from his piggy eyes. But the price he mentioned made the other catch his breath and cough.

"Well Knorre, you fucking thief" he said, "calling that a fair price's worse'n calling this catspiss wine. Not a chance. Maybe we could talk at, let's say, fifteen percent, but even then . . . "

"Lars, my friend, Lars . . . " the Dane shook his head. "Lars, we been friends for how long?"

"I wouldn't go that far" protested Lars. "Same game maybe – but you bastards've pinched the ball these days, ain't you just?"

"Not me, Lars. Not any Dane. *Your* king's levied the import tax, not me. Can you deny it?"

"'Course I can't" muttered the other. "Why's the little bugger ruining honest Norse merchants, that's what I can't work out?"

"Well, my friend, not s'long ago the boot was on the other foot. Your king Hardraada jus' about fucked all Danish trade anywhere. Maybe his son's got a fit of conscience."

"Nah" came back Lars, "Kings and Danish merchants don't have consciences. Just counting-frames an' deep pockets. How's your conscience?"

"It's not a fifteen percent conscience my friend" chuckled Knorre. 'In fact, I'm struggling not to suggest you take it or leave it."

"Look" said Lars, "maybe fifteen's a bit hopeful. Tell you what – gimme twelve, an' I'll call in a promise I'm owed at a knock-shop I know. Been saving this little trollop for m'self, but . . . a deal's a deal. This girl . . . she can pick up corks."

"Corks? Wine-corks you mean?"

" 'S right. Wine-corks."

"Lars, Lars – why would I beggar myself to watch a slut picking up corks? I can do that myself! Anyway, what's the point?"

"Eh? Oh – sorry. Should've explained. This slut's from the Inland Sea, y'know? An' when she picks up the corks – she don't use her hands. Know what I mean? 'S her party trick – seen it myself. Seen her work her way along a bench collectin''em an' droppin''em in a bag."

Knorre choked. "Fuck! True?"

"True. But she works too,'course.'magine that . . . an' you can have it; I'm owed an hour of her time – did her a favour, never mind what. Interested? Twelve per cent?"

"Seven"

"Ten, fuck you!"

Knorre spat on a palm and held it up for the clasp. "No thanks – I'll let her do that!"

Nidaros, Norway, July 1067.

The Scraeling nodded to the sentry, who grounded his spear, swung a forearm across it in salute and shouldered it again – all without looking at him, the Scraeling noticed to his amusement. He scuttled under the archway marking the threshold of the area set aside for ministerial residences and swung along the roadway with the lurching gait that was always freer in summertime. The Scraeling hated the cold, for it had caused pain in his twisted and shortened leg throughout his life. *And to think I once lived in Shepetovka and other places in the Rus* he thought, and shuddered inwardly. But no more. Now, cold meant a warm and stone-built house with a fire – and Elisabeth. Above all, golden Elisabeth.

The door opened as he stepped onto his threshold and Olga, Elisabeth's favourite maid, took the scrolls he carried from him as he stepped through. "Thank you, Olga" he said with a smile. "Won't need those until the evening."

Olga bobbed her head and waved towards an inner doorway. "My lady awaits you, lord Ranulf" she said with an impish smile that made him lift an eyebrow. "I'm to discover if you're in a good mood before showing you through. If not, says my lady, I'm to offer you this" and she indicated a large goblet on a table by the door.

The Scraeling laughed. "I've never been in a better mood, Olga. But you can offer it to me anyway!" Laughing, Olga handed him the goblet; he sniffed at it and said "Mmmm – Falernian, at a guess – and since I'm the only one I know in Nidaros who keeps Falernian, I think I know where it came from too. What are we celebrating, Olga?"

"Ah, lord Ranulf – my lady has something to ask you, and she wants you well pleased before she does."

"Then let's allow her to make her own guess, favourite maid, and thank you for my greeting!"

Laughing still, the Scraeling stepped into the room and paused for a moment to look at Elisabeth as she turned her face to him from where she sat embroidering by the light from the big window. He felt the visceral thrill that ran through him when she smiled at him, and the moment of utter disbelief that this perfect and golden goddess could love him, crippled in childhood by the kick of a destrier, with a leg twisted and wasted in the forty-odd years since as it clung to a crudely-set pelvis.

"Olga tells me you have something to ask me, my darling. You're not going to suggest that she takes over your duties again, are you? This time – I might let her!"

Elisabeth giggled at their memory of Olga's offer of years before when, with Hardraada at home during the winter months that put an end to campaigning, the maid had volunteered to assuage the Scraeling's 'needs as a man' through the services of herself and the côterie of ladies that the Princess Elisabeth had brought from the Rus.

"You're all talk, my man and my love, and we both know it. But in a way, you're close to the mark." She rose and came to him, took the goblet from his hand and sipped the rich white wine within it. "Your favourite, dearest – didn't I choose well?"

"Yes, and it's got me worried" admitted the Scraeling. "Terrified, even. Before I burst – what's this favour you want from me? It's yours, my love, whatever it is. You know that, surely?"

"Well, I know you'll grant it – but a girl prefers her man to ask her" said Elisabeth, her eyes dancing as she slipped an arm around his neck.

"Elisabeth, dearest, lovely, golden woman of my heart – just what d'you want? What do you want me to ask?"

"Ask me" murmured Elisabeth, "if you can make an honest woman of me. There's no reason, other than the formal year of mourning, why we shouldn't wed, my love – and I want to wake up for the rest of my life as Lady Ranulf de Lannion."

The Scraeling smiled. "I'd had it in mind, darling" he agreed, "but the mourning period's a nuisance. Still – it'll be over in the third week of September. Would you care to keep Christ's Mass this year as Lady Elisabeth de Lannion?"

"Is that a formal proposal?" asked Elisabeth archly, and the Scraeling gave a mock-weary groan.

"Very well" he sighed and got down on his sound knee, taking her hand.

"Elisabeth, princess of Kiev and queen of Norway. I love you beyond all people and all things. Will you make me the happiest man on earth in taking me for your husband? Please?"

"Of course I will, darling. Whatever made you think I wouldn't?" And the two of them burst out laughing as she hauled him, lurching, to his feet and into her arms.

The royal palace, Nidaros, the same day.

Styrkar came through the door to the king's private antechamber and bowed to the figure in the padded chair. Magnus lifted a hand in acknowledgement and waved him to a seat.

"Let's not stand on ceremony, Lord Styrkar, for we don't have time" he said. "We've given orders that you're to be shown into our presence whenever you wish because we're going to be relying on you more than a little, from now on. You understand?"

Never the brightest of men, Styrkar frowned. "Aye, majesty. Whatever you want, I'm here to do. Er . . . was there something I can do right away? Perhaps?"

Magnus looked at him. "Yes, lord marshal, there is. What's the present state and condition of our military strength? As far as you can say?"

"Hasn't changed that much since . . . oh since January last, majesty. You recall what the Scraeling said then? He pointed out that . . ."

"Yes marshal, we know what lord Ranulf pointed out" interrupted Magnus. "We merely seek to know if a military man – a proper military man – agreed with the opinion. Do you?"

Jesus thought Styrkar, pretending deep thought. *The man who built the Landwaster's army isn't a proper military man?* But aloud, he temporised.

"Well majesty, I'd have to agree with most of it" he said. "It's gonna take a generation for our strength to come back anything like it was. Why, right now the *drakkars* that brought the army back f'm England – all thirty'f them – they'd still do to take the army wherever it was needed. With spare room and all if you want the real truth."

"Yes, lord Styrkar, that's what we want" mused the king. "The truth. Sometimes a king gets less than that. He gets what others want him to hear, for whatever reasons they want him to hear it. What's your opinion of our trading policy? As it was discussed at that same meeting?"

Styrkar blinked, caught off-balance by the question. "Trading, majesty? Ah – well, the Scrae . . . that is, Norway, we've deliberately opened ourselves up t'the Danes to keep 'em happy, haven't we? By way of an import tax?"

"We know that, lord Styrkar" said Magnus patiently. "What we wish to know is your opinion of how it's working. Well?"

"Our merchants're suffering, no doubt about it majesty" said Styrkar, making it up as he went along. "People too, from what I hear – they've no option in goods and precious little in the prices they pay, is what I hear."

"And, speaking of Denmark, what's your view of the threat posed by Svein and his ambitions?"

"Don't rightly know if he's got any ambitions as yet, majesty" said a perspiring Styrkar. "Whole point, as I understood it, was t'keep the Danes happy so they'd not develop any . . . ah, ambitions."

"But there's no guarantee they won't" said Magnus. "Once it sinks in how weak we are? And we are, aren't we?"

"We're all of that, majesty" agreed Styrkar. *What the fuck's going on here? Talk about a bee in his bonnet . . .*

"Hmmm. So if I hear you correctly" said Magnus, "we can't discount a military move against us by Svein of Denmark; we're in no condition to prevent it, and in the meantime our trading policy's causing resentment within our kingdom. That's what you're telling me, isn't it, lord marshal?"

"Who, me? Eh . . . aye, majesty. That's . . . that's . . . what I think" said Styrkar, who had no idea of where the conversation would go next.

"Thank you, lord marshal. A king needs the soundest of advice, and that's what we feel we get from you" said the king. "We won't trouble you further at the moment, but should any further evidence of discontent among our people come to you, remember that your place as our trusted counsellor gives you the right of unrestricted access to us. Won't you?"

The Raedwaldsson estate, Reading, England, the same day.

"No, master, the secret's ramming a little at a time – earth once round the post's enough, y'see, then ram. Every layer. Bit'f water on top helps it all sit home, aye?"

"Post-holes seem so deep, Garth, and a layer doesn't seem to fill it much!" said Osmund ruefully, reaching for the rammer and wincing as he opened his hand.

"Here, young master, lemme see your hands, eh?" came Garth and he turned over the boy's hand. "Thought so. Blisters. Two things there, lord Osmund – allus shift the tool slightly in y'r hand every stroke. Stops y'r skin wearing in same place until it's harder, see?"

"And the other thing?"

Garth turned faintly pink. "Well . . . it's how to toughen y'r hands quickest way there is, lord . . . ah . . . well, see . . . I don't rightly know how to—"

"Garth! I'm no use to you with blisters! How do I harden my hands?"

"Lord Osmund, you shouldn't be doin' this at all, so you shouldn't! My wife hears 'bout this, she'll . . . I'll get . . . the lord workin' with his hands . . . she'd die o' shame she would – but she'd settle me first!"

Despite himself, Osmund burst out laughing. "And Aelfgifu able to reach your chest if she stood on a bench!" he said. "Fear not, warrior man – I'll not tell her! *Now, how-do-I-toughen-my-hands?* I'll keep asking till you tell me, Garth, and we both know I will, so—"

"All right, all right, lord. You piss on them!" said Garth in a mumble.

Osmund stared. "Did you say 'piss on them'?" he demanded, and the big farmer nodded reluctantly, sending the boy into gales of laughter.

"Just the thing for a cold day!" he declared, wiping his eyes. "Or for dirty hands!" and he was off again while Garth smiled at the thought of how good it was to see a smile again on the face of a boy he loved as his own.

"Well" said Osmund, "better get on with it – bet it stings open blisters though!" And Garth turned away to pick up the shovel as the boy fumbled at the flap of his breeches. "Why doesn't Brother Edmund teach me useful things like this instead of Latin and numbering and writing? It's be— ow! . . . ouch! . . . I was right about the sting! . . . Oooohhhh!"

"Tell me Garth" he said over his shoulder, "you grew up with my father. Am . . . am I anything like him? When he was my age? He would have been bigger, of course, but . . .?"

There it is thought Garth, *always his father, God rest him,* but he leaned on the shovel and said, "Lord Penda wasn't allus big, master. Up t'your age, you an' him, well, y're much alike – 'cept you're like y'r mother, bless her. You're dark like Lady Gytha, but he took after his father. Lord Raedwald, he was very fair, aye."

"But size-like, no, not much different. Not till he was fifteen'r so – then he started growing like a plant in spring, he did. Both ways – up and out. Up till then, I c'd wrestle him easy 'cause I was allus bigger'n heavier. But that all changed. Changed real quick, aye!"

He turned to where Osmund waited, and said firmly, "And you're gonna be just like y'r father, lord Osmund. You're comin' up for fourteen, aye, so you've a year in hand yet, but you're like him already'n the way you walk and the way you're so quick on y'r feet."

"You think so Garth? You know, Uncle Ranulf said that once, when he was here and we played keep-the-wicket. He said I'd be in Dad's class as an axeman one day. I remember it very well – I was proud of that."

"So y'should be, young master" said Garth gruffly. "Lord Penda was Angel o' Death with an axe in's hand. Wasn't foul with a blade, neither, but he preferred the axe, aye. When he swung an axe it sang. Axe's all about balance, strength an' speed. An' that was lord Penda right enough. An' your uncle Ranulf'd know that because they was comrades-in-arms in Micklegarth[2] an' other places too, like enough."

"I miss Dad, right enough" said Osmund wistfully, and for a second the grave young face belonged to a child again, "but I miss Uncle Ranulf too. I wish he'd come again."

"Been big changes where he bides too, lord" said Garth, picking up the shovel. "Might be . . . maybe he's . . . "

"Oh, I'm sure he's alive" said Osmund, lifting the rammer. "Dad always said that on Judgement Day it'd be Uncle Ranulf arguing with God for the sinners. You remember he and Dad spoke after Stamford Bridge. They spoke with King Harold and the lord Gyrth, and King Harold asked him ah . . . who's that, Garth? They're armed and on our land . . . who are they?"

Garth turned and peered away to where the road wound by the edge of the woodland. A column of horsemen was just visible, the trees behind them breaking up the hard outlines of shield, lance and hauberk. His mouth went dry at the sight he hadn't seen since one of them loomed over him on Senlac Ridge.

"Normans!" he said harshly. "Fucking Normans, lord Osmund! Come on – fold in the ground down t'stream there. Leave the tools – get 'em t'morrow. Come on!"

But Osmund didn't move. "Garth, this is our land. I'm lord of this manor since my father died, and I won't run away on my own land. Or anyone else's" he added, and Garth caught his mood in the instant. Quietly he put the shovel aside, moved his dagger from plain sight round to

---

2 *Micklegarth (Saxon) = Miklagard (Norse) = Constantinople. (Greek).*

the small of his back and picked up the rammer to lean casually on it. The boy stood on tiptoe, shading his eyes as he saw for the first time the men who had killed his father.

Someone in the Norman troop must have had eyes as sharp, for the note of a horn split the air and the head of the troop swung to the flanker who had seen the boy and the man by the row of posts marching across the meadow. In silence they awaited the troop cantering towards them, and the only movement that came from either of the pair was when Osmund drew himself up and put his hands on his hips.

On and on they came, and it wasn't until the pair on the ground could see the white flecks around the muzzles of the destriers that the rider at the front flung up a hand and the column drew rein to stare down, as the horses shuffled and stamped, at the two on the ground.

"Don't you Saxons move out of the way of men on horseback then?" he demanded. "You may not be so lucky a second time!"

"You have all my land to ride across" returned Osmund flatly in perfect French. "Why do you ride where I'm standing? *You* may not be so lucky a second time."

This brought a guffaw from the Normans within earshot, and the leader sniffed. "Well, well. You speak our language. That's a start."

"Not the start of anything I want to continue" said Osmund. "As well as a warrior my father was a learned, travelled and cultured man who had me taught because he admired all things French. Until he tasted your culture on Senlac Ridge. In all his life my father made only one mistake, and admiring you people was it."

"Your father fell at Hastings . . . ah, Senlac?" asked the leader, removing his helmet with the broad nasal bar.

"As I've said" returned Osmund. "With his father, and his brothers, and his king."

The leader unlaced his coif, threw it back and ran fingers through his cropped hair while he thought. Then he said, "Young man, my sympathy for your loss. May I know your name? And that of your father?"

"I am Osmund Pendasson. My father was Penda Raedwaldsson, and his father was Raedwald, who traced his descent from Hengest himself."

The leader inclined his head and said, "I am Valery-Michel d'Avranches, young man, and I am a vassal of Walter Giffard de Bolebec, lord of Longueville. I am commanded to search out, in this area, the lands and buildings that belonged to those who bore arms against us, and to inform those who presently inhabit them that they are forfeit to King William. With whom do I speak, in the case of the lands of the rebel Penda Raedwaldsson?"

"With me" returned the boy. "I am lord of the manor of Raedwaldsson. And if my father is a 'rebel', messire, tell me this – is the 'King William' of whom you speak, he whom I know of as 'the Bastard of Normandy, grandson of the Tanner'?"

There was a growl from the troopers behind d'Avranches, and he lifted a hand to still it as he smiled thinly.

"I was about to remark, lord Osmund, that you seem rather young for such responsibility. But you forestall me in proving that with your tongue. May we treat each other with civility? Now favour me in two ways. First, tell your man behind you to be careful how he holds that posthole rammer lest he arouse suspicion of his intentions. Then tell me where I may find lord Penda's widow, for I would speak with her."

The Raedwaldsson manor.

D'Avranches settled his weight on the wooden seat, swung his sword-belt aside and reached for the cup. "Thank you for your courtesy, Lady Gytha" he said.

Gytha's mouth twisted. "I cannot resist you, messire" she said in French. "Senlac saw to that. It's as well, then, to learn to bear what cannot be changed."

The cavalryman inclined his head. "As you say, my lady. And I may say that I understand, for I have a wife and children in Normandy." He hesitated, then "For myself, I would wish that another had this duty. But I am charged with making the will of my masters known in this part of the kingdom, and I may not set that task aside, for soldiers do not."

"And what is your task, messire?" asked Gytha, drawing herself up to her full height as she stood by the window overlooking the yard in which D'Avranches' troopers were watering their horses. "What is the will of the victor for the conquered? And the widows? And the fatherless?"

D'Avranches grimaced at the bitterness in her voice. "My lady" he began, and paused. "My lady, I have no words to soften this, so may I tell you as shortly as I can. This is the manor of Penda Raedwaldsson, is it not?"

Gytha turned to face him and lifted her chin. "It was the manor of my father and his fathers before him. It passed to his only child upon my father's death and to my husband, lord Penda, upon our marriage."

The Norman inclined his head again. "And Penda Raedwaldsson took up arms against the rightful king of England and died in battle?" he asked. "Is that the case?"

Twin spots of fire appeared in Gytha's cheeks. "No, messire, it is not the case! My husband defended the rightful king of England against those who would have usurped the kingdom. Twice! For he fought the Landwaster also before returning to confront the Bastard, and I care not who holds otherwise."

D'Avranches shook his head. "Then we differ, my lady, but this is no time to speak of oaths sworn and broken, nor of promises made, nor yet of offers made by a Witan that had no power to make them. None of this now matters, for as you yourself say – it cannot now be changed."

"Very well" said Gytha, turning back to the window. "You say you have no words to soften your message, so tell me, my master –" and there was a world of scorn in the last two words "– tell me what you must."

"As the estates of a rebel who opposed the king and died in doing so" said D'Avranches harshly, "this manor is forfeit to the king. He has given it to Walter Giffard de Bolebec, lord of Longueville in Normandy. He will give it, in turn, to whom he pleases."

"And my children and I?" demanded Gytha, "Are we to be turned out?"

"No, my lady" said the cavalryman after a moment's hesitation. "King William's quarrel was with a forsworn usurper, not with the laws and customs of England, his new kingdom . . . and he would honour them. Since it is the law of England that women may inherit once they are of age, and since these lands passed to you upon your husband's death, they will pass from you again when . . . when you marry again."

Gytha frowned. "When I marry again? And if I . . ." She stopped as she guessed his meaning. "I . . . I am to be married to a Norman? To the man this . . . this Giffard chooses for me? With no say in the disposition of my lands or people? Messire, this cannot be true!"

But she saw her fate in the set of his face, and the deliberate placing of his cup back upon the table sealed it as nothing else could.

The Scraeling's residence, Nidaros, Norway, late July 1067.

The Scraeling put down the sheaf of papers and reached for his cup. "I can't get over it" he said, and Elisabeth looked up from her sampler.

"What, dearest? What can't you get over?"

"What I might call the Danish Policy" answered the Scraeling. "On one hand it's taken Norway by storm. The demand for Danish goods – everything Danish, and I mean *everything* – has never been higher, I'm told, and I'm also told there's no sign of it slackening. You and your ladies have been wonderful darling. Well done!"

"It's little enough, sweetheart" said Elisabeth dismissively. "And in fact it makes me just a touch worried about how easy it is to shape people's opinions. Look, all I did was make a list of a dozen ladies of the Court who've got homes elsewhere as well as here, buy a lot of Danish ware, and entertain them often while you're scribbling away at the palace or reading your eyes out. Keep telling them how new and fresh and . . . *better* . . . the Danish stuff is, and they believe. Then when they go back to the provinces and people there ask them what's new at Court, well . . . it all falls into place really, and just grows. Like children making snowmen by rolling up a snow-ball."

The Scraeling smiled at her and silently raised his cup in her direction. She put down her sampler, opened her mouth, closed it and picked up the work again.

"What?" asked the Scraeling curiously.

"Nothing" she returned, and the Scraeling rose from the chair, set down his cup and crossed to her.

"My love" he said, and kissed the top of her bent head. "My love, you've just said 'Nothing' in a way that really says 'Everything'. So – " and he gently took the sampler from her hands, laid it down and took her hands in his. "What is it?"

"Children" she said in a small voice. "I said 'children' just now, and I . . . I . . . oh Ranulf, I don't just want to be Lady Ranulf de Lannion. I want . . . to have your children dearest . . . *our* children. Lots of little de Lannions. Well, a boy and a girl at least. Am I silly, darling? You see, once upon a time I couldn't even begin to think about it, but now . . . am I being silly?"

The Scraeling opened and closed his mouth, genuinely shocked.

"Darling Elisabeth, I haven't ever thought about it. Are you sure . . . sure, er . . . can you . . ."

"Sure I'm not too old?" finished Elisabeth with a note of asperity in her voice, "Oh yes Ranulf. I'm not ready for my shawl yet, and yes, I'm still capable of bearing children. As long as they're yours, my man. But who knows for how much longer?"

Light dawned and the Scraeling said, "Ah . . . is that why . . ."

"Well yes. And no. I mean – I want to be your wife anyway, whether we can have children or not. But if we married, dearest, I wouldn't have to . . . I mean, I feel guilty every time I . . . but let's just leave it. We'll marry as soon as we can, and just see what happens? Is that all right Ranulf?"

"Better than 'all right', darling" said the Scraeling and he kissed the top of her head again, savouring the scent of her hair. "It's wonderful. And I'll have time to get used to the idea of being a father. Me! A father!"

"You'll make a wonderful father, Ranulf dearest. For all the reasons I love you. But before I shock you any further – what's the 'but'?"

"Eh? The 'but'?" asked a mystified Scraeling.

"You began by saying 'On one hand' and complimenting me on how well the Danish policy's going. There's got to be another hand, darling. What is it?"

The Scraeling shook his head in admiration. "Where did I ever get you?" he said. "Yes. There's a distaff side, dearest, and it's this. All around the country, Norse and Danish merchants and traders are falling out. Sometimes it comes to blows, sometimes it stops at warehouses burned and vessels damaged. In those papers is a summary taken from the regional chiefs in the trading provinces – in one of them" he said, rummaging on the table, "in a town . . . ah . . . yes, here it is – in Tonsberg, the oldest trading town in the country for goodness' sake, a Danish merchant was set upon in a brothel, beaten within an inch of his life, robbed and accused of 'unnatural vices'!"

"Well perhaps he had some, dearest" offered Elisabeth and the Scraeling snorted, holding up another paper.

"Just for the sake of it, the regional chief looked into the accusation and he wrote a note to the effect that not only was the trader blameless so far as he could make out, but it was more than a possibility the man was set up deliberately. The woman in question was a skilled and practised harlot given to performances that I'm not even going to *think* about in your presence. Yes, it's all here. And as she was from the Inland Sea, she was hardly an outraged daughter of Tønsberg either. No – the Danes are catching it, at a local level, for the success of the general policy."

"And it *is* succeeding – the numbers of Danes asking for trading licences is through the roof. And we're getting revenue from the import tax too, although that's something of a bonus. There's no knowing what'll happen."

"I suppose you can't blame our people though" said Elisabeth. "They must be bewildered, to say the least."

"You're right, my dear. As always" he added with a grin. "Next step is to sweet-talk the Danes so they'll keep up the supply – and then it'll be time for good king Magnus to earn a few cheers by graciously rescinding the import tax – as a show of his willingness to listen to his people and govern in their interest. Danes can't complain because they've had a start and, thanks in part to you, will still have a demand – and our merchants will work twice as hard to make up the leeway. That'll keep them quiet too."

"Darling, you're downright devious" said Elisabeth. "Come and tell me how you arrive at all these schemes."

"Well" said the Scraeling, raising his cup to her again, "I've got a beautiful golden accomplice who's got amazing talents in a number of directions . . ."

The royal withdrawing-room, Nidaros, Norway, the week after.

"You can't blame our people though, lord Ranulf" said Prince Olaf. "You've talked to me yourself about fairness and the right to fairness, and they must be wondering why their lawmakers treat them so."

The Scraeling spread his hands. "No argument, highness. And that's the second time your point's been made to me lately. Or one very like it. You're right, of course. It hasn't been fair. But it's been necessary, and sometimes in a royal life – well, kings, and those who do their bidding, can't manage both."

"We're the first to admit" said Magnus, fiddling with a loose thread on his sleeve, "that your policy seems to have kept the Danes happy, and that's as important as it ever was. But is there no other way of doing it? The reports you've handed us concerning the brawls and affrays in our trading towns – well frankly, lord Ranulf, we can see then adding up to undoing all the good. After all, open brawling between Dane and Norseman isn't what we're after, is it?"

"A fair question, majesty, and even better than fair. It's exactly right. I've been thinking about that . . ." and the Scraeling went on to discuss the plan he'd outlined to Elisabeth, ending, "So if I might have your majesty's permission to go to Svein with the new trading protocols, the lifting of the import tax can be announced while I'm away, if it pleases you."

Magnus smiled. "It'll please us a great deal, lord Ranulf. And you have our permission to depart just as soon as you can. In fact—"but with that, he was overtaken by a paroxysm of coughing that went on and on despite the wine the Scraeling poured and offered him to sip. At last it was over, and Olaf peered anxiously at his brother.

"Magnus, brother, that cough isn't improving, is it? And it's high summer – what'll it be like in the winter months, then? Shall I have your physician fetched?"

"The Arab? He'll only bleed us again Olaf, and that hasn't stopped the cough so far, has it? No thanks. Lord Ranulf, please make your preparations. Deliver us a copy of your proposal – which we are confident will be excellent – and take from us a personal message of goodwill to our brother sovereign of Denmark."

The Scraeling bowed himself out, and when the door had closed behind him Magnus turned to his brother. "Olaf, what's your opinion of lord Ranulf?"

"My opinion" temporised Olaf, "In what way brother?"

"In all ways. Or as few as you wish. You had dealings with him during the invasion of England, didn't you?"

"More after it" returned Olaf. "But right from the time of the army's assembling at Orkney I was taken by the way he worked. He missed nothing, Magnus. No detail was too small to take his attention. Oh" he hastened, "not that he insists on doing everything himself. Quite the reverse – but he insists on being responsible for everything, and he follows up. Must be a terror to work for."

"What about after the battle?"

"Ah. I saw even more of the same then. He's not a warrior in the same sense as father, or Eystein, Ivarr or Haakon, who all died – or Styrkar, who didn't. They were leaders of men and fearsome killers of men, but the Scraeling matched them in his own ways. He's a thinker, a planner, an organiser, a director. Look – when the news of the disaster at Stamford came in, he was the one to call the base-camp garrison together and snap them out of the disbelief."

Magnus frowned, and Olaf hurried on. "He told them that until we knew better, I – *me*, Magnus, for God's sake – had decided that we needed to put Riccall in a state of readiness to receive wounded, to load them aboard the fleet and to hold off the English while we did that. So in less time than I can tell you about it, he had men cutting down trees to heighten the palisade and to entangle attackers, others checking water, food and moorings aboard ship, a watch atop the highest hill around – he overlooked nothing and thought of everything, because then he suggested I get among the men to order this and direct that because it was good for them to be under orders, and good for me to be seen giving those orders. As if I knew anything about it! He's a marvel, Magnus."

And he's also dangerous, thought Magnus. *He's clearly got Olaf and Styrkar won over, but I'm not sure I can live with the competition he brings me. If the monarchy's going to survive what we've done to some of the most important people in Norway* – for the king had no illusions about the importance of trade to a country that struggled to produce enough food to feed its people – *it might be well for our lord Ranulf to take a back seat for a while. Yes – while he's away I'm definitely going to rescind the import tax, and I'll make sure it's trumpeted as the king easing the burdens of his people. Burdens imposed by insensitive advisers. Yes, that's it. That's the right note.*

"Quite a man, by your account" remarked Magnus, "and I know father thought highly of him, too."

"Certainly" said Olaf. "Why, he was with father most of his life. And from the evidence of my own eyes, I've more than a suspicion that our father owed a lot of whatever successes he had to that man."

"High praise, brother" commented Magnus *but more and more I find myself doing this because the Scraeling presses for it, and that because lord Ranulf advocates it, and the other because the council of ministers can't see past him either. Might be time to show everyone that the king has a mind of his own. Nothing personal though. Well, not very personal.*

Aloud, he said, "Right. Think I'll have the rest of that wine warmed up and spiced. See if that holds the cough at bay."

Reading, England, early August.

"That's it, master, that's it." The axe slammed again into the iron-bound wooden shield. "Let axe draw you onto your foeman. Speed, strength, balance –" *Wham!* "Aye, that's it – that's it – stroke, master! But whoa, hold a minute!"

Garth lowered the shield and stepped back to look at an Osmund crimson-faced and gasping. The boy lowered the big farm-axe and leaned gratefully upon it, his arms on fire and his shoulders screaming.

"Speed, strength, balance. Speed, strength, balance. Them three things, master. That's what y'r Dad was all about –'s what he'd be tellin' you now 'f he was here 'stead o' me. An' look – you got the speed, you got balance like a cat, but you ain't got the strength. Not yet. You will have, but not yet. So don't try 'n stop the axehead, lord Osmund – go with it, twist under it, let it slow, bring it back t'other way, keep y' feet movin. Use y'r speed an' y'r balance, an' wait for the strength t'come. Now – still tired? Good. Again!"

He hefted the shield and motioned with his free hand for the boy to move in on him again, and as they began the shuffling dance of mock combat the woman who watched from the corner of the byre found herself torn two ways; her pride in the son who grew taller and stronger each day, fought with her fear of what he was doing and what it might lead to. *Son of my warrior husband* she thought, *how I love you! How I love you, my darling! What will become of us, my son, my firstborn?* – and it was not until the echo hung in the air that she realised she had whispered aloud.

At last the weaving, shuffling figures halted and she heard Garth say, "Enough then, young master. 'Nuff for today –'s that last bit, when you're so tired you can't hardly lift the weapon – that's the bit that makes you stronger, like. 'S the man who c'n last just a bit more that kills the man who can't. You be that man, master – you last the bit more. You work just the bit harder. Lord Penda'd like that, so he would."

"His mother would prefer that too" said Lady Gytha clearly as she stepped out from behind her corner and the two spun to face her, dismay and embarrassment plain on their faces.

"Osmund Pendasson, that good man Brother Edmund has been waiting an hour to begin your Latin instruction, and it is not meet that we treat our folk in that fashion. No, young man –" and her hand went up in denial of his protest, "when what we *would* do wars with what we *must* do, duty must win. Ever. So go, and quickly. My son – " as he bobbed his head and turned away, "your mother believes that her son has manners enough to make apology where he has given offence. So . . . no, Garth, bide you there – I seek a word." Slight as she was, Gytha Raedwaldsson was not one to be denied or argued with and both men knew it.

Osmund departed at a fast trot with the heavy axe, Gytha noted, held up at its throat in one raw-boned fist. "Tell me, Garth" she said, her eyes still on her son, "I understand that the axe my son carries is heavier than a true war-axe of two edges. Why is that?"

"Bless you, Lady Gytha" said Garth cautiously, "farm-axe must be heavy f'r what it does. It's weight – an' a sharp edge helps, 'course – what sends axe through wood. But wood don't move an' swerve an' fight back, see. Men do, so y'gotta have balance, aye? An' a war-axe be light enough to give a warrior balance, but it cuts better 'cause. . . 'cause steel's better f'r one thing, an' the edges're curved so they bites through . . . well, anythin' in their way. An' that's why" he ended.

Gytha looked up at the big farmer. "Garth, I would that my son not become a warrior, for warriors die. As did his father." For a second the bitterness was in her voice, but then, "But I know, as a warrior's wife, that life and death are but two sides of the one coin. I know, too, that had he lived Osmund's father would have had him doing what you do with him ere now. So I thank you, man of ours, and bid you continue."

"Work him hard, Garth, work him hard enough to make him a warrior such as his father was. No – make him better, for if I cannot turn him from the way of the warrior, I would have him live when others die. So teach him well, Garth. Make my son invincible!" Her voice shook with the force of her emotion, and Garth dropped to his knees to avoid seeing the tears for her slain husband in her eyes.

"Aye, m'lady" he said, and his own voice was husky, "as best I can, I'll make the lord of this manor a warrior. One lord Penda'd be proud of."

Gytha cleared her throat and when she had herself under control she said, "Garth, Garth, what would this manor be without lord Penda's spearbearer? Faithful servant, man of my lord and me, rise that I may speak to you of what the future holds for all of us."

The royal apartments, Nidaros, Norway, early August.

"We've asked you here, lord Styrkar, rather than to the formal chambers, to impress upon you that what we discuss here tonight must remain absolutely confidential" began Magnus, and Styrkar bowed his understanding.

"Kingship requires constant vigilance, marshal – vigilance of an order known to you from your experience of being in the presence of the enemy, we fancy. So it is for those of us called to the higher duties of state. You follow?"

"Aye, majesty. Just so." *I've been in the presence of the enemy, but I'm buggered if I know when you have, you play-actor. What's this about?*

"Good. In our present condition, marshal, we find ourself torn in two directions – each of them, in our mind, equally unpalatable. You recall our previous discussion of the sufferings endured by our Norse merchants due to the policy of imposing an import tax on all goods coming into the kingdom?"

"Er . . . aye, majesty – but not goods brought in for resale by Danes, if I recall rightly."

"You do, lord Styrkar. You do. We have favoured the Danes in order to placate them; to keep their minds from notions of conquest, from a war we cannot hope to win. Yes?"

"Aye, majesty. As you say." *And you're a pompous arsehole too, speaking down to me like that. Your majesty.*

"That policy must cease, marshal. Our people won't have any more of it. Reports are reaching us from around Norway – reports of assaults on Danish merchants and the destruction of Danish goods. Clearly, this is the work of Norwegian merchants who see their livelihood disappearing and who are moved either to do this themselves or to have it done by others."

"Er . . . and you want me to stamp it out, majesty? I'm not sure I . . ."

"No, marshal. We can't have the nation's sword and shield moving against the very folk he protects. We are minded to end the import policy that favours the Danish merchant over the Norse one. Immediately."

Styrkar blinked. "But won't that defeat the very end the Scrae . . . lord Ranulf wants to achieve? Keeping the Danes happy? Majesty?"

"Ah" said Magnus, steepling his fingers as he leaned back in his chair. "Lord Ranulf may yet come to see the error of his ways and the short-sightedness of his policy. We certainly hope so."

"And . . . and the Danes?" ventured Styrkar.

"The Danes" echoed Magnus, his eyes far away. "Since you tell me we can't live with them in battle, we'll need to come up with something else to 'keep the Danes happy', as you put it. And we have, marshal, we have. One of those decisions, those hard decisions, we spoke of previously, my friend. Lord Styrkar, we intend to make an alliance with Denmark and to cement it with the very blood of our royal family. You approve?"

"Blood, majesty? Blood . . . ah, how? I mean . . . in what way?"

"We intend to offer a member of our family in marriage to Svein of Denmark, marshal. It's the perfect solution, for Svein is unmarried – we might say he doesn't have queens enough – and we have a surfeit of them!" Magnus laughed at his own joke while Styrkar looked mystified. "We have two dowager queens, marshal. Two!"

Light dawned. "Ah yes, majesty. Your mother, Queen Thora, and Queen Elisa –" He stopped at the thought that had sprung into his mind.

"Yes, marshal. Queen Thora and Queen Elisabeth, first wife of our father. No land needs two queens. Three, in fact, when we marry."

"True, true majesty" said Styrkar, his mind racing. "Er, which . . . that is, who will you . . . honour with the Danish alliance?"

Magnus looked down his nose at him. "Really, marshal! We can hardly virtually banish our own mother, can we? Elisabeth, of course! Queen Elisabeth will perform this service for her adopted land."

"Ah, majesty . . ." faltered Styrkar, "Queen Elisabeth . . . strictly speaking, the *lady* Elisabeth by your father's wish on his marriage to your mother, in fact . . . in fact is . . ."

"Is eminently suitable for this idea of ours" broke in the king. "Yes, we know she is. Do you see any impediment to that?"

Not fucking much! thought Styrkar. *Only that it's probably safer to kiss a viper than cross the Scraeling.* But aloud he said "No, majesty. None of any importance."

Magnus smiled thinly. "Good" he said. "We are aware, marshal, that there might be some slight resistance to the idea from the lady herself. Oh, nothing she won't get over with time and a little thought on the nature of the service she's performing for Norway . . . but some, initially. That's where you come in, and why we seek your assistance to make this plan of ours work, for the good of the country. We want you to take Queen Elisabeth under your personal care and protection, in the first instance, and then to provide us with an outline of how she is to be housed, cared for and convoyed to Svein. All – that's *all*, marshal – in the greatest security. You understand?"

"Aye majesty. Er . . . the timeline for this? When's it to happen?"

"That depends upon your arrangements, lord Styrkar. The offer of the lady's hand in marriage is about to be made to Kobenhavn. This is going to happen, marshal. Believe us."

Freya's shiny tits thought Norway's marshal, *it'd better happen while the Scraeling's out of the country then. There's less chance of him lying down for this than there is of finding a nun in a brothel . . .*

The Scraeling's residence, Nidaros, Norway, early August.

"There's a *drakkar* waiting for me at the harbour, darling" said the Scraeling. "The first time I've set off from there since – since the fleet sailed for Orkney. You remember?"

"I should" said Elisabeth. "I was there, terrified for my man going off to war but not able to show it. Do *you* remember?"

"I'll never forget it" said the Scraeling, "but what I remember most was the pain of not being able to speak to you properly. You needn't have worried about me though – I'm very much a headquarters sort; not really a soldier. Never have been."

"Not even when you're filling Scythians full of steel in Miklagaard alleyways? Nor breaking a regiment of enemy footsoldiers with only twenty archers about you? Not really a soldier, eh?"

"Mere incidents" said the Scraeling, taking her in his arms, "only part of a regiment, it was, and you don't want to believe all you heard from Penda – he was just trying to impress you because he thought I needed the help. Anyway, he was big enough to shelter behind, so I did. Often. But look, my love, I've left a seaman muttering about the tide and a good wind, so I'd better go before he decides to use me for bait once we get out there."

"Now – once I'm back from what I'm sure will be a very successful embassy, I'll ask the king for your hand when the period of mourning ends in September. That should be a good time to ask.

Think Olga's up to organising a wedding?"

"Darling, it's half-done already" murmured Elisabeth, looping a slim arm round his neck. "She's already managed to get a promise of three casks of Falernian from your wine-merchant, and now she's working on the food. The meat's still running around at this moment, mark you."

The Scraeling shook his head in admiration. "The woman's a treasure. She's never failed . . . hang on – *three casks?* Impossible! Snorre swears blind he can't get me more than two at a time, and they're six months apart. How's she going to get three out of him for eight weeks time? Or shouldn't I ask?"

"Better not" giggled his promised one. "Olga's very persuasive. As you might have discovered once – but not all men are as high-principled as you, my darling!"

The Scraeling blushed. "Ah, but I had you to wait for" he managed. "No contest. None at all."

"Thank you, my darling man" said Elisabeth. "And now I'll wait for you. Godspeed, my love."

Wessex, England, about the same time.

"You're in the shit" said Ivo de Bois flatly. "In fact, you couldn't be in more shit if you walked behind your destrier for a month. In your place, I'd quit and leave the army now. No, yesterday."

"And do what?" snarled the man he faced. "And over what? Fuck's sake, she's an enemy. And she was asking for it. You can't tell me these people don't know what's what, and what sort of behaviour'll keep them where they need to be."

De Bois sighed. Part of him noted the fine early morning weather and told him it would be another hot day of riding, but he wrenched his mind back to the task at hand, a task he found more than disagreeable.

"Ralph de Courcy, you're a fuckwit. Son of my cousin though you are – and that's the only reason I'm taking the time to speak to you now, 'cause we're related – you're still a fuckwit with all his brains hanging off his belly. What, by the good God, came over you when I detached you and your six yesterday? Take your time – tell me it all, and tell me slowly, because I'm the only chance you have right now. The next person you tell this to'll be

Giffard himself – and if you get any of it wrong, God help you because Giffard won't! Speak!"

"You detached me and my section" came back the sullen answer, "an' told us to sweep the tributary there to find out who owned what, to make a list of those and to find out which of 'em had fought against us at Senlac. Right?"

De Bois nodded. "Right. Go on."

"Second manor we came to – about noon, aye – we grabbed an old bugger sitting on a stump sharpening a scythe, an' he told us straight off the manor belonged to Aelle Aelfricsson, who'd died at Senlac. Serve the bastard right, I thought, but the Englishman you gave us asked him who ran the manor now an' he started laughing. Hard to understand, he was, 'cause he'd no teeth, but in the end he said the lady of the place ran it, because all there was in the house was women. Six of them. Seven counting the widow."

"Anyway. He gave us directions and we found the place. The widow was more'n reasonable – we talked, I give her the message 'bout forfeiture. She never shed a tear, y'know. Just drew herself up an' thanked me in a voice that would've frozen water – didn't need the Englishman to show me that – and offered us a noonday meal. Well, I said no thanks, as per your orders, but she said we'd want to water our horses, and maybe ourselves, so I couldn't see anything wrong with that. Her way of getting rid of me, I thought."

"Fair enough" said de Bois. "No-one can call that looting or pillage. What next?"

"Well, this tall piece came over while we were watering, an' said she'd make us free of the barn while we ate from our saddlebags. Rations, y'know? Said there was hay in there, for the horses. She spoke good French, too. She said there was cider in the press-room we were welcome to, an' could I come an' have a look t'see how much I thought we wanted? Well, I saw no reason not to – we'd delivered our message and we'd be off after we'd eaten, so . . . Anyway – soon's we got inside the press-room she dropped the bar across the door an' – she grabbed me."

"Grabbed you?" said de Bois, "How? Where? Hang on – how were you dressed?"

"Eh? Oh. It was hot. I judged no danger of ambush, so I'd ordered the undress, and we weren't mailed. Nothing wrong with that, is there?

So . . . I was wearing tunic and trousers An' she grabbed me round the neck an' told me something about not wanting to die a virgin, and how . . . how she envied my horse."

"Oh fuck" said his commander wearily. "And you fell for it!"

"Look, cousin" said Ralph. "Put yourself in my place. I'm twenty-three, been fighting since last September, part of an army that's got no women in the train 'cause Duke William – *King* William – who's twice my age an' forgotten what it's like, says we're on crusade against a perjurer. None of the whores in London'd have anything to do with us last Christmas, not that we were allowed to go near them anyway . . ."

"All right, all right!" snapped de Bois. "Go on!"

"Right. By then, she'd . . . she'd . . . her hand under my tunic an' on the laces of my breeches-flap. Panting and carrying on about how strong I was or something"

"What'd you do?"

"Are you serious? What would you do, cousin? I pulled the laces out of the front've her dress and popped her tits out. That enough detail?"

De Bois grimaced. "Didn't occur to you that this supposed virgin seemed to know her way about?"

"Look – it's easy to ask questions now, but at the time . . . when a woman's panting for the very thing you haven't had for a year . . . and she's got her robe picked up with one hand and your cock in the other . . . you don't stop to wonder. And I didn't."

"Didn't what?"

It was the younger man's turn to sigh. "I didn't wonder. I didn't stop. And I didn't disappoint her as far as I'm concerned; not from the noises she made or the words she said."

"Well, she's saying different words now and so's Aelle's widow" snapped de Bois. "The girl's her oldest daughter, and according to her you dragged her into the room, barred the door, tore her gown – I've seen it by the way – and raped her. When did you knock her about – before or after?"

"Knock her . . . what? I didn't hurt her at all – Jesu, I didn't need to!"

"Well, she's got a black eye and a split lip – says you did it to stop her screaming. When she defended herself."

The young man laughed harshly. "Defended herself? She was going up an' down like a puppet on a stick if you want . . . hang on! – 'to *stop* her screaming' you said? To *stop* her? That means she screamed, does it? As well as *defended* herself?"

De Bois' forehead wrinkled. "That's what mother said. What're you getting at?"

"Well, a manor-house that size's got servants about. An' the press-room wasn't far from the barn where all my men fed out. Ask *them* 'f they heard any screaming. Or saw anyone getting dragged anywhere. And while I'm at it – see any marks on me? I mean – if I had to knock her around that much, wouldn't I have scratches? Teethmarks? From her *defending* herself?"

"Ask the servants you can find. Compare the stories, 'cause I'm telling you cousin, that bitch – both of them – are lying in their teeth. But I'm buggered if I know why. I mean – in the end, what's she got to gain?"

"You might be surprised" said de Bois, rubbing his jaw thoughtfully. "Look – it's well known by now that we're not exactly going to ravage anything or anybody; just confiscate rebel lands. And the rebel families with them. Now if anyone's got a beef under law . . . well, the widow might see that as meaning we'll go easy on them, maybe. It's a possibility. Anyway, I'm bound to look into it – can't avoid it."

"Not much of one in my book" said the younger man. "You mean she'd . . . she'd whore her own daughter on an off-chance? I can't see it!"

"Well think about it. She's got six daughters and no men. She's probably desperate to keep a roof over their heads – she might have thought that laying us under some sort of obligation would help her do that. Oh . . . I don't know. Bugger it – it's too deep for me. But look, you young goat – keep your cock in your pants from now on, y'hear?"

Ralph grinned. "You think I might get accused of rape again?"

"That's the least of your worries de Courcy. Because I think mother might decide to try her own luck next time. An' if she does . . . you get her. And that's definite!"

The Court of Denmark, August.

The Scraeling's embassy to the court of Denmark's Svein went as well as he'd hoped. They were old acquaintances, for the Scraeling had danced attendance upon Svein and his whims during the protracted peace negotiation of four years before – four years that now seemed to belong to another life – when Hardraada had sent him to deal with the slippery Dane.

In truth, the Scraeling had liked Svein Estrithsson then, and he liked him no less now. Nephew of Cnut the Great and a distant relative of the Scraeling's own Elisabeth besides, Svein was a cheerful and clever man who was as unlike Hardraada as might possibly be. No warrior, Svein fought only when he had to – but a formidable talent for strategy and an impish impudence had seen him embarrass the fearsome Landwaster on more than one occasion. In fact those who knew how close the sea-battle off the mouth of the Nissa had come to being Hardraada's last fight would never again underestimate the cunning of the short, round Dane, nor his talent for doing the unexpected in the blink of an eye.

More, though, Svein was a good companion. He could converse on a range of subjects and had an amusing story for each and any of them, but none of his drollery hid the fact that he had a first-class mind and was deeply perceptive also. Men liked Svein, and his talents were the cause of that. That liking had kept him ahead of Hardraada's many attempts on his life both on and off the battlefield, for in a career that saw him have far more rough than smooth in his contest with the Landwaster, his ability to find refuge among people who loved him had been constant.

"Well Scraeling, you're off home tomorrow. What d'you do with yourself now you've only got one king to hob-nob with, hey?" and he laughed uproariously. The Scraeling had told him of his interview with Harold Godwinsson after Stamford Bridge – not all of it, of course, because even Elisabeth was ignorant of the extent of his part in Hardraada's downfall and the Scraeling saw no reason not to let the past keep its secrets.

"Oh I'm busy enough, majesty. I make myself as useful as I can to King Magnus, who's a genuinely good young man, and his brother Prince Olaf, who's the same. Neither's anything like the father, so if God is good there'll be peace in this our Scandinavia for many years. That's what we all wish, anyway."

"Amen to that, my friend. Magnus has said so in so many words in that letter of greeting you brought me. You'll take one back for me? Good, good – my thanks. Not easy being a king, you know, never mind what it looks like from your side." He paused to sip reflectively at his cup.

"Even when one's as well-served as Magnus is, having you. Y'see, if royal policy goes right, the minister gets all the credit because everyone knows who's behind it – I mean, look at your own reputation, man. Other hand – if the policy fails, suddenly it's the king who's the bad bugger 'cause it's *his* policy. You can't win. And you can't duck responsibility, 'cause that goes with the crown. But that sort of thing never bothered Hardraada, God rot him. He was big enough, hard enough, ready enough to tell the whole world to bugger off when he wanted. Magnus, now . . . different story altogether. He needs to cut his own track, just to impress, y'know, Scraeling. You see if I'm not right." He drained his cup and the Scraeling murmured something sympathetic.

"Here – let me offer you some of this . . . but back to you. Tell me – we've known each other long enough for this not to come as too much of a shock I hope – would you consider bringing your family to Denmark? To work for me? All the world knows what the Scraeling did for Hardraada, and frankly I've always been a little in awe of your talent for getting things done through sheer organisation, patience, planning and forethought."

The Scraeling sat stunned, and he went on, "Denmark's just beginning to recover from fifteen years of war, and we're nicely on the up. But to be honest, you know, there's no-one like you available to me. No-one with your range of talents to make sure we keep going forward. Y'see, Danes work hard enough to get by and while they're getting by they don't look ahead. That's what you're good at. One of the things you're good at anyway. So – you and yours? You won't find Denmark ungrateful! Well – cat got your tongue, or d'you dislike my wine that much?" And he roared again.

"Ah . . . I've no family, majesty. And . . . and as for Norway, well . . . as you know, I promised Harold Godwinsson I'd help make a Norway that no-one need fear. That I'd keep his northern flank in return for mercy for young Olaf . . . 'course, that's all gone now, with the Bastard in control of England, but I can still offer my help to Magnus – and Olaf too, I suppose . . . no, majesty, my heart's in Norway. But thank you. Thank you – you do me great honour."

"Ah well – if you don't ask, you don't find out, eh? If you ever change your mind, well . . . anyway – how're the two queens getting along now Hardraada's not there to keep them apart, hey? Elisabeth's a relative of mine somewhere along the line y'know. Round about our shared grandfather's time, or great-grandfather or something. Can never get my head round that sort of thing."

Which was nonsense if ever the Scraeling heard any, for Svein Estrithsson's head was as deadly in its own way as Hardraada's axe had been in its.

The Chronicle.

I should have listened harder, though. In fact I should have accepted. But if we knew then what we know now, we'd all be wealthy I suppose. In later months I realised that Svein was trying to tell me something despite the constraints that kings used diplomacy for. And I hadn't given the wily Dane enough credit for knowing as much about the gossip of neighbouring courts as I'd have wanted to know in his place, because he surely hadn't raised Elisabeth's name simply to tell me he'd no head for family history.

No, I certainly wasn't blameless. I'd become used to being at the centre of the web, you see. I was well aware that Svein hadn't gilded the lily in what he said of my ability to run things – oh I knew what I could do and what I was worth, all right – and if I thought about it at all I suppose I thought that he was simply trying to buy my talents in order to avoid the work of developing his own. And that conceit cost me dear.

At the time, though, all I could see was the end of an embassy and the beginning of the happiest time of my life. I even dared wonder how fatherhood might be. Yes, I was that far out of touch with reality.

Reading, England, early September 1067.

Gytha closed her eyes to shut out her son's pain, and behind her eyelids there came the picture of the four-year-old Osmund's tears on the day he kicked his prized pig's bladder hard into the gnarled old thorn bush that alone remained of the woodland that her grandfather had begun to clear. "Garth shall make you another, if you ask him politely" she had assured the heartbroken boy as he stood with the holed and limp leather in his little hands; and so he had. But now her son had seemed to deflate at his mother's words of a moment before, just as the bladder had ten years before, and he sat now with his face in his hands by the empty fireplace.

At length he raised his head, and the tears started to Gytha's eyes as she saw the pallor of his face. "Mother" he whispered, "oh mother, tell me ... tell me that there's another way. Please. Please. Anything is better than ... what would ...? No mother, you can't. Not a Norman. They killed my father ... my father and your husband. *You can't!*"

"My darling, my darling, there's no other way" Gytha whispered. "If you knew how many nights I've not slept trying to find another way, and the time is almost upon us ... believe me, there's no other way. I must submit."

"No, mother. Never that! Rather than that, I'd ... I'd rather leave here. Yes. Yes. Why don't we move away, mother? We can do it! My father has relatives ..."

"None in any better case than us, Osmund" and Gytha's voice was sad, defeated. "For defending his king's body and cause; for fulfilling his *hus-carl*'s oath, your father is termed 'rebel' by the victors. Had he lived – as no *hus-carl* could with his lord lying on the field – he would have been outcast, for the winners decide what's meet and what's just. D'you hear me my darling? *The winners decide!*"

"And everywhere, even in our own land, the custom is for the property and lands of a rebel to be forfeit. So the Normans claim that they follow our Saxon custom even as we would – as the man d'Avranches was at pains to point out to me on the day you and Garth led him here – you recall?"

The boy nodded, mute and despairing, and Gytha went on. "Aye, your father had relatives where I have none – but Osmund, their lands are forfeit also and they have the choice as we have, for all the men of your father's family are either dead or attainted as rebels through having sons who fought at Senlac."

She drew a shuddering breath. "Osmund, we can't change this fate or avoid any of it. D'Avranches explained to me— and I swear to you, he was much more gentle than he need have been— this manor is forfeit to William of Normandy, and he's given it to one Walter Giffard. Giffard will give it, in turn, to an unmarried vassal of his own, who will ... who will become my husband. As I say – we can't change this, and we must accept it." Her mouth twisted. "Ask Brother Edmund to explain what *vae victis*[3] means, my son."

"Then ... then we'll ... we can go elsewhere, mother!" exclaimed her son, starting to his feet. "We can ... I can – hire myself to a Saxon lord who

---

3 *Vae victis: woe to the conquered. (Lat.)*

has his lands still. Mother, we needn't live under any man's yoke!"

"Osmund, we all live under one yoke or another. The time isn't right for you to support a family yet although I know, beloved son of your father and me, that you'd die trying. And that's what frightens me. Besides, there's more."

"What more can there be?" Osmund flung back bitterly, "Normans will live and walk where my father lived and walked. I, who would have been lord after him, must see one of those who killed him lord it over my lands and my people. What more can there be?"

"Just this, my beloved" said Gytha gently, and she reached up to him. "See, my son, how tall you grow – a little more each day, and your shoulders broaden even as I look at them. I see my man more and more in your face with every month that passes, and that will never change. Aye, Osmund – even if I had no other to remind me of the man I loved and whose memory I'll love until my last breath – I would still have you, and it would be enough."

"But I have – we have, my son – your brothers Gyrth and Aelric also. And she whom you love more than anything or anyone in the world – your sister Sunngifu, who was not yet born when your father kept faith with his lord king, so that yours are the only man's hands, yours the only man's voice, she has ever known. And even if I were willing to lead them into a cold and cruel world, Osmund, there's one other thing I can't ignore or put aside. Or, say, many things."

Osmund frowned, put his hands over those of his mother where they lay on his shoulders, and raised an eyebrow. Gytha smiled sadly.

"Dearest son, how often I've seen that same look on your father's face when I perplexed him! Those 'many things' are the folk of this manor. They'll have a new lord whether I stay or go, will they not? But if I stay here, if I remain the lady of this manor, if I am my new husband's *adviser*"– and again her mouth twisted – "many hurtful things that might be done from ignorance . . . may not be done. Osmund, the folk of this manor were ours – your father's, mine, and they would have been yours one day – and it's our duty to care for them even as they care for us. Can you flee and leave Garth, Aelfgifu and their twins to face new masters? Can you, my darling? No. I thought not. Your father's shade won't let you!"

"But mother . . ." said Osmund hesitantly, "all you say's true. Aye, I know it – but mother, the price of all that is . . . well, it's you. You. A Norman will be your husband and your lord. A Norman will . . . will share your bed. The bed you shared with my father!"

Gytha flinched, and her small white teeth fastened on her bottom lip. She closed her eyes a moment, and when she opened them Osmund saw the tears brimming within them. "My son, my son, you're so young to be speaking of such things . . . but it's true. You're right. You're the man of this house, and I must remember that."

"Osmund, you're right and you're wrong at the same time. Yes, a Norman will be my husband and my lord. But he'll never be my man, for my man died at Senlac. Yes, a Norman will share my bed – but it won't be the place I shared with your father. Without my man, your father, in it, a bed is no more than a bed." She drew a ragged breath.

"Osmund, I went as a maid to that bed, and the maid, the woman and the wife died when your father did. And I will be dead until the Lord Jesus unites us again in His kingdom. Until then, Osmund, I'll live for the people dependent on me. That's how I'll keep your father's memory within me. It would please him, for your father never stepped back from his duty. Not ever, my darling son. So – nor must we."

The neighbouring manor, at the same time.

De Bois was uncomfortable in what he was doing, and the trouble he had in pronouncing the name of the Saxon woman who sat opposite only made things worse. Frithuswith Aelfricsson seemed to sense that, and de Bois fancied he could see a gleam of pleasure in her ageing and watery eyes.

"Look" he said doggedly to the interpreter, one of three that Giffard had organised for his troop, "tell Lady Frisfrith . . . ah, Friwith . . . tell her again. I've spoken to my men. Individually. And none of them heard anything untoward coming from the press-room in the barn, even though three of them noticed her daughter going in there with my soldier." He waited while his words were translated and noticed the gleam of amusement on the wrinkled face before him as Aelle Aelfricsson's widow replied. *Something wrong there* he decided. *Parent or no parent, if someone raped my daughter I'd be a lot less composed than that. No. I don't believe her. But what's she up to?*

"Lady Frithuswith says that's to be expected" reported the interpreter. "She also says that, if it comes to it, she can produce a servant who both heard the noises from inside and saw Wynfrytha, the daughter, leave the press-room and run to the big house after."

"After what?" asked de Bois, and the gleam of amusement returned as the Saxon woman replied "After he'd had his way and as soon as she could stand. After he and his soldiers had left the barn, because she didn't want the soldiers to mock her further."

"Right. Tell her to produce him." Lady Frisuwith turned her head and spoke to the maid who sat over a sampler at the window, and the girl left the room. As they waited in the uneasy silence, de Bois studied the woman opposite as best he could without seeming to and his sense of unease wouldn't go away. Lady Frisuwith Aelfricsson was no beauty, and she wasn't young, either. *Yes – she's too composed by half* he decided. *Ralph might be all I think he is, but there's a question or two to be asked here just the same, and I'll ask it.*

"Lady Aelfricsson" he said. "Your husband fell at Hastings, yes?"

"At Senlac" she corrected him, and he spread his hands in acknowledgement of the correction..

"Leaving you here with six daughters, I understand?" She assented, and he grunted. "Got something right, then. Now ask her how old she is. Go on!" De Bois grunted again when the interpreter made it clear that the lady admitted to being fifty.

"So she married late, if her eldest's eighteen?" he asked and the man admitted that it appeared so. "And she's had five other daughters in – what – those eighteen years, then."

The door opened and the maid reappeared with a young man whom de Bois judged was a groom, from the straw stalks that bedecked his clothing. At Lady Aelfricsson's nod, the man repeated for the interpreter what he claimed to have heard and seen from outside the press-room.

No, he hadn't seen the couple enter the room but, yes, he'd heard sounds from within it. Sounds of a blow – perhaps two or three, he couldn't be sure, and yes, he'd seen the soldier leave and ride away with his men. As soon as they had left the young mistress had emerged, crying, from the press-room and run to the big house, certainly, but he'd still been able to get a good look at her.

"Describe her" de Bois ordered the interpreter, "and listen, friend – you're already shit with your own kind for the work you do, so just remember where your future lies. I want your impressions as well as your translation, got it? Now tell him to describe what he saw."

The interpreter nodded, and put the question. The groom answered vehemently, and from the corner of his eye de Bois saw what he could only describe as a small smile of satisfaction steal across the face of the lady of the manor. *Too pat by a long way* he decided.

"Put this to him exactly, and fast" he said to the interpreter, and took a deep breath. "Right" he said. "You saw Wynfrytha come from the room, her right eye already swelling, her mouth cut, her hair dishevelled, and weeping. Then she ran to the big house. Was she running quickly?"

Yes, it came back. Yes, messire had it exactly. She'd been running as quickly as anyone in terror, and she was certainly knocked about, exactly as messire said. And he thought her gown had been torn, yes, but he couldn't be sure.

"Because she was running too fast, perhaps?" suggested de Bois, and the man agreed.

"Now you're as sure about what you've told me as you can be? Think about it, or it'll be the worse for you, man." The interpreter spoke; the man thought carefully and then nodded.

"Very good" said de Bois with a glance at Lady Aelfricsson, then he turned to the interpreter. "Tell him to go. And what d'you think of his story?"

"Seems to be quite clear about what he saw" said the interpreter. "There was no hesitation at all."

"Noticed that" said de Bois, "and something smells. Here's a groom – his only experience of Normans is hearing one rape his master's daughter, and here he is in a room with a senior officer asking him questions. And out it comes, with no loose ends? No hint of panic? No unease at all? Don't think so. But anyway – there are one or two loose ends, as it happens."

He swung to look coldly at Lady Aelfricsson as he spoke. "Tell the old crone this. I find her story, and that of her daughter, improbable, and I'm not going to take the investigation any further. My reasons are as follows."

"One. Her witness, the groom, got the damaged eye wrong. When I first saw Wynfrytha, it was her *left* eye that was blackened. But he got a good look at her, remember? Two. He wasn't sure that her gown was torn. You wouldn't miss that if you did see a rape victim immediately after the event. Because he got a good look at her, remember? Three – and finally. She wants us to believe that a virgin of eighteen who'd just been beaten into submission so she could be raped was *capable* of running so fast that a witness who was waiting there after being alerted fully by the sounds of this brutal act couldn't see details of her injuries, or even of her dress? If she'd just been raped, she wouldn't have been able to stagger, let alone sprint, for much, much longer than she waited in that press-room to leave."

He waited while this was repeated, and was gratified to see the woman's face lose its look of amusement. "Now" he instructed, "tell her this. The groom may have seen Wynfrytha coming from the press-room, but he didn't see a black eye, or a split lip, because she didn't have those injuries. She didn't have a torn gown, although the laces may have been pulled through. And she didn't have any difficulty in moving because she hadn't suffered any abuse she didn't want. Her daughter offered herself to my soldier, just as he told me."

Frithuswith Aelfricsson shook her head violently, any trace of amusement gone. She harangued the interpreter, who held up his hand in the end and turned to de Bois. "She won't admit it, messire – keeps on about the justice of the conqueror and no mercy for the conquered, that sort of thing. Swears her daughter's a good girl who was a virgin before our troop arrived. And so on. And on."

"If half of what my man says is true" returned de Bois, "she wasn't a virgin by a long day's march. But I've put time into this whole thing – time that's been wasted now, and she's going to hear from me. But I need to protect my man, for I've an idea what's behind this, and this old trot might decide to take it to Giffard himself. So she needs to know that I'm on to her. Calm her down, will you, and ask her to listen to me carefully?"

The royal court of Denmark, mid–September 1067.

The king of Denmark put his feet up on a stool and thought how blessedly good it was to be alone for the first time in the day. *There's always something* he thought; *someone wanting a signature or a decision or a favour or a judgement or . . . anything and everything.* But for the rest of that day, there was nothing. Nothing he knew about at that moment – *which isn't to say it can't change at any minute, but still . . .*

He could, he reflected, think about his impending marriage. For he was going to marry. Oh yes – he couldn't afford not to, much as it would cause grief to a man he genuinely liked and even respected. To the man he had just farewelled, the Scraeling.

He reached sideways to the cabinet that stood by his favourite chair, placed where it caught the longest light from the big window, and fumbled in the top drawer until his fingers found the sheet that lay on top. Magnus' personal letter to him.

Bloody cruel to make the Scraeling bring it he thought. *Not worthy of the man he thinks you are, Magnus. That must make you one of the Scraeling's rare mistakes. Ah well. . .* He unfolded the letter and scanned through it until the key section leaped up at him where he held the paper to the light.

. . . desirous of binding our kingdoms as closely as they should be, dearest brother, for the good of both . . . that end, and knowing of your unmarried state . . . hand of my stepmother, and Dowager Queen of Norway, Elisabeth, who was once Princess of Kiev also . . . . period of state mourning for a twelve-month following the death of my father in battle, ending . . .

Svein was under no illusions over why Magnus had sought to flatter him in this manner, for he was as wily as the Scraeling had always held him to be. Being perfectly aware of Magnus' parlous military situation, he had noted the imposition of the import tax with wry amusement and full encouragement to Danish traders to take as much advantage of it as possible. *Tell them 'Fill your boots while it lasts'* had been his advice to his chancellor. Why not, if it kept them happy and off his back? Wasn't as if his coffers couldn't stand the revenue from the eagerly-sought trading licenses, after the years when Hardraada had nearly ruined trade permanently.

But Magnus has nothing to worry about from Denmark, if only he knew it mused Svein. For neither Magnus nor Norway had anything Svein wanted, even though England's Godwinsson had savaged the Norse army to the point where the king of Norway and his counsellors started in panic whenever a Dane or a Swede broke wind. But Godwinsson himself had been savaged a scant three weeks later, by the Bastard of Normandy, in the closest-fought battle imaginable . . . *and if Godwinsson hadn't been so battle-happy he'd still be king, and it'd be William rotting in the rain for the past year* thought Svein. *When you think about it, anyway, I held off Hardraada for years with a lot less to work with than Godwinsson had – and the Landwaster was a better soldier than William'll ever be, no matter how long his Norman arse points downwards.* Yes, the king of Denmark had something quite other than invading Norway in mind.

For William had his troubles in England, just hanging onto the place, and Svein was of a mind to multiply those troubles. After all, Hardraada had trumpeted the justice of his claim to England's throne through his scant connection with Cnut the Great, who'd ruled England, Denmark, Norway and parts of Sweden – *cheeky bugger wasn't even related to Cnut. I am!*

England was still the richest country in Europe – all that had tempted Hardraada was still there to tempt Svein and, come the spring of the following year, Svein was going to take the field for the first time in the five years since he'd narrowly failed to nail Hardraada at the battle of the Nissa.

But let's not put temptation in the path of a young and headstrong king he had thought, *especially one who's a Haraldsson, even if he's only got one or two notable hard men left.* Hence his concern with developing lasting good relations with Norway, but now – now, fortune had smiled on him as never before, because Magnus was young enough and pompous enough to let a dynastic alliance bind him forever. Marriage into the Norwegian royal family! – *hang on, she's never been more'n an unwanted queen anyway. Hardraada allowing her and the Scraeling proves that, an' since Stamford – well . . . But don't look a gift horse in the mouth. What d'you care?* And it gave him a claim to the Norwegian throne no less strong than Hardraada's claim to England had been.

Also, it proved the value of having eyes and ears in the right place. Hard luck for the Scraeling, though. *All I can find out says he and Elisabeth are a happier pair than most married couples.* The royal hand smacked the arm of the chair in frustration. *I did give him the chance* he told himself. *If he'd taken me up on my offer, he could've brought his Elisabeth to Denmark and welcome. I'd give more'n a royal bride to have the man who built the Norwegian army mastermind my invasion of England . . .*

But what could he have done? Taken the Scraeling into his confidence? No chance. That sort of tidings altered history. *No, majesty, my heart's in Norway* said the voice in Svein's head. Figure of speech, or what? Was he talking about Elisabeth or Norway itself? *Story is, he talked Godwinsson out of blinding young Olaf and killing those hard men of Hardraada's who survived, after all.* Maybe his years as Hardraada's man had made him Norway's man too.

The palm smacked the chair again. No middle way. He needed Elisabeth to cement the alliance that would leave him free to act. *I did my best* he told himself. *Sorry Scraeling – no middle way, I'm afraid. Sorry, my friend.*

The Aelfricsson estate, near Reading, England, mid-September.

Aelle Aelfricsson's widow subsided at last and sat glaring at a stoic de Bois, who turned at length to the interpreter.

"Tell her" he said, "that I'm not going to take her complaint any further, as I said, but that she can if she wants. Tell her that the area commander is Walter Giffard de Bolebec, lord of Longueville, and that he's a friend of the king and a man known for his fairness and sense of justice." He waited while the interpreter did his work, and then spoke again.

"But she knows that, because she's taken the trouble to look into what we're doing by the king's command. So if she does go to Giffard" he resumed, "tell her I'll give my conclusions to him also, and they'll be what I've said in front of her. And I'll add what I believe to be the reasons why she did what she did in accusing a young soldier of something that might have led to disgrace and dismissal. Good God, our king dismissed a noble of the army for something that occurred at the end of the biggest battle anyone who fought in it can ever remember! So she'll have some explaining to do of her own, and she's going to regret the whole thing, assure her!"

The two English spoke for a moment and the interpreter turned back to de Bois. "Messire, Lady Frithuswith wishes to know what you mean" and the Norman nodded.

"Very good. I'm happy to tell her, but I'm not going to mince words. This is how I see it. Lady . . . Lady Friswith has heard of the king's policy that widows holding land will be married to landless Norman soldiers, and she doesn't – or she may not - want to marry again, because her childbearing days are over. She's also heard that our king has had the Pope declare this campaign a crusade – she may even have heard that our king is an upright and scrupulous man. Which he surely is. And I think she saw that being the wronged party might get us to leave her lands alone. But there's no chance of that, tell her, and there never was. So what she did – and my soldier termed it 'whoring her daughter', was as hopeless as it was wrong. Tell her."

So the interpreter spoke, and de Bois watched a tear escape the old and tired eyes to slide down the graven cheeks. He leaned forward. "Lady" he said, looking directly at her and holding her gaze as the tears flowed freely now, "your lands are forfeit, as was told you by the man you wronged when he came here first. Nothing will change that. Your lands will take a Norman master, as will you and yours, and that is your fate."

The Court, Nidaros, Norway, late September.

Magnus hawked up the phlegm and spat it into the bowl held for him by the physician. He got his breath back under control and sipped at the spiced wine while the Arab took the bowl to the window and peered into it.

"Well?" demanded the king, "there's blood in it isn't there?"

"Oh yes, majesty" agreed the doctor, "but it's nothing to worry about"

"Nothing to worry about?" asked Magnus, "our lungs are bleeding and you tell us there's nothing to worry about? What d'you bloody mean?"

The doctor winced. "The blood, majesty, isn't from your lungs. You've been coughing a good deal of late, and I suspect the blood is throat lining. Nothing more. Throat lining."

"Throat lining. Nothing more" mimicked the king. "It's *our* bloody throat lining and *our* bloody cough, doctor. What're you doing about it? All of it?"

"Ah . . . the spiced wine – as you have it there – and the same heated as well before your majesty retires should bring relief. Also—"

Magnus lost his temper and his royal reserve at the same time. "Well it hasn't so far, you fucking quack. Nor your bleeding – Christ, man, between your bleeding and my cough, I'm about due to run out of blood altogether! Not good enough!"

The Arab cringed. "Majesty, I have an infusion for you. Prepared with my own hand. A mixture of moss and lichens from your own land and certain dried herbs from the Inland Sea. Most efficacious in all previous situations where I've tried it, I do assure you. May I show you how to use it?"

"No, you can't. What you can do is take yourself away, because I've work to do. When I'm ready, I'll send for you. And if this doesn't work – we'll give it a week, my man - you're going to be the new pox-doctor to the trading ports of Norway! Close the door behind you."

The stricken Arab bowed himself out and Magnus walked to the large desk in the corner where he picked up the letter with the big and ornate seal of Denmark in the bottom corner.

Brother Magnus, Greetings . . . fully agree . . . new era of peace and mutual prosperity . . . amicable trading between all . . . forging alliances based on goodwill where once we forged weapons . . . mistakes of the past . . . king's duty to marry where best he can for the good of his people . . . end of the period of formal mourning is quite acceptable . . . Her Majesty settled in her new kingdom by Christ's Mass and the new year . . .

Nidaros, about the same time.

Nothing changes, decided an amused Scraeling as he shuffled past the same sentry who performed the same salute with a complete lack of expression. But not so, he caught himself – wasn't he about to become a married man for the first time in his life? Busy as he was these days, wasn't that enough change for anyone? Right or wrong, he decided, it was all the change he needed or wanted at that time. With the import tax a thing of the past, it was time he turned his attention to building a picture of what was going on in England.

True, the leading men of England had submitted to William at Christmas last, but if there was anything he knew of England and the English it was that they were a stubborn, proud and determined race who cherished their independence and that, he decided, meant that the Conqueror – to use the name that was now commonly used for the erstwhile Bastard of Normandy – wouldn't sit easily in his saddle for a time yet. At the least, he told himself, it wouldn't hurt the Scraeling to know what was going on or what might go on.

Well – if truth were told there was more in that than simple prudence. His first reaction to the disaster that was Senlac had been to return to England – but to what? His cousin Penda was surely dead with Harold Godwinsson, even as he had told Elisabeth, and while he'd had some notion of doing what he could for Gytha and Penda's children, he had had no idea of what it might be.

In the back of his mind he had a half-formed suggestion that he might personally undertake a formal embassy to England – why not? He had done no less for Hardraada, to the court of Edward whom men called the Confessor, in the days when he ruled. And, he would advise Magnus, it couldn't hurt for the new king of Norway to be among the first to offer greetings to the even newer king of England.

Aye, that was it. What had Svein said? *Magnus, now . . . different story altogether. He needs to cut his own track, just to impress, y'know?* Just so – good wishes from the young king of Norway were likely to be warmly received by a still-embattled William of England, who would doubtless honour their donor both then and in the future.

Nothing disloyal to Penda's memory in any of that, decided the Scraeling as he drew near to his own door, for no amount of regret would alter the verdict of Senlac, and anything that brought, or helped bring, stability and peace to England would bring the same to Gytha. And while he was over there, he'd certainly discover what her situation was. She might even decide – for Elisabeth was sure to . . . but no, he chided himself, he mustn't make plans for Gytha's future . . .

His door flew open as he reached for the handle, and a sobbing Olga tumbled through it to fall at his feet. "Lord Ranulf. . . my lady . . . to the palace, and an escort — my lord, they bade me pack her clothes, and I've done that . . . but oh my lord, my lady bade me stay and speak to you . . . my lord, what does it mean, for my lady didn't know either!"

"Stop!" commanded the Scraeling. "Olga, stop! Listen! Listen to me, yes?" And he drew the sobbing maid up into his arms and then away to the stretch of his arms where he shook her gently.

"Peace, girl, peace. Now . . . ?" Olga gave a racking sob, gulped twice and took a deep, deep breath. The Scraeling nodded and shook her gently again.

"That's the girl, Olga. Now – begin again please. Where is my lady?"

"Two hours ago, lord. Two hours. An escort came from the palace, and said they were commanded to bring her there. And they wouldn't even wait for her clothes – said they'd come back for them and I was to pack them – all, lord Ranulf, and my lady bade me wait here with them and hope that you came home, and I saw you through the window just now, and . . . oh . . ." she broke down again.

The Scraeling tried to think clearly through the whirling of his head. "It's the end of the period of formal mourning for Hardraada, Olga" he said. "Perhaps it's something to do with that. Look, nothing's easier than for me to find out. Cheer up girl"

But even as he said the words a cold hand clutched at his stomach. He was one of the most powerful men in Norway and he had had no inkling of what had been going on as he scribbled away in his office in that same palace. None whatever. *What was it?*

It had been his intention to bathe, dress and return to the palace to seek audience of the king, and he had already advised the chamberlain of his intention to do that. At that interview he intended to ask for Elisabeth's hand, and he . . .

Ah, that was it! Magnus was a step ahead of him and had divined his intentions. He wanted to give Elisabeth to him on the spot as a reward for his service at the Danish court, and had decided upon a surprise. Yes – he and Elisabeth were probably smiling together over his supposed panic even at that moment.

"I have it, Olga – dry your eyes, lass" he said, and explained his thinking. When he had done, Olga flung her arms about his neck and hugged him to her own great embarrassment when she realised what she'd done.

"That's all right" laughed the Scraeling over her protestations. "You know, you're a real waste – you should be making some man the happiest fellow in the world, Olga! Have a bath drawn for me, my dear, and I'll practise being suitably astonished and pleased while I'm having it – our secret for evermore, mind!"

An hour later he was ushered into the royal presence, and to his surprise Magnus was alone. The king made a few complimentary remarks on the success of his embassy to Svein, but the Scraeling's instincts caught something more than a hint of awkwardness in his tone.

Well – the Scraeling took a deep breath. "Majesty, you do me more honour than I deserve. Svein is a pleasant man and a wise king, and I'm certain we'll travel very well together. Now, majesty, if I may, I'd like to turn to a personal matter."

Magnus ran the royal tongue over the royal lips and nodded for the Scraeling to continue.

"It won't have escaped your majesty's attention that your stepmother, the Lady Elisabeth, and I have . . . have an attachment to one another. Nor that this was so in your father's time, majesty. What you may not know is that your father . . . your *late* father . . . encouraged me to . . . to meet with your stepmother in the days after he had decided to take your majesty's mother to wife. He – King Harald – made it plain to me that his marriage to Queen Elisabeth was . . . was to continue only for the sake of giving no offence to her family." *What's he doing? He's sitting there not even blinking. Is he listening?*

"As I say" resumed the Scraeling, his lips dry, "the Lady Elisabeth and I have an attachment – a long-standing attachment, majesty, that found favour with your royal father" – *that's stretching it a bit. Hardraada certainly knew about it though, because he'd torment me with it when he was in the mood* " . . . no longer young, and we . . . Lady Elisabeth and I . . . widow, would regularise our union if your majesty would . . ."

Magnus stirred. "Queen Elisabeth" he said, as if waking from a dream. "She's Queen Elisabeth. You said so yourself. Just now."

"Majesty? Ah . . . quite so. Queen Elisabeth, aye." *Ah, so you were listening. Good.* "Well, majesty. I would formally ask . . ."

"Yes. She's a queen, lord Ranulf, and there's no getting away from that. As a queen, she's a member of the royal family."

"Quite so, majesty, quite so." *I should bloody hope so. What's the matter with him tonight?* "And as the head of that family, majesty, it's for you to . . ."

"But as a member of the royal family, lord Ranulf, she's more than a queen and more than an individual. You might say she's a state asset also. Yes – an asset. Don't you agree?"

The Scraeling blinked. "Well majesty, I'd never considered her in quite those terms. I can certainly say that lady . . . ah, Queen Elisabeth is an asset to me. And naturally, I'd try with my life to be one to her." *This is going wrong* thought the Scraeling. *It's bizarre, at the very least. Anyone'd think she was a bolt of cloth or something.*

"Majesty, in so many words . . ."

"No, lord Ranulf. She's a *state* asset. Princes, princesses, and especially queens, are a *state* asset. Whatever they are to the rest of us. Elisabeth is a *state* asset, we say, and as a matter of fact . . . we have contracted a state marriage for her."

"Eh? You've what . . . your pardon, majesty, I thought you said you had . . . for . . . for Queen Elisabeth? I've misunderstood."

"No you haven't lord Ranulf. We have contracted a state marriage for the Dowager Queen Elisabeth. When the period of state mourning for our father, King Harald III is over. As it will be in a week or so, will it not?"

The Scraeling shook his head like a man deafened. Magnus' voice seemed to come from far away. ". . . defence of the kingdom . . . binding tie of friendship . . . very highest level of kinship. Service . . . not limited by earthly life . . ."

"Stop!" said the Scraeling for the third time that day. "Stop!"

"What was that?" snapped Magnus, "what did you say?"

"I said 'Stop', majesty. I – I have misunderstood again, I fear." His head felt full of porridge. "Do I understand that your majesty has arranged a marriage between Elisabeth and . . . and . . . whom?" *Oh Christ, let him say 'You, you dolt!' Let it be a clumsy royal joke!*

"Svein Estrithsson of Denmark" came the words, each one dropping into the Scraeling's consciousness like the hammer of doom.

"No!" choked the Scraeling. "I was with Svein only days ago, and he spoke no word . . . that is, he said . . . he would have said – " . . . .*Elisabeth's a relative of mine somewhere along the line y'know. Can never get my head round that sort of thing . . .*

"We asked him to discuss the offer with no-one. No-one, lord Ranulf. And as one sovereign to another . . ."

"But this is the highest affair of state, majesty" croaked the Scraeling, his head spinning, "I would have drafted it . . . been involved in it . . . in some way, surely . . ."

"You were, lord Ranulf. The letter of offer was drafted by another. You delivered it from ourself to king Svein."

A hot ball of flame ignited in the Scraeling's belly and he doubled over in a pain such as he couldn't remember ever experiencing. *I should have listened . . . really listened– Svein made me that offer . . . where's the way round this?*

" . . . not for those of base birth, lord Ranulf . . . risen high, but . . . limitations . . . hope . . . highest levels of our court . . . but not that level . . . what?"

"I said" answered the Scraeling rising painfully to his full height, the knot of fire still in his stomach, "I've served your family faithfully and well since I was fifteen, and more recently since . . ."

"It's your place to serve" snapped Magnus, "and no-one can say you've suffered by it. You're a wealthy man, and the power I allow you is—"

" . . . a new king who found himself on the throne in dangerous circumstances . . ."

"Hah! I have other advisers, other ministers . . ."

"And it seems your majesty calls on them when you wish to break faith with —"

"Break faith? *Break faith, you insolent cripple?*" Magnus fairly screamed the words and he broke into a paroxysm of coughing that flung him back into the chair from which he'd started in his anger. And perhaps that was the best thing that might have happened, for it gave the Scraeling a moment to come to himself, a moment in which he realised that his right hand was clenched fast under his left forearm and the heavy throwing-knife he'd learned to keep sheathed on its underside in the years of his wandering with Hardraada's viking band. But it wasn't there, and hadn't been there since his return from England and Stamford, for that life of treachery and betrayal was over. Wasn't it?

The Scraeling handed Magnus a goblet of wine and the king caught his breath and spoke weakly. "Lord Ranulf. This kingdom stands in peril, and none knows it better than you, for you brought back our army from the wreckage of England. Norway needs a strong alliance with one whom you admitted is perhaps the strongest king between ourselves and France . . ."

"Majesty. Svein has no designs upon us. What would it profit him? *Nothing!*"

Magnus set his jaw. "Has he told you this? Have you discussed it? Do you have his oath in writing?"

The Scraeling felt his temper rising. "Of course not! Were a simple question infallible, majesty, what would be the need of spies and the divers other ways I gather the information that permits *you* to make decisions? And have I yet failed you? Aye, *have I?*"

"And you will not fail me in this, lord Ranulf. You will stand aside from any hope of marriage to the Dowager Queen Elisabeth. That is my word!"

The Scraeling fought for control, and when he spoke it was as reasonably as possible. "Majesty, it's poor reward for my service to you. It's even worse in that you've revoked the gift of your predecessor to me" *which was one way of putting it* he thought, "and that is not a custom of kings, for all that . . ."

"How dare you!" exploded Magnus. "You would—"

"Yes I would!" interrupted the Scraeling. "It's my function – it's *been* my function – to advise you, as I advised your father. In my time I've done that as best I can, even when you didn't want to hear the advice – aye, both of you!"

"And it's gone to your head, Scraeling! You'd do well to remember — "

"Magnus of Norway, your father was a greedy and selfish pagan – but I never needed to tell him that a king keeps faith with those who serve him well. In revoking his gift to me, you've broken faith and done what isn't fair. And no loyal servant should be treated so!"

"'Fair' my lord? 'Fair'? Let me remind you of what you said of unfairness in this very room. You admitted that the import tax had been unfair, and then you said, *But it's been necessary, and sometimes in a royal life kings, and those who do their bidding, can't manage both.* Do you remember that?"

The Scraeling tasted the bitterness and gall of his own words as Magnus went on, "You will doubtless reply that your tax was for the good of the state – as you saw it. Can you guess, lord Ranulf, how I'm going to argue next?"

There was nothing to say, but the Scraeling lifted his head and said, thickly, "Majesty, pray you pardon my words. Majesty, I humbly ask that you allow the lady Elisabeth and myself to leave your lands and dominions together, never to return. And if you will allow this, I will forfeit all my land and possessions to the crown, and swear on the holiest of relics never to seek their return or recovery."

Magnus gestured impatiently. "Lord Ranulf, you haven't understood. I don't seek to beggar you, or to cause you distress. Well, it's not my *intention* to cause you distress. This is a matter of state, my lord, and nothing else. Try to see it as that. And in that, recall that you are who you are but the Dowager Queen has been royal since her earliest days – aye, both in her homeland and . . . what?"

"I said" returned a Scraeling looking into the abyss of complete despair, "I'm descended from those who were kings of Brittany in the ancient times – when your majesty's forefathers lived in caves and wore bearskins that smelt worse than when they belonged to the bear. That's what I said. Did you hear it that time?"

Reading, England, October 1067.

The axe crashed into the reinforced shield in a flurry of blows so swift that Garth broke ground before them, leaping backwards and sideways to break off.

"Hold! Hold, master! Chris' bones, what power! It's happening, lord Osmund – jus' like I said, 'member? It's happening!"

Osmund dropped the axehead and leaned on the clumsy implement, grinning. He was scarcely breathing hard, noted Garth, even as he grinned back. "Y're hitting hard, master, and y're hitting often! An' well I c'n see why!" He nodded at Osmund's bare arms - arms that had, seemingly overnight, sprouted muscle and sinew along their length and were still giving promise of more to come.

"That's the tree, Garth" said the young man. "I can feel the muscles burning as I hang there, but there always seems to be some left. Just the way you showed me. See?" And he put the axe down carefully and trotted across to the oak tree where he leaped to seize a lonely and sturdy limb and drew himself up, the weight of his body depending from the branch, a dozen times without apparent effort before he rolled out a wrist to fling one hand to the front of the branch and then the other to hang on the branch like, Garth realised, a crucified Christ. Then, to Garth's utter disbelief, he raised himself – once, twice, three times on his arms alone – until the branch touched the back of his neck and the muscles of his back stood out like knotted cords.

Osmund crashed down to the grass beneath the old oak, groaned and stretched. "Jesu, Garth, they hurt! Three's more'n I've ever done, though"

"Naught amiss'n that" said Garth in bemusement. "I never taught you that! Never seen anythin' like it, master – no wonder y'r filling out!" And he looked again at the hands that were no longer those of a child and up the sinewy arms to the broadening shoulders.

"Before God, y'r lord Penda's son, master Osmund" he said, "an' right proud of you he'd be this moment. But that's all f'r today, I think. Let y'go early, eh?"

"You sorry for me, then, Garth?" said Osmund with an impish grin on the face that was Gytha's, and Garth grinned back.

"No master. But I'll be sorry for me 'f we do any more. You've split the shield, even with the axe-head reversed."

The Chronicle.

*M*agnus would not allow me to see Elisabeth. She was gone from me, he insisted, and there was an end of it. Nothing I said could shake him, and in the end he rose and summoned his chamberlain to have me shown out. Aye, I was all-but thrown out of his presence. I, the Scraeling, Norway's chief minister – but in that moment I would have given it all for a fisherman's estate and hut if I could have had Elisabeth to share it, for I didn't doubt that she would have done so and gladly.

It was months before I saw Magnus Haraldsson's action for what it was – the assertion of a man living in the shadow of his mighty sire and desperate to be recognised as his own man. And perhaps the angry railing of a sick man against the fate that condemned him to be a weakling. Did he know then that his doom was already upon him? No matter – whatever his reasons, understanding them brought me no comfort.

I had known despair in my life before. The long-gone night when viking wolves burst from the sea, raping and pillaging upon the convent that had been my home, bringing me within a second of Skallagrim's knife tearing across my throat as I waited on Hardraada's whim as to whether I lived or died. And until I realised that I had a use to him and his cut-throats, I had known both fear and despair often enough after that. But slowly and gradually I had come to realise that one goal remained to me – to work for, plan towards and plot the day when I would cause Hardraada's fall, and with it the world that had produced him and his kind.

And God had been good to me, for I had done just that. Because of me, Hardraada had been drawn down to England. Because of me he had set off across enemy territory, he and the bulk of his army without their mailed byrnies. And because of me and my planning, the army of England caught him and slew him, slew the Landwaster.

And I had my new world. In it I still had a goal, something to work for and towards – as I had told Svein, aye and Harold Godwinsson before him, that was to be the making of a Norway that would be a threat to none but fish, and a good and peaceful neighbour to all.

But not now. Without Elisabeth, without the woman Hardraada had cast aside and who had chosen me, there was nothing. Nothing but an abyss of such depth, such width and such blackness that it must surely swallow me. And her?

What of my golden Elisabeth? Was she, who was everything to me, to become again a chattel in yet another game played by kings?

There was no justice in it. Kings had ... well, they had servants like myself to do their thinking and to unfold their dreams. But "He needs to cut his own track, just to impress, y'know, Scraeling. You see if I'm not right" said Svein within my head.

I would not accept it. I'd find my way to Elisabeth somehow; nothing ought to be beyond the man who'd outfoxed the commander of the Varanger Guard, the ferocious Landwaster, and brought him to the dust. Aye. All I needed was to find a way, and we'd leave Norway forever. But together.

Nidaros, early October.

"It's no good, Scraeling" said Skuli Bergrsson. "Styrkar's taken personal charge of her 'safety'...'s what they're calling it. An' he's taken her to a royal hunting-lodge until she leaves for Denmark. They've guessed you'll have a go, like. Well, they're expecting it."

"Hunting lodge? Magnus hasn't the balls to get on a horse" said a brooding Scraeling, thickly. Skuli sighed.

"No. 'S one of Harald's. Look, Scraeling, does it matter who owns the fucking lodge? Come on, man – sort yourself out. An' leave that alone" And he picked up the wine flask and put it firmly out of reach. "You've got the brain that built the best army in the world – fucking use it, eh? Look – I reckon I can get you into that lodge to see y'r lady. What you do after that's up to you. But if you want to snatch her – I've got a *drakkar* in the harbour. Inner harbour, mind, but still."

"That's good of you, Skuli. Very good of you. But from what I hear, there're guardships across both harbours – fact, I've seen the deployment. Never mind how, but I've seen it. They're using my fucking system, f'Christ's sake, the one I put in place when Hardraada's fleet was hosting here. How's that then?" and he laughed bitterly.

"Right, right. Leave that f'r now. Want me to get you into the lodge?"

The Scraeling frowned as he fought the effects of several large cups of wine. "How'll you do that Skuli? Good of you, but ... why?" and he belched.

"I'll do it – don't worry. Why? Might be 'cause I owe you something f'r being the man who led a hundred of us into the middle 'f a Bulgar army and then dropped the bad bastards' leaders one by one to encourage us. Or maybe I owe you f'r getting me away from England when you should've cut my throat at the anchorage, me with that many wounds an' raving out of my head. Buggered if I know why, Scraeling."

"But I do know this – I don't see that man here tonight. I haven't seen him all week. What I have seen is someone who reaches for a flask like he used to reach for a pen. You're a funny bugger – you never gave up on me 'cause you never give up on anyone, Scraeling. Why the fuck're you giving up on y'self? Eh? Well? Odin's balls – get a fucking grip! All right?"

"Not that easy Skuli" muttered the Scraeling, repressing another belch. "Bastards're waiting for us, y'say. Need to think about it eh?"

Skuli glanced at him and shook his head more in pity than despair.

The port of Nidaros, the next night.

The marshal of Norway had asked himself several times lately whether or not he should change his ways to match his new lifestyle. The king had certainly shown him many marks of favour since their conversation in the palace, and Magnus was more than a little straight-laced. He certainly wouldn't approve of what Styrkar was doing at that moment, which was tightening his grip on the large and fleshy hips of his favourite whore as she knelt on the creaking bed in the upstairs room of the dockside tavern.

On the other hand, he told himself as he thrust hard enough to elicit a grunt from the woman, the simple soldier he was had commended him to two kings – why change a winning habit? *Because you have to stay up with things* he decided as the fire building in his loins made him increase the tempo – *hah, nice choice of words there* – until the rhythmic slap of flesh on flesh filled the room.

The whore moaned in protest, but Styrkar gripped her even tighter and pulled her to him as he slammed harder into her. "Settle back and enjoy it, you bitch" he grunted, "long way t'go yet . . . got a real man on y'hands tonight!" The whore made a sound that might have been either protest or pleasure, dropped her head and spread herself even wider before she reached back between her legs to find him. Styrkar stopped considering any future beyond the next five minutes and addressed himself to the task of trying to drive her through the wall.

But he was thinking about it two hours later as he went to the stables – thinking so deeply that the figures materialising from the dark backyard took him completely by surprise. Slammed back against the wall and pinioned there by four strong men, he felt a hand relieve him of dagger and sword – "Check his boot-top" – came a voice he hadn't heard for a long while, and the hand groped round his sealskin ankle-boots before reporting them clear.

"Well, Styrkar – you randy little bugger, you. Y've kept us waiting, you old goat. That because it takes you longer these days – or 'cause she couldn't get enough of you, lucky girl?" said the voice from the dark, followed by sniggers from the men who held him.

"Skuli" said Styrkar, "Skuli Bergrsson. Freya's tits, man, are you in trouble or what! Y'know who I am these days, don't you? Course you do!"

"Course I do" snapped the voice. "I know *what* you are too. You're a backstabbing little shit who potted Haldor Snorresson to get where you are now. He's still alive, Styrkar, still governor of Iceland and still keen on visiting you – or having you visited – one dark night to thank you for his . . . ah . . . promotion. He's still got the temper of a bear with a sore arse, by the way. Some things don't change, old friend."

" 'Fuck's it got to do with you? Me and Haldor?" asked Styrkar belligerently.

"Couple of reasons. Three really, Styrkar. First of them is you being prepared t'do anything that'll get you a leg up. *Anything* I said, 'specially jailing women."

"Second – remember Ivarr Todrsson? From the old days? Aye? He married a cousin of mine y'know, an' their boy, Haakon, he fell out with his old man. But he came back in the end, they let bygones be bygones an' young Haakon impressed Harald to where he got a seat on the Army Council. Remember? Just after you shafted Haldor, it was. So he soldiered 'longside his father, he did – made us all real happy."

"But they both died at Stamford, Styrkar, same's I nearly did. Same's lots of good men did. But they needn't have, 'cause their battle station was under the Landwaster banner with Harald hisself, y'remember, and they wouldn't have died if your division'd supported young Eystein when Orri's Storm went in to get the king's body back.[4] But you chose to stand off!

---

4 *See 'The Landwaster'*

Didn't you? Don't fucking lie, Styrkar. *I was there!*"

"Someone had to cover the retreat" said Styrkar sullenly. "So where were you then, you clever bastard?"

"Taking a wound that near killed me trying to *prevent* a retreat in the first place, y'arsehole! An' I lost my division to those bastard English *huscarls* doing it!"

"Let the *skalds* sing about the past, old man!" snapped Styrkar. "Why now?"

"Now? That's the third reason, friend and comrade. What was left of my axemen got me back to Riccall – most of 'em died along the way mind you – and the Scraeling got me aboard a *drakkar* just alive, an' he kept me alive on the way home. An' when I found out you'd cheated Odin's ravens again, Styrkar, I'd have come for your head there an' then, but he talked me out of it. Said we – Norway – had lost enough an' it was time to rebuild, an' find new ways, an' . . . an' a whole lot of other shit. Still don't know why I listened, but he's got that way about him, the Scraeling, eh? An' in the end, well, he talked me out of you, like I said."

"So I retired, an' you carried on kissing arses. You were always good at that. But how've you repaid the man who saved your fucking head, Styrkar? You've locked up his woman, that's how. Never mind" and he clapped Styrkar consolingly on the shoulder, "your dirty habits are gonna give you the chance to pay a few debts, you horrid little piece of shit. Listen carefully . . ."

Giffard's headquarters, Wokingham, England, October 1067.

"So there you are" concluded de Bois, shifting his weight in the hard wooden chair and wincing as the blood rushed back. "That's what it was all about. Mother couldn't face being married off again, so she put daughter up to crying rape. And it was your bad luck to be the next good-looking young chap along."

"My good luck to have a troop commander who'd look so closely into things, though" mused Ralph de Courcy. "Thank you, cousin."

"Mind you" said de Bois reflectively, "Whoever gets that manor from Giffard'll earn it. Lady Frisso-witha-something-sson isn't young, or attractive come to that, and she's had a hard life that shows."

"That's no way" said the younger man in mock hauteur, "to speak of the woman you promised me!"

"Eh?" said de Bois. "I what?"

"Just after you advised me to keep my cock in my pants – remember? Or I'd get the mother? No?"

"Did I? Believe me, cousin, you'd think twice. Even a randy young goat like you."

"I might, if she's what you say. But – " said Ralph, greatly daring, "I could handle a bit more of the daughter."

De Bois sat bolt upright. "You young bugger – you've missed disgrace by the skin of your teeth, and already you're looking for more! Now look – I'm going to say this once, and only once and it's something your father should have told you before you left home. Your cock's got one eye and no brain, and that makes it a fine servant but a poor master. All right? Keep it out of trouble!"

Ralph held up a placatory hand. "Hang on, cousin, hang on. I'm thinking past just banging Wynfrytha. That manor'll go to someone who Giffard regards as useful, yes?"

"That's usually what happens" said de Bois dryly. "And you're interested?"

"Not if you are" said de Courcy. "You've served Giffard well these many years. And the duke – sorry, the king – too. You could expect it."

"Not me" said de Bois firmly. "I'm a member of Giffard's household, and I'm well content with that. There'll be work for a soldier here for all the years I've got left."

"And what then, cousin?" sought the younger man. "Wouldn't it be nice to have someone make a bed warm enough to crawl into on a cold night?"

De Bois sighed. "How do I put this, Ralph? D'you eat bread?"

"Bread? Of course I do – we all do! What's that about?"

"Do you buy the oven when you want bread, or just the loaf?"

"Eh? I buy the loaf, of— oh! Oh! I see! Well put, cousin!" And Ralph de Courcy flung back his head and laughed.

"But let's get back to you. Would you really take on a woman so much older, whose name's a nightmare?" asked de Bois, and de Courcy shook his head.

"No – but I'd think more than twice about the daughter. Well why not? She'll inherit the manor one day won't she? And if the old lady wants a home for the rest of her life, that's fine, and that's still within royal policy, surely. And if I'm her husband, the manor'll pass to me then . . . not to mention the oven!"

De Bois rubbed his jaw. "It's just possible, I suppose" he conceded. "You were one of the first to join the duke at the Normandy muster, you fought at Hastings, you took a leading part in quelling that riot at the coronation in London last Christmas, and you've given good service ever since, this last piece of nonsense aside. But no one your age's going to get a manor that size. Not unless you do something spectacular for Giffard, I'd think."

"Or unless someone with Giffard's ear puts in a good word" argued de Courcy. "And that's you. You're his senior commander, and a lot more than a 'member of the household'. You'd be in line for a manor yourself if you were the marrying kind, cousin, and you can't deny it. More'n that – you're well known as William's man too, through and through. You're more like the king than the king is!"

"You've got a lively imagination, Ralph. But I'll speak to Giffard about the matter, because I'm going to tell him the whole story before he hears it from someone else. I'll tell him, too, that I'd have gone into it for anyone else, anyone who happened not to be a relation, but who was an officer of mine."

"There you go, cousin – scrupulous to the end!" shot Ralph, and de Bois grinned.

"Too old a dog to change my ways now, and besides – yes Bruno? Come in." The last to the man who'd just knocked and stooped through the doorway.

"I hear Giffard's name just then, Ivo?" asked the newcomer, "What've you been up to? Wants to see you soon as you can – he muttered something about widows and manors."

In the hills behind Nidaros, the same night.

The party's hooves drummed up the track and slowed for the sharp bend up to the last level. "Stand!" came a hail from the darkness above, and Styrkar drew rein and raised his voice. "Styrkar, marshal of Norway and a party of four."

"Tonight's word, lord Styrkar?"

"Eystein. And the second is Viken. And the Viken was Eystein's regiment, so stand aside."

"Come forward to be recognised" after a silence during which the sentry had presumably registered the rasp in Styrkar's voice.

"Eystein? Viken? Styrkar, you're a cheeky bugger as well as a treacherous one, aren't you?" murmured the man who leaned forward from the marshal's left. "Let's go, but recall your head's been forfeit to me since Stamford. And remember that, whoever lives beyond tonight, you fucking won't if anything goes wrong. Got something up my sleeve – no kidding – and it's just for you. Scraeling taught me that trick when he pulled it on me one time in Sicily, an' I never even saw it till it was tickling my nose, eh? Half a chance, Styrkar – that's all I want, 'cause it's all I need."

They walked the mounts forward to where an officer raised a burning torch from the brazier that kept the early winter chill from the half-dozen men who clustered around it. The man held up the torch, Styrkar turned his face to it, the officer came to the salute and waved them through.

Magnus was taking no chances, Skuli thought. This was the fourth checkpoint they had passed on the way up the track, each demanding a different password and each sited where the terrain flattened to allow the possibility of another way up into the high woodlands. Cutting their way out would be noisy, bloody and difficult, and he wondered which of the options they had discussed the Scraeling would take. Beyond that, he decided as they kicked their horses into movement again, only one thing was certain – Styrkar wasn't going to see the morning.

They drew up before a steep-roofed and heavily-timbered building at the end of the track. Its front was bathed in the flickering glow of a dozen torches that would burn through the night, replenished as needed from the bundles lying on the porch of the lodge. Here again were soldiers aplenty, and an officer strode forward as the party came to a halt.

"Lord Styrkar? You aren't expected, sir" he greeted them and Styrkar turned to him as he slid down from his horse.

"Yes, Einar" he said, "the queen's baggage and a maid of the household. We'll see her, late though it is, because her movement orders've been changed."

"I can't allow that, lord marshal" said the officer crisply. "She's to have no visitors – by your own order, and that of the king as you reported it to me.

Your orders were quite clear, sir."

"Aye, no visitors but me" snapped Styrkar. "We won't keep her long."

"No visitors" repeated the officer firmly. "'None' was what you said, lord marshal." Turning, he snapped, "Sections one and three to the ready!"

"Oh fuck" said Styrkar wearily. "I'm not subject to my own orders, you dolt. I gave them, and I can un-give them, got it? Listen carefully – have the queen wakened, apologise for me, and tell me when she's ready to receive us. Move!"

"I'm sorry, marshal" said the officer, and his head lowered like a stag at bay. "You'll need to give me a formal order before a witness cancelling your previous ones, then another concerning what you now wish. Until that happens, I'll stop any of your party who move towards the house – however I have to, sir, I'll stop them. I hope you—"

"Damn your bloody eyes!" snarled a Styrkar now quite beside himself, "That's it! You can consider yourself relieved—"

"Hold on there Styrkar" broke in Skuli. "Your name Tambarskjelvar, young man?"

"That's correct, sir" returned the officer, white-faced before Styrkar's fury.

"What're you to old Einar Tambarskjelvar then? The one who told Hardraada to go fuck himself 'cause he wasn't up for being bought?"

"My great-uncle, sir. I'm proud to say I'm named for him" returned the young man.

Skuli chuckled. "See, Styrkar? Runs in the family!" Turning to the officer, he said, "Young man, I'm Skuli Bergrsson. You've never heard of me, but I crossed blades with your relative once or twice. And I'm bloody glad it was only once or twice. He was a man amongst men, young one, and he died for a principle too if I heard right. I see him in your face, and I'm glad to meet another Tambarskjelvar – just as bloody-minded as the other one!"

"Styrkar, if you'll take some advice from an old comrade, you'll promote this officer instead of breaking him, because you haven't got any more like him – and we need lots more like him. Up to you. Now – I'll witness the new orders, so can we get on with it? Be daybreak before we've got indoors."

Young Tambarskjelvar bowed to Skuli and faced Styrkar wordlessly. Styrkar said "You've made your point young man. I withdraw my previous orders and issue you the new ones I spoke of. Well done." and walked past.

The Raedwaldsson estate, Reading, England, October 1067.

"Then you'd better get on with it" said the Norman sergeant, his face unyielding. "Days're drawing in and the digging's only going to get harder once the ground freezes. How many've you got?"

"Not enough to finish the harvest an' put up y'r building at the same time" Garth told the shifty-looking English interpreter. "Hundred all up."

"Add in the women too" came back the answer. "They don't work, they don't eat. This castle's to be ready by the new year. There it is –" the Norman gestured to the pile of wooden walls and frameworks left by the just-departed ox-train – "but it's no good like that. 'S well as the ditch we talked about, them walls need to go up on its inside, and the footings're a man an' a half deep. I'll give you a month to get the ditch an' footings dug."

"Told you I haven't got that kind'f workforce" retorted Garth. "even countin' the women. How about that?"

"No problem" returned the Norman, "you'll need to get some in – say, next manor, I dunno . . . anywhere you like."

"An' how'm I gonna feed them?" demanded Garth. "Last year's harvest was buggered by your troops, an' this year's hasn't been that good either."

The sergeant shrugged, thickset and bulky in his hauberk. "Your problem" he said. "Maybe you c'd feed them what your wives an' kids won't be having seeing they don't work? Up to you. I'm gonna pace the line of the bailey, an' peg it – don't say I never done nothing for you, Englishman!"

"Real good of you" muttered Garth sullenly, and the Norman showed broken teeth in a sardonic grin.

"Nah" he said. "I lied. Not doing it f'r you. When your new lord gets here after Feast of our Lord, I want him t'see his walls standing high 'n proud, got it? Well what you waitin' for?"

The hills above Nidaros.

"Help you down?" said one of Styrkar's party, holding up his arms and the maid, hooded and muffled against the night chill, slid down from her sidesaddle perch.

The man held out an arm and the maid took it as the two large cases came from the frame on the packhorse's back, and they moved towards the house. The sentries under the porch saluted and stood aside and those within were crisply dismissed by Styrkar.

As the door closed behind them the party moved deeper into the lodge where they couldn't be seen through windows and the maid said, "Well done Skuli. That young man nearly buggered things completely. Fancy tripping over one of old Einar's brood here!"

"He's a good man" said Skuli. "I wasn't joking either, Styrkar – you really should promote him. If you live long enough" he added. "Now take the riding-cloak – nothing in the pockets I hope – sit there by the fire and keep your hands where we can all see them. Or we tie you up, please yourself"

"No, nothing in the pockets" said the Scraeling, emerging from under the cloak and tossing it to Styrkar. "Thanks for your arm then, Arneirr – tidied things up nicely" and the man spoken to grinned briefly without taking his eyes from a sullen Styrkar.

The Scraeling tapped on the door to the next room, eased it open and walked through. Those outside heard a woman's cry of surprise before the heavy door closed to, and Skuli waved Styrkar and Arneirr to a settle by the glowing fire.

"Get comfortable" he advised, "and Styrkar – did y'ever meet Arneirr here properly? Him'n my nephew Haakon I told ya about grew up together, but Arneirr missed Stamford an' stayed at Riccall 'cause he took an English arrow in the shoulder at Fulford, week before. Y'know, he helped the Scraeling get me into that *drakkar* I told you about. You two jus' have a good chat 'bout old times, eh? An' he's a bit keen on cutting ya throat, so don't forget the hands Styrkar. Don't forget the hands."

In the next room the Scraeling clutched an Elisabeth who was weeping and laughing at the same time. "My darling man" she managed, "I thought I'd never see you again – Magnus said I wouldn't, ever again – and the thought of going to Denmark without seeing you – that was worst of all but you're here – oh you're here my love – and nothing will ever be bad again. Oh my darling Ranulf . . . what did my clever, clever man say to make him change his mind?" and she kissed him fiercely.

When they came up for air, the Scraeling said shakily, "Darling, we haven't got long. But we won't need long. Magnus hasn't changed his mind. About anything. Fact is, the last time we spoke he threw me out after telling me I wasn't royal enough for you." He gazed deep into her eyes and kissed the tears from her cheeks.

"My love, I've got the marshal of Norway at knife-point in the next room, courtesy of a friend from the old days. I told you about Skuli – ah, never mind now ... but we're supposed to be here to advise you of a change in your travel arrangements, so we haven't got long. I want to get you out of here – I came in as your maid – and we'll get out the same way and be down the mountain before you're missed. Then Skuli's going to take his *drakkar* past the guardships down at Nidaros – they'll expect that, once someone here remembers his name – but you and I with four men I've got waiting at the foot of the mountain – we'll ride hard for the border and Sweden while Magnus chases Skuli. Darling Elisabeth, if we're steady and ... what is it, my love? What?"

She had gone rigid in his arms. "Ranulf ... Ranulf darling— it won't work!" she exclaimed. "Don't you know ... that man, the horrid one ... aye, Styrkar ... he's part of your plan? Is he? *Is he?*"

The Scraeling frowned. "Yes darling – an unwilling one. He doesn't know about Skuli and us splitting up, of course – we'll make sure he thinks we'll ride for the harbour once we've dumped him at the foot of the mountain. Why?"

"Why? Because he knows how Magnus is going to take me out of here. He *knows*, darling! Magnus is going to deliver me personally to Svein. He told me so himself before he had me brought here – sure to impress my new husband, he said, to have a fellow-king bring him a royal bride. Something like that – oh darling, I was in such a state I couldn't be sure, but that man, Styrkar, confirmed it when he came to me yesterday."

The Scraeling shook his head. "Darling, start at the beginning. Please. I know nothing of this. Take your time" and he kissed her again, a kiss that she returned.

"Darling man, Magnus is going to ride up here with an escort, to take me down to the harbour. Then he'll – we'll – board a *knorre*, a royal one, sail out of the harbour, pick up an escort of *drakkars* and sail south for Denmark. And he's doing this so he can claim to Svein that he's personally escorted me every foot of the way to my new home, darling. That's what Styrkar told me, and I'm certain it's what Magnus said the day he tore me from our home."

"Well – and I'm sorry darling – bugger Magnus and bugger his plan too. We'll change that, for a start, so . . . what is it, darling?" She lowered her head to his chest and began to weep again.

"There's more" she whispered. "Magnus told me that if I resisted, or if you resisted in any way, it would be treason. He said treason . . . treason's anything affecting a king. And as his stepmother, treason is what it would be if you . . . you . . . and for treason, you'd, you'd suffer death in front of me. Darling . . . darling, I think he's a little . . . well, he's either mad or this means so much to him . . . that's why I was so . . . so surprised to see you."

"Leave that to me" said the Scraeling. "We haven't come this—" but she interrupted him, her eyes brimming with tears.

"No Ranulf." And the finality in her voice stopped him dead. "No, my love. Think about this. Styrkar knows how I'm going to be moved, and it's obvious that his soldiers know too, so they'll insist on seeing me still here as you leave. Styrkar knows that, don't you see?"

"If we do what you've planned, they'll take us before we mount. Then you'll fight, and I'll see you cut down before my eyes. And if you don't fight, they'll deliver you to Magnus and I'll see you executed for treason in front of me. And Ranulf, Ranulf darling, I couldn't bear any of that . . . don't ask it of me, my love, please . . ." And her plea dissolved in tears.

"What's the alternative?" cried the Scraeling in anguish. "I let you go to Svein? I never see you again? Elisabeth, Elisabeth my golden love, I'd rather die! If Magnus wants to kill me, let him! I'd rather die trying to keep you with me than live without you, as God's my judge and witness! I'd rather die, because for me there's no life without you!"

"Dearest man" whispered Elisabeth, "it's just that way for me too. But I would be kept alive, because Magnus' plan can't work without me. You're . . . you're a soldier, and you've . . . seen things that I haven't . . . and I can't know about because I'm just a weak woman. And that's how I know that I can't bear to see you die. You – the gentlest, wisest, kindest man in the world. You – the man who's been my only love these eighteen wonderful years. You – whose children I want to bear. You – the man whose face I'll see and touch on my deathbed. Don't ask me to watch you die, my love. No— anything but that. If you love me – anything but that!"

The Scraeling bowed his head because he knew there was no answer. Elisabeth sensed his despair and held him tightly. "My love, my love, I've thought of killing myself" and she felt him go rigid. "But . . . but it's a sin under the church, dearest, and it would mean we could never be together again . . . after. So I put it from me. Darling, look at me." She took his face between her slender hands and stared into his eyes.

"Darling, before I say this, I want to tell you that I believe in our Lord and His Father and His heaven, but you know that." The Screaling nodded mutely, for he was well aware that Elisabeth was a devout woman.

She went on, "But darling, I've also known heaven on earth, and I know it when I'm in your arms. I've known it for eighteen years my love, and those are eighteen years I wouldn't have had if you hadn't caught me when I threw myself at you. Princesses are what Magnus said, darling – no, he was right, believe me. Ranulf de Lannion, only my good fortune in being loved by you has made me any different from any other princess."

"Now, darling . . . now it's time to return to what Fate's had in store for me all along. I'm going to a royal marriage – just as I did before, and the fact that I'd never thought to do so again's got nothing to do with it. Ranulf, I'm in front. I'm in front by those eighteen years of wonder when you made me the happiest woman in the world. Every day of the years I knew you cared for me, my love."

"And this – this is what I want to say to you, and the promise I want to make you, my darling man. Ranulf de Lannion, husband of my heart and owner of my soul, know that I can face all things where I go if I know that you're alive and well and thinking of me sometimes. And I'll do this, I swear to you, all the days of my life on earth until God brings us together again. Ranulf . . . darling Ranulf, will you think of me?"

The Screaling nodded, aware and unheeding of the tears streaming down his face. He tightened his long archer's arms around Elisabeth and squeezed her until she gasped. "Think of you my darling?" he whispered, "Before God, I'll think of nothing else if you forbid me to die for you."

"No, my love, I don't want you to die for me" came back the answer. "I do want you to live for me, though, because that will give me the faith in us and in our shared eternity that I'll need to get through the life marked out for me. And I can't avoid it, my love."

The Screaling nodded blindly, for he knew there was nothing to say. Nothing to do, nowhere to run, no action he might take. He, the wiliest of strategists and the most subtle of planners, was hard up against the wall built by an apprentice king and a devout and loving woman.

"No, I can't avoid it, darling. But there's one thing we can do about it, and if God truly cares about Ranulf and his Elisabeth, then it'll happen. And it'll happen tonight. Ranulf, I want you to kneel with me in prayer and then I want us to make love for whatever time we have. And if God answers our prayer, my love, your seed will find root and I'll go to a loveless marriage with your child within me. And then you'll be with me in form, as well as memory, every day."

London, November 1067.

"We're looking at our second Holy Season in England" said the king of England, glancing around a council table where no-one would meet his eye, "and from here, it's worse than the first. Much worse. Then, they'd just lost, they'd submitted, and they were staggering. Now, rebellion's all around us and has been all this year."

He held up a thick index finger. "First, Peterborough. Next, Eadric and those bloody Welshmen –" heads rose at the unaccustomed bad language. Another finger. "Third, that Godwin witch, Gaetha, encouraging the west to rise to join Eadric. She's kept me busier this year than her bloody sons did, and that's a fact. Fourth – Dover and that idiot Eustace. Why do I put up with him, anyone tell me? Odo, you did that well, brother – my thanks!"

"Pleasure" mumbled the warrior bishop of Bayeux. "Something about Eustace makes me want to kick his arse and keep kicking it." The rumble of laughter that followed the remark lifted the tension in the room and William went on.

"Fifth – we had to teach the north a lesson too, and I've a feeling we'll need to do it again properly one day because they're a queer lot up there. Aye, Robert, just as you're always telling me. I agree – I always did, brother. Right – change hands" And he held up another finger.

"Then there was Godwinsson's sons raiding the west country, not two months ago. If they hadn't been so greedy, and too stupid to realise it, that could have been serious. They could be back. And finally – there's Edgar the Aetheling. The Witan recognised him, for all he submitted to me, and the monks of Peterborough hailed him as king besides. Now he's claimed sanctuary from that bastard in Scotland, and he's sitting just over our border, biding his time."

Christ's wounds thought Fitz Gilbert, *that's two 'bloodys' and a 'bastard' from William, and that's more than I've heard in the last five years, nearly. He didn't even curse like that when he heard Godwinsson'd snatched the throne, so he—*

Fitz Osbern cleared his throat in the silence that followed William's outburst. "Not quite that bad, majesty" he said, and raised a finger of his own. "We're still here. It's been a hard year, but we're through it – and nothing's going to move until spring, and we'll be ready then too."

Giffard nodded in agreement. "One other thing, lord king" he said, "It's easy to look at the bad news – but Godwinsson's sons were seen off by the *fyrds* of the west and they're – well mostly – Englishmen, aye, and only a few Normans. We shouldn't overlook that."

"What're you getting at, Walter?" asked Fitz Gilbert, and Giffard turned to him.

"Just that what we're doing's working, Richard" he said. "We've treated the English fairly, and they know it. The king's policy's to do things through legal means – that's *their* legal means — far's we can, of course. The only folk we've dispossessed are those who supported an oath-breaker and a heretic against us."

"But as the king's just said" returned Fitz Gilbert, "we've had our hands full all year. That sound like success to you?"

"Well" said Giffard, "look at where the trouble's coming from. The north, the south and the west and— "

Fitz Gilbert snorted. "And that's good? Bones of Christ, Walter, that's—"

"That's nothing new for this land" said Fitz Osbern. "As Walter was about to say. Weren't you?"

"Aye" said Giffard. "Look – Godwinsson had trouble with the north, and trouble bad enough for him to kick out his own brother. We know he had trouble with the Welsh in the west too. And we gave him something to think about in the south. And then, of course, there was Hardraada. What I'm saying, Richard, is – this land's had strife since Cnut himself. And probably before that too!"

"But Walter's real point" said Fitz Osbern, leaning forward, "is that whoever holds the heartland – aye, here, around London – holds the country. Even Godwinsson knew that. I shouldn't have to tell the soldier you are that, if he'd fallen back on London and locked us up on the coast, we'd have had to sail home or die."

The king, leaning back at the head of the table, reached out and tapped a finger on it. "Well spoken, William" he said. "It's the more needful, then, that the lands of the rebels – and that's all of the Godwin territories here, in Wessex, come under our control before spring brings more of the same problems. All of you, settle the men who owe you service, *now* – take the land I've given you and parcel it out. I want no land left in rebel hands by summer."

The Raedwaldsson estate, Reading, February 1068.

Gytha held up her needlework and squinted at it in the weak winter light from the window. No – it wouldn't do because she had overstretched the cloth in the frame and the line she had sewn wasn't level. She sighed, fought back a moment of nausea and reached for the small blade to unpick the stitches, changed her mind and laid down the work.

"What is it, my lady?" came the voice from the fireplace and Gytha forced a smile as she turned.

"Oh, some careless work here my lord" she replied, "a moment's foolishness when I set the cloth in this frame. Nothing that can't be reworked – when I have the mind for it."

"Here – one of these on each side should make light enough" returned her new husband, fixing two tapers into holders on the small table where her work lay. "You shouldn't strain so to see – it grows darker by the minute."

Gytha smiled at him again. Ivo de Bois was a decent man, she had decided, and she might have done a good deal worse in Walter Giffard's choice of a husband for her. He had been a member of Giffard's household all his life, never seeking anything but the life of a professional soldier until Giffard's decision that a man so useful to him ought to have a status that reflected the esteem in which his lord held him.

In truth, and although Gytha didn't yet know it, de Bois had protested the decision in telling the Norman lord that he had never thought to marry and wasn't sure he was cut out for it or for fatherhood. At which Giffard had hooted with laughter and told him, in the forthright way for which he was notorious, that throwing a leg over a Saxon heiress would be much more enjoyable than throwing the same leg over a destrier, and had promised to find a 'suitable mount' for him.

Giffard had kept his word and had found for his most prized troop commander a young widow with a fine manor in the very heartland of England. In her thirty-fourth year, Gytha Raedwaldsson was in the bloom of her womanhood and her childbearing years. "And d'Avranches, who listed the manor, tells me she's pretty, too – small, dark and tasty" had been his description, and on his coming to the manor just before Christ's Mass, de Bois had been forced to admit the truth of his lord's description.

By nature a serious and reserved man who'd never accepted that the brutality and profanity of a soldier's life should extend beyond active service, Ivo de Bois had found the circumstances of his situation as lord of the Raedwaldsson manor difficult. More difficult than impressing a young duke of Normandy by rallying two shattered sections of Norman infantry in battle at Val-es-Dunes as a seventeen-year-old, much more difficult than storming the ridge at Senlac in the dying light of an autumn day, and infinitely more difficult than teaching his troop that humility rather than arrogance well became soldiers who had won a great victory by God's grace and the narrowest of margins.

The man who fussed with the tapers had found other things difficult also. He had found the sullenness of the boy – the young man by the size of him – who was now his stepson hard to accept, even though he accepted its inevitability. It was hard, he thought, because of Osmund's implacability. De Bois wanted to get on with the young man because of the clear and obvious bond between his wife and her firstborn. Nearing forty himself, de Bois had accepted that he would never have children of his own and had in fact long determined that, after he could no longer answer the call of the trumpets, he would end his days in a monastery. Yet here he was – head of a family, even if it was by Giffard's decree and not God's.

And there was something else about family, something that made him conscious of the flush rising from the tight neckband of the ankle-length indoor robe he wore. The wedding ceremony had been simple enough and the celebrations that followed carefully restricted to pledges of friendship and wishes for long life and health. De Bois had ordered it so in deference to Gytha's feelings at being summarily married off to a man she had known only for the four days since his arrival on the manor, and that to a representative of the race that had made her a widow. Indeed, he thought, she would never know if her new husband had crossed swords with her late one on the battlefield – come to that, nor would he.

That had made their wedding night even more difficult. De Bois had known whores in his career, but as was the case with every other part of his simple and straightforward life, his relationships with them had been transactions – quickly concluded, fully paid for and dutifully confessed to be paid for again as sins of the flesh. He had wanted nothing but release, and that had suited him and the guilt of his own weakness in requiring it. Needless to say he had found his wedding night different in that any intimation of tenderness was hard to articulate, and the flush of his embarrassment intensified as he thought back to his fumbling attempts to lodge in Gytha's body.

For her part, Gytha had gone to her wedding bed conscious that this was where she began to pay the price that service to her people and her folk demanded of her. *The price of all that is— you* said Osmund in her head. Even as Penda had paid his price, she told herself, I won't hold back from mine. She had sent her maid away and waited, alone in the large bed, *without my man and your father in it, a bed is no more than a bed* . . . in a room lit by a single taper, until de Bois had sent his well-wishers away and entered the chamber.

He had disrobed quickly and although she had turned her head away from his seamed and scarred warrior body she had seen, too, his eagerness and the sight of it had repelled her as Penda's eagerness never had. He had got in beside her with only the briefest of pleasantries and despite herself Gytha's body had locked up so that she started violently when he reached for her.

"I'm sorry, my lady" he had said. "Did I startle you?" and she had made some answer, conscious, first, that she spoke his language while he did not speak hers and, second, of the foolishness of the thought. He put his hand back, reached for her shoulder and pulled her over to him so that the front of her body came up against his and the rigidity of his maleness and, despite herself, she shrank from it, gasping "No!" and pulling away.

De Bois lunged back and over her, and she felt his leg swing across her body as his full weight came upon her. Suddenly she was helpless beneath his weight and into her mind came the picture of all the scars she had seen in the light from the taper and she shuddered with revulsion. . . . *yes, a Norman will share my bed—*

She bucked to throw him off, her intentions forgotten in the storm of emotion that filled her mind, but his weight pinned her to the mattress. She struck his broad back with her fists and squirmed beneath him to drive away the knee that sought to prise hers apart, and as they rolled to and fro in the big bed he pulled her savagely to him, gave a mighty groan and went rigid. For a brief second Gytha thought he had had a seizure but then she felt the hot flood of his seed spurt across her belly and thighs, then another and another while he gasped out his passion into her face.

Stunned, Penda Raedwaldsson's widow turned her face away and the tears came as she wept silently for the life she had lost, and doubly for the one she had found. Ivo de Bois glanced at her closed eyes and noted her clenched fists where they lay on the coverlet and, rolling away to lie on his back and stare up at the ceiling, he had said,

"My lady . . . Gytha . . . this is not what either of us would have chosen, and neither of us brought ourselves to this place. Yet . . . yet here we are, and it's not for us to judge what or who brought us here. My lady, I'm the master of this manor and I have been commanded to marry you so that it should pass to me in accordance with the laws and customs of this land which allows its women the right of inheritance."

"If I could please myself, I would do it by pleasing you. And I think I would please you by not coming to your bed, thus I would not do that. But man and wife are commanded by God to be one flesh, my lady, and we – I – dare not disobey that command, for soldiers do not . . ."

— Yes, a Norman will share my bed – but it won't be the place I shared with your father screamed Gytha inside her head

" . . . disobey commands. I am your husband before God, and I would be your man"

— my man died at Senlac —

". . . and use you kindly. My lady . . . Gytha . . . we must go to bed at the end of every day, and I would be to you as a husband. Will you be the same to me?"

— I went as a maid to that bed, and the maid, the woman and the wife died when your father did—

"Will you, my lady?"

Gytha had turned to him, in helplessness rather than love, with a sob that she could not repress. He had put an arm across her shoulders and drawn her to him for them to lie together in quiet for a time. And when that time was over, Gytha de Bois began to pay the price of keeping faith with her dead husband.

Off the coast of England, March 1068.

The Chronicle.

*T*he lookout's call turned me from my practice at the cask bobbling on a line in our wake. Yes, there was a smudge of land on the grey horizon where a sullen sky met a freezing sea, and if I could have found anyone to take the bet I would have wagered five gold pieces that it was Flamborough Head. That was ever Skuli's favourite landfall on the English coast, and his skilled seamanship and navigation had made it again.

For a moment I envied my captain's simple certainty that the only things worth having in life were a stout ship beneath his feet, enough beer to see him to sleep and a warm woman on a cold night. He looked for nothing beyond those things, and was content to follow a leader he liked – which was why, he told me, that he would take me a-viking again if I wished,

As it happened, I did wish and that is why I peered at Flamborough Head on a cold morning in March when winter gave no hint of slackening its grip on the Shallow Sea and my whole world had been the cask and my determination to put as many arrows into it as possible. I glanced away over the low freeboard of 'Nordvedr', the 'North Wind', to where the cold grey water curled past her flanks and thought how little difference there was between the water and what flowed through my soul. I knew that in those waters at that time of year a strong man would live perhaps five minutes, and there had been many times since a horse had carried me, unseeing, down a mountain behind Nidaros, that I had not wanted to live even that long.

I have no memory of the Christ's Mass when Elisabeth went from me to Denmark and only scattered recollections of that whole time when, I was told, the winter held Nidaros in a grip of white iron and the outer harbour froze as well as the inner. No memory, I say, because I spent most of that time in the embrace *of the waters of Lethe since I could not have the embrace that was dearer to me than anything in the world. Aye, I drank myself back into oblivion whenever I awoke and it took the love and dedication of a servant to change that, for I could not shift for myself and beyond another flask of wine I sought only death itself.*

February 1068, Nidaros, Norway.

The Scraeling lashed out at the shadowy figures looming over him as he awoke, but his arms were seized in grips of steel and he could not resist being dragged from his bed. He hit the floor, his knees gave way and he sagged to the ground only to be dragged upright again.

"Outside with him" he thought he heard, but all sound was coming down a long, fuzzy tunnel and when he opened his mouth to scream his anger at the shapes he felt his stomach rush into his mouth at sickening speed and he retched helplessly and painfully, for there was nothing in his stomach to come up. Again and again he retched, bringing up only a thin acid-tasting bile that he could feel running over his chin, through his beard and onto his chest.

"Fuck me!" came a familiar voice. "Would you look at him? Smell him? This's the cleverest man in the world, Heggr – the man Hardraada himself called 'the most dangerous little bugger alive.' Hold him up." Through his helplessness the Scraeling felt his clothes grasped at the front and the hiss of a blade slicing through them, and heard, "Right. Outside" as his clothes fell away.

Still his tongue wouldn't answer his urging and he tried to spit but failed. Then he was conscious of shuddering cold as the darkness lessened and he knew himself outside. Outside, in the depths of a Norwegian winter, but even as his fogged mind registered that fact he felt himself picked up and thrown bodily through the air to land in something that engulfed his naked body. *Snowdrift*, he thought as coherent thought returned to tell him he was spitting out snow – *I'm in a fucking snowdrift* – but he was seized by the ankles again, drawn back, lifted and hurled again as one of his assailants gave a whoop of laughter.

"Once more" said the voice, "but mind his left leg you hearty bastards – there's not much of it. Just one more . . . maybe" And for a third time the Scraeling flew to plunge into a drift deep enough to take his body from head to shins. Strangely, it wasn't cold – well not as much as his cringing mind told him it would be – and the outside air was much colder.

"Fuck you, Skuli" he panted as he was dragged out again to shudder in the icy air, "What're you bloody playing at, you fucking pirate?"

"That's my Scraeling" said Skuli as he draped him in a blanket and picked him up bodily, "always a sweet talker." And he towelled the Scraeling hard enough to drive the protesting breath from his body then said "Oh, just one more" and whipped the blanket away for the two big men with him to seize the Scraeling and pitch him, yet again, into the huge drifts that were deep-banked behind his house. This time he came up snarling.

"That's it! That's fucking it, I'm telling you! What the bloody hell— " and Skuli roared with laughter and held out the blanket.

"Come on, man – before your dick falls off –'s already turning blue, ain't it boys?" At which his companions roared in their turn and the Scraeling snatched at the blanket and scurried indoors as fast as he could. Inside the door he swayed and clutched at the doorpost as the warmth came to greet him.

"You all right?" came Skuli's voice and a firm grip on his arm.

"Fine" answered the Scraeling. "Shit – stinks in here though?" He stepped to the fire, over the clothes Skuli had cut from him. "My head's floating, feels like."

"Not surprised" said Skuli. "You've drunk enough wine recently to float a dozen *drakkars* all by yourself. Rub hard with that blanket Scraeling – my old uncle knew a man who'd lived way up north. He told my uncle the scraelings up there – Suomis, he called 'em, something like that – dive in an' outta snowdrifts all the time, 'cept they whip each other with tree branches first. Aye, rub harder – till ya skin's red."

"No thanks" said a Scraeling sobering by the second. "Tree branches?"

"So he said" nodded Skuli. "Mind you – the scraelings up there're cannibals too, I've heard. Funny things they do. Get him some clothes, Auti – that big cupboard in the wall there, eh?"

"Not the only ones" said the Scraeling turning too quickly and staggering so that the man Heggr had to reach out to him. "No. What . . . what're you doing here?"

"Here – put those on" said Skuli, gesturing to the clothes Auti was holding out. The Scraeling took a robe and shrugged into it. "Drink?" he said as his head came through the neckband. Skuli shook his head firmly.

"No" he said. "You neither. Y'can have all the water you want though. Now – what'm I doing here? I'm here 'cause I hadn't seen you in a month, so when your man through there came t'see me an' tell me you were sick, I came straight away. I went back straight away too, t'pick up these two – you don't remember Heggr an' Auti? They was up the mountain with us . . . no?"

The Scraeling shook his head. "No. Go on though."

"So I came back a second time. Today. T'get you sober an' keep you that way."

The Scraeling pondered. "How'd you get past the sentry?" and Skuli shrugged.

"He'd seen me pass with your man, an' didn't blink when I came back with the boys. There's lotsa people interested in you an' what y'r doing, Scraeling. Lots. You hungry, by the way?"

The Scraeling's stomach heaved, but he fought it. "Could manage some bread. Not much."

"A start" said Skuli. "Your man says you haven't eaten since you started drinking. Not properly. Still. That's all over now."

"Really?" asked a rather nettled Scraeling. "Who says so?"

"Me" said Skuli. "And them. We're moving in, so smile an' look happy. I'm just looking after myself, Scraeling – never know when I might need you to put me back together again, do I?"

Giffard's headquarters, Woking, Wessex, March 1068.

"Are you mad, or what?" asked Raimund de la Mor. "De Bois'll break you for that – relative or no, Ralph! And I don't blame him – after he hauled your arse out of the fire the way he did. What're you thinking of?"

De Courcy sighed. "Hang on, Raimund. I've been through this with Ivo" he said. "To begin with, he didn't understand any more than you do. It's the manor I'm after, not the daughter, although she'll make a good start. And Ivo knows just what I'm up to. Think he disapproves of so much naked ambition, actually, but that's his lookout."

De la Mor frowned. "You want the manor? Fat chance, Ralph. People like us don't have the seniority."

De Courcy was unmoved. "Think so? There'll never be a better time.

The king doesn't have a lot of choice, does he? He's hanging on to England with bugger-all men because the king of France's taking advantage of his troubles here to play hell with Normandy's frontiers. Your brothers still with Montgomerie in Brittany?"

Raimund nodded. "Far's I know" he said. "That's after fighting Angevins and French along the way."

De Courcy shrugged. "Makes my point then" he said. "And I doubt if we've seen the last of English resistance, come to that. I've heard Giffard say that we'll need to clean out the north before we're much older. And what's all that prove? Just that Giffard's going to need good men around him."

"But – a manor?" asked de la Mor unbelievingly. "They go to . . . well . . . to people like your uncle!"

"Cousin" corrected de Courcy. "And it's odd you should mention him, because I put the very same thing to him. He swore he wasn't interested; that he was quite happy as a member of Giffard's household, soldiering until he couldn't mount a destrier any more – that sort of thing. But guess what – Giffard virtually ordered him to take over the manor right next to the one I've my eye on! And he agreed, reluctantly, and married – also reluctantly, just after Christ's Mass. As you know. But what you probably don't know is that I've never seen a bigger change in a man. Amazing what a regular roll in a warm bed'll do for you, eh?"

De la Mor whistled and rolled his eyes. "I've just about got used to living like a monk" he said, "so no-one'd need to ask me twice! About the manor or the marriage-bed! So you'll be neighbours as well as relatives!"

"Well not yet" returned de Courcy. "Cousin Ivo's agreed to put in a word for me with Giffard, but he says it's a long shot that'll probably have more to do with service than good opinions. So I'm going to be a model soldier, aren't I? And useful in all sorts of ways, to anyone who can get me a leg up."

"So what're you about, sneaking in and out of the very place where they accused you of rape?"

"There's no suggestion of 'sneaking' Raimund. Fact is, de Bois encouraged me. Sort of. My line's that I bear them no grudge – can see what the old lady was up to; defending her home the best way she could; want to establish good relations with the locals; king wants to treat all his people equally – you know the sort of thing" said de Courcy. "We've all heard it enough to vomit."

"Certainly – but I never thought I'd hear you prattle it!"

"Ah. For one thing, young Raimund, there's a manor at stake. For another, I'm not averse to return jousts with Wynfrytha."

"And have her screaming rape again? You *are* mad!"

De Courcy waved his hand. "That's all in the past" he said, "and mother wouldn't dare. Matter of fact, the first time I bundled Wynfrytha, right there in the barn, I got the idea she'd enjoyed it. And" he said raising his eyebrows archly, "I'm happy to say I've had her screaming since. But not 'rape'. If you see what I mean?"

De la Mor goggled. "You've had her . . . again?"

"Half a dozen times. Over three visits. The first visit I spent with mother, feeding her all the twaddle about how we all need to get along; royal policy to look forward; quite understand her wish to protect her home and family. What you called 'the prattle'. But I ended up asking her if I might pay court to Wynfrytha and hinted that I had high expectations."

"Well, bugger me!" exclaimed de la Mor. "How are you for cheek? But what'd she say?"

"Had Wynfrytha in, and gave us her blessing. She's all for it, you know. That's both of them. Well, why not? If you think about it, my getting the manor keeps it in the family until we get the sisters married off and the old trout dies. So she . . . ah, she leaves us alone when I visit. Which I do quite regularly."

"And Wynfrytha?"

"Has a healthy appetite for pork, and more ways of consuming it than it's decent to think about" said de Courcy smugly. "And tomorrow we're back on detachment with de Bois, so sometime in the next week I'm going to let her consume it again."

De la Mor shook his head admiringly. "You've got it all sewn up, Ralph. Woman and wealth. You know, I'd no idea you wanted to settle down so much."

"Who's settling down? With the revenues of that manor behind me – and they're worth a bit, if I'm any judge, don't you worry – I can do anything I like. And I will, believe me. Wynfrytha's just a first step, and a pleasant one she is too. The manor's the second."

De la Mor raised his cup. "And the third?"

"Power. The wealth of the manor'll help, Raimund, but you get power by being noticed, and I'm going to be noticed all right. Anyway, I'll need something to do while Wynfrytha raises the brood I'll enjoy putting in her belly, won't I? But I've got to get there first. And I will, Raimund, I will."

Reading, England, the previous month.

Once there was a time thought Gytha, *when things stayed the same for a while. Not like now – now's always becoming then, and things change all the time. Penda leaving with lord Tostig. Coming back before Stamford, then on the way through to Senlac. His death, with the leaders of all Wessex. Sunngifu's birth – very early because of the shock, and her so small and weak. Widowhood. Being father as well as mother to my boy, lord as well as lady to our people. Then our home taken. Marriage to a Norman. And now . . . pregnancy.*

For she couldn't avoid the fact any longer. Her four previous pregnancies told her what two missed courses and the nausea that never quite left her meant. She was pregnant to Ivo de Bois, and if it hadn't happened on their wedding night, it had been soon after. She buried her face in her hands for she saw, in a blinding moment of clarity, what it would mean to Osmund, her first-born.

She was quite aware of the tension between Ivo and Osmund and, like her husband, she accepted it as inevitable. She had also seen how de Bois had tried hard to be conciliatory towards the young man and she had blessed him for it, but now her condition was going to force them all to confront what had been only a shadow at the back of her mind since Valery d'Avranches told her that she was to lose the manor.

What would become of her son, the lord of the Raedwaldsson estate? For a time after she realised that de Bois was a good and decent man she had dared to hope that he would take Osmund as his own and that, in time, Osmund would succeed to the manor that was his already through Penda. But now . . . now, with a child of his own to be born, how would de Bois react?

More, how would Osmund react? Gytha thought she knew, and the knowledge filled her with dread. For despite de Bois' best efforts, Osmund was barely civil to him, and that only for the sake of the pleading in his mother's gaze when they were all together. He had taken to absenting himself from the big house for hours at a time, under pretext of assisting with the earthworks necessary to the erection of the timbered castle not far away. And it was true that the manor was short of labour due to the toll that Senlac had taken of its men, and true also that Osmund had assigned himself a man's part in the backbreaking labour of digging the ditch and throwing up the spoil to form the mound, but still . . .

So deep in thought was she that she wasn't aware until he spoke that de Bois was in the room and as she started up he laughed and put up a hand to wave her back into her chair. "No, my lady, stay there pray you. Truth to tell, you make a lovely picture there against the light, so lost to all. Tell me – what makes you ponder so deeply?"

Gytha stood, a wave of light-headedness coming over her as she did so, and she swayed a moment. De Bois leaped forward and caught at her arm. "My lady, you . . . you're so pale. What is it, Gytha? Has there . . . is there . . . some mishap? Ill news? What?"

And whether it was his obvious concern or even the use of her name by that formal and reserved man Gytha never knew, but straight away she bowed her head and the tears came as she said haltingly, "No, my lord . . . no ill news and no mishap. Nothing that's not like to happen between a woman and her husband . . . my lord, I'm almost sure . . . sure that I carry your child."

For a moment he stared at her and she back at him, seeing as she had never done before the faint welt of thickened skin down the spine of his nose where the nasal bar had rubbed over the years of his service, and the thick and greying hair cut just above his ears to cushion the weight of the heavy helmet. Then he exclaimed something that her French wasn't quick enough to catch, swept her into his arms and said.

"A . . . a child? My lady, a child? . . . us? Me— a father? No! I . . . I cannot—" And her stomach turned over in dismay.

"My lord, you don't . . . ? You cannot – you don't want . . . ?"

"No, my lady . . . I mean, of course I do! Me a father . . . ? I'd never thought to . . . I don't believe it . . . are you sure, my lady, truly sure . . . ?" And his arms were tight about her.

"Every sign, yes . . . and I know the signs, for—"

"Of course, my lady, of course. Yes, yes. Oh Jesu! What news! What . . . what may I do . . . ?"

She replied without thinking. "You can stop calling me 'my lady', my lord. My name is . . ." and the incongruity of what she had just said occurred to her and she burst into laughter. After a second it occurred to de Bois also, and his laughter joined with hers so that nothing in the world seemed more natural than that he should take her again in his arms and that she should go willingly as the bearer of the most precious gift in the world.

And that was how Osmund found them as he stepped through the same doorway. His Norman overlord with his mother in his arms, and the sound of their laughter hanging in the room. In an instant Gytha saw the look in her son's eye and caught her breath, but de Bois missed it.

"Osmund, welcome! Welcome and welcome again, today of all days! Osmund, your mother brings me the most joyous of news. You are to have a brother – another – and we are to have a son to make us truly a family! What does my stepson say to that, young man?"

Osmund's eyes shifted to his mother, and Gytha shivered at what she saw in their depths. He said nothing for a long, long moment and then he looked again at de Bois. "Your stepson says that the world may call me a member of your family, messire, but I do not. I am of the line of Hengest himself. As was my father, and his father before him."

And he turned back through the doorway.

That night.

"Know what I'd do" said Ralph. "He's been cock of the walk here long enough and he can't get used to being anything else. And he *is* something else now. Me, I don't care who his father is – or who his father *was*. If it takes a good hiding to teach him the difference . . . well, good enough!"

De Bois shook his head in exasperation. "Ralph, you're all balls. Fair enough – you're a young man. But how's that going to sit with his mother? She's going to make me a father, for Christ's sake!"

Such blasphemy from Ivo de Bois startled his young cousin for he knew that, while de Bois never shrank from calling a spade a spade before his men, he was more than a little straight-laced and a pillar of rectitude in private. So he thought a little more before he spoke again.

"Cousin,'s up to you of course. But if you want my opinion, Giffard's got you here for life. You're not a wandering soldier now. You're still a soldier, aye, but you won't be moving on as you've done all your life. Your life's here now, isn't it? I mean – it's your manor. And it's only going to get more so if you're going to have kids of your own. And it seems you are, you old goat!"

De Bois smiled thinly and Ralph hastened on. "Now. You've tried hard with Gytha's brat. I've seen you. And I've seen him giving you shit, too. Oh aye, just the right side of enough, granted. But the way he looks at you – me too, and any Norman come to that – tells me he's trouble. And the older he gets the worse he'll get. 'S why I'm saying – sort it out now, cousin."

"Look, tell you what – what if I push him into it and then I give him that good hiding? You could let it go 'til you think he's had enough, then call me off and kick me out for a while. Gytha's grateful, maybe the little bugger himself realises he's got something to thank you for . . . yes . . . it could work. What d'you think? Be glad to do it – in fact I'm itching to do it, cousin. No charge!"

De Bois laughed again. "Yes – known for a while there's no love lost between you and Osmund. Aye, it could work. Where would you go when I kick you out, though?"

"Next manor. Wynfrytha can't get enough of me – so much for me raping her, eh? – and the widow's hoping Giffard'll give me the manor."

De Bois refilled their cups. "He might too. I know he's thinking about it because he asked me who I'd like for a neighbour. I did use your name, but he seemed to think you're a bit young. Wouldn't hurt your cause to impress him – keep your name in front of him I mean. He's not in a hurry."

"Nor am I cousin. If I do get it, I don't want the widow as part of the deal, though. Wynfrytha, now – she'll turn my hair the colour of yours in half the time it's taken you!"

De Bois shook his head and smiled. "You randy young rip" he said, raising his cup. "Giffard was right, though."

"In what?"

"Oh . . . " said de Bois, colouring slightly, "something he said about marriage. Anyway – I'll think over your suggestion. It's not a bad one."

Off the English coast, March 1068.

"Remember how we came here before, Skuli?" asked the Scraeling, looking at the coast of England sliding past *Nordvedr* on the starboard side.

"Aye" came the reply, "you were off t'see Penda as I recall. Terrible hard man that – head like a rock an' a belly like an empty keg. Never known his like."

"Me either" said the Scraeling. "I still miss him. Did you know we were related?"

Good, thought Skuli, *at last you're thinking 'bout something else. Someone else.* Aloud, he said "Ah . . . think you did mention it once. An' I noticed you call him 'cousin' once or twice. That right?"

The Scraeling nodded. "That's right. We've – we had – an ancestor in common. Long time ago though. Long time."

"Doesn't matter" said Skuli. "Blood's thicker'n water now, an' it was then too – no matter how long ago it was." Not for the first time, the Scraeling marvelled at the simplicity of Skuli's thoughts on life.

There had never, he realised, been any question of Styrkar outliving his usefulness on the night he had got them past the guards and into Elisabeth's prison. Never. And Skuli had stilled his scruples by reminding him, after the deed, that Styrkar had known that the scheme they had hatched to get Elisabeth off the mountain was foredoomed – "And he would've let it happen, Scraeling, an' wouldn't Magnus have called him a good boy an' offered to let him cut your balls off? Wouldn't he just? Nah. Styrkar's had it coming for a while. A real man would've died at Stamford, 'cause Hardraada's marshal had no business living where his king died. Your cousin Penda didn't shirk, now did he?"

The Scraeling became aware that Skuli was looking at him curiously. "Eh? What? Sorry!" he said. "Somewhere miles away – thinking what a philosopher you were, matter of fact."

"Aye?" said Skuli doubtfully, "That good? What are they anyway? Fill-a . . . what?"

So the Scraeling explained what a philosopher was and Skuli grunted, unimpressed.

"Sounds like bullshit to me. Either you know what's what or you don't. What's anyone want to spend his life askin' questions for then? I remember you askin' me once what we were doing pissing on a tree in Sicily, Scraeling, an' I said then you had too much education, didn' I? Remember?"

The Scraeling laughed, and Skuli was glad to see it. "I do, old friend – I certainly do. And you answered me with one of life's great truths – 'A man's got to piss somewhere' you said!"

"True then and true now" noted Skuli. "But what I was askin' was – we going to see Penda's family again?"

"Yes. Yes, we are" said the Scraeling and Skuli waited in vain for further explanation before saying

"Think we'll take the shorter way in then. Off the Thames, y'know?"

But the Scraeling didn't answer, for he was somewhere else entirely.

Reading, Southern England, the week before.

There was perhaps an hour's light left in the short winter day that changed Osmund Pendasson's life forever, so he and Garth had called an end to the day's work on the castle footings and sent the workforce to woodgathering for the night ahead while they worked on alone, as they often did.

"What a difference an edge on the spade makes" said Osmund, picking up a whetstone, and Garth grunted agreement from further along the trench. He began to play the stone along the cutting edge of the blade, and as he fell into the rhythm he let his mind call up images he would sooner have blocked – but, young as he was, Osmund Pendasson was a realist who believed in grasping the nettle when confronted by a problem.

And the first image he called up was of his mother, in the Norman's arms and looking happy about it. Laughing, even. But she had stopped laughing when she'd seen the look on his face. Had she come to enjoy her Norman, then? Did she do her duty to her folk more willingly now – *it's our duty to care for them even as they care for us* – in the bed she'd shared with his father? *Yes, a Norman will share my bed* – and when a man and a woman shared beds wasn't it bound to happen?

That brought up another image, and Osmund recoiled from it before he accepted the necessity of facing it, because it had happened, aye – the short-cropped and thickset Norman on top of his mother, between her legs, thrusting himself into her and she welcoming it, writhing beneath him as they wrestled towards his discharge deep within her. *Fucking* him. Aye, that was the word. He was *fucking* her, and she him. Osmund had heard the word but never its ugliness until he pictured his mother opening her body to the Norman's thick cock as he had seen the cows welcome the bull and the mares the stallion . . . *Fuck! Fuck!* Was Penda, son of Raedwald, – *whose memory I'll love until my last breath* – so soon forgotten? *Fuck!*

"What?" demanded Garth, and Osmund came from the misery of his dark thoughts of betrayal to find the farmer looming over him, one large

111

hand outstretched for the whetstone and a question on his face. "What'd you say, master?"

"Nothing" muttered Osmund, his face on fire and his mind a whirl of black misery and tortured thoughts. "Nothing. Just thinking." And he turned away to where he was deepening a section of the footings for the timber walls. Garth watched him for a moment as he began to play the whetstone himself, and noticed the savage energy behind Osmund's drive of the sharp spade into the earth and the way the big shoulder-muscles bunched for each stroke. *Something not right there* thought the spearman. *Let him come to it himself. He will, when he's ready. And best I can . . ."*

"What the fuck's this?" broke in a loud and coarse voice, and Garth turned and flung up a hand against the low and blood-red sun to see the Norman sergeant standing, hands on hips, above him on the edge of the trench with the interpreter a pace or so behind him.

"What's what?" answered Garth, and the sergeant gestured impatiently.

"Fucking trench isn't deep enough by two feet. I told you this'd to be finished by Christ's Mass, didn' I? An' it wasn't! Nor by a month after, an' it still fucking isn't! *Is it?* Where's the workers? Get outta that fucking trench!"

"Not our fault the winter lasted so long" Garth pointed out as gently as he could while he and Osmund scrambled out. "Ground was frozen hard – you know that – y'saw it!"

"Aye, an' I warned you 'bout that too! Last October, it was. Did you start right away? Did you buggery, you lazy Saxon shit!"

"Last October was harvest" came back Garth defiantly. "Can't do anything then 'cept harvest – not even you clever Norman bastards c'n do anything 'cept harvest – what you gonna eat through winter, fuckhead? Eh?"

The sergeant's grasp of English was rudimentary, but it certainly included the word 'fuck' in all its associations. "What? What'd you call me?" snarled the sergeant, while slow grins spread across the faces of the two men-at-arms behind him and the interpreter looked worried.

"I called you a fuckhead" said Garth turning his face to the interpreter. "And before that I called you a clever Norman bastard. But I didn't mean that bit 'cause I've seen horse-shit with more brains than you. 'Course, it came from a Saxon horse. Now tell him that, you little arsehole – and get it right! Just like I said it!"

So the interpreter did, and the sergeant's eyes bulged. "Right, that's it!"

he snarled. "You're the village big boy, so you're up for it. I'm holdin' you responsible for the fact this job's behind, an' once the village's seen your ribs through the skin'f your back, we'll see if they work any faster. Or any longer'n the day." He turned to his men as the interpreter drew breath and snapped "Grab him boys – while the interpreter's talking, on my word— !"

"Stand fast!" Osmund's voice cut through the others and everyone stopped talking. "Sergeant, there's no need for that. This man's taken more than his share of the work, and he's got the villagers to work miracles besides. You've little idea of just how few of a workforce we've got. You've got more reason to thank him than punish him, believe me!"

"Why should I?" snarled the sergeant when he'd got over Osmund's command of French, "and who the fuck're you anyway – his son?"

"I'd be proud to be his son" came back the reply. "But I'm Osmund Pendasson, lord of this manor."

"No you ain't" said the sergeant, smiling. "Ivo de Bois is. An' you're the by-blow o' the rebel that got his at Hastings, fucking good riddance. Was he a perjurer like his fucking king? He piss on any holy relics too?" And only Garth's huge hand in his chest stopped Osmund as he stepped forward into a red mist of rage. The sergeant smiled.

"Well boys" he said, turning to his companions – "What've we got here? I'll tell ya – we've got a lazy bugger an' a cheeky bugger who fancies his chances. Let's take 'em both down th' village for a flogging, aye? Tell you what . . ."

But Osmund had exploded into motion and shoved Garth hard enough to send him sprawling into the trench. Leaping past him, he swung up the spade and let fly a cut at the sergeant's head. The man wasn't helmed, and the sharp spade took him just above the eyebrows to slice through bone and flesh like the top coming off an egg while Osmund whirled past him to drop a shoulder into the second man and send him also into the trench on top of a Garth scrambling to his feet.

But he was now facing a combat veteran and, slight though the pause on the way through had been, it was enough for the Norman's blade to *skreek* from its scabbard. He broke ground to assess the threat, snarled and came in fast with a swinging cut at the boy's legs that Osmund was quick enough to catch on the steel blade of the spade rather than the four-foot wooden shaft. He exploded upwards to beat the Norman's blade up into the air and the man's head lifted with his tight-clenched blade, leaving his chest and throat open and exposed. Like lightning Osmund thrust hard under the Norman's chin and the keen blade of the clumsy weapon sliced into and through the man's throat, well-nigh severing his head and loosing a hard-pumped spout of blood from his neck that hung for an age over him before it followed the body to the ground.

But Osmund had no eyes for that, because even while the dead man was still on his feet he had spun to the trench where the last Norman was stumbling to his feet over a Garth who had fallen again under the man's weight, took careful aim and thrust hard downwards at the exposed neck. But he struck the man on the shoulder, feeling the collarbones break under the blade and as the man screamed he swung the spade one-handed for the edge to crash down onto his head and the screaming stopped.

"Master!" came Garth's voice and he swung round to see Garth leaning from the trench with the interpreter fast by the foot with the man making mewling noises in his terror as he tried to break the grip. Osmund hesitated only a moment before he swung the spade again and those noises stopped too.

He dropped the spade and slumped to his knees, then to the ground. Four men had just died in an explosive blur of motion, and he began to shake uncontrollably.

"Lord Jesus!" whispered Garth, "I never saw the like!" and he scrambled from the trench to where Osmund lay trembling violently, to take him in his arms. "Oh Jesus!" said Garth, then "Oh Jesus, oh Jesus, oh Jesus . . ." as he rocked the quivering boy back and forth for long moments. Then as sanity returned, he sat up and shook Osmund gently.

"Master! Master! Lord Osmund! Hear me – listen! We must! You must!!" And he shook the boy again. Osmund turned a white and wide-eyed face up to him, but there was life in the eyes again and even as Garth stared into them in the fading light he saw awareness come back into them from where it had fled during the burst of feral fury that had taken four lives in as many seconds.

"Master! We must bury 'em. We c'n do it right here – down there!" he said, pointing to the trench. They'll never find 'em there – 's all dug over anyways! An' we never saw 'em anyway, did we? They were never here! You all right? Are you? Jus' you stay there – let me dig the hole an' then you c'n give me a hand to get 'em in it! Stay there!"

"No Garth. No – think!" Osmund's voice was unnaturally calm. "Four men can't just disappear. They can't. The whole village knows we're up here tonight, and sooner or later someone'll give it away. When they can't be found anywhere else, someone will settle on the fact that this was the last known place they went. It's what I'd do, Garth, how I'd think."

"Aye, they'll be found, and it'll all come out. And when it does, that's it for you and me – me because I killed them and you because you watched me do it and helped cover it up. The Normans will kill you, Garth. They will. No – burying them won't do."

"Then – what?" whispered Garth. "What do we do now, master? All the same anyway, isn't it?"

"No. There's a way. It's why I killed the interpreter too. We keep it simple and we keep it true. Mostly true. This is how it was – the Normans came here right enough, and started in on us over how slow we're being. This one – " he indicated the sergeant – "insulted my father. I went for him and you threw me back. They began laughing – I hit you with the spade to get you out of my way, and that's all you know because you woke up in the trench. When you did, you saw – this" and he gestured around them. "We leave them just where they fell. Garth. We don't shift them, so that someone can put it together just the way you describe it. All right?" And the voice was as calm as if they were discussing the grain yield. Despite himself, Garth shivered.

"All right master. But what about you?"

"Me? I'm going, Garth. I don't know where, and I wouldn't tell you if I did, because you can't tell what you don't know. But I need your help to get food, clothes and weapons together for wherever I'm going."

"God above, master Osmund, you're only fourteen! You can't . . ."

"Fifteen in June, Garth. Fifteen. That's much better than fourteen."

"Lord Osmund, I can't . . . I . . . let me come with you! Aye! I served your father—"

"I know, Garth, and you served him well. His people too. And that's why you must stay. There's Aelfgifu and your children. And there's the village. And there's my mother. Now I can't do for them what my father's son should do for them, Garth – so you'll have to. They all look to you, and so they should, because you'll die before you let any of them down. That's it.

That's how it must be, and I know you'll get the true story to my mother."

Garth's shaggy head drooped and he began to weep softly, but Osmund went on in his supernatural calm.

"Tonight, and until you get me what I need, I'm going down to the shepherd's hut by the river. That'll be safe enough for a little while because the Normans don't know about it yet and probably won't until summer. Anyway, as soon as the fuss has died down a bit and they've spread out to find me, I'm going to take a horse from the stables one night and find a way through."

"Now – there's one more thing, Garth. You'll need a mark because I hit you, remember? Let's say I hit you with the flat of the spade, aye – on the forehead, I think – that'd stun you. You'd better have a bruise to show – and some blood, but there's plenty of that over there. That rock there – aye – should make a mark. Sorry, Garth. And thank you. Thank you. Thank you for serving my father, and my mother – and for what you've taught me. I'll take a dagger and sword from those things yonder, and I'll see you tomorrow night? Good. Now – ready?"

Somewhere off the English coast, March 1068.

"Go to England" Elisabeth had said. "I don't want you grieving for me, my darling, and I doubt you'll ever serve royalty again. You've got to do something, so go and see what you can do for that wonderful man's family. They're your family too if they were Penda's – did you think of that?"

Not in so many words, thought the Scraeling, *but it was true enough anyway.* Yes – he would go to England because he had nowhere else to go and nothing else to do. He was fifty-one years old and the rest of his life stretched before him featureless as the ocean on their seaward side. More so, even, for out to sea he could see a small fishing-fleet.

Now Osmund would be – ah, born in June fifty-three, so he's fifteen this year. And Gytha was eighteen when she married Penda in fifty-two, so she's . . . aye, thirty-four this year. What about the other boys? And Gytha was about due at the time of Senlac — Anyway, he'd find out soon enough.

Skuli had got him on his feet and able to face the world without wanting to drink it dry, but it had taken a month or two. And in that time he had thought much about what he wanted to do and where he wished to go, so that Skuli's half-joking offer to take him a-viking again had fallen on fertile soil.

For his part, Skuli had confessed himself bored. "I've been all m' life a wanderer, Scraeling" he had said, toying with a horn of beer. "That nearly stopped at Stamford, but thanks to you it didn't. Well I'm over that now, an' what've I got? A *drakkar* an' forty of a crew who don't fancy fishin' any more'n I do. Got no idea'f buying or selling, an' people who keep cows an' pull tits for a living can help themselves far's I'm concerned."

All of which had been a prelude to his offer to take the Scraeling anywhere he wished. "Aye, the old days've gone," he had said, "an' they won't come back. But I always reckoned, Scraeling, that wherever you were, there was . . . ah . . . interestin' times, you might say. There was allus somethin' going on. And you're a bloody handful you are – bilking whores, cheatin' amber sellers – remember how you put it over that Greek arsehole, the general – oh, y'know, Hardraada's mate, him what thought he was so fuckin' important? Shit, was that funny or what! Aye, an' you puzzlin' out how to get Mad Karl an' his boys into that castle . . . through the shithouse in the end, remember?"

So here they were, and here he was – all he was worth riding in a stout chest under the half-decked rear of the *drakkar*. But he had managed one final challenge before leaving Norway.

When they had left his home for the last time, they'd stopped in front of the sentry at the end of his street and the Scraeling had stared at him fixedly until the soldier began to sweat gently. Still the Scraeling stared, and the man grew redder and redder while Skuli and his men tittered until in the end he had said, "Yes sir? What is it?"

And the Scraeling had crowed in triumph and said, "Nothing, soldier. I just wanted to see if you were awake. My friends here tell me you're asleep and you salute in your sleep. Will you salute for me and wish me good morning? Eh?"

So, probably on the basis that the sooner he got rid of this lunatic and his hairy friends the better, the sentry had crashed to the salute shouting "Sir, good morning sir!! Good morning!!"

Whereupon the Scraeling had thanked him and produced a roll of paper before enquiring of the sentry if he knew which house belonged to the Scraeling. On being assured that he lived in the sixth house down on the left, the Scraeling had gently corrected the man.

"I *used* to live there" he had said. "You do now, my friend, and this is the deed of title. I'll fill in your name for you in a moment. Now you probably won't be allowed to keep the house – this street's set aside for minister's residences, and the court's full of complete pricks, starting with Magnus himself – but you can sell it because it's yours. And please yourself whether or not you sell the contents first, because they're yours too. Enjoy the wine, won't you? Here you are, my man. And thank you again for my salute."

"See, boys?" Skuli had demanded as they rolled the handcart off down the road, "Didn't I tell you he was a fucking legend? That sentry's grandkids'll hear about the Scraeling till they're sick of it, and we're going a-viking with him. Odin, smile on us, 'cause we c'd do with a hand through the troubles he'll get us into………"

The Raedwaldsson estate, Reading, England.

Osmund wrinkled his nose at the musty smell of the season-old bracken in the corner of the shepherd hut, but blessed the shepherd who hadn't bothered to clean out after himself last autumn. He unslung the sergeant's swordbelt from where he carried it across his chest and laid the weapon down by the deep-piled bracken. He glanced out to where he would see the river when the moon rose, unfolded his cloak and spread it on top of the bracken.

He was hungry, he realised, but there was nothing to be done about that because he had eaten nothing but the handful of bread and cheese snatched up on his way from the big house, his mind full of Gytha in the Norman's arms and the voice in his head – *most joyous of news* – for whom, Norman? Yourself, surely? – *a brother, a son* – my mother, Penda's woman, birthing a Norman so we would be – *truly a family*! Truly? Aye, a family in which Penda's son would yield Penda's manor to a half-breed . . . no family of mine, Norman!

To his mortification the tears scalded his eyes as he thought of the look on his mother's face as he came through the door. Of her laughter. Of her obvious happiness. Angrily, he dashed them away from his eyes with the back of a hand, and lay down on the cloak resolved to empty his mind of all except what he intended to do tomorrow.

Despite himself though, he remembered the explosion of hatred in his head at the sergeant's words and the white light that had powered him into action, going through Garth and at the taunting Norman, the spade swinging back like the axe of his drills with Garth but so much lighter so that the sergeant was dead on his feet even as he turned back to taunt him again. And the savagery of the parry that picked off the second man's slash at his legs, while through the red mist leaped the picture of an open and inviting throat that had offered only the slightest of jars as the hard-driven spade sliced into and through it.

They had been the immediate threats; the other two the longer-term threats and he had decided on the order of their deaths with an icy calm he could clearly remember and even wonder at. But what he recalled most clearly of all was the look he had seen on Garth's face as he came from his trembling fit. The big farmer had been looking at him as though he had never seen him before – Garth, whom Osmund had known all his life, whose big hand had been as familiar to him as that of his own father as the toddler had become a child and the child a young man. Garth had looked at him as he might have looked at the Devil himself had the Horned One appeared from a hedgerow or even the ploughed earth itself.

But what had been most remarkable of all was the way his mind had worked immediately afterwards. He couldn't remember working out what he would do. No, it had been there, completely formed in his mind, unbidden and not consciously sought. He had *known* – that was all there was to it, and he knew that Garth had seen that too. But now, now, all he wanted was to be rid of the thoughts in his head for he was weary as never before in his life.

Osmund closed his eyes and summoned the face of his father from a long-buried memory of Penda's smile as he listened, ale-horn in hand, to Uncle Ranulf quizzing an eleven-year-old about his pony, and sleep took him quickly.

Thames-mouth, early that morning.

The estuary was as busy as Skuli remembered it and he ordered the big square sail dropped at its mouth to send *Nordvedr* on its way under oars alone. He was aware that the very appearance of the dragon-ship in the estuary would awaken old memories and no small amount of apprehension, and the last thing he wanted was to excite curiosity in a land now ruled by men who were even more foreign to him than the English had been. So the sleek and low-slung *drakkar* pulled quickly through the banks of roundships that Skuli knew as *knorre*, a wolf prowling a sheepfold, and the multitude of smaller craft that plied between ship and ship or ship and shore stayed well away from its snarling prow and the bank of oars that bit into the water with a power and purpose that only underlined her menace.

"Not changed that much" said Skuli to the Scraeling who stood beside him on the steering-deck. "I hear this place's always busy, an' it was last time we were here."

"Different world then" returned the Scraeling absently, and Skuli knew by the tone of his voice where his thoughts lay.

"Anywhere, anytime's what y'make it, Scraeling" he said gently, then "What're we up to at lord Penda's place, then? Any idea?"

The Scraeling shrugged. "What I want to do" he said, "is find out how things are with Gytha, Osmund and the family. Whether they need help. Whether they're still there even. Suppose they will be. What I heard in Norway was that the Bastard was marrying off land heiresses to his favoured men."

"Clever" grunted Skuli. "In time . . ."

"Exactly" agreed the Scraeling watching a lighter in the grip of the current pull madly across it to keep away from them. "Keeps his treasury happy at the same time as it holds down the land he's stolen. And it's all legal according to English law, because they let their women inherit land."

"Quick road to a fuckin' mess," muttered Skuli. "Lettin' women inherit anythin'."

The Scraeling snorted with laughter. "Now, master – how far up the Thames do we go?"

"First, to the harbourmaster. That's your end o' things, boss. Dunno if things're still the same, but if they are there should be an earldorman in charge. I think we should report t'him an' tell him we're visiting relatives – well, we are, you reckon – an' let him see we're no threat. Then, if he's happy, 's about forty of their miles – fifteen leagues if I remember – to where another river branches off t'the left. That's the Kennet, so the captain I spoke to in Nidaros told me. Somewhere up the Kennet's the place we want. You don't recall?"

"Not clearly, Skuli – had a bit on my mind then." *Aye – making an end of Harald Hardraada was indeed quite a lot to have on your mind,* he thought, *and best not mentioned in this company at least.* A long way to go yet, a good day or so, and he set himself to look for signs of damage suffered in the city's recent past.

The Raedwaldsson manor, Reading, the next day.

"I don't believe it" said Ivo de Bois flatly. "Those men came through Hastings and the best that Harold the Forsworn had. You want me to believe that Osmund – a boy of . . . what, fourteen? . . . killed three veterans of that business?"

"I know, sir, I know!" said his second, Giso, in exasperation. "But what other explanation fits? There were six people there and only two're still breathing. And we've got one of'em, and he's had a smack on the head that, by the size of the bruise, would've killed anyone not built like the Saxon ox he is."

De Bois shook his head. "Again" he commanded, and Giso began. The ox, Garth, had stumbled into the village just after dark the night before, weaving from side to side and with his face covered in blood to raise the hue and cry over murder done at the castle site. On hearing it Giso had taken a sergeant and half a dozen men with torches there, and they had brought back the story that was the source of de Bois' disbelief.

According to Garth it seemed that the dead sergeant had intended to flog both Garth and Osmund – *wouldn't have happened* thought de Bois, *but he didn't know that* – as an inducement for the village to co-operate, but had insulted Osmund's dead father also. Garth was sure of that, for when the boy had snatched up a spade he'd attempted to restrain him, turning away for a moment to curse the sergeant, and turning back into the swing of the spade. "And that's all I knew till I woke up an' saw . . . what I saw. What's still there."

"Four dead men" said Giso, and ticked them off on his fingers. "Trebas with the top of his head peeled back and his brains all over the place. Lamoulle's head still attached by a strip of skin – throat smashed in, spine cut through. Genvier with a deep cut down through his left shoulder to his chest and his head split from side to side. Oh, and that interpreter fellow – the Englishman – had his head stove in completely. All axe wounds in my book, aye. Now, there was no axe there – but there were two spades; our ox says they had one each, but the one nearest the bodies was covered in blood and brains. Covered."

"And you think?" said de Bois. Giso puffed out his cheeks.

"Dunno" he said, "but if you're asking, messire, I'd say the Devil himself was loose up there. As you say – our men were combat veterans, no argument, but only one weapon was unsheathed – oh, Trebas' sword, belt and dagger're missing, by the way – so what happened, happened bloody quick."

"So let's see" said de Bois, still struggling with the implications for him personally. "You're saying that a fourteen-year-old took a spade – a spade, for Jesu's sake – to three veterans and *killed* them? Assuming for a moment that any farmer with a farm-tool could do that – why couldn't it have been the ox? What's his name again?"

"Garth" said Giso. "He's the village leader – headman, whatever you like. Yes, thought of him. Even thought he could've faked that bruise and all the blood – God knows there's plenty of it around up there, but I had a look at him when I came back and he's cut all right. Dent in his forehead you can get two knuckles in, but there's no doubt – he's got the power and strength to inflict wounds like that. But if it was him – where's the young man? Where's Osmund? And if it was Garth – where's Trebas' weapons? He hasn't got them and they're not lying around."

De Bois shook his head in mystification. "What d'you think, Ralph?" he asked the silent figure by the window.

Ralph stopped gnawing the thumbnail he'd been working on, wiped his hand absently on the front of his robe and considered. "Torn two ways" he said. "I can't believe Osmund could or would do that. But Giso's right. If it wasn't him, where is he? Giso – did you look around for sign of fresh digging?"

Giso's brows came down and he looked his puzzlement. Ralph went on, "I mean – let's assume Garth's our axeman and for some reason he killed them all. How's he going to get away with it? Blame Osmund? That'd mean Osmund'd need to disappear. Just as he has, because he hasn't come home, has he? And then Garth runs his head into a few rocks, covers his face in blood, comes down and tells his story."

"Let's not forget" he went on, warming to his theme, "there's so much newly-dug earth up there – who's to know what any of it covers? I'd say we need to sit down and work out how much time Garth had to do all this – we know when the villagers were sent down, don't we? And we know when it got dark, so . . . how much could he do in that time? And we go at it on that basis."

De Bois looked at him with respect. "Well done, Ralph. I like that – it'd answer a few questions right enough. I think we need to get a digging party up there – and no-one mention this to Gytha until we know more. And even then – leave it to me. But well done, cousin – you might have something there."

Dig all you like thought Ralph as Giso bustled from the room. *You won't find Osmund on the site. You won't find him because he did it all right, the little Saxon bastard, and now he's either running or in a bolt-hole somewhere. Oh yes, he did it – and if cousin Ivo can't believe it, it's because his brain's still between Gytha's legs. There's no fool like an old fool. And to think he once told me all my brains were in my cock! If that's what marriage does to you, I might have to put Wynfrytha on rations. Still, if I do this right, it could be all the convincing Giffard needs to put me into that manor . . .*

On the Thames, the same day.

There's been damage all right thought the Scraeling watching the occasional patch of charred ruins slide along the bank as *Nordvedr* surged confidently upstream, *but a while ago because there's green growing through most of it.* And that confirmed what the harbourmaster's man had said as he passed them through upriver.

William's coronation had been an occasion of misunderstanding; blood had been spilled and homes set afire but it had all been smoothed over. "And now?" The Scraeling had asked and the man had shrugged. "We get on with it" he had replied, handing over a paper that they were to show if required. "Least, we do here in London. Well, not much choice really – but I hear different from other places, from the ships that come in from around the coast, y'know?"

"I can imagine" said the Scraeling, "and I can guess how all that talking dries the throat. Here's our fee for this paper – and a little more to make up for the strain on your throat for telling me where and why things are different elsewhere – " and four silver pennies had appeared in his fingers as if by magic, with the result that it had been some time before he reappeared to walk down to the dock in the weak spring sunlight.

"Thought they'd locked you up" said Skuli, "what kept you?"

"Just seeking a little information" returned the Scraeling, "you never know when you might need it. And you can never have enough information, Skuli." And he answered the other's shake of the head with a grin and a wink.

"So – all over here, but not in the west, the north and the east. What you'd expect, really – this's where the Normans are strong; here and in the south – and they're stretched in those other places. Agrees with what I heard in Norway about William's settlement policy. But Reading – smack in the middle of the area that's strongly-held; at least they're in no danger from fighting back and forth."

The Raedwaldsson manor, that night.

The moon rode high in the nigh-freezing air, but the man who left his own hearth and stepped quickly into the darkness with a bundle tied tightly into a cloak and slung over one brawny shoulder, knew where he was going. He looked swiftly around him before setting off south across the manor, keeping to the shadows as he moved through the village so that none saw him go.

But there was none to see him go in any case, because the man with an interest in him was already up ahead, buried in the forest rim overlooking the wide plain leading down to the river where the sheep were penned in summer for shearing. "Come on, come on!" he thought to himself, his eyes never leaving the track from the village. "Osmund'll be starving by now – if I'm right he's been there a full day with fuck-all to eat, and either he's coming out tonight or someone's going to him."

Ralph had guessed what had happened, almost as soon as he had heard of the discovery at the castle-site, for he was no-one's fool. He knew of Osmund's feelings towards de Bois – towards all Normans in fact – for the young man hadn't troubled to hide them. But he knew one or two other things also.

Ralph's passion was the chase, and he was adept at reading game tracks. Some weeks before, he had come across what he was certain were boar tracks in a patch of woodland exposed enough to the sun to thaw before freezing hard again at night. Since he had happened upon the tracks he had fallen into the habit of checking them almost on a daily basis, confident that he would ride them down in late spring or early summer, and on his third such visit he had pulled up at the sound of voices on the other side of the hill. Moving quietly to the crest, he had gazed down into a clearing where Osmund and Garth were about the training that the farmer had promised Gytha.

Ralph had watched, astonished at the way the young Saxon had sent the blunt side of the clumsy axe whistling in at the newly-reinforced shield harder and faster than he would have thought possible; hard enough to make Garth stagger under the force of a full strike and swift enough to make him keep the heavy shield in constant motion anywhere from over his head to down at his ankles.

Oh yes. Ralph was in no doubt whatever that Osmund Pendasson was capable of taking three or four men, given the advantage of surprise. He moved like shifting light, his full weight behind the axe-head as it went home but weaving and spinning to turn a blow glancing from the target into another that came in while his opponent was staggering from the first, always perfectly balanced, always with the menace of the axe-head before his eyes so that he had weapon and target continually in his line of sight.

And the arms – God in heaven, Ralph thought – the arms were like twisted ropes, able to send the axe-head cutting right or left without benefit of a clumsy swing, and as the young man spun to face the shield that bored in at him continually, the bunched muscles of the shoulders slid to and fro like snakes under the tunic that stretched to its utmost over them. At last the exercise had ended, and Osmund had paused only to lay down the axe before striding to a tree limb and beginning a punishing series of arm exercises.

For an hour Ralph lay watching and listening, and when the others had gone he lay half an hour more, thinking, until he was certain that they were well away. What he had seen convinced him of two things – the first, that Osmund Pendasson was likely to be more than a match for him with a weapon in his hand, and the second, that Osmund and Garth were as close as father and son.

And that was how he came to be lying under a tree on a night that

125

was much colder than he liked them. Ralph was convinced that Osmund was capable of cutting down the four men at the castle-site like so many saplings because the blazing speed and aggression he had witnessed from the cover of the forest above their clearing had been unequalled in his experience, an experience that had included a long day at Hastings. And he was equally sure that Garth had either helped, or was covering for his young lord, because the realities surrounding the slaughter at the site were no less clear to Ralph than they had been to Osmund.

That's the only way he had told himself. *The only way Osmund can disappear, and unless he's gone without food, clothing, weapons – and on foot! – he expects to get them soon. And you don't—*

There. At the head of the path there had been a movement where a patch of blackness had detached itself from a deeper patch, and Ralph could see it raise itself to stare backwards to where anything following would be lit by the moon when it cleared the shadow of the last hut. For long moments nothing moved, and Ralph could well-nigh see the man who watched swing to scan the emptiness of the long meadow before him. Ralph knew where he was going, for he had discovered the shepherd's hut in his search for the boar's lair weeks before.

Then the figure was off, hugging the trees that fringed the river and flitting from shadow to shadow until it disappeared into the clump of trees at the end that sheltered the hut from the wind that blew towards it down the open area. Ralph had little doubt that the figure was Garth and that he was bringing Osmund the provisions he needed, and he realised that what the two Saxons did would determine what he himself did next. If they reappeared together and made for the stables he had two choices – either to accost them himself or to fall back, rouse those elements of the garrison handy to the house, and then take them. But the first was too dangerous and the second likely to deprive him of the credit he deserved for bringing in a dangerous rebel.

The very sort of credit that would see him in the Aelfricsson manor by midsummer.

The shepherd's hut.

Garth pursed his lips and whistled softly, twice, as he approached the hut black against the water beyond. He jumped as an answering whistle came, not from the hut but from the trees to the right of it.

"Master? Young master?" he whispered and a low chuckle came to him.

"Expecting anyone else out here, Garth? Saw you from halfway across the meadow, moon's so bright."

"Thought y'might've been asleep, master" said Garth and he felt rather than saw Osmund shake his head.

"Too hungry, Garth" he said. "Come in. What'd you bring to eat?"

Garth unslung his bundle of clothing and handed Osmund another of food; while the youth chewed hungrily the farmer placed a bow and quiver full of arrows against the wall. Then he picked up various articles of clothing and listed them for the listening Osmund. "Trousers. Leggings. Jerkin. Hoods. About all y'can carry an' keep a hand free, master – but this bag here, Aelfgifu sewed it up – 'f you cut the stitching down the sides it opens out into 'nother cloak 'cause that's what it was before she sewed it."

Osmund squeezed his arm in the darkness. "Bless her for a good and thoughtful woman, Garth. And you. How's your head?"

"M'head? Well enough master – had worse from wrestling your father, no error. But look you – that Giso's had me over an' over today – what happened, what I saw, what I heard, where you might be – all o'that, an' more t'come I reckon. Master, will you go tonight? We c'd get a horse from stables an' – if y're gonna go – I c'd see you on y'way tonight."

Osmund shook his head. "No Garth. Tonight I could be hiding nearby, hungry, tired, desperate enough to try for a horse and I'd wager they're watching the stables for those reasons. Another day or two and they'll assume I've got away a bit further at least, so the search'll go further also. That'll give me space to take a horse and get through them from behind." A pause, then, "Has ... has my mother spoken to you?"

"Aye master, that she has. An' ... an' I told her what I told ev'ryone else. God forgive my lyin' to Lady Gytha, but there was others hard by. But master, I'll make some excuse t'see her soon's I think it's a good idea. Spring planting's comin' up soon ... something'll serve. An' ... an I'll tell her how you got away."

"Garth, tell her . . . tell her I'll return one day. That she'll be in my prayers always, and my brothers, and little Sunngifu. Tell her . . . I'm not ashamed of what I did, because I did it for my father as he did it for his lord. And tell her . . . that I've run only because I don't want her to see me die, and . . . her new husband . . . would have no choice. Can you tell her that, Garth? Please?"

"Aye, master" and the big farmer's voice was husky. "Aye, I'll tell her. Now look'ee – eat all that food tonight an' tomorrow, for I'll be back tomorrow night."

"Thank you Garth. Thank you for it all. You're much more than I deserve, for I've let my mother down. I've failed in what she asked of me, and that was to do my duty as my father did to his king and she is doing to our folk. Will you look after her for me? Please?"

"To m'last breath, lord Osmund. My hand on that." And two hands clasped, the boy's scarcely smaller than the man's.

An hour later, Ralph grunted in satisfaction as he saw a lone figure steal along the treeline, and he waited until it had gone from sight back towards the village before he slid slowly backwards, rose to his feet and stretched cramped limbs.

"That's it then" he said softly to the cold moon that looked down on him. "Tomorrow I win a manor. And do my good cousin the favour he hasn't got the balls for at the same time."

The same night.

"We've done the best possible" said Ivo de Bois, "and we're sure . . . that is, there's no . . . no sign . . . of Osmund on the castle site. So" – and he sighed, "so that proves he's still alive. Unfortunately it also seems to prove the truth of what the man Garth told us. Osmund killed four men. Three soldiers and an interpreter. My lady . . . my dear . . ." the word felt thick and unfamiliar on his tongue but he ploughed on, "my dear, do you think Osmund could – is he capable . . . could he have done what we think he's done? I'm so sorry, truly sorry, could he?"

Gytha lifted a ravaged face. "Capable? *Capable*, my lord? Osmund would have died for his father, because my boy worshipped him. Senlac took my man, then my little boy, my firstborn, and made him a man at thirteen!" she sobbed.

"Do you know, he set himself to do all the things his father had done – even to the lighting of the lamps in this house at evening, because Penda did that to signal the end of the working day and the time when we could be a family. *Capable?* My lord, if your men indeed taunted Osmund with his dead father and he had no other weapon, his teeth would have sufficed!"

De Bois took a step towards her, concern plain upon his face, but she flung back her head. "*Capable?* Garth has done for him what his father would have done were he still alive. Garth has made him an axeman, and I saw, and I . . . I begged him to make my son invincible, that . . . that what befell his father . . . would never befall my son. That he would not be bested by any man, weapon in hand. And Garth knew the craft of the axe from his lord, Penda. From the best axeman in England! Oh aye, my lord, Osmund is 'capable' and more than capable, boy though he is!"

De Bois shook his head. "My lady, his age will not save him if he's taken. He's killed three Normans and one in Norman service. I can do nothing for him . . . to save him. My lady, pray with me. Pray that Osmund runs far, fast and successfully. I would give all I have that this might be undone. But it cannot, so I again I ask you . . . pray with me for your son."

In the same house at the same time.

"Congratulate me" said Ralph de Courcy, holding up his cup.

"Congratulations" returned Raimond de la Mor, clinking the other's cup with his own. "Er, why? What for?"

"For winning a manor. Tomorrow morning" said de Courcy, draining the cup with a flourish. "I'm going to bring in a rebel and a murderer. Least, I'm going to bring in his body."

De la Mor goggled at him. De Courcy laughed at the look on his friend's face, refilled his cup and explained what he had seen that night and what he intended to do the next morning. "Want to help? Do you no end of good with Giffard. Osmund's a murderer, so his life's forfeit to the king's justice anyway, and I can't see him coming with me quietly. And it does neither of us any harm to be seen as strong enough to deal with problems like Osmund."

"Won't do either of us any good with Gytha, though," muttered

Raimund, "and unless I'm much mistaken, not with your cousin either."

"But that's the point" said Ralph. "At least one of the points. Cousin Ivo's in a cleft – and this time it's not Gytha's – " he sniggered, "who's it up to, to do justice? Cousin Ivo. Who's married to the criminal's mother? Cousin Ivo. So you see, I'm doing him a favour by saving him a decision that'll break someone's heart. Not that I care, when all's said and done. Bugger Gytha and all her kind. Our kind's what's important, Raimund. So my question – want some of this?"

De Courcy held his breath as he sipped again, because for all his apparent carelessness he doubted his ability to confront and kill Osmund. In fact, if de la Mor turned him down he had already decided to kill Osmund from ambush. That would make the deed harder to justify, of course, but he could always point to the boy's outlawry. If it came to that, he'd have Garth taken and tortured until he confirmed what Ralph had already come to believe – that the two of them had conspired to kill the four Normans. But yes – de la Mor's help would make that unnecessary. "Well?"

De la Mor nodded slowly. "Yes" he said. "Yes, I do. What d'you have in mind?"

The next morning.

They had anchored in the stream well short of the village of Reading itself, Skuli being unwilling to go further up an unfamiliar river, and a tributary at that, in the darkness. Now here they were, sliding through the mist of the early morning to ease gently across the current and under the steering-sweep alone towards a mooring by the thick forest that ran down to the river's edge, while the Scraeling gave due consideration to how best to approach the man or men who now ran Penda's estates. For some reason – and the Scraeling had no idea of what it was, although he had noted it – *Nordvedr* was ghostlike in her total silence as she ran in under a thick and drooping willow to bump her snarling prow gently into the bank before the grapple-hooks flew and she was hauled broadside-in.

The years fell away and the Scraeling turned to Skuli and spoke, "That's it, Skuli – other side of these trees there's a path that leads to the village. Now, I'd better go myself – one look at any of your cut-throats and they'll send for the Bastard himself. I'll take only half a dozen with me, so if you'll pick them for me . . . and you'll be putting another half-dozen ashore, of course?"

Skuli looked hurt, and the Scraeling resolved to give up teaching a born pirate his business. He dug into his sea-chest to produce a comb, a looking-glass and a cloak of better quality than the salt-stained effort he was wearing, and set about making himself look presentable. But he had hardly begun when a cry of "Skuli! Scraeling! Quick!" split the air from the bank and he dropped everything to leap over the bulwark and up to where one of the shore party was gesturing frantically and looking away down the meadow to its end.

The Scraeling followed his gaze to see a man bursting clear of the brush at the treeline at the end of the meadow and sprinting up the green expanse as if his life depended upon it. Which it surely did, decided the Scraeling, as two men mounted on ponies exploded from the thicket behind him, wrenched boar-spears from the saddle-boots that held them and thundered up the meadow behind the flying man.

"The trees, fuckwit, the trees!" hissed Skuli beside him. "Get into the trees!" But the same thought had occurred to at least two others at the same time for even as the flying fugitive altered his angle to cut into the trees the rider on the right hand did the like and rowelled his mount to send it bounding forward. The runner decided his chances of getting into the woods before being run down weren't good enough and swung back to the open ground, bringing a French yell of triumph from the rider and a flourish of his spear. "Stand, Pendasson, stand! There's nowhere to go – stand or die!"

Skuli felt the Scraeling go rigid beside him, but he couldn't tear his eyes from the scene before them. The swerve away from the trees had taken the man squarely into the path of the left-hand rider and as another triumphant shout split the air the fugitive skidded to a halt, spun and faced the charge of his pursuer balanced on the balls of his feet, big hands away from his sides and his head up. The rider whooped, lowered his spear to the couch and charged in at the figure before him.

At the instant before the couched spear crashed into his chest, the man on the ground swayed away from its glittering point. One hand slammed across the shaft of the spear behind the head and the other came up from underneath to lock on to the weapon in a muscle-cracking heave that brought the rider, his hand entangled in the leather sling attached to the spear, flying from the saddle like a bird rising into the air.

"Hey! See that? Feet never fuckin' *moved!*" burst out Skuli as the rider hit the ground head-first and bounced to a standstill. The fugitive was on him in a flash and scrabbling to free the spear from his hand, but had to break off to twist away from the charge of the second man by dodging under the very nostrils of his mount to the side opposite the rider's weapon-hand.

"Y'won't do that twice, son" muttered Skuli, and the fugitive must have reached the same conclusion, for as the swearing horseman thundered past he turned to bolt for the woodland again, tripped over the outflung and unmoving arm of the man he had unhorsed, and sprawled on his back dazed, helpless and exhausted.

The rider completed his circle and pounded down on him, adjusting his grip on the heavy spear to plunge it down overhand. "I win, Osmund! Die like your fucking father!" he screamed as he hung over the white-faced man on the ground, and his spear-arm had started downwards when his face bloomed outwards from the centre as a large hole appeared in it, his arms flew apart, the spear clattered down across Osmund and Ralph de Courcy toppled slowly backwards over the crupper of his saddle.

Skuli blinked and whirled to where the Scraeling was already tying the sling back round his waist. "Get those ponies" the Scraeling said to the men about him. "Slowly – they'll be trained to stand but they don't know our smell so – slowly, yes? And someone check that other bugger that came off first. Get them both out of sight. *Move!*" He glanced up and down the meadow and lurched forward in his shuffling gait to where the fugitive, up on one knee, had turned to the sound of voices.

Odin's balls! thought Skuli as he sent men to the horses and went forward himself, *Didn't I say it? 'But I always reckoned, Scraeling, that wherever you were, there was interestin' times.' Well, didn't I just?*

"Osmund, my boy!" said the Scraeling from five yards away. "Well met – how you've grown!"

"Ohhh ... Uncle Ranulf! I ... I'm ..." said Osmund, and fainted.

Aboard 'Nordvedr'.

"He's *how* old?" asked Skuli in disbelief as they looked at the figure on the sleeping-mat.

"Fourteen. I'm almost sure his fifteenth's in June. Certainly about then" said the Scraeling, running his hands over Osmund's limbs and ending by peeling back an eyelid to glance at the eye beneath.

"Fourteen" mused Skuli. "Look at them shoulders! Never seen anythin' like that footwork either. Or the strength – see how he hoicked that bugger out of his saddle? Way those two handled their spears, I reckon they were real soldiers – and your boy made a right fool of them anyway. No, never seen nothing like him for speed!"

"Yes you have. You saw Penda in Miklagaard. Against the Scythians. Osmund's his boy, don't forget."

"'Course!" breathed Skuli. "Shit, yes. He's Penda's boy all right. Wonder what he c'd do with an axe in them hands?"

"That's the interesting part" said the Scraeling absently. "I'd wager Penda never taught him what we saw today, Skuli. Think about it – Penda died when Osmund had just turned thirteen. Someone's taken his boy in hand. There's another dangerous bugger somewhere about."

"Garth" said Osmund, his eyes still closed. "Garth's the truly dangerous one." His eyes flicked open. "Uncle Ranulf! Is it really you, then? Really? Sir, I'm . . . I'm truly glad to see you— welcome. Welcome!" He tried to sit up, but lay back with his head swimming.

"Stay a moment" said the Scraeling, pressing him down gently. "There's no hurry, and you don't begin every day by fighting two armed horsemen for your life – most of us break our fast before we break any necks. As you did with the man you hauled from the saddle, by the way. Normans?"

Garth nodded. "Ralph de Courcy – he was the one you struck down. The other – one of his friends, I think. I've seen him, but I never knew his name. What . . . where are they?"

Skuli bent a forefinger down in the most eloquent of gestures. "Well weighted" he said. "And they'll stay there for months. Two'f my boys have stripped the horses, swum 'em across the river an' turned 'em loose on the other side. Be a while before they're found."

"Thank you sir. I'm Osmund, son of Penda, and I'm in your debt sir.

Thank you again."

"I'm Skuli Bergrsson, Osmund, and I'm not used to anyone calling me 'sir'. Specially ones who c'n handle themselves like you. 'Skuli' – all right?" And he held out a hand.

"Thank you – Skuli, then" came Penda's smile from Gytha's face, and Osmund held up a hand that was little short of the size of Skuli's, noted the Scraeling. He cleared his throat.

"Osmund, I hope we'll have a long time to talk – but now, I think, first things first. Tell me why those men were trying to kill you." And he signalled to Auti to bring food while Osmund sat up slowly.

So between mouthfuls Osmund told them of Gytha's marriage, and of their situation. He told them of the events of the past two days and even the Scraeling blinked in shock at his matter-of-fact mention that he had killed four Normans. "But I underestimated Ralph, Uncle Ranulf. He must have known about the hut, because he couldn't have found it by accident – I mean, at that time of the morning?"

It was only through luck and a full bladder that he'd escaped being taken in his sleep. He'd arisen with the earliest light and had just finished relieving himself, he said, when he'd heard a horse cough and recognised it at once. Whirling round, he had been in time to see de Courcy and his friend materialise from the dripping forest and immediately clap heels to their ponies. By the grace of God, a rabbit had erupted from a bush under the very nose of de Courcy's mount to send it plunging and skittering, and without further thought Osmund had seized the chance to bolt round the hut and away. "Should have come through the trees, though, when I think about it – but I didn't think, uncle." and the Norsemen had seen the rest.

"Mmm. Are those two likely to be missed soon?" asked the Scraeling and Osmund shrugged.

"Ralph often goes to the Aelfricsson manor and spends some time there. I've no idea what he does there – never been interested enough to find out. Whatever it is keeps him away for days sometimes. He's a relative of my . . . of my mother's new husband, so he's treated a little differently. But that was before. Now . . . now the Normans will be combing every inch of the manor for me, I suppose, and they're doing it themselves, Garth tells me, because they don't trust the manor-folk to hunt me down. So . . . I don't know how long it'll be before he's missed."

"Doesn't matter" said the Scraeling. "They'll not be found where they are, and if Ralph was the only link between your manor and the one across the river, the horses will be fine there for a while too. Yes. But I asked because someone's going to notice our presence here before long, and I think we should announce it before we're discovered, Skuli, especially since Osmund's going to be hidden among the crew, eh?"

Skuli grunted assent, and the Scraeling went on,

"I've a mind to see your mother again, Osmund. So I'll go and do that after I seek out Garth, and I'll tell her you're coming with me – and you'll have to, my boy, because you've done enough to merit hanging six times over in Norman eyes. And if I can't speak freely to her " – for the Scraeling hadn't missed the tone of *my mother's new husband* – "I'll make sure Garth does. She'll need to know. She deserves to know."

"Aye, Uncle Ranulf. Er – where are we going then?"

"No idea, my boy" said the Scraeling. "But we'll find trouble somewhere, doubtless. Your father had a nose for it - and you're so obviously his son!"

The Chronicle.

I set out along the track to the village with six of the better-dressed of Skuli's band, and found Garth with little difficulty. I greeted Penda's spearbearer with real joy, for we had met during my previous visits to the Raedwaldsson estates and I knew he had loved Penda as I had myself. For his part he seemed to return my feelings for he declared, with tears in his eyes, that God himself had surely sent me there – and when I told him of the events of that morning he paled and crossed himself.

Quickly I assured him that Osmund was safe and would continue to be safe, both because I would bear him beyond the reach of any pursuit and because there would be no trace of the Normans who had vanished that day until the horses were discovered on the Aelfricsson estate. Garth swore that Giffard hadn't yet disposed of that manor and that, since that was so, he could arrange for the ponies to disappear into the Aelfricsson stables as though they had never lived elsewhere.

And, hands shaken on that promise, he bore me off to the big house I remembered so well from happier days – the house where I had played with Penda's children and plotted the defeat of the world's foremost soldier. On the way there I asked of Gytha's new husband and found, to my surprise, that Garth

*thought well enough of him as a fair man who had been a good fighting soldier
and who deserved the respect due to such a one.*

*I must have looked my surprise, for the big Englishman hastened to assure
me that, while he would never love or even esteem his Norman conquerors, he
saw daily the widow of his beloved lord treated with respect and kept in dignity,
and for that consideration he would deal always as fairly as he could, with and
for Ivo de Bois.*

" 'Cept where lord Osmund's concerned, 'course".

The manor house.

Gytha clung to the Scraeling and sobbed as if her heart would break.
Perhaps it had broken at the sight of him, for while she had had both
husband and son taken from her, he had appeared like a wraith from the old
days of happiness and youth. The youth had fled from the woman who wept
in his arms, for her hair showed traces of grey and the tear-stained face was
no longer that of the child-bride he remembered.

"Oh Ranulf, that you should come here now . . . this day . . . I mean, at
this time" and he remembered how she had exclaimed at the sight of him
and rushed into his arms without pausing, "this time, of our greatest grief.
Truly, God has sent you—" and he shushed her and laid a finger across her
lips.

"Gytha, beloved of my beloved cousin – I've spoken with Garth, and
so know all. What I want to say is that . . . that my vessel is moored by
the sheep meadow, and Osmund is safe aboard her." She gazed mutely at
him, uncomprehending, and he said, "Osmund is safe, my dearest. Do you
understand?"

Her lips trembled and she said "How? How in God's name, Ranulf,
did you find him when my husband's soldiers can't? How?" And something
told the Scraeling not to relate the details of that morning's work, for what
Gytha didn't know she could never tell, whether impelled by conscience,
confession or duress.

"He found me, dearest lady. He found me. And it may well be as you
say – perhaps God did send me here this day, and if that's so, it may be
why your husband's abroad after Osmund even now, so we may speak. But
Gytha – should that come to an end, I would know – and quickly – if you

and your children will come with me, now, even as Osmund comes with me. Flanders awaits you, and even France itself, for neither have any cause to love the Normans. You could be safe there, you and Osmund both, and I have wealth enough for you all. It's yours, Gytha, whatever you need or want, for I know Penda would do that for me or mine. It's yours."

She had stepped away from him while he spoke, the better to look up at him – he wasn't a tall man, but he'd only ever met two women smaller and slighter than Gytha – and after he'd finished she lowered her head, hands by her sides, and wept again, the picture of utter misery as the tears ran unheeded down her face and onto her gown. It seemed that all the sadness of the world ran from her then, and the Scraeling stepped forward to her again.

"What is it, Gytha? Why do you weep so? Come away with me. Let me take Penda's family with me. Let's return to the happiness we knew before Senlac. Before Stamford even. What does my lady say?"

She raised her face to him and sobbed, "Ranulf, Ranulf, none of us may do as we wish. None of us. Osmund and I . . . have spoken of this, and I told him then that my duty . . . to his father . . . the only man I'll ever love, Ranulf, and I know that you loved him too . . . my duty will keep me here to look after the folk . . . who were the folk of Penda, and who loved him as we did." She broke off and wiped at her eyes, but before he could open his mouth in protest she went on.

"My duty – aye. My duty to my lord, Ranulf, keeps me here. And remaining here means that I must marry the man my overlord chooses for me. And marrying that man means I must share his bed." And all the while as she spoke the tears rolled down her face. "And sleeping with him means . . . means, Ranulf, that I've carried his child within me these three months past. I am to birth a Norman's child, Ranulf. I, who bore my lord four children of our own. And my son hates me for it, Ranulf – he – he hates me for it, for I've seen it in his face!"

"I can't . . . can't believe that, Gytha" said the Scraeling. "Not Osmund. Osmund loves you fiercely – he always did, and I'm sure nothing's changed."

Gytha laughed a laugh that had no mirth in it. "Nothing's changed? Ranulf, dear Ranulf, the whole *world's* changed! The king's changed! A Norman walks where my father and my husband walked! A Norman shares my bed and my body! And nothing's changed? Ranulf, *I* haven't changed.

I'm doing what I swore to do when I married Penda as a girl – to be a good wife to him and the keeper of his house. Well, both he and his house have been taken from me, but I'll serve his memory until God leads me to him as He did once before. Even though the son I love thinks me a Norman whore because of it!"

"Gytha! Oh Gytha, my lady! That's . . . that's just fooli— my dearest lady, you're not yourself! And little wonder, for what you've been through! Gytha, Gytha, think again. Put all this behind you, please. Come away with us – we can talk of this later, when we're away. And what we want, can happen. We'll make it happen! You'll see!"

"Will it? Will it dearest Ranulf? As I've said – none of us may do as we wish. And if we can have what we want . . . forgive me Ranulf, but . . . but if we can truly have what we want, why isn't the first minister of the king of Norway offering me and mine safe haven there? Why Flanders or France? And why has a lone *drakkar* slunk into the river that girds the Raedwaldsson estate?"

The Scraeling paused with his mouth open in sheer astonishment, and Gytha smiled for the first time that day, albeit sadly. "Something's wrong, isn't it Ranulf? No. I won't come with you. But I want you to take my son, and when you think the time's right, explain to him that sometimes duty's about doing what you have to do rather than what you want to do. Sometimes duty means living for your people instead of dying for them or for your king. And sometimes it asks you to live on your knees instead of dying on your feet. You'll make him see, Ranulf. You're a very wise man."

"So. That's decided. Tell me about Elisabeth. What's gone wrong?"

Cornwall, England, March 1068.

The stopper squeaked as Leo shoved it back in his water-bottle with an emphatic smack of his hand, swilled the liquid round his mouth and gargled it slowly down his throat. His trumpeter hid a grin and thought how the boss never varied his approach to battle. The ritual with the flask was part of it, and the trumpeter had once heard Leo explain to his friend Odo that, while a soldier couldn't do much about what faced him in battle, he could do lots about a dry mouth and a sweaty grip.

Leo nodded at the trumpeter. "We're in first" he said, "so keep an eye on me because I'm going to pace the horses much's I can, right?" The trumpeter knew to the second when Leo would call for the "Trot" out of the "Walk" and the "Charge" out of the Trot, but he acknowledged as though it were new to him. More ritual. He didn't need to be told, but the boss needed to say it.

Leo looked across the valley to where the brightly-painted shields of the raiders were gathered in the traditional Saxon shield-burg, and as they saw the stillness that preceded action come over the Norman ranks, the shout of "Out! Out! Blood, Out!" carried across the valley-floor and Leo made a show of twisting in his high saddle and spitting.

"Not up to much, are they?" he called across to Odo, who sat his horse in front of his troop and Odo made his reply as loud.

"Nah. Remember Hastings? Now *that* was a battle. Come to think of it, that was a war-shout too. Not that it did 'em much good though."

"Right, brother" called back Leo, perfectly aware that fewer than a third of the men at their backs had been on the field at Hastings, "we dropped the men there – now we're dealing with the boys. The Godwinsson boys themselves!"

"And look – cheeky bastards've got another Dragon Banner! There, in the middle!"

"That's mine!" called Leo. "Ponthieu got the real one – I want this one!"

"Not if I get there first!" returned Odo, still deliberately loud and aware of the sniggers from behind them, and Leo guffawed.

"Fair's fair!" he called. "Tell you what – if I get it . . . I get it. If you get it . . . we'll dice for it tonight!"

The sniggers became outright laughter, and the trumpeter said urgently, "Messire, signal!" and Leo looked away to the left where de Penthievre's guidon was coming back to the vertical. He watched it dip twice more, recognised his designation and ordered his own standard bearer to acknowledge.

"Trumpet! Walk-march!" He touched spurs to his destrier and the huge beast he had been controlling without thinking as it fidgeted and stamped throughout the period of waiting for battle, moved forward and his bridle-arm took the strain of holding it in check as it responded to the peal of the trumpet.

He heard the rumble, clash and jingle behind him as three troops settled into the walk-march and he worked the muscles of his face to settle his heavy helmet into its final position even as he laughed at himself for this little act of superstition. There was nothing wrong with his helmet's fit and it wouldn't move by even a fraction, because he had done up his own straps before seating his mailed gauntlets on his hands and rubbing the wrinkles out of them so that they lay perfectly flat. Nothing had been left to chance, and nothing but a lightning-strike or God's intervention would prevent the mass of bone, flesh and steel that was the Norman heavy cavalry from smashing into, over and through the footsoldiers who awaited them.

"Trumpet! Trot!" *How was it for them?* he wondered *What do we look like, coming on? Any of them wishing they'd had a piss before they lined up? How many've them—- concentrate! Passing through the infantry divisions . . . yes . . . yes . . . guidon to right and left . . . a good boy that.* "Bearer! Stay close by me, y'hear?"

Three troops split into column of twos as they cleared the infantry squares . . . *Come on, fuck it, come on!* . . . "Trumpet! Sound 'Diverge'. Again!" Odo, Waleis and their respective troops bore away from Leo's troop at an angle, their aiming-points spread to left and right of the Saxon centre and as 'Diverge' pealed out for the second time each trooper moved to the outside to line up his inside leg with the outside leg of the man in front so that each troop became a long and deadly arrowhead.

A last glance to right and left, and Leo set himself to choose his personal target. "Trumpet!" and his mount, veteran of two dozen charges as it was, suddenly bounded forwards— "*Charge! Charge!*" – and there it was, beyond the bar of the helmet's nasal, an immensely broad Saxon in the front rank, startling blond hair spilling from under his helmet and an eight-foot spear held over one shoulder in the posture from which it could either be launched or used to stab. The man's mouth worked as he waited, and although he could hear nothing over the roar of hooves and battle-shouts, Leo knew the man sang his ancestry in defiance of the enemy cavalry thundering towards him and shaking the earth.

At the last, cavalry and foot leaped towards each other at unbelievable speed, and Leo switched his own lance over his mount's neck and pulled hard back on the sling to couch the shaft solidly into his body with all the strength of his right arm in the underarm grip that many of his soldiers were beginning to prefer to the overhand stabbing grip. At the same time he thrust a braced left arm forward to receive the shock of the Saxon's spearhead as far from his body as he could, and in the very instant of the spear slamming into the kite-shaped shield he flicked up his lancehead to send the point leaping for the Saxon's face.

The Saxon spear slid from the heavy wooden boss of the shield a second before Leo's point went home under the Saxon's chin and the man simply vanished somewhere in the press to leave Leo with the impetus and weight of his mount scarcely checked crashing on deep into the Saxon ranks. From the edges of his vision he could see the heavy Norman swords swinging about him as his troop forced itself deeper and deeper along the path it had carved into the shield-burg, but he clung to his lance to keep the wielders of those terrible axes eight feet away. At last the weapon splintered on a shield; he dashed it into a bearded face whose mouth snarled soundlessly and ripped his own sword from its scabbard. *Come on, Penthievre* he thought, *where the fuck are you?* as their momentum finally died and he became a machine that hacked down first on one side and then on the other at the shapes that milled around him, pressed forward from the front.

Can't withdraw – can't disengage. We're stuck, too deep. It was true. Their charge had been so successful that they were set deep into the Saxon ranks, and the original plan of hitting hard and withdrawing to induce a pursuit while Earl Brian hit the Saxon right and rolled it up wouldn't serve any longer. *Right – go forward.* Leo stood in his stirrups, smashed down at a helmeted head trying to drive in under his shield and bellowed at the full pitch of his lungs, "Trumpet! Sound 'Charge!' Sound 'Charge'! With me, Breton men! With me, sons of the Vexin! On me! On me!"

The trumpet pealed and Leo snarled at his guidon bearer to signal the advance. From behind and on the sides there came a mighty roar and Leo's three troops, unbelievably, shook themselves and began to plough forward like an armoured serpent, step by step and then foot by foot and yard by yard with gaps beginning to appear as the Saxons were squeezed tighter and tighter between the Norman arrowheads grinding on before the trumpet's over-and-over demand for a charge.

Then, like the crash of winter waves on a rocky coast, a storm of cheering away to the left announced hot work going on there also, and the tides of warriors before them seemed to roll back so that at last Leo broke through into empty ground, the Dragon Banner squarely ahead of him and under it a tall figure in gleaming mail that caught the eye even amid the *hus-carls* surrounding him.

Godwinsson! thought Leo. *One of them anyway. Can't be anyone else, not with the Wessex dragon. Got the bugger!* With no further thought he swung the sword round his head, pointed it towards the banner and jammed in his spurs. The destrier screamed in pain and shot forward, leading the remnants of three Norman troops in a wild charge that crashed into the ranks surrounding the figure under the banner, overwhelming the men on foot with weight and speed so that the circle round the leader shrank and pressed ever back as his bodyguard fell where they stood.

For the rest of his life Leo never recalled what passed between his realisation that the *hus-carls* were cracking and the moment when he awoke from a nightmare of hewing and hacking to find himself, shieldless and on foot, with the Dragon Banner in his hand and the man who had stood under it now lying at his feet.

That evening.

Earl Brian de Penthievre poured a cup of wine for Leo with his own hand and set it before him. Leo inclined his head in acknowledgement of the honour, but did not pick up the cup until de Penthievre had picked up his. "St Brieuc, I've never seen anyone do what you did. Never. All hail, and honour!"

"All hail, and honour!" echoed his household knights, in the salute reserved by warriors for warriors; from those who had witnessed to those who had done. De Penthievre drained his cup – forcing all present to do likewise – then gestured for refills and again set his hand to Leo's cup.

"You should be dead, because you charged from a complete standstill" he said, offering the cup. "What made you do it?"

"Couldn't think of anything else, to be honest, my lord. We were in too deep to break off" said Leo, concentrating on the cup to avoid the eyes looking at him – some in admiration, others in envy and one or two beyond that in jealousy. "They seemed to . . . melt, I suppose, at the onset. Suddenly, there we were – in and stuck. Nowhere to go, and couldn't withdraw, so . . . we pushed on."

"Sounds like an ideal wedding night" commented de Cournaille. The tent erupted in laughter and Leo was happy to join in for he found this sort of attention difficult to manage. "But Jesu, you hit them hard enough with that new formation of yours to begin with – that's where you did the damage, I think." There was a buzz of agreement and de Cournaille went on, "Where'd that manoeuvre, that arrowhead, come from anyway?"

"Something we discussed" said Leo, now on surer ground. "Wanted to cramp them, y'see. We don't mind the spears – after all, we've got 'em too. But those axes . . . well." He fell silent, and heads nodded. "And it takes room to swing an axe four, five foot long. So we thought – catch the axemen between two columns of horsemen, and then they've got no room."

"And once you're above them" nodded de Penthievre, "and they've got no room, and you're standing in your stirrups . . . aye. Well done, St Brieuc. You're a thinker. The king should find a use for you."

"The king . . . what, my lord?"

"The king. Sending you to him with my report of the death of Ulf Haroldsson and the rout of his army. They're scraping the bottom of the barrel – most've them we killed today aren't Saxons at all. Mercenaries – Flanders, Ireland, Denmark – all over the place. King needs to know that, and you're the man to carry the report. And to give him that –" and he gestured to the Wessex Dragon standing against the tent wall. "Now he's got a pair."

The Chronicle.

*O*smund came with us as we dropped back down the Thames, and he spent much of the way sitting under the half-decking, reading and re-reading the hastily-penned note that Gytha had given me for him. I would not know until years later what it had contained, but I could make a fair guess. In any event it was Osmund's farewell to his home and to his childhood both, and the young man who came to stand by me as we slid down the ebbing tide towards the great pool where the ships clustered at London was in low spirits.

On the river Thames.

"I've made a mess of things, haven't I uncle Ranulf?" said Osmund, staring across at the far bank.

The Scraeling thought carefully before he spoke. "Well, let's see" he replied. "We could say you've only brought forward a decision that needed to be made sometime. If Ivo de Bois is the man that Garth and your mother think he is, he'd have looked out for you when you came of age. The Raedwaldsson estate – whatever it's called now or in the future – might in that case have been your home for life. On the other hand, if de Bois decided in favour of a child yet unborn, why you'd have had to make your own way, just like now."

He paused and stared down at the water bubbling along the side. "And there's the thought" he went on, "that de Bois isn't his own master. If you'd tied yourself to him and the manor, you might have regretted it later because what I hear is William's got problems in other parts of England. Problems that'll see him call on the very people who're in his debt for their lands – people like Ivo de Bois. Fancy riding behind your stepfather against a band of Saxon rebels? Thought not. Well, now you won't ever have to."

"One other thing – the way things have turned out, I'm here now when I probably wouldn't have been then, so you're not on your own. And I know you're tough enough not to care – " and he reached out a hand to ruffle the young man's hair – "but it's a comfort to your mother. And she's still the second most important woman in all the world to me."

Osmund grinned. "I'm glad of your help, uncle. Very glad, and grateful too, and I'm not too tough to say so. Have you . . . are we, ah . . .?"

"No. I've no idea" admitted the Scraeling cheerfully. "One thing at a time. It's not quite two days since you hoicked a soldier from his saddle and broke his neck for him. And not quite a week since you killed four others with something designed for digging holes. Hardraada used to refer to me as 'the most dangerous little bugger alive', but he never met my nephew, did he? No my boy – no plans yet, but then planning comes after knowledge, and we're off to get some knowledge from a man in London."

London, at the same time.

"This makes good reading, St Brieuc" said the king of England, looking over the parchment and pawing it like a bull about to charge.

Leo inclined his head and mumbled something to drive from it the ridiculous memory of how his last words with William of Normandy had been passed on the latter's first morning as king of England while he eased the royal bladder at the edge of the Hastings battlefield.

"Yes – covered yourself in glory according to Earl Brian. He's well taken— what's that?"

"I said" answered a flustered Leo, "Earl Brian's too kind, majesty – my men and I did what we'd trained to do, no more. And we were lucky."

"Horse shit!" said William vehemently, and several of those who attended him blinked their surprise at the rare crudity. "Horse shit, St Brieuc. Good soldiers enjoy good luck, because good luck's a matter of training, planning, and thinking ahead. Good luck's all about knowing what you're doing, knowing where you're strong, and working on your weaknesses. Nothing chancy about it. And we'll talk about your training and planning later, you and I. More wine?"

Leo had been warned about that, for William's loathing of drunkenness was famed. "No, thank you majesty. I haven't eaten yet, and one's enough until I have. But thank you."

William grunted and put the paper aside. "I'm not going to keep you from your meal" he said. "In fact, you're going to eat with the household tonight, because I want to know about this manoeuvre you've invented, according to Brian. But just so you can be thinking about things, I'll tell you now I've got a job for you. You got your three troops because of what you did for me day after Hastings, and I didn't put you in charge of that by accident either. I like winners, St Brieuc, people who succeed."

Hardly surprising given what you've faced down in your life thought Leo, but the king was speaking again "— take you all your time. But if you succeed – *when* you succeed – you'll not find me ungrateful. Even to a Breton." And those who surrounded the king laughed at one of his rare quips, for William's troubles with the Bretons were well known. "Now – more later, but what I've got for you will see you in charge of more than three troops, so be thinking about who you want as your staff . . ."

The Chronicle.

*I*t's always the quiet little men who know things, and the man in the harbourmaster's office was a quiet little man. Day by day he wrote papers, scrutinised manifests and issued passes for upriver and downriver, and day by day his knowledge of what was going on in and around the biggest port in the land built and grew. But, being only a little man, few credited him with any knowledge whatever, and certainly no-one ever sought it.

But I did both, for knowing a little about many things had seen me become indispensable to one of the world's most formidable soldiers, so I didn't hesitate to sound out my acquaintance of our passage upriver. And in all truth it was scarcely necessary to palm him a few silver pennies – although he didn't refuse them – as I asked him what areas around London were good for an honest trader to avoid. Even while I led him to believe, by inflection and wink, that I was nothing of the kind. In fact, without trying too hard I managed to convince him that the half-decking of my Norse drakkar hid crates of swords, byrnies and spearheads, all surplus to a destroyed Norse army, and like to be of interest to any who needed such, but lacked them.

And it emerged that trouble had recently flared not too far from London itself, in a part of the country known as the Fenlands. But it need not inconvenience one engaged in the coastal trade, he assured me as he played my game, for the Fenlands was the name given to a great area of marshland created by the confluence of some four rivers – big ones, aye, all navigable, by the way – flowing to the sea in the region of the old North Folk, which was northabout from London itself. Best avoided, it was, for the lands of the Fens were home to groups and bands of desperate men who set at naught, from behind their marshy and tidal barriers, the laws and ordinances of the Norman masters of England. And he shook his head at the wickedness of some, even as he pocketed my money and I thanked him gravely for giving me information that could prove to be my deliverance.

I returned to Nordvedr with much to occupy me. I had no fear of Osmund's discovery so far from his home or anywhere the young man was known, but what had happened at the Raeldwaldsson estate had occurred so quickly that there had been no time to plan for anything that might follow our getting him away. I had some idea of lying low to see how things turned out when the search for him was abandoned, and while sense dictated that this be done near to his home and among those not favourably disposed to the Normans, the idea was no *more than that.*

Skuli helped me in that for he assured me that we might reach anywhere there was three feet of water to float Nordvedr. And as to my notion of seeing how things would turn out for Osmund Pendasson, he simply asked what else I might be contemplating doing with forty men who had naught else to do but follow where I led?

So, a day after leaving behind the Pool of London and my informative friend, Nordvedr nosed carefully into the great estuary known as The Wash, to see what friends might be made among those who were no friends of the Normans.

The Fenlands, England, April 1068.

"That's it" said Skuli in a low murmur as *Nordvedr*'s sharp keel bit into the mud for the fifth time, "that's as far as we go, Scraeling. There's no getting her off this time. Not forwards, anyways."

The Scraeling nodded, recognising Skuli's sailor's awareness of what lay beneath his keel. "Let's get her round, then, eh? In case we need to leave in a hurry?" He realised that he had dropped his voice to the same low murmur as Skuli and for an instant he wondered at his foolishness, but even as the thought occurred he noted how the air of the great swamp pressed in on him as tightly, almost as the winding channel they had followed from the sea held the sleek *drakkar* in its grip. More – no bird disturbed the heavy air of the marsh and even the slap of the tide against the sides of the vessel had ceased, proof enough that sea had yielded place to swamp.

He wasn't the only one who thought so. Skuli's wolves sat on their rowing benches in unaccustomed silence, heads twisting this way and that as they strove to penetrate the marsh-grass that reared on all sides of the waterway.

"Good idea" said the viking and then, "Look sharp, you handless arseholes! Every second man over the side, slide her back and lift when I tell you. You other buggers, lift her on your sweeps and gimme all you got, or you'll go over too!"

Chest-deep in the water, the Vikings pushed up on the strake that ran along *Nordevedr*'s side while their fellows dug their sweeps deep into the bottom of the waterway and heaved back until the dragon-ship shuddered and broke free to coast backwards. "Easy!" snapped Skuli from the steering-oar, "Hold your way!" and *Nordvedr* lay still on the sullen water, "Well come on if you don't want to swim!" and the vikings hauled themselves free of the mud and inboard.

"Give way" ordered Skuli and pulled hard on the steering oar to send *Nordvedr*, live again, dancing across the waterway to a tongue of solid land on the other side.

Royal headquarters, London, June 1068.

"There's trouble in the Fenlands" William said. "Know where they are?"

"Five days from London, I think, majesty?" hazarded Leo, who had only a very hazy idea of English geography.

"Half that" grunted William "and they give on to the sea at the Wash. So – they're a back door, always open, and pointing directly at London. Anyone with the balls to take a fleet in there could find himself an easy march from the capital, and I can't be waiting for that to happen, now can I?"

"Svein of Denmark tried that, majesty – and he couldn't do it" said Leo, greatly daring.

The Conqueror snorted, and again Leo was reminded of a bull. "Svein's all wind and piss" he retorted, and Leo's eyes snapped open at the expression. *He's worried.* "He wasn't serious – never was. All he wanted was danegeld as a buy-off, and maybe five minutes of importance. No – forget Svein. He's top dog in Scandinavia now, St Brieuc, and that's where he'll stay, because he's shot the only bolt he's got."

He paused, and sipped again at his second cup. *That proves it* thought Leo, who'd nursed one cup for half an hour, *he's worried all right.* "Svein's got what he wants" he said, "but Godwinsson's boys, the ones who got off your field, still worry me. Their mistake was to land in the west instead of the Wash because it was nearer their base in Ireland and easier. I don't have to remind you that landing in the Wash would put them near enough to the Godwin heartland of Wessex, too. That *would* be worrying."

The king set down his cup and looked at it for long enough to tell Leo that he didn't see it, and the younger man realised with something close to shock that he was seeing the Conqueror in a rare moment of doubt. But before he could think of anything to say, William spoke again.

"And the chance of the Perjurer's sons doing something right for a change isn't all of it, St Brieuc. Sadly. As I said, there's trouble in the fenlands. There's a band of rebels there, led by some thegn or other who slaughtered our people and took refuge in the swamps around Ely Cathedral. Now, I don't know the ins and outs of it – I don't even know how our people came to be there in the frst place, because I didn't authorise it and nor did any of my top commanders. For a start, it's against my policy. But that alters nothing, St Brieuc, because the fact is that they're there, and they're a bloody nuisance."

Leo frowned. "But majesty – aren't they contained? I can't see them being much of a problem to us penned up in a swamp? Surely?"

William picked up his cup again. "Quite right. They're no military threat, St Brieuc, but it's what they represent that's the problem. As long as they're free, they're a temptation and an excuse. A temptation to the Godwinssons to come down the Wash and an excuse to support men fighting to rid England of the invader. And they're a problem we don't need at this time."

"Look, it's not yet two years since you and I fought Hastings. But they've been hard months. We've had trouble in the west, the east, and the north. We've had trouble with Scots, Welsh, the sons of Godwinsson, their bloody mother, and even with our own – and don't ask me why I let the Count of Boulogne live, because I don't know myself. Yes I do. I let him live because I don't need any more trouble across the Narrow Seas, not with Philip of France and Conan of Brittany giving us plenty there already."

"And now? Now I'm waiting for the north to rise in favour of the Aetheling – because they will, you know; I can feel it in my water – and Malcolm the Scot will probably come in too. I'm going to settle with the north, St Brieuc, and when I do none of them will ever forget it! Nor will any of their grandchildren, even supposing we leave enough of them alive to have any!"

He rubbed his forehead in a gesture that was more eloquent of weariness than words could have been, and glanced round at Leo. "Yes, St Brieuc – this thegn, this Hereward's a problem we don't need. And you're going to solve it for me."

Leo ran his tongue over his lips. "Majesty" was all he could think of to say.

William slid the flask across the table to him. "Oh go on" he said, "I've had one more than you – make me feel better!"

And he outlined the task he had for Leo. It was to carry the fight to the rebels in a manner that would deny them the use of the swamp for anything other than concealment while it became obvious that the rebellion in the fenlands was doomed, and its extinction no more than a matter of time. "And all that to be done with as few men as possible, for between ourselves, St Brieuc, I'm stretched to the limit in Normandy between Philip and those bloody Angevins."

"It's cruel country" he had said, "and the task won't be easy. I'm not putting in one of my senior commanders, and there are reasons for that. First, putting in Mortain, Fitz Osbern or Giffard would do this Hereward more honour than he deserves. Second, I need those men in other places, given how thin we're stretched, St Brieuc".

"But third – and most important to me – they're all proven commanders who're the best on any battlefield in the world at what they do. But they've never done this, or anything like it. Nor, I suppose, have you – but you're a thinker and a planner, and you've got a talent for getting things done and for coming up with other ways. You've proved that, and Brian Penthievre sings your praises. Not just for your new manoeuvre, but also for the way you take things on. And that's the fourth reason, St Brieuc. I like winners, and I've not chosen you by accident. So get on with it, and you won't find me ungrateful."

"There it is, then. You can have anything you want, or can get, within reason. Just hold that bloody Englishman until things settle down for us. And if you can get your hands on him, so much the better – but just hold him and deny him to the Godwinssons."

The De Bois estate, Reading, September 1068.

The pain was worse, much worse, than anything Gytha had ever known and in the moments of lucidity between the wrenching, tearing pangs that she was sure would split her body asunder she found time to wonder why. *Four* she told herself, *I've borne four children and I can bear this one . . . I can bear this one . . . I can, I can, I . . . Oh God help me, here it comes again . . . oh God, my God . . .* and her riven body twisted and arched from the surface of the bed as the scream came from deep within her.

Two rooms away, Ivo de Bois knelt before the crucifix on the wall of the chamber he shared with Gytha and prayed. *You, who knew Your own agony for all mankind; You, who suffered for the sins of others; You, who offered forgiveness to thieves and all manner of men who believed in You – forgive Gytha her agony, for she believes in You as staunchly as any, and she pays now for my lust . . .*

"That's it, m'lady, that's it!" Gytha heard through the miles and miles of space that separated her from the body that writhed and twisted on the bed, "Just push, m'lady, push hard's you can!" *Aelfgifu, Aelfgifu, I've nothing left. Nothing – this baby will come to the world through me, not out of me, and I can't push, I can't, I can't, I can't . . . for I'm going to be riven apart . . . oh God, my God, I'm dying, I know I'm dying— Penda, Penda—*

"One more push, m'lady! For Lord Penda. For Lord Osmund, m'lady, just one more! The babe's coming; I can see the head! Oh push, my lady!" Gytha took her last breath and braced herself for an effort she knew she could not make, and then Penda was there before her eyes.

Penda, tall and wide as ever, Penda holding out their son to her, the babe lost in his huge hands, Penda smiling blue-eyed and flaxen-haired at her. *Gytha, Gytha, Gytha my love, see what you've given us. We'll name him for your father, aye? Osmund he shall be.*

Osmund he shall be she whispered, smiling up at the blond giant, *Osmund, Osmund, Osmund, aye.*

"M'lady, a girl! A girl! It's a girl!"came Aelfgifu's voice, and Penda smiled once more at her and stepped backwards away from the bed where she lay. *My love, my man, where are you going? Don't go to Senlac, stay a moment with me – ride tomorrow; the king cannot want more – stay, stay my man, my Penda, my husband—* but he moved to the wall and through it before Gytha's very eyes, and she wept. *Penda, Penda, Osmund . . . .*

The Isle of Refuge, Ely, the Fenlands, at the same time.

The man blundered past an Osmund spinning away from his charge, a foot slammed hard into the back of a knee and down he went. A moment later the sky was blotted out as the young man's weight crashed down across the other's upper body, and the roar of the onlookers announced their recognition of a fall and a fair pin. Osmund rolled off him, scrambled up and extended a big hand to draw his opponent to his feet.

"One each, Osmund! One more!" insisted the other, and the clamour of those who'd lost money the moment before supported the demand. The Scraeling opened his mouth; Osmund looked directly at him and gave an imperceptible shake of his head. The Scraeling closed his mouth again and Osmund turned to his opponent.

"One more, Hereward" he agreed, and the lord of the Fenlands smiled and held up a hand for Osmund's slap before moving off the usual five paces.

Osmund crouched, facing Hereward, and his gaze bored into the other's eyes, shrugging off the moment of surprise that came with the sight of one blue and one grey eye looking back at him. *Concentrate* he told himself, *Hereward knows folk'll look at his eyes, so watch his knees 'cause they'll move first* . . . and Hereward came forward like a striking snake. Osmund met him in a flash, sliding in below the outstretched and thickly-muscled arms to slam his shoulder into the open mid-section.

But there was no flinching and none of the sudden explosion of breath he'd hoped for. Instead Hereward grunted and flung his arms around the young man's mid-section, pulling him forward and deeper into his own middle and burying his face against Osmund's back to guard against an upwards explosion.

Watching, the Scraeling knew with sickening certainty what would come next, and it did. Hereward's arms tightened and he heaved against Osmund's body-weight to bring his feet off the ground and drive him head-first into the earth before dropping on him to claim the pin. But even as the Scraeling's mouth went dry, Osmund's legs straightened with explosive power to send his hips high into the air and his legs curling over Hereward's shoulders.

For an instant Hereward tottered, holding Osmund upside down, before the weight of the younger man's legs told and Hereward crashed to the ground on his back, still locked fast with Osmund while the onlookers roared again. Then, in a blur, the tableau blew apart as the men scrambled to their feet, each seeking the advantage of height, with Hereward the faster by a heartbeat for he hurled himself from a crouch at Osmund's back to send the boy toppling headfirst to the ground under his greater weight. Osmund's head disappeared between Hereward's hip and the unyielding ground, and the Scraeling saw in the limpness of his body that the impact had been severe enough to knock him out.

Hereward claimed the pin and rolled, panting, off Osmund as the Scraeling scuttled forward with a water-jack.

Osmund's eyes flickered open as the Scraeling crouched over him, and Hereward's hand was there under his arm. "What . . . oh . . . how . . . " said the young man, then his eyes cleared.

"You all right?" demanded the Scraeling, and Osmund grinned painfully. "Been better" he said. "Lost it did I, Hereward?"

"That you did" said the lord of the Fenlands, taking the jack from the Scraeling, uncorking it and offering it to Osmund, "I fell on you and pinned you while you were out. Didn't mean to, but you're too bloody hard a man to let get back up again, so I thought . . . well, why not?"

Osmund laughed, and the Scraeling was glad to see it. "Sure you're all right?" asked the Scraeling again and Osmund probed gingerly at the side of his head, wincing. "Nothing some of that water won't fix" he said, and Hereward clasped his hand and leaned back to draw the young man to his feet, where the two men embraced as money changed hands, some of it for the second time.

The de Bois estate, Reading.

Ivo de Bois had never been happier, and he marvelled at it. There was a time, he mused, as he stood by the window looking at a view he didn't see, when personal happiness had to do with a well-turned-out troop of horse, or the feel of a young and powerful war-horse beneath him. Not any more. Now, happiness was twofold; a woman he adored and the pink bundle brought to him for his approval by the woman Aelfgifu. Aye, Matilda. Matilda de Bois. *Matilda de Bois, my daughter. My child.* God be thanked, and God be praised. God be praised, too, for His answer to de Bois' prayer in bringing Gytha through the ordeal of childbirth, for Aelfgifu had assured him that his lady no longer bled and that rest would restore her. And that was the second part of happiness.

He bowed his head in acknowledgement of the vow he had made that, were Gytha delivered from her ordeal, there would be no repetition and no more children. Gytha's children would become his, and his in every way.

And it would be enough.

The door opened, and he turned. "Aelfgifu?" he said, the word strange and unfamiliar on his tongue.

"Lord Ivo" said Aelfgifu slowly, "my lady is awake and rested. She asks for you."

The Ely marsh, the next day.

"How's your head?" asked the Scraeling, and Osmund came from his daydream.

"My head? Oh, it's fine uncle. Why?"

The Scraeling sighed. "Thought from the look on your face you might be suffering" he said. "Not every day you have someone the size of Hereward – or anyone else, come to that – bounce up and down on it, is it?"

"No. No, I wasn't suffering. I was thinking that, if I'd been a bit faster turning I might have got out of his way and dropped him again, same way's I did before. Hereward's not that quick, y'know, and I've noticed he sticks to the same moves. Well, he's so strong he doesn't need much else. That's why I tried to run him around a bit, and it worked the first time. Should've worked again if I hadn't been so slow. Well – next time, eh?"

The Scraeling shook his head in a mixture of admiration and exasperation. "You're amazing" he said. "You ought to be too frightened to get into the ring with Hereward, because you're fifteen years old and he's a grown man. Granted, you're as tall, but you're a couple of stones lighter – you lost with honour and took ten years off my life doing it, and now you're talking of doing it again? I should get Skuli to lock you up somewhere!"

Osmund laughed Penda's laugh. "Oh come on, uncle Ranulf – he's not that much heavier, and I reckon I'm quicker. Most times anyway. I've watched him wrestle a lot, you know. I've just got to find a way of staying away from his weight and his strength. And I will, you'll see."

"Well, while you're thinking about it, you might go and check our set lines. I'm off to promise Ossa's wife some of what you bring back for a loaf or two.

Osmund pulled a face. "When this is all over" he said, "it'll be a long time before I eat fish again."

The Chronicle.

I *sympathised. In fact, I agreed. I was as sick of fish as Osmund, but none who lived on the Isle of Refuge had much choice. We lived on wildfowl, their eggs, fish and a very occasional rabbit. Grain was a luxury that we got through barter with the good folk outside the marsh, for there was no land available to us to grow it ourselves. Hereward refused to allow any pillage of the marsh-folk or their livestock and he was right in that, for we needed their goodwill. Besides, he said, it was an ill thing for a thegn of England to steal from the poor when he might steal from the Norman rich with a willing heart and a clear conscience.*

Hereward was a man I found interesting. Rumour had it that he'd been exiled at the request of a father who'd found the wild and headstrong youth too much of a handful to avoid being outlawed one day. Whether or no that was correct, it was true that he was determined on his own way to a fault, and couldn't bear losing in any regard. The story was that the young Hereward had returned from exile after the Conquest to find his inheritance gone and his brother's head nailed above the manor-house door. And he had taken a terrible vengeance in his turn, harvesting fourteen Norman heads and nailing them in place of the one he had given reverent burial before his flight into the depths of the wild and treacherous fens where the sons of the dispossessed had rallied to him in the Isle of Refuge at Ely.

Ely was reassuringly and formidably safe, since sea-going vessels could reach it via the Wash and River Ouse, while swamps and a network of hidden waterways guarded its connections with central England. It was a castle without stone and a fortress without walls, a strong place that might only be taken by cunning and stealth rather than fire and storm. And its defenders had the cunning and the stealth in the men of the Fens, the men who knew the paths and the trails through the morass that awaited the unwary foot or hoof; the men whose knowledge was life or death to any who sought a way across the Fenlands.

And there they waited, but without any clear idea of what they waited for. From time to time the men of the Fens broke from their watery fortress to raid and harass Norman garrisons, possessions and, at the first, livestock. But they soon tired of trying to drive the beasts back into the swamp for the creatures shied and balked at the narrow trails when all their instincts told them that death lay there, and in the end the swamp men stopped trying and bought, begged or bartered for meat from the folk outside.

The De Bois estate, Reading, Christmas 1068.

"Congratulations, Ivo. Congratulations, Lady Gytha" said Walter Giffard, his hard soldier's face creasing in a leathery smile. "Beautiful child – takes after her mother, eh Ivo?" and his snort of laughter accompanied the raising of his cup to the parents who had just seen their daughter christened in the manor-house that had been home to Penda, and Gytha's father before him.

"Our thanks, Walter" said de Bois, marvelling inwardly that his status as a landholder gave him the right to address Giffard by his name instead of 'Messire' as he had been accustomed to doing for years. "It's good of you to honour us with your attendance when you're so busy. Our thanks for that too."

"Aye, we're busy Ivo. Always. And some of us will be busier this year yet. But some things are too important to miss, and your little Matilda's hope of heaven's one of them. Especially since I couldn't attend the wedding of my best divisional commander to his beautiful English wife. Thought I'd make up for that this time."

De Bois coloured at the mention of his wedding, fearing what it might bring up in Gytha's mind and Giffard sensed it. "Anyway" he continued, gesturing to the fur cloak that hung from a peg in the entrance-way, "something for the little girl" And at his signal one of his companions delved into the cloak and brought out a cloth-wrapped object which he handed to Giffard.

"This is for little Matilda" said the Conqueror's hardest-hitting cavalry commander. "May she use it for many, many years and perhaps pass it to her own children. And may those children mean as much to this land as yours, Gytha and Ivo. No, let me, my lady – your hands carry a precious burden!"

Giffard turned back the folds of cloth to reveal a silver cup, elaborately chased and decorated around the initial "M" in the centre. Gytha's eyes widened and de Bois stammered his thanks, which Giffard waved aside.

"It's a copy of the queen's favourite cup" he said. "I've seen it often, and found a good English craftsman in London to make me one to my description. Soon's I had your invitation, Ivo, I got him started, and he's done well. Not as well as you and Gytha, of course, but who among us does that well? Anyway – long life and happiness to your beautiful daughter!" raising his cup again, with his retinue following him.

"Now, Ivo" he said, setting down the cup, "'fraid I can't stay for your board, old friend. That busyness we spoke of. But – I'd like to take you from your guests just for a moment?"

Wondering, de Bois indicated a small room that he'd had set aside for Gytha to sew in because it had a north-facing window, and the two men moved inside.

"Apart from my wish to honour your invitation and see the child of my most trusted man" said Giffard without preamble, "I wanted to see what a year of marriage has done for him. And it suits you well, old friend, it surely does. Despite your gloomy forebodings. Remember?" he asked with a chuckle that extended to poking de Bois in the ribs.

De Bois laughed in his turn. "Aye, Walter, you were right. Right in all things" he added, turning slightly pink again. "But" he said hastily, to cover his allusion to Giffard's joke about a 'suitable mount', "do we ride again in the spring?"

"Aye, we do. This spring. *We* do. You don't" said Giffard. "In fact, your soldiering days are over, Ivo. Unless Godwinsson and Hardraada both return to life. Then we might need you. But, short of that, grease your hauberk and lay it in its case."

De Bois frowned. "Surely you jest, Walter" he said. "Is the king so blessed with fighting men that he has no use for another?"

"He has a better use for you" said Giffard gently. "He knows of your marriage, and I took the liberty of informing him of your family news. The family you and Gytha have begun. He's delighted, Ivo, and he commands me to tell you so, for the babe is his policy for the settling of England made flesh. Now – you swing a mighty sword, and have ever done so, Ivo de Bois. But from now on, you'll use quite another weapon to much better effect."

That time, Ivo turned more than slightly pink.

The Isle of Refuge.

Osmund said little of his mother and family, and during those first weeks in the marsh, remembering Gytha's words to him, the Scraeling believed that to be because he had turned his back on them in anger. But gradually he came to realise that the boy was punishing himself for the savage outburst of fury that had led to his exile and to his mother bearing the burden of

Penda's legacy alone. Nothing he could do or say would ease Osmund of that conviction, for he wore it like a hair shirt and the Scraeling recalled how, even as a young child, the depth and quality of Osmund's thought had been one of the most remarkable things about him.

You'll make him see, Ranulf. You're a very wise man said Gytha within the Scraeling's head, but Osmund saw perfectly already, and from all the Scraeling could see, the young man honoured his mother for the choice she had made as much as he scourged himself for letting her down.

And so the Scraeling resolved to let time heal the scars and set himself to be a father to him in all the ways he could – for his sake in chief, but for that of Penda, and Gytha, and – aye, for Elisabeth too. *Oh the plans, the plans we once made and the certainties we foresaw, we who were sure that the world we fashioned would be an honourable and just place!* But he could hold to part of that world, for with Elisabeth gone from him – and, despite every effort he made, she did go from him until not even the dark reaches of the night would bring her back – there was nothing else, no other plan, no other care, to fill it.

Osmund won the respect of the hard men of the marshes, as much for the punishment through which he put himself as for his readiness to learn the ways and the lore of the Fens and his willingness to put himself in the path of danger when the war-bands sallied out of their marshy fortress. He trained long and hard with sword, spear and axe until few remained quick enough to match his speed of foot, or strong enough to catch the thunderous blows of his axe on the heavy shield, or brave enough to face even the blunted and tipped spearhead he could make move faster than the light coming off the waters that surrounded the Isle of Refuge.

The Scraeling saw himself to Osmund's instruction in bow, sling and throwing-knife for the lad's father had once described him as — *five foot seven on your tiptoes, one leg useless, not a man for axe and mail but fucking deadly with anything you can throw, launch or shoot*— and he could think of no-one better to receive the benefit of anything he could teach than Penda's son. And under his uncle's steady urging and insistence that sinking shaft, stone or blade into the middle of a target was much, much better than merely winging it Osmund, still a boy in years, became a man in physical stature among the dispossessed and the rebellious of the swamplands, at the same time as his surprisingly old head on young shoulders saw him turned to by those much his senior for counsel and opinion.

Early January 1069.

Lonely, troubled and muffled against the chill, Gytha walked the path past the ancient thorn-bush. *Osmund's bush* she had called it, since the day he had burst his pig-bladder ball upon it. She stopped and looked at the gnarled old bush, thinking of what it had seen on the Raedwaldsson estate – aye, since long before it had passed to Penda Raedwaldsson on their marriage, even – and wondered what it would say to her if it could speak.

Would it upbraid a Saxon mother of a Norman's child? Would it speak of her father, the widowed Osmund who had never married again after his beloved Godiva had died giving Gytha life? It had the right, she decided. Anything so long part of the Raedwaldsson lands had that right for it, no less than the land and the people, was the heart of her vow to keep faith with her lord as he had kept faith with his king. Unto death. *Unto death,* and her shiver had nothing to do with the freezing January air.

A little over three months since she had nearly died herself in giving birth to Matilda, and she thought she knew why. She had had nothing to live for, nothing that lay beyond the agonies of birthing, and nothing would change next time. For there would surely be a next time, and she shuddered to think of it.

Nothing, without Penda. Her others hadn't taxed her so, for Osmund, Gyrth, Aelric, even Sunngifu, born though she was in the nightmare desolation of Penda's death, were the children of the man she loved as she had loved nothing and no-one else, and that love had brought her through.

If she looked at it coldly, Matilda had brought her the agony and the travail and nothing behind it. Matilda was part of the price of her vow, part of her penance for being a Saxon noblewoman sworn to the service of her folk as her husband had been sworn to that of his king.

But she couldn't look at it in that way, for the memory of the pink and helpless little bundle Aelfgifu had placed in her arms no less than the joy in her woman's heart as she pulled her second daughter to her breast would not leave her. *I'll live for the people dependent on me* she had sworn to Osmund, and at the time of its uttering it had been Penda's folk she had meant, aye.

But wasn't Matilda dependent on her also? And wasn't it God's will that Matilda had become part of her life? Did God want her to turn from her vow and become the wife of Ivo de Bois and the mother of his children in spirit as well as fact? For she couldn't. She could honour de Bois for the kindly and gentle soul at the core of the hard Norman conqueror, but she could never love him. She could even make him free of her body, but she could never love any man as she had loved Penda.

In the whirl and tumble of her thoughts she felt utterly alone, bereft and spent; too spent to wipe away the tears that started from her eyes to slide as quietly down her face as all life, all hope and all future was sliding from her also. Surely God wouldn't ask so much of her when all she had wanted was to die and go to Penda? Was there no . . .

Penda. *Penda.* In the moment of her greatest puzzlement she stopped in mid-stride as it came to her. In her torment she had called on God and He had sent her dead husband to her. Hadn't Penda appeared to her at the very moment when she would have died, split asunder? Hadn't he spoken to her of life, and hope, and love? Hadn't his love and his life-force given her the strength to birth her daughter as she had the others?

Of course. Of course. It was how she could – how she *would* – keep the vow she had made. *Yes, a Norman will be my husband and my lord* was what she had admitted to Osmund, and to the Scraeling she had said, *And marrying that man means I must share his bed . . .. and sleeping with him means . . . I am to birth a Norman's child, Ranulf. I, who bore my lord four children of our own.*

And Penda knew that. He knew that, and a God who'd heard her prayer had sent Penda to her, to help her, to give her his boundless strength. And he would come again. Penda, the love of her life, would help her stand by her vow as he had stood by his. And because of that, she would continue to be wife to Ivo de Bois, regardless of where it led. *That's how I'll keep your father's memory within me, Osmund. It would please him, for your father never stepped back from his duty.*

She sank to her knees heedless of the muddy path and stared unseeing at the thorn-bush, and that was where a flying Aelfgifu found her moments later. "M'lady! Lady Gytha! What is it? I saw you from the big window! Where's the pain m'lady? My lady!"

Gytha looked up and smiled for the first time in what seemed like weeks. "Pain? No pain, dear Aelfgifu. Not any more."

Later that week.

"My lord" said Gytha, offering de Bois the cup, "have I displeased you?"

Her husband jerked upright. "Displeased . . . ? No, my love, not in any way! Why do you say such a thing?"

"I ask, my lord, because we have not . . . we have not been . . . as man and wife since Matilda's birth. And I wondered . . . if the Sieur de Longueville's visit for her christening had anything . . . " Her voice tailed away and she looked at him.

"Giffard? Giffard's visit? No, dearest Gytha, no! In fact, he commended us on Matilda's birth, and in fact . . . also . . . he told me that the king himself knew of our daughter's birth and offered us his congratulations in like manner. Giffard? Oh no!"

"Then, husband . . . then why . . . why have you not come to our bed? Why do you sleep in the chanber that was Osmund's?"

De Bois set down the cup and walked to the window, where he gazed at the iron-grey day that was fast deserting the snow-covered land. He cleared his throat twice before he spoke. "Gytha, dearest, you suffered . . . suffered so greatly in the birth of our beloved daughter. You must have time to recover, must you not? Your woman . . . Aelfgifu . . . said that rest would restore you."

"Husband, Matilda is over three months old, and baptised into the church. Your wife is well rested, and ready for you to return to her bed. Our bed."

"I'm glad . . . glad for you that . . . .that your body is . . . restored, my love. During your travail, I prayed for you . . . that you might come through your ordeal. An ordeal that I caused you."

"Husband?" The puzzlement in her voice. "Ivo, you didn't . . . cause my ordeal. *We* caused my ordeal, for what happens between husband and wife is like to do that. Is it not?"

"Aye, it is!" He swung from the window to look at her for the first time and the passion in his voice brought her upright in her turn. "Aye, it is. And at the height of your pain, when I feared for your life; feared I would surely lose you, I vowed . . . I vowed that there would . . . that I would not put you through such travail again. And I will not!"

Gytha walked to him, took his hands in hers and looked up at him. "Ivo de Bois, was it not you who said to an unwilling wife that we were commanded to live together as husband and wife? And that a soldier was accustomed to obeying his orders? Did you not?"

He nodded, gripping her hands. "Aye, even so. But . . . my lady, I fear that my coming has caused you nothing but pain, and . . . and I would cause you no more" and he looked away.

"Husband," said Gytha gently, "why do you speak so of pain when all know that childbirth is a woman's lot? Why?"

De Bois shook his head. "Not the birth alone, my lady. Because of me, your son and your firstborn is fugitive. I speak of Osmund, of course."

The word hung between them in silence. *He's a good man* thought Gytha *and he loves his daughter and he loves me.* She took a deep breath. *I can use that. Use it to seal my word to Osmund. To Penda also.*

"Husband" she said, "husband, pray you look at me. As I told you that you alone did not cause the pain of childbirth, so I tell you that you alone did not make my son fugitive. A Norman would be master here in any wise – you, or another. What happened would then have happened in any wise, would it not?"

"And husband, know that I believe myself fortunate that you, and not another, are Giffard's choice for me. And know also that those dear to me – my children and my folk, Aelfgifu and her man Garth, and the other folk of this manor – believe this also and esteem you for a fair and just lord." She saw the play of emotions across his face; saw the dejection change to surprise, then to pleasure then to delight.

In that moment Gytha realised the power she had over Ivo de Bois. "Husband, it is so" she assured him, and chose her next words carefully. "And I will be a good wife to you in the same measure, Ivo, as he who is lord over us is a good lord to us. To Garth and Aelfgifu, to little Sunni and her brothers, and to Matilda her sister. This I promise, as I promised to obey you on the day we were wed. Aye, this I promise."

"Gytha . . . oh Gytha, my love, my love. I will. I promise you— and those you named— that I'll be such a lord. I promise" choked de Bois, holding out his arms.

The Isle of Refuge, February 1071.

Five of the six men were weary, but if Osmund was also it didn't show in his walk as he moved to the meat-shed and slid the carcase from his shoulder on to the butchering-block with never a sign that he'd carried it a good three miles through the bitter cold of a February day. The Scraeling, whose crippled leg was on fire, shook his head enviously as he shrugged free of the folded and sewn cloak that carried all the grain they'd been able to coax from the peasants who farmed the abbey lands on the fringes of the great marsh.

He groaned as he stretched and flexed his shoulders and Osmund, his burden already yielding to the knives and saws of the butchers, grinned at him. "Getting old, uncle?" he asked. "Want a rest somewhere soft and dark and quiet, then?"

"Don't think I'd fit inside your head, nephew" retorted the Scraeling, and the rest of the forage-party chuckled. "It's like I always sa— "

"I know, I know" said Osmund with mock weariness, "Youth's wasted on the young, yes?"

"At last. I've told you often enough" said the Scraeling, working his shoulders. "Jesu, that grain weighed more than the Bastard's sins! Hereward anywhere about?" This to one of the butchers, who jerked his head without looking up from the joint he was easing from the carcase.

"In the hall" he said. "Got visitors. Abbot and some new folk."

"New folk?" said the Scraeling. "What sort of new folk?"

"Coupla real important ones by the looks" said the butcher. "Here, you've done well this time Scraeling. Plentya meat on this one. Them others the same?"

"Not quite" said the Scraeling. "This's the biggest, so we gave it to Osmund. Carrying it stopped him eating it, didn't it, nephew?"

"Not by much" agreed the young man. "Reckon I could eat it now. Raw!"

The Scraeling glanced affectionately at the towering youth. *Buggered if I know how he's grown so big* he thought *on what he gets to eat around here.* Food was their consuming passion, for there was never enough of it during the winter months. The party had had to bargain hard for what they'd got, and the carcase Osmund had carried had been expensive. That was why the party had been entrusted to the Scraeling.

"Anyway" said the Scraeling, "how many new folk?"

"Not sure" said the butcher. "But here's Hereward now. Ask him yourself." The Scraeling turned to see the lord of the Fenlands striding towards them.

"Ah, you're back, Scraeling" said the powerfully-built Saxon, "and you've had success! Good, good!"

"Some" acknowledged the Scraeling, "but it was expensive. That big carcase there was supposed to be breeding stock according to its owner."

"That right?" said Hereward, "how'd you get it then?"

"Talked him out of it" said the Scraeling briefly. "But as I said – it was expensive. Hear we've got some more, then?"

"And not just anyone" chuckled Hereward, who was clearly in a good mood. "Ever heard of Morcar? Morcar of Northumbria?"

And that made the Scraeling forget all about his shoulders and his leg. For he certainly knew of Morcar, although he'd never met him.

"Heard of him" he admitted, "but never met him."

"Come and meet him then" invited Hereward. "He's in the hall with a couple of others you should meet."

Well, well. This'll be interesting the Scraeling thought, for if Morcar had only known it, he owed his earldom to the Scraeling. Tostig Godwinsson's demotion from the earldom of Northumbria had been part of the plan that the Scraeling had woven with Tostig, his brother and king Harold Godwinsson, and Penda Raedwaldsson. The plan to bring the Landwaster down upon England. The plan that only the Scraeling was still alive to remember.[5]

Wonder if he'd thank me for telling him? The thought brought a chuckle, and Hereward raised an enquiring eyebrow.

"Nothing" said the Scraeling. "Just a thought."

That night.

But Morcar's presence wasn't 'nothing', the Scraeling thought as he rolled that night into the crude bed that Osmund quietly ensured was always topped with a resewn cloak stuffed with enough marsh grass to offer a soft

---

5   *See 'The Landwaster'.*

lodgement for his uncle's crippled hip.

Wager he thinks I haven't noticed thought the Scraeling, glancing affectionately across to where Osmund's sleeping length nearly filled the other side of the hut. *He's a wonderful boy, and I can't see this Northumbrian blowhard being good for any of us. Osmund, Hereward, any of us.*

For the evening hadn't been one to fill the Scraeling with hope for the future. In fact it had filled him with nothing but dismay, because two things had become obvious to him shortly after meeting the newcomers. The first was that no-one in Morcar's retinue, starting with the earl of Northumbria himself, had the slightest grasp of the realities of the swamp-men's position in the last enclave of free England. The second was that none of them, and especially the earl of Northumbria himself, would let that fact deter him in any way from proposing the most hare-brained schemes imaginable.

Sweet Jesus, I was sore put not to laugh out loud when he started blathering about marching on London thought the Scraeling as he waited for sleep, *and when he talked of sending emissaries to the Godwinssons in Ireland, I nearly asked him why he hadn't done just that when the Godwinssons were closer at hand – say four and a half years ago?*

But it wasn't his business to antagonise Morcar – unless something happened to make it his business – and perhaps Morcar had sensed that there was nothing going on in the swamp. For there wasn't. In all the time he and Osmund had been in the swamp, and try as he would, the Scraeling couldn't divine any plan in what they did from day to day. Hereward's only aim seemed to be to exist from day to day and month to month in defiance of the Normans. In fact, since the Danish army sent by Svein had allowed itself to be bought off by the Conqueror – *you always knew a good deal when you sniffed one, Svein* – and sailed away in the months before the Scraeling and Osmund had arrived, that defiance had taken no active course whatever.

And that's all about Hereward thought the Scraeling. *He's no patriot, really. He's a young man who doesn't like being told what to do; who reacted in exactly that way when he came home after the invasion; and who's out of his depth now. And that's him. That's Hereward.*

But that opened other possibilities, chief among them being that direction of the band's activities might pass from Hereward to someone more vocal. Someone like the ex-earl of Northumbria.

That bugger blights anything he touches decided the Scraeling, drowsing, *and nothing I heard tonight convinces me other. We're staying well out of any scheme he launches, for it's bound to be half-baked and bloody dangerous for everyone in it except himself. So I'll watch him like a hawk, and if I have to, I'll take Morcar myself.*

Ely marsh, Cambridgeshire, May 1071.

The Scraeling pointed right, then left before moving his hand gently forward to send two teams of men sliding noiselessly forward through the long grass of the fenland to where the sentries, full of their afternoon meal, half-dozed at their posts around the huge pile of stakes, fascines and logs.

In the long, crackling silence that followed Osmund finished checking the contents of the bag he carried then looked sideways at his uncle and raised an eyebrow. The Scraeling nodded and held up a finger in a gesture that said "Any minute now" and the young man grinned. His hand shot to the dagger in his belt as there came a rustle in the grass before it parted to reveal the nut-brown face of Ossa, who had spent so much of his life in the Ely marshes that Osmund had accused him, only half in jest, of being a duck who walked in preference to flying. He grinned, and passed the edge of a hand across his throat. The Scraeling nodded.

"What kept you?" he murmured, and Ossa spat.

"Six sentries" he said. "Not four. I checked first – found the other two asleep. Prob'ly watch and watch, through the night – four on at a time, like?"

"What'd you do with them?" asked Osmund and Ossa spat again.

"Not that much. Still got their eyes shut, ha'n't they?" he said briefly, and the young man recalled being told how a troop of patrolling Norman infantry had taken turns at Ossa's wife until in the end he had agreed to lead them through the trackless swamp. He had led them onto an island of firm ground in the middle of a bottomless bog before escaping to bring a dozen of Hereward's archers to solid ground thirty paces away, and from there they had offered the Normans the choice of how they died. Only two had attempted the crossing, and one of those had got within spitting-distance of safety before a punt-pole pushed him back in and the ooze reached his screaming mouth.

"Right" hissed the Scraeling. "Guard'll probably be changed at dusk. Now's a good time." And he set off through the grass behind Ossa,

Osmund and his bag following.

He's a natural rascal thought Osmund affectionately; *he can't help himself. But he never leaves anything to chance, and he makes sure others don't either. Who'd ever have thought I'd be fighting beside him as my father once did?*

For there was no doubt in the young man's mind that the Scraeling was involved with the band led by the man known as Hereward the Wake for Osmund's sake rather than Hereward's. In fact the Scraeling had no great love for Hereward because, as he'd pointed out to his nephew, Hereward's dispute with the Normans stemmed from self-interest before anything else.

"Look" he'd said one night as he carved away at an interesting piece of bog-oak he'd rescued from the kindling-heap, "remember that Hereward's on the run for the same reason you are. He killed the man who was given his family's lands, remember? And nailed his head above his father's door?"

"He had right on his side, though uncle" Osmund had said. "He'd suffered a wrong, surely?"

"That's what I mean. Don't ever" said the Scraeling, carefully deepening a curve in the wood with the point of a small dagger, "believe that Hereward's doing all this for England, or Godwinsson's memory, because when all's said and done, Godwinsson's England outlawed Hereward for being a fucking menace to it all. No – Hereward'll give all this up, soon as William offers him his family land back and a pardon for all the Normans he's killed. And when William gets sick of it – or when he realises Hereward's price – that's just what he'll do. Why? He can't afford trouble here, so close to London – so he'll put an end to it sooner or later. He's just turned most of the Danelaw into a graveyard, hasn't he?"

That was no less than the truth, thought Osmund, if the stories brought by the survivors of Norman reprisals for the northern rebellion were to be believed. Anything that moved in the great swathe between the ancient towns of York and Durham had been slaughtered – man, woman, beast or bird, and anything that might provide shelter had been razed. Anything or anyone William's soldiers missed, fell prey to famine and the pestilence that came from rotting and unburied bodies. The north of England had simply disappeared as a place that would support life, in a manner that had caused the Scraeling to remark that the spirit of Hardraada the Landwaster had surely been kept alive by the Devil.

And their turn was coming. Hereward's bands were less than a pinprick to a king bent on securing his northern and western frontiers, but their very presence was an affront to his majesty and his control both, and they would not be tolerated much longer – the more so since the devastation of the north had sent notable rebels such as Bishop Aethelwine of Durham and Earl Siward Bearn into refuge at Ely. And Morcar of Northumbria. Aye, Morcar above all.

"Morcar" the Scraeling had brooded aloud, "welcome as the pox, and twice as dangerous. He was the downfall of Godwinsson, and a man who can't lie straight in bed." He'd passed off the remark when Osmund had asked him what he meant, but the young man would recall it later. There was—

Ossa made the whistle of a plover through his cupped hands and listened for a reply. It came, and the party emerged from cover to see men lowering their bows and nodding in welcome.

Up close the stockpiled timber was even more impressive than when seen from the cover of the scrubby trees. It towered to well over the height of a man and stretched for a hundred yards, comprising fascines, stakes and logs for building a cordwood road through the swamps of the Fenlands. It was the product of many hours, days and weeks of impressed labour, but Osmund had no thought for that as he thrust the pitch-soaked rags deep into the piles of brushwood that would in turn be placed among the stakes and logs and turned to glance up and down the vastness of the pile to where others were doing the same, while here and there men coaxed fire from flint, steel and timber.

Willing hands moved logs from the great pile and buried the brushwood within them before replacing the logs atop them, and when the Scraeling was satisfied that all was ready he nodded to Osmund, who took a brushwood torch, thrust it into a fire and swung it gently round his head so that the embers flared into life before thrusting it at the full stretch of his arm into a space between two logs, to where a brushwood fascine waited. The brushwood flared almost at once and Osmund withdrew his arm to leave the torch buried in the fascine and a thin trail of smoke spiralling upwards.

"Anything we want from the sentries?" demanded Ossa of the Scraeling, who was frowning thoughtfully at a pile of timber, and he gestured to a small pile of weaponry nearby. "Didn't want their mail, did you?" he enquired and the Scraeling came from his reverie and chuckled.

"Not me" he said, "It'll only fit a big strong chap like you!" Ossa laughed, for he was a thought shorter than the Scraeling, then turned away and signalled the withdrawal. In less than a minute the only living things in the middle of the small pocket of hard ground were the flames.

The Fenlands, May 1071.

Leo kicked at the pebble to send it skittering into the pool with a plop that betokened deep water. He sighed. Half the problem, he thought, was the depth of the water in some parts of the fenlands. The other half was its shallowness. *Very clever* he told himself, *can't hide much from you, Leo,* and he was honest enough with himself to grin at the obvious nature of the thought.

No, it's true enough he decided. The swamp was bottomless in some places and anything but in others – and those places could be half a mile apart or a mere three feet. Fortifications surrounded by water were difficult, but not impossible, to reduce and Leo understood the process very well, cavalryman though he was. But fortifications surrounded by water, mud and the odd stretch of land that offered the defenders the chance of escape were something else again. They took months – years, even – of wearying and dangerous toil in a nightmare world of stinking mud and lurking quicksand with a hideous death one unwary step away.

But month by shuddering month and through the best and the worst of England's fickle weather, his infantrymen and dismounted cavalry had drawn the net around the fenlands tighter and tighter and the rebels of the swamp had sullenly and reluctantly given back before them. Now he was poised for the last push, and one way or another it would be successful. He chipped another stone into the tarn with the toe of his heavy shoe and let his thoughts drift back to the day when he'd dined with a king and the Conqueror had given him his mind and his task.

Just hold that bloody Englishman until things settle down for us. And if you can get your hands on him, so much the better – but just hold him and deny him to the Godwinssons. But he'd done better than that, thought Leo. He'd neutralised the rebels, tightening the ring round Hereward and pushing him inexorably back into the swamp, and now he was ready to take the step that would finish him. He'd taken casualties, certainly, chasing men who had known the marshes since birth and fighting for control of the maze of tracks, paths and ways through the swamp, but now he was poised to take the last step. And that was to fix his quarry, to hold their attention through a threat they couldn't ignore, to offer them a target that would draw them down like a moth to a candle. And once the moth was fixed, Leo would crush it.

The Isle of Refuge, Ely marsh, May 1071.

"Uncle Ranulf, what did you mean about Morcar doing for King Harold? That's the 'Godwinsson' you meant, right?" asked Osmund as they enjoyed the twilight outside the long hut.

The Scraeling stopped his whittling and looked round at the young man beside him. *God's bones, Osmund would be a prodigious size full-grown if the seventeen-year-old frame beside him was any indication.* "All I can say from my own knowledge" he said, keeping his voice low, "was that Harold went out of his way to placate Morcar and his evil brother, Edwin. Even to the extent of preferring them to his own brother, Tostig." That was close enough to the truth to do for now, thought the Scraeling.

"Because they held the earldoms of the north" mused Osmund. "And King Harold needed strong men there. Because of the threat of Hardraada." The Scraeling glanced at him sharply, but Osmund was far away.

"I've been speaking with Earl Siward" he said, and the Scraeling felt the warning prickle of trouble. "Do you know Siward at all?" and at the shake of the Scraeling's head he went on, "Interesting man. Took a bad spear-wound at Fulford Gate – says Morcar wasn't keen on fighting there, by the way – and that's why he limps still. But what I found even more interesting was what he had to say about Morcar's reluctance to follow the king down the London road. 'Course, Siward was out of it by then because of his wound." And by now the Scraeling's prickle had grown into certainty.

"Siward says that Morcar and Edwin swore their duty was to the north, not to any other part of England" went on the young man, "and in fact they didn't get anywhere near here until weeks after Senlac. Ever heard that?"

The Scraeling nodded reluctantly. "I have" he admitted, "and from what I was able to discover from Norway, I believe it. If you pressed me I'd have to say that Morcar and Edwin sold Harold out. But Osmund, things aren't always that cut and dried, you know." Osmund raised an eyebrow, and the Scraeling plunged on.

"To begin with" he said, "I've always believed Harold needn't have fought at Senlac. He could have trapped William there at Pevensey. Bottled him up. Let lack of grazing take care of the Bastard's war-horses, and the autumn gales make sure he got no supplies from Normandy. Even if he did fight, he could have put it off until Morcar and Edwin got there. They'd taken casualties at Fulford and Stamford against Hardraada, you know."

Osmund shook his head decisively. "Can't agree there, uncle. Siward tells me the troops Morcar committed at Fulford weren't more than a fraction of his strength. What was he doing with the rest? And he didn't commit any at Stamford – that was the royal *hus-carls*."

"Well, I can't help you with that" said the Scraeling. "I wasn't at either. But tell me – why d'you want to know? Where's this going?" But he knew perfectly well where it was going.

"Garth's told me often enough" said Osmund, "how Senlac turned on just half an hour of daylight. Darkness, he said, would've allowed my father and his sword brothers to get the king off that ridge. Morcar's *hus-carls* would've bought him that time. And the London troops arrived next day, he says, so the king would've been able to go after the Bastard with fresh men to his exhausted ones. So" he went on with relentless logic, "we'd still have a Saxon king, uncle Ranulf. And I'd still have a father, a mother, a family and a home. Yes?"

The Scraeling puffed out his cheeks. "You can look at it that way, my boy" he said. "Nothing surer. And I can't argue with any of it. Except to say again – Harold needn't have fought, you know."

"Fair enough, uncle" said the young man quietly. "But that was the king's decision, wasn't it? And once he'd made it, wasn't it up to those he'd made powerful to support it?"

"Loyalty demands that, aye" admitted a Scraeling with nowhere to go.

"Not just loyalty, uncle Ranulf. Honour, too" returned Osmund. He got to his feet, stretched and announced his intention of trying for a fish at their evening feed, leaving the Scraeling marvelling at the age of the head on such young shoulders.

The de Bois estate, Reading, at the same time.

"Is Matilda still sick Mummy?" asked Sunngifu and Gytha reached gingerly down past her swollen belly to stroke the long flaxen hair of her older daughter.

"Not so badly now, darling" she replied. "Not now it's summer and the warm weather's here. She's much better."

"Well can I play with her then? Now she's not sick?" with the remorseless logic of a four-year-old.

"Not today, Sunni. Today she's sleeping. But tomorrow – we'll see. Now – let's dress your hair, because you know how much Daddy likes to see it plaited and wound round your head, don't you?"

"Yes" giggled the little girl. "He says I look like a queen wearing a crown. Do I?"

"Of course you do" smiled her mother, "a little Saxon queen." *With Penda's hair and eyes* she thought, *yet you call a Norman 'Daddy'. Well, it'll come to that for us all, won't it? Or perhaps not all. Oh my son, my son, my firstborn, my darling, where are you? How are you?*

Cambridge, a week later.

"How serious are the losses?" asked William as he peeled the apple, "and what're you doing about them?"

"Not serious, majesty" replied Leo, "because they're burning the material we've left far enough out in the marsh to be tempting for them. And it's not good stuff – my carpenters tell me it's second-grade timber, some of it rotten, and we've left an awful lot of brushwood out there too. As to what we're doing – the first-grade timber's all stored at this end under tight guard. No, majesty – Hereward's welcome to what's put there, and while he's playing with it we'll keep on adding to what we've got here, because it's obvious we'll build the causeway as we go – from this end."

William nodded, his attention concentrated on getting the peel off in one long strip. "And losses in men?"

"That's the worst part, majesty" said Leo. "Detachments out there've got to be light enough to encourage the rebels to have a go, but not light enough to be silly. Swamp duty isn't popular with the men. One other thing." He paused, and William looked up.

"There's a rumour" said Leo, choosing his words carefully, "and it's come from at least three parts of the marsh – a rumour that one of Hardraada's ex-lieutenants is involved with the rebels. His secretary . . . ex-secretary . . . I'm told. A cripple."

William frowned and bit into the apple. "Can't see it matters" he said shortly. "Not if they're still burning the decoy timber. And I'd wager gold that Magnus of Norway hasn't sent him. He's not the mischievous type, from what I'm told."

"So you don't see any Norwegian involvement, majesty?" asked Leo and William grunted.

"No. What I hear about that treacherous swine Morcar joining Hereward worries me more than a hundred Norwegians, because where there's the earl of Northumbria, there's trouble. He was trouble for Godwinsson. I was stupid enough to trust him on that basis, and he's been trouble for me just the same."

"No, you're doing fine, St Brieuc. Just keep containing these rebels as you're doing, and piling up the materials we'll need for the autumn. Don't worry about Norway, and forget about Hardraada's cripple, whoever he is or was. I've got the best man around here as my area commander, and that's you."

The Isle of Refuge, Ely marsh, May 1071.

"He's coming over" said Ossa. "All I see out there tells me he's coming over. And he'll come from Aldreth, 'f I'm any judge. He'll build a roadway of some sort – you'll see. He'll have to. Y'can't get cavalry mounts in anythin' that'll float in our waters."

"Y'r right there Ossa" put in Skuli. "*Nordvedr*'d struggle to get steerage in most of that. A roadway of some kind it is. He'd have to build it, an' I can just see Hereward here letting him. Eh?"

Eyes swung to the Lord of the Fens at the head of the crude table, who smiled. "Not likely" he said, "but William must know that. He must know he'll take big casualties in the building, and even more if he gets across. Why's he doing this?"

"Because you're an affront to him" put in the Scraeling. "That simple.

173

He's a king of England with a rebel nest three or four days' easy march from his capital, and now he's sorted out his frontiers and beaten his rivals, it's time for the lesser problems. That's us."

"Lesser problems?" demanded Morcar from his self-appointed position near Hereward, "*lesser* problems? Don't you Norsemen know anything? By anyone's strategy I'd say we were one of his greater problems – we've been here three years!"

"True. And where are we going?" asked the Scraeling mildly. "I might not have your grasp of strategy, Morcar, but in all humility I'd say we're less of a problem to the Bastard than Godwinsson's sons, Godwinsson's mother, Malcolm of Scotland, Edgar the Aetheling, you and your late brother, and any of the others he's seen off during the time we've been sitting here with our heads up our arses. That's what this Norseman knows."

"Heads up our arses?" snapped Leofric, one of Morcar's thegns, "I'm not having that. We've been a thorn in his side for three years, man!"

"Some of us have been" returned Skuli. "Some others've been here a bit less time." At which Leofric flushed and his hand went to his dagger.

"That's enough!" snapped Morcar. "Regardless, Scraeling, you can't deny we've been a problem to William. Why, you've led the raids on his building-dumps yourself!"

"True" agreed the Scraeling. "And if you'd been on any you'd have seen what I've seen. You could probably build a cattle-pen with the sort of timber we've been burning, Morcar, but I wouldn't keep any of *my* cattle in one. No, the Bastard's been keeping us busy and limiting us to a bit of looting and plundering – sacrificing the odd detachment of soldiers here and there, just enough to keep us from looking further afield and becoming really dangerous by joining up with some of the others I mentioned just now."

"*What?* Where the fuck d'you get these ideas from?" demanded an exasperated Morcar, and the Scraeling smiled.

"Believe it's called strategy, Morcar, and I thought you were good at it. Consider – how'd William like an army of, say, Danes, coming in through the Wash, met there and guided by us down the three, four, days' march I talked about just now, closer to his capital than his arse is to his saddle? Eh?"

"But he doesn't need to worry about that, because he's got us burning heaps of spare timber for him. The real stuff – the stuff that'll make his roadway – that's where Ossa says it is, at Aldreth five miles away. Yes, Morcar, he's taken us out of every other game going. Well . . . not William, but the man he's made area commander here. Don't know his name, but he's a cunning bugger and a good soldier. I hear he's a Breton, too. Nothing against him for that, though – I'm one myself, matter of fact."

"How'd you know that?" asked a clearly nettled Leofric.

"I talk to people, Leofric, and I have other people talk to people I can't talk to. But I listen more than I talk, see?" came back the answer.

Hereward had been listening in admiration. *Jesus, no wonder Hardraada set such store by this one* he thought. *Nothing gets past him, does it?* He tapped the table and said, aloud, "So – unless we decide to move elsewhere, all we can do is wait until William begins building. Then make him pay for it, hard as we can. That it?"

Around the table heads nodded. "If we're gonna move" said Skuli, "no reason to do it right now. See the building begun, make him pay like you say, pull out jus' before it's finished. If it costs him enough, he won't do it again."

The Chronicle.

*I*t was true, and it weighed on my mind. Ever since our arrival in the marsh we'd been busy doing very little of consequence, and the people we found there were an ill-assorted lot. There were survivors of Senlac who had been hunted from their homes in consequence, men who genuinely held the Saxon cause as theirs – not that there had ever been many of those, and even fewer now as England settled down under the new masters. There was the usual assortment of landless and vagrant hoping to find riches the quick way, and there was a notable number of young men either attracted to desperate deeds for their own sake or, like Osmund, disinherited.

And there was Hereward himself, and all my thinking came back to him like a pigeon to its loft. Hereward was an interesting character, being well-educated and well-travelled even if only by circumstance. As a consequence he had a fund of amusing travellers' tales and these, coupled with an engaging personality, a ready laugh and a generous nature, won men to him with ease. He was skilled in arms and that won him as much respect as his formidable strength, for although he was no Penda in that regard he was more than capable with sword, axe or spear.

But Hereward had a weakness, and to me it was a serious weakness. He was a warrior born, yet not a commander, for anything that touched his honour made him insensible to any other consideration and where some praised his singleness of purpose, for myself I saw it otherwise – as I've already noted.

Hereward's nature had dictated the vengeance he took upon the despoilers of his father's hall just as surely as it had dictated the crimes for which he had been banished as a young man scarcely older than Osmund. And – as I'd warned Osmund – because vengeance, rather than conviction, had dictated his outlawry, his outlawry would end when either he or William deemed enough to be enough and became reconciled.

To offer him justice, Hereward himself might well have been aware of his impulsiveness as a shortcoming, for when Nordvedr had ghosted deep into the Fens, he had been glad enough to offer shelter to forty likely-looking ruffians and the silent young man of impressive size who came with them.

But he was no less than delighted to hear from Skuli, on the quiet and at my instructions, that the cripple who accompanied him was no other than the legendary Scraeling, Hardrada's former henchman, and I found myself admitted to his council and my opinion sought from the very beginning of our time there. More often than not decisions were made in accordance with what I recommended, but that altered more than somewhat when Morcar and his followers arrived after William harried the northern lands with fire and sword.

But I cared little for Hereward's cause – whatever it was – and even less for any cause Morcar espoused. My cause was the young man I had quickly come to love as a son, and as long as we could move if we had to in the time it took to raise Norvedr from where she slumbered, weighted, beneath the murky water of the Fens and set her mast into her, I would help Hereward where and when I could.

In the marsh.

Osmund spoke more of his father than of his mother, and he was endlessly interested in his time with the Scraeling in the service of the eastern empress. At other times he sought knowledge of his father's service to the sons of old Earl Godwin, and at those times the Scraeling had the strange feeling that he was telling the boy of things he already knew, most likely through Garth, and that he was drawing a picture of his father within his head. But there remained things – notably those things surrounding

Penda's decision to accompany Tostig Godwinsson into exile – over which the Scraeling warned myself to guard his tongue, for he was now the only man alive who knew the secret of that decision,[6] and he saw no need to alter that.

But, with the grace of one much older, Osmund drew from the Scraeling his own story of the years since his father and his uncle had parted on the eve of Senlac, and he was noble enough to commiserate on the ruin that the Scraeling's life had become, although, thought the Scraeling, in all truth and all respects his own tragedy was much, much worse. The cripple esteemed the young man for that, and in particular for the comment he made one night just before his eighteenth birthday when, in answer to the Scraeling's question concerning where he wanted to pass his nineteenth, he remarked,

"Not here, uncle. This fight's over. As much over as the England of my father's over. And though I wish it wasn't, the Raedwaldsson estate's behind me now forever, because Ivo de Bois can do nothing for me, even if he wanted to for my mother's sake. I know that now. But I believe he would if he could. Aye."

He paused a moment, then said, "But Uncle Ranulf, we're alike in so many ways. We both loved Penda Raedwaldsson. We both have respect among our comrades; they respect the skills you've given me with weapons and in battle – " and he said that with no hint of brag or boastfulness, " – and I've seen how they seek your mind on this and your advice on that. Most of all, we've both twice lost the things that mean most to us in all the world – and the first time that happened to you, you were younger than I am now, am I right? And as often as I think about what my father told me of your early life, I tell myself that if you could overcome your loss to become what you have, then so can I. And because that's so, uncle, we need to find another world. D'you think there's a world somewhere that'll take the Scraeling and Penda's brat?" And Penda's smile flashed from his face.

"Surely, my boy" said the Scraeling, hearing the huskiness of his own voice, "but if we can't find one – we'll make one. I promise!"

---

6 *See 'The Landwaster'*

Aldreth camp and depot, Ely marsh, June 1071.

The right-hand pulley wheel squealed as the pile-driver smashed down to send the pointed treetrunk sliding down half its length into the ooze before the shed.

"Up!" came the word and both pile-drivers rose ponderously into the air, the right-hand one again emitting a long squeal that might have been a protest.

"Forward!" and the shed inched forward on its wheels another six feet. "Down!" and again the pile-drivers thundered downward to send the treetrunks plunging down into the mud of the Fens.

"Up! Rails!" Two lighter trunks were manhandled forward to bridge the gap between the two pairs of new piles. Stout leather straps were threaded through the holes awaiting them near the tops of the piles, drawn tight about the rails and quickly spiked into place with long, hand-made iron nails, William's siege-hardened engineers and sappers never pausing for thought or uncertainty. *Ah, I see* thought Leo, watching each strap soaked in swamp-water, *they'll shrink as they dry and bind the rails to the piles even more tightly. Always more to learn, isn't there?*

He watched the men step forward, each pair bearing a slender post for the corduroy road that would take the army over the ooze of the Fens, bend to the rails and nail them home, outer edge first, to drive the logs as tightly as might be back into the one before, then the inside edge.

Six feet of roadway completed, the shed inched forward again at the word, the pulley screamed and the weights smashed home anew. Odo leaned towards him.

"Looking good, Leo. They're into the rhythm of it, eh?"

Leo grunted. "Aye. No danger of fire this time – bastards burned everything there was to burn last time." Which was no less than the truth, for the fire that had swept out of the Fens had been stoked by the prevailing wind to an inferno that consumed everything before it – vegetation, shed and roadway.

"Right" agreed his lieutenant. "They won't be doing that again" He turned away to order the outside of the timber-walled shed, already covered in hides against fire-arrows, to be doused again with water drawn from the marsh.

Leo winced at the memory of the king's reaction to the rebels' use of fire against the first attempt to bridge the marsh. *But in all truth*, he reasoned, *even had it been foreseen it could hardly have been prevented.* As it was, the framework of the moving shed had been saved and he was thankful that the rebels had shown their hand in time for the attackers to get the shed back to safety instead of when the cumbersome shelter was in the middle of the marsh.

No. All things considered it might have been worse. He watched the shed inching forward and back, the logs smashing down into the depths and the roadway creeping forward. There was an inevitability about the steady progress that fascinated him, cavalryman though he was, for it spoke as nothing else could of the iron determination of the race that had built an invasion fleet from scratch and standing timber then armed it, provisioned it, garrisoned it from the adventurers of Europe and finally brought it across a strip of water that was still greatly feared by sensible men, to win a kingdom against all the odds.

"Good progress Odo" he pronounced. "Keep them at it. And have that fucking pulley-wheel greased, can you?"

Further back in the marsh.

Osmund crouched at the edge of the rushes and peered through at the distant progress of the causeway. There was no doubt – it was appreciably nearer, and there was no chance of approaching under cover to within arrow-range.

Thanks to Morcar he thought. *If he had to set fire to the marsh he might've done it a bit later.* All, he reflected, that had been achieved by the earl of Northumbria's action had been a day's delay while the Normans had made good the damage to roadway and shed, while the cost had been the removal of the only cover allowing men to get within bowshot. *Probably didn't want to get any closer, gutless bastard.*

There was no love lost between Morcar and Osmund. Under normal circumstances there would have been few meetings between an earl and a homeless warrior, thegn's son though he was, but the Isle of Refuge was anything but normal. There was one acknowledged master and that was Hereward. For the rest, all were members of his war-band although some, and Morcar for instance, considered themselves to be something more than that. That conviction had already led to heated words between the earl and the young man when Osmund had spoken up against Morcar's proposal that the causeway should be destroyed by direct storm.

The young man had pointed out, in the face of Morcar's scorn, that a daylight approach was out of the question in the face of the firepower that would surely be directed against them, even if they could muster sufficient boats and punts to bring an attacking force close enough in numbers great enough to be effective. The nods and grunts of agreement that had accompanied his words had annoyed the earl to the point of recklessness, for he had questioned Osmund's right to speak at a council of "his elders and betters". At which the young man had simply risen to his feet and walked silently from the room to a mutter of triumph from Morcar's cronies and a thoughtful shake of the head from the Scraeling.

Osmund shook Morcar from his thoughts. *What'll they have in behind that causeway?* he wondered. *Archers, certainly. Probably two or three siege engines too, to keep us away from the causeway?*

"They'll get across all right" came a murmur from behind him and he nodded.

"Nothing surer, Uncle Ranulf" he returned. "And there's nothing we can do about it. Unless we're as stupid as Morcar."

The Scraeling chuckled. "Now, Osmund" he chided, "there's always something one can do. What about building a siege engine and using it to throw the earl of Northumbria at the Normans? Hey?"

Osmund snorted in laughter. "You're in a good mood" he said. "A much better mood than you ought to be with a Norman army coming to teach you not to mock your betters. What're you up to?"

"Just an exercise" said the Scraeling. "An exercise in seeing the possibilities. Have a look at how the thing's built, my boy. A careful look. When you've worked it out, come and tell me. I'm going to see if I can help Heggr make a stew that doesn't taste of swamp water and duck shit. Don't frown so, young man – you'll get wrinkles before your time." And off he went.

Ely Abbey, June 1071.

"Give me wisdom, Lord, that I may save this house to Thy glory and Thy work" intoned the man on his knees before the high altar of the abbey. "Give me, also, the courage to face the wrath of men even as Thy Son faced the wrath of men in Thy holy name, if this is what Thy will requires."

"Amen" came a chorus from behind him, and one voice continued. "Lord God, we Thy servants of Ely, beseech You to send Thurstan, our father and abbot, the wisdom for which he asks and the courage to do Thy will. And we ask for that courage for ourselves as we support him in the doing of Thy will and word." And there came another chorus of amens as the monks of the Fenlands swung in behind their leader.

Thurstan prostrated himself before the altar and led his brethren in the Lord's Prayer before rising stiffly and turning to face them as they scrambled – some of them even more stiffly, he noticed – to their feet. None was getting any younger, he realised, and the tumultuous times of the past five years had aged some visibly. He smiled at them and raised his hand in the valedictory.

He caught the eye of his second and lifted an eyebrow. The other, Wulfstan, nodded imperceptibly and hung back as the monks filed from the chapel. "Thurstan?" he murmured and the abbot fell in beside him.

"Have you considered what we discussed?" asked the abbot, and Wulfstan tucked his hands inside his wide sleeves and nodded.

"Yes, Thurstan, and I've taken it on myself to keep watch on them. As a result, I fear your suspicions have foundation. Both brothers constantly find excuse or cause to be in each other's company, and they move themselves from one roster to another to make that possible, quite as they please. There is also ... talk ... among our brethren that one visits the cell of the other by night."

Thurstan stiffened. "Have you taxed either with what you know?" he asked, and again his deputy nodded.

"Oh yes. They don't deny any of what I've told you. In fact they glory in it, for they hold that God's will is clearly that Norman William is to rule over us, that our support of Hereward and his ilk is therefore ungodly and contrary to God's manifest and revealed will, and that this abbey should lose no time in supporting the true king with its prayers, its treasure and its brethren."

"Do they so!" said Thurstan. After a moment he asked, "And the visitations by night?"

"Prayer together" returned Wulfstan. "Prayers that the eyes of the abbey's great ones be opened to God's manifest will. So they say."

Thurstan snorted. "And what of their vows of humility and obedience?" he demanded. "What of them? And these two scarce tonsured! Are you sure they're not lovers?"

Wulfstan shrugged. "Who knows?" he returned. "They're young, so they know everything. And the young these days aren't as they were in our youth. We've discussed this often enough, Wulfstan – the whole generation's gone to the pack. All of them think they have the right to dictate rather than to ask; to be listened to instead of listening. None has any notion of what it is to serve before they rule."

Thurstan nodded, for it was a familiar conversation for each of them. "So" he said. "They're two only. But truthfully, Wulfstan, I find myself wondering if they're not right. 'Manifest will', eh? I can't deny – no-one can deny – that William's still here. He's been winning for five years, in spite of everything. He's seen off Godwins, Danes, Scots, Edgar, the Welsh and even one or two of his own barons. Is that God's will, do you think?"

"Who can say?" said Wulfstan as they came to the refectory and he paused with his hand on the latch. "William's causeway is a-building. Perhaps God will answer your question in its success? Or not."

Thurstan clucked in frustration. "All very well, Wulfstan, all very well. But if William's Normans have to fight their way over the marsh, they're not likely to be too fussy over what they do to anyone, or any thing, here. Understand?"

"Only too well, father" said Wulfstan, returning to their formal public relationship, "only too well."

The Isle of Refuge.

"The bindings" said Osmund, "where the rails sit on the piles. The bindings're your 'possibilities'. They can't drive spikes through the thickness of a tree-trunk, so they've used bindings. Wide leather strips – bound tight, nailed down, wet so they shrink again as they dry, and bind the rails tight to the piles. And they're really only bearing weight from above, so they're not going to move very far."

"Well done" said the Scraeling, peering into the cauldron as he stirred its contents. "So tell me why the bindings are a weakness, if they're so good."

"Because they can be cut" said Osmund patiently, "where the piles, rails, or roadway can't. They can be cut from below. By swimmers."

"Mmmm" said the Scraeling. "Here, try this. Need thickening?"

"Not for me" said Osmund. "It's good. You're a man of many talents, uncle."

"You're too kind, my boy. I know a little about many things, I'll admit that. But I don't know who the best swimmers in our little band are. D'you think you could help me there? Say, by this evening? So I can put it to Hereward?"

Three nights later.

"Now remember" said the Scraeling, "their torches're to light up the water around the causeway so men in boats can't approach, not to look for swimmers or reeds sticking up above the water. The same light will bounce off the water and hide you. But even so, don't go shallow anywhere near it – get your chests on the mud until you can come up under the roadway, yes?"

The four men in front of him grunted assent and carried on coating themselves and each other with a mixture of fat and soot while the men who would ferry them to their drop-off point smeared the same mixture on their faces and hands.

"Lastly" said the Scraeling, "a spare dagger each? Sharp?"

"Fine, thanks uncle" said Osmund, looming big in the starlight, "I think we've got it. Aye?"

"Aye" came back the other voices and the Scraeling felt foolish.

"Right then" he said. "Who's got the blacking?"

Across the marsh.

"That's it then" said the sergeant as the last torch settled down to a steady burn in its holder on the causeway. "No wind tonight, so they'll do nicely. Ya got a bowshot in every direction, so yous archer buggers can earn ya pay for a change and nail any fucking thing that comes outta the dark, got it?

And if it happens, scream ya heads off and my boys'll be here while yous're still peeing yourselves. Questions?"

The six archers looked at each other, decided there was no point, and set out along the roadway. "Relief?" asked one of them hopefully, looking back.

"Relief? You thinking 'bout relief already?" scoffed the sergeant. "Two hours on, two off – I'll tell the other girls on m'way back, and they'll spell you in two hours – if they c'n stay awake. But I'll be round any old time, an' if I catch ya dozin'... well, don't let me!"

And he marched off down to the landward end of the causeway that thrust into the marsh like a long wooden finger, feeling the solidity of the timber beneath his feet. *Settle those fucking Saxons this time* he thought, *an' about time too.*

In the dark shadows beyond the light from the torches, the Scraeling leaned to balance the punt as Osmund slid into the water to join Ossa. "Where's your reed? Got it?" he whispered, and Osmund sighed.

"Here" he whispered. "Where it's been since we left! Uncle!" And he stuck the foot-long reed in his mouth, blew to clear it of anything that had crawled into it, and felt for the daggers at the small of his back.

The Scraeling was glad to change the subject. "Oeric must be in position by now" he hissed, and he looked round to check their position under the north star for the last time. "When you're ready. God speed!" And the two men who clung to the side of the punt slid down and away with hardly a ripple.

"And now we wait" murmured the Scraeling to his boatman, and bent down to bring his eye nearer to the waterline. No – there was no ripple to betray the reed breathing-tube sticking up above the water, and in his mind's eye he saw Osmund and Ossa stroking powerfully beneath the black surface, just as they had practised.

Four or five minutes to the edge of the torchlight, thought the Scraeling, then a dive to the marsh-bed for the distance to the causeway, coming up where they needed to in the cover of any of the reed-clumps that dotted the waterway where their roots clung to the mud. If all went as planned, he realised, he would know no more until Osmund's head broke surface beside him where the punt waited under the brightest star. And by then, William's causeway would be crippled and waiting to die.

No – there was nothing else to be done, so he let his mind wander back to the last battle with Morcar. *What drives that man?* he wondered. It was as though the earl of Northumbria approved of nothing that didn't come from him – yet he rarely took a direct part in any of the band's ventures and he had shown no sign of any talent for leadership at all.

Morcar had been against the Scraeling's plan to destroy the causeway under the weight of the men who would cross it, claiming that there was no glory in it and that its destruction in such a fashion would send no message to those in England who still resisted William.

"And who are they?" the Scraeling had demanded. "Godwinsson's boys've never come back, the Danes likewise, the west's held by William's best soldier and the Bastard himself's turned your earldom into a graveyard. Don't you understand? We're the last, Morcar. The last little detail, the candle at the end of the night if you like. And William's about to snuff it out."

"Buggered if he'll snuff me out" said Morcar belligerently. "He'll have a fight on his hands if that's what he wants."

"Of course. You're probably ready to give him one, seeing you've been stuck here in the middle of a swamp for a while" said the Scraeling neutrally, but several of the listeners guffawed just the same.

Morcar had flushed. "Your vikings aren't the only ones capable of striking a blow, y'know" he said, "and when we do, we'll make sure it counts!"

The Scraeling had shrugged. "Well enough" he said. "There're plenty of Normans to go around, so help yourself. Just leave the causeway alone, got it? Hereward?"

The Wake had nodded. "Aye, Scraeling. Fair enough – your target if you think your team can do it."

And in all truth there were plenty of Normans to go around. For months, it seemed, there had been a steady build-up of Norman numbers at the outer edges of the great marsh. There were no easy targets these days, for convoys were guarded in double and sometimes triple strength, while patrols comprised cavalry where they could operate, as well as infantry, and raiding supply dumps had become risky and difficult. It pointed to one thing and one thing only, the Scraeling brooded, and that was William's determination to bring an end at last to the affront to his dignity lurking in the Ely Marsh. And why not, he thought, because now—

The peal of a horn shattered the silence of the night and he leaped as if he had been stung. Men's shouts split the air and before the Scraeling's unbelieving eyes a dozen boats raced out of the darkness and into the torchlit circle around the causeway. Each was full of men and even from where he sat the Scraeling could see the gleam of torchlight on weapons and mail. They were Saxon, without question, and the Scraeling's shock gave way to an all-consuming anger as he realised he was watching a full-on surface assault on the causeway.

"Morcar!" he exploded. "Now *fuck* him for the useless, treacherous, arrogant by-blow of a dockside whore he is! God, strike that man blind! He was told—" but his anger evaporated before the fear that clutched his bowels at the thought of a battle raging above and around the young man he had come to love more than anything or anyone in the world, and he found himself mumbling prayers for Osmund's safety; that he might have the sense to turn for the darkness and leave the torchlight for Morcar and his fools; that he might turn in his track and swim back to the boat; that the Normans would be too busy with the obvious to look beneath the surface.

In the event, the last was what happened. Driven by the screaming horn, archers poured onto the causeway and the attacking boats attracted a veritable storm of arrows that, at such short range, quickly found the chinks and the gaps between shields. Stricken men rose to their feet and toppled over the side or sprawled among their fellows; oarsmen were hit and sent their craft careering round in circles; two of the attackers capsized, hurling men into the water where they were quickly filled with Norman shafts as they struggled in the water. Not one boat got closer than twenty yards, and the Scraeling saw with something approaching disgust that Morcar's thinking had not extended to covering the charge of his axemen with archers of his own.

As it was, the attempt on the causeway was no more than live practice for the Norman archers and some of the better marksmen scored even at long bowshot and in the flickering shadows. Morcar's boats broke under the relentless hail of shafts and fled for the darkness to the jeers of the Normans on the causeway.

At last their sergeants got them under control and promptly stood half of them down. " 'Bout them, sergeant?" called one, gesturing towards the bodies floating in the water. "Fish them out, or what?"

"Whaffor?" came back a sergeant, "not likely t'have anything you want, lad. Nah, leave 'em for the eels. All the bastards're fit for anyway!"

"Reckon they'll be back sergeant?" called another, and the sergeant spat into the dark water.

"They c'n suit their fucking selves far's I care" he said. " 'f they do— well I've got you ladies t'look after me, ain't I? Just like you did that time. Me, I'm going to get my head down. 'Night!" and he left to a series of good-natured catcalls from men proud of their own showing in battle. *Which was exactly what he'd intended*, thought the Scraeling as he crouched in the darkness with an icy ball of fear in his vitals.

What could he do? There was now less hope than ever of approaching the causeway, or of going in underwater himself, for the chances of being spotted by a garrison wide awake and itching for action were as high as those of coming across Osmund were negligible. No, all he could do was sit and wait. And pray – there was always prayer.

The de Bois manor, the same night.

"William" said Ivo de Bois. "He shall be called William, my dear. If you agree?"

Gytha smiled wanly. She was so very tired, for the birth had been more difficult than she would have thought given that William was her sixth child. And Penda, her Penda, had come to her and for her again with the love shining from his eyes and encouragement in his voice. But still, *Too old, Gytha. You're too old at thirty-seven* she thought, and raised her eyes to where her husband stroked a tiny pink fist with his own little finger. *He's a good man* she thought, *much better than I might have hoped for. Since the only man I hoped for is dead, áye.*

"Yes, my lord. And thank you for seeking my mind. William it shall be" *And then we'll have our own William and Matilda. Why not? My England – Penda's England – has too.*

De Bois took her hand where it lay on the cover and raised it to his lips. "My dear" he said, "It's for me to thank you, more than my words can say, for this gift. I know our William isn't the . . . the first son of English and Norman in this land, but . . . but I hope he'll be a sign, perhaps? A sign of two peoples living in one land so . . . one day . . . they'll be the same people. And William and Matilda – they're native born. Native to this land.

As . . . as are your other children, my dear."

"Even so, husband" said Gytha, forcing a weary smile. William woke, and gave a thin, high cry. She brought the babe to her right breast and his little mouth found her nipple right away. "See, how he claims his birthright already!"

"My dear" said de Bois, "you needn't do that if you don't wish to. There are wet-nurses aplenty in the village, surely?"

Gytha frowned, and spoke slowly in English. "Husband, that's not the custom of the English. And if it were, it still wouldn't be my custom. This is a child of our bodies, Ivo, and he'll be fed from my body. Now – you spoke of two peoples becoming one, didn't you? If you mean that, husband, learning and speaking English would be the best way to start I can imagine. And when William grows beyond his first year . . ."

He followed her words with effort and, when she'd finished he thought for a moment and then nodded slowly, looking at the suckling child. "Gytha, you have right" he said, also in English. "I . . . I try today . . . and tomorrow, and each day . . . I am speaking . . . speaking a little. With you. And to William. Aye?"

"Aye" said Gytha, smiling up at the man who doted on her, *and you'll keep your word. And our folk, Penda's and mine, will think the more of you for it. But who'll make a world for our first-born, Penda's and mine?*

She was tired, but when William had been fed she'd see him asleep then seek sleep herself. And Penda.

In the Ely marsh.

The Scraeling stared miserably through the reeds to where a wide-awake and very alert troop of archers paced to and fro on the causeway. It had been at least an hour since the attack, and the ball of ice in his stomach had grown larger with every moment of it. For his life he could think of no way in which he might discover what had become of Osmund – and with a guilty start he realised that three other men were somewhere between him and the causeway also. No – he knew that, in half an hour he would slip over the side himself because he would — the boatman hissed "Hear that?" and the Scraeling realised that a nightbird had called somewhere nearby in the marsh.

"The bird?" he asked and there came another hiss.

"Plover. They sleeps at night. 'S them. One o'them anyways." And he gave the same warbling whistle, and then another. A faint splash broke the crackling tension among the reeds, and the Scraeling strained to see, off to his left, a half-imagined ripple in the water. Then a hand grasped the gunwale of the low-lying boat and another came in, searching for a grip. As he reached for it two more heads bobbed suddenly into view and a voice murmured "Ossa, lord. Lean back."

The Scraeling hauled on the hand as he leaned back and Ossa slid into the boat as if he were indeed half-duck. "Well met, Ossa!" whispered the Scraeling. "Is — "

"Right behind, lord. Rounded us all up under the causeway, he did, an' sent us off first. Said . . . " but the boat rocked as a big hand grasped the gunwale and another reached into the boat. Ossa and the Scraeling grasped hand and arm and leaned back to pull Osmund inboard.

"Oh my boy!" said an overjoyed Scraeling, "No trouble then?"

"Easy" said Osmund. "All the bindings cut three parts through as we agreed. Don't want it falling over until as many of the bastards as possible're on it, do we? But what happened? We'd have been back a good hour ago, but for Normans running all over the place above us."

So the Scraeling told him what had happened as the two low-lying boats melted back into the reeds.

Aldreth camp and depot.

"So what happened?" asked a frowning Leo, and his lieutenant, Waleis, shrugged.

"Boats came out of the marsh and headed for the causeway" he replied. "I dunno if they meant to burn it, chop it up or dance on it – they didn't seem to neither. No archers, so no cover barring a few shields. Result? They lost a couple of dozen men for nothing. None got close to the causeway, and we hit them hard. Been good for the men too, especially after the bastards set the marsh afire that time. Men enjoyed hitting back."

"They would" nodded Leo. "But this's the clumsiest attempt I can imagine. Too clumsy for men who've had us by the balls more than I care to remember. Did you check everything?"

"Nothing to check, messire" said Waleis. "Like I said – the only Saxons within ten yards of the causeway were dead and floating. I sent two squads've infantry back up along the Aldreth road 'cause I thought the attack was bound to be a diversion. Just like you did. But it wasn't – it was a fuck-up right enough, a plain and simple fuck-up. You think they're getting desperate?"

Ely Abbey.

"They're getting desperate" said Wulfstan. "Last night cost them dearly. Perhaps the Normans are closer than we think, Thurstan?"

The abbot didn't answer for a moment and when he did his voice sounded tired. "I remember when it was 'we', Wulfstan. When they fought with the blessing and under the banner of this church. What's happened?"

Wulfstan pondered a moment, then he blew out his cheeks. "I'm glad you ask that, because I've been giving a lot of thought to what our own two rebels had to say to me, if you remember. What's happened, you ask? Well to start with Hereward mismanaged things to the point where his Danish allies made off with most of the treasures of this abbey. But that's not important, and never was because it can be replaced. It *will* be replaced – if the abbey survives. And *that's* important."

"And, touching that" he went on, "there's another important thing, and it's this. There's no cause any more, Thurstan. When Hereward came here, took refuge here, well, enough determined men under a competent leader might have – *might have* – been able to stay the Normans. A Godwinsson, say, or Morcar or his brother perhaps, or even Svein the Dane if his men had been interested in anything but easy loot. Perhaps even Hereward himself if he'd been serious."

Thurstan nodded. "Yes. Hereward took vengeance for the slight on him. Not because he sought to deliver England from the Conqueror. I see what you're saying. But where does it leave us?"

"Leave us? Why, in a swamp, surrounded by Normans, waiting for the end and hoping we and this abbey won't be part of it" returned Wulfstan. "If you're asking me, I think we ought to be part of the answer, not the end."

"And by that you mean . . . ?" came back the question, and Wulfstan sighed.

"William doesn't have to build his causeway" he said. "We both know that there are ways through the marsh that will bear the weight of soldiers even as they bear the weight of Hereward's marauders. Let me say it plainly. I think we should preserve this abbey and the folk it serves by holding the wrath of the Normans from them. And us. I'm saying that we should show the Normans the secret paths. There."

Thurstan was silent for a long time. "I know the arguments for that, and for serving the man set over us by God's will" he said. "but I think we should await a sign, Wulfstan. Perhaps we should see whether the causeway will bring about God's will, if His will is the taking of this isle? Aye, a sign."

Make up your mind thought Wulfstan as he choked back a grunt of exasperation. *That God's will is the taking of this isle is beyond doubt. Men don't call William 'the Conqueror' because he's easily put off. Sometimes God's will needs a nudge, father, and I'm going to provide it.*

The Isle of Refuge, later that night.

The Scraeling couldn't remember seeing anyone move faster in his entire life. One moment Morcar was hunched over on a stool whittling a piece of wood as he laughed at some sally one of his circle had made, and the next he was sprawled on the ground looking up at the figure that towered over him, dagger in hand and with a foot pinning one of the earl's arms to the floor.

"What the fuck d'you . . . why you little bas— "

"That's not for the men you killed tonight, Morcar" said Osmund flatly. "No, don't get up till I say you can – and tell *him* to sit still, because it's your nose that'll come off if he doesn't, right?" And Leofric sat back down again.

"No, that's not for the men who died because of you. They were your men and anyone stupid enough to follow you has it coming, so they're no loss. The reason I'm about to kick your arse is the other men you put in danger – me and my three. And the plan you put in danger. You were told to leave the causeway alone. *Well weren't you?* Hereward told you, and I heard him. *Well didn't he?* What'd we do to deserve you, you fuckhead?"

"Leofric, he's told you once already" said the Scraeling mildly from the other side of the table. "If your arse rises any further off that seat, my man, I'm going to see how far up it I can shove this dagger. Please yourself."

"What're you talking about?" snarled Morcar, "my attack took attention from your band of heroes didn't it? What's the problem with that?"

"I've heard about your attack" replied Osmund, bearing down a little harder, "from people who couldn't believe how clumsy it was. Even the Normans must've wondered what was going on, and a halfway useful watch-officer would've checked that causeway on the spot and found the lashings cut mostly through. *That*'s my problem with what you did. Thank Christ, Morcar, we haven't got all the fuckwits on our side, because they've got one at least on theirs. And that's why I'm only going to kick your arse instead of cutting your throat – but there wasn't a lot in the decision, believe me, so don't trade on it."

He lifted his foot from Morcar's arm, drew back the other and slammed it into Morcar's side. The earl of Northumbria doubled up with an agonised grunt and Osmund took advantage of that to yank him over and sink his boot, hard, into Morcar's upturned behind twice. Leofric and Morcar's other cronies bounded to their feet but stayed there as Ossa, Skuli, Auti and Heggr loomed up beside the Scraeling with steel in their hands.

"That's two" said Osmund, "and you put four men in danger. I'm a fair man, Morcar, so here's another two." And he suited action to word as Morcar squirmed across the floor. "What about you?" he snapped at Leofric, "Fancy your own chances next, d'you?" Leofric stopped straining against the Scraeling's grip and stood very still.

Morcar bounded to his feet, white with rage, and leaped for a sword-belt hanging on the wall. But the Scraeling was quicker, and a dagger slammed into the wall by the sword-hilt an instant before Morcar's hand snatched at it, and the earl froze.

"That's the one from my boot, Morcar" said the Scraeling into the silence. "Now listen carefully. Osmund has a dagger, so you're welcome to mine, 'cause I'm a fair man too. But soon's you touch that sword, you'll get my other knife as well – anywhere you like. Got a preference?"

"What the fuck's going on here?" came a roar from the doorway, and Hereward strode into the hall. "Morcar! What's —"

"This little bastard jumped me!" snarled Morcar, still white, "And he—"

"He *jumped* you? What's going on? Osmund?"

"I did" returned Osmund, his eyes never leaving Morcar. "Then I kicked his arse, hard as I could, four times. But I shouldn't have. I should've offered my men that pleasure. Sorry, Ossa. Sorry, boys."

"You ... kicked ... sorry? What in Christ's name are you talking about? Scraeling?"

So the Scraeling explained, briefly, and Hereward's eyes bulged. But before he could speak, Morcar found his tongue again.

"Hereward, I'm an earl of England and I've been manhandled. I want this—"

"No you're not" came another voice, and eyes turned to Siward. "You *were* an earl of England, Morcar, but you stopped being one when you abandoned the man who made you earl, to die at Senlac." There was a deathly hush in the room, for Siward rarely spoke in public.

"And then you shit on his memory – and your own honour" continued Siward into the silence, "when you knuckled under to the Bastard. *You*, that hated anything of Godwin, of the family that alone kept Norsemen and Normans from us. *You*, that raised the storm that drove Tostig Godwinsson from the land. *You*, that were made earl in his place. *You*, that were the most powerful man in England the day after Senlac. *You*, that held back his fighting men – for what? After Senlac, Morcar, *you* could have raised the Danelaw, declared for Edgar the true king, swept the Bastard from London and kicked his arse back to Normandy. But did you? Did you *buggery!*" Siward spat on the earth floor and continued in the hushed silence.

"If all that makes you an earl of England, Morcar, I'll give up my claim to that rank now. No – I'll go further. If *any* of that makes you an earl of England, I'll go and see the abbot about taking holy orders tonight. An earl? *You?* Earls lead fighting men, Morcar. Like Osmund did! I wouldn't ask you to lead the abbey's cows down the pasture, you sad little, sorry little, hopeless little coward!"

Long before he had finished, Morcar had turned white with fury, but Siward turned to where Hereward stood frozen.

"Hereward" he said, "this is your hall and I should have sought your permission to speak in it. I ask pardon for the haste of my tongue. But not for what it said. This earl of England holds that the young man here did your bidding at the risk of his life. This earl of England further holds that what Osmund did after was well enough merited. And that's my word if you want it."

Hereward shook himself like a dog emerging from water. "Not good enough Siward" he said, at length. "I don't know who did what to who before Senlac, because Edward banished me long before. Fact is, I don't care. *Now*'s what concerns me, and now we've fallen to fighting among ourselves."

"But there'll be no more of it" he said, meeting and holding Osmund's gaze and then Morcar's. "No more. If there's bad blood between you, I can't help it. But I won't suffer it either, because it doesn't help anything we do here. Stay away from each other – and if you can't do that, stay away from the Fenlands. Got it?"

The Chronicle.

*S*ince coming to the marsh I had often reflected that the two years between Stamford Bridge and my departure from Magnus' court were as if they had never been. That was my time with Elisabeth, a time when I had looked forward instead of back, when the joy I took in her love had driven away from me the wariness, the suspicion, the talent for plotting and scheming that had attended me since I was fifteen. But in my time in the marshes I had returned to weighing men's words, watching their faces as they spoke them and judging the motives behind them. In a word, I had returned to the dark side of men's natures, and it was what I saw in Morcar's face that led me to counsel Osmund to spend more time watching the Normans than with Hereward's band on the Isle of Refuge.

For his part, the young man flatly refused to go in fear of the earl or to defer to him in any way, but I had foreseen that and I couched the advice to him in terms of the part he and his skills could play in delaying and harassing the Norman advance across the swamp. And there I needed no support, for all could see the causeway creeping closer and closer with each passing day so that I began to wonder if our raid had achieved any purpose. For all the weight of the great castle and the crashing and shaking that went on within it, the causeway appeared as solid as ever as it inched forward and the roadway that would bring the Norman infantry grew ever longer. And there was no moment, by night or by day, when an attack of any sort by the defenders of the Isle might have succeeded, for Morcar's first attempt upon it had removed all cover that once existed.

There came the day when the probing arms of the causeway entered the shallows where the Isle rose from the marsh bottom, and we knew our days were numbered.

The Isle of Refuge, mid–June 1071.

"Knee-deep" said Ossa as they watched the work. "I reckon they'll stop at knee-depth and build a ramp. What d'you say Osmund?"

"Yes" said Osmund, "agreed. They'll want to get ashore quickly, and I wouldn't be surprised if they flung a troop of cavalry ashore first."

"Cavalry? You think so?" came a new voice and the young man turned to see Hereward behind him.

"I think so" he said. "Put yourself in their place – last thing you want is to get stuck on a narrow front with all your men behind you. They've always had the numbers; we've always had the ground. They've turned that around now – that causeway's given them the ground." He was silent a moment and then "It's like my father's spear-bearer said about Senlac. Once the Norman cavalry got onto the ridge, that was it. Our turn now."

"Maybe not" said the Scraeling. "They had nowhere to go at Senlac. We've got the marsh behind us, don't forget. By the time the Normans get here we can be long gone. There're other places in the marsh where we can regroup. Make them do it all over again?"

Hereward grunted. "We can't argue with their cavalry" he said, "that's certain. I'm not even sure we can argue with the numbers of foot they'll bring ashore. Wants thinking about."

As if you haven't been thought the Scraeling, but aloud he said, "Sooner rather than later, I'd say. I'd give it two days at the most – the very most – before that castle's sitting on our bank."

Aldreth, the same day.

"Tomorrow, messire" said Waleis, "definitely."

Leo raised an eyebrow. "You sure of that?" and the other nodded.

"No error" he said. "The castle'll be ashore tomorrow. And that leaves you to say what's coming out of it when the front drops down and makes the ramp."

Leo nodded. "Your troop for a start, Waleis" he said. "You've taken this all the way through, and it's only right you should have the honour of leading us ashore. Behind you, three hundred infantry – Norman, Breton, and Flemish mercenaries. They're ready, and they've been ready for days. That'll give you the numbers, and the cavalry will give you the shock power."

It was Waleis' turn to nod. "Right enough" he said. "I'll take holy orders if they stand against that. Where're the rest of us going?"

"Odo's got his troop and mine along the edges of the marsh where we agreed the Saxons'll come out" he said. "Y'see, we don't expect them to stand against you – fact is, we don't believe they can. They'll break, all right, and scatter. And when they come out of the marsh . . . only problem we have is judging where those exit points'll be. That's why I've kept two troops on firm ground."

"Now – I'm staying here with the reserve and a section of gallopers. I want this to be your operation, Waleis, because the king'll be grateful. We all know this is the last of it, and bloody hard work it's been since Senlac – but this is it. Tomorrow night, England will be William's – and the men who did it will be barons soon after, mark my words."

Ely Abbey.

"They're here" said Wulfstan. "Well, all but here. And the talk is that Hereward's not going to stand."

"Not going to stand?" repeated Thurstan, "Not going to stand? He'll surrender?"

"No" said Wulfstan, "he'll run's what I hear. So there'll be no battle."

"Run?" asked Thurstan, "Where to?"

"Do we care?" asked Wulfstan, "No battle means we welcome the Normans with open arms. No battle means this abbey and what treasures it has left is safe. No battle means reconciliation with the king – and he is the king, Thurstan, no matter what the likes of Edgar the Aetheling and Hereward say, because Senlac is long behind us and William's the power in the land. The only power in the land. You agree?"

"Aye, I agree" said Thurstan. "Surely this is the sign we sought, Wulfstan. God has answered our prayers and revealed His mind to us."

"Amen, father" replied Wulfstan, and Thurstan was too delighted at having the decision made for him to notice any irony whatever in his deputy's voice.

The next day.

The causeway stretched towards the Isle like a great serpent, just as it had for days, but today it was alive with mailed men, shields raised to deflect the shafts that sailed towards them in desperation rather than hope.

"Feel that?" asked Skuli of no-one in particular, and around him heads nodded. The concussion of the great pile-drivers could be felt through the ground, and the Scraeling turned to Hereward.

"Well, leader? We've got an hour, I reckon, and then— "

But Hereward didn't even glance at him. "Look there" he said, gesturing towards the far end of the causeway. "My imagination, or . . . yes! Again!" and the Scraeling followed his pointing hand.

"Look at the right-hand edge, there . . . y'see? It's shifting – it's bloody shifting! Tell me I'm . . ." and even as he spoke the causeway lurched, settled and lurched again.

From the causeway there came a babble of sound that contrasted with the grim silence that had until then accompanied the inching progress of the causeway. There came the scream of a trumpet as it cut through the chorus of shouts and for a moment all was still until the causeway lurched again, bringing another tumult of noise, and this time the whinnies and screams of horses unsettled at the trembling of the ground beneath their feet. Then the trumpet split the air again and again, in the same call.

"That's their 'Retire'!" said one of Ossa's companions.

"Eh? You sure?" asked the man beside him, and the other spat.

"Heard it all fucking day at Senlac, didn't I?" he said. " 's the 'Retire' all right."

From the far end of the causeway there came a mighty groan and the watchers on the Isle saw the causeway tip slowly sideways as the rails slid from the bearers that held them and the shouts of the men on the causeway turned into screams as the outer ranks slid helplessly over the edge. The roadway rippled down its entire length as it twisted like an enormous snake and threequarters of its length slid sideways from its piles to crash down into the waters, taking its burden of armoured men with it. For a moment the left-hand edge resisted the tremendous pull of the twisting roadway, then piles came surging from the marsh-bed under that irresistible force and the whole roadway turned over, flinging men and horses into the marsh in a shouting, screaming mass.

"You must've missed cutting that last tie, Osmund" remarked the Scraeling into the awe-struck silence of the watchers, "Shame on you – knew I should've gone with you!"

"Archers!" shouted Hereward, "Now's your time!" and flight after flight of shafts whistled towards the men – the very few men – who struggled to the surface, and one by one as the shafts found their mark they sank again until nothing living moved on the surface of the Ely swamp.

Inside the castle.

Bedlam reigned as the destriers, terrified at what they could feel through their great feet, plunged and reared in panic.

"Dismount! Dismount!" screamed Waleis. "Horses' heads! Their heads!" And his troopers flung themselves from the saddle down among the flailing feet and threw all their weight on the bridles of their mounts to drag the head down in a madness of screaming, kicking horses and shouting men. From the rear ranks two chargers broke loose, turned and leapt headlong into the swamp dragging their riders with them, mailed feet skidding helplessly on the timber flooring, through the reins wrapped round their straining forearms. For long, long moments it was touch and go as to whether or not the others would follow, but gradually the horses quietened and the commander could look back through the castle to the outside.

What he saw appalled him. The castle was on its own, the causeway behind it for as far as he could see almost totally under the murk of the Ely swamp with nothing moving on the surface of the water.

Fuck thought Waleis, *what now? Defence – limit the damage.* He fought down the urge to giggle as the thought occurred to him that there was precious little left to damage, and that— "Orders, messire?" came his second, and Waleis blinked.

"Horses held in threes" he snapped into the silence. "Everyone else, get those piles dragged across the rear – form a barrier, make it high. Move!" But before any could move, a voice came from the outside in perfect French with a Breton accent.

"In the castle, there! How many, and who commands?"

Waleis paused, irresolute, and the voice came again. "If you cause me to come and find out for myself, I'll bring four boatloads of archers to help me ask the question. Once again – how many, and who commands?"

Waleis raised his voice. "Twelve troopers. Waleis de Sambry in command" *and how he wishes he wasn't* he thought bitterly.

"I see the front wall of your castle is designed to drop" came the voice. "Listen carefully, and live. First, remove your hauberks and put your weapons to one side – the left side as you face the front. Next, send your horses to the rear, held by three troopers. Third, release the front wall and send it down. Finally – repeat my instructions now."

Seething, Waleis did so and the voice replied, "Excellent, messire de Sambry. Carry out my instructions."

The Norman side of the swamp.

Leo's tongue was stuck to the roof of his mouth in horror. *Oh Jesus* he thought. *Sweet Jesu, this can't have happened. It can't.* He stared out across the swamp to where he could see right through the castle, sitting crouched on what was left of the causeway. *A half-troop of horse and two hundred foot-soldiers* he thought, and his mind struggled to comprehend it. *Gone. Fucking gone.*

"Thank God you held the last third back, Walter" he said to the grim-faced Breton beside him, and his own words seemed to come from far away.

"They should've been on the causeway" said his commander, "And they would've been if Mesnille had been able to make up his mind about their order of march. So I suppose you could say it was just another fuck-up, messire."

"One that went in our favour" said Leo bleakly. "Just for a change."

Ely Abbey.

"Well, brethren" said Wulfstan as the door closed solidly behind the second of the two monks. "Have you reflected upon my counsel to you?"

The two looked at each other for a second before the shorter turned to Wulfstan, his jaw set and thrusting upwards.

"We have considered it, Prior Wulfstan – and we have rejected it."

"Have you so?" said Wulfstan mildly. "And your vow of obedience?"

"Does not apply to God's manifest will, Prior" cut in the other. "It cannot, for is not God's will revealed to all?"

"Certainly not" came back Wulfstan, "for were that so, what need would there be for such as we? Do we not minister to those who cannot know the word of God for themselves? Tell me that?"

"Yes, Prior" said the first, "most certainly. But those are common folk, after all, who have not had the will of God revealed to them through knowledge of the scriptures, prayer, fasting and learned discourse. As have we."

Wulfstan barked a laugh. "I see your vow of humility sits as lightly as your vow of obedience. Very well. Let me summarise what I know of the revelations made you by God, shall I?"

"First – you hold that God gave the land into William's hand at Senlac, and that the Holy Father's banner that they carried was a sign of that. Next, and since that is so, rebellion against the Normans is rebellion against God's will. Third, that our support of Hereward and the blessing we give him defies God and His will. As does defiance of the lawful king. And that, for all these reasons, the brethren of this abbey should submit themselves to the king's majesty. Yes?"

The two looked at each other before the taller turned back to Wulfstan's raised eyebrow and nodded. *Jesu, he's arrogant* thought the older man. *When I was his age a word from Prior Athelstan was an order, not a suggestion. Different world today.*

"So" he said reflectively. "Has it occurred to you – either of you – that the more than two hundred hardened rebels in the Isle of Refuge not half a mile away might have something to say about your determination to carry God's will into effect? Eh?"

"You see, God has us work His will through fallible, weak, ordinary men. Men who don't have our advantages – you know, 'knowledge of the scriptures, prayer, fasting and learned discourse', I think you termed them. With a little more experience" he said, unable to resist it, "you'll come to know that reality must always temper God's will. No, get that look off your face – it's not blasphemy, and I'm your superior under God and in this abbey. So get used to it."

The two monks lowered their heads submissively, but Wulfstan could easily imagine the black looks on their faces. "As it happens" he continued, "that's what I want to talk to you about. Pragmatism. Reality. Something much more ordinary than your interpretation of God's will. Or my interpretation. Or even Abbot Thurstan's interpretation." The heads came up, the faces clearly puzzled.

"Now I've got your attention" said Wulfstan slowly, "I need to say that the most important thing in all this is the abbey and the work it does among the people of the Fenlands. This house holds St Etheldreda's legacy. It has done for four hundred years, and if we don't carry it forward for another four hundred, it's not going to be our fault. When the Normans storm the Isle – and they will – they're going to carry all before them. In the heat of battle there's going to be no difference between monks, rebels and stray dogs. They'll kill everyone here and burn anything standing. Including this abbey if they need to, or if the rebels give them cause."

"So" he finished, "your way is the right one. Not" he added as the two young men smiled at each other, "because you interpret God's will more accurately than your betters, but because it's the sensible thing to do. Sensible for reasons much less lofty than yours, but sensible all the same."

"But that doesn't excuse your presumption in this matter" he went on, "and because of it I'm going to award you a penance that'll bring home to both of you what humility and obedience really mean. However – I'm prepared to remit that penance if you serve the abbey and its guardians as they want. And 'as they want' is up to *my* interpretation, not yours; got that?"

"Now listen carefully. Tomorrow, you're going out of the swamp to visit the Norman camp. Why? To hear confessions, should you trip over any of Hereward's rebels on the way. But as well you're going to carry a message to the Norman leadership and seek a meeting, and this is what you'll tell them . . ."

The Isle of Refuge.

"This won't finish it, you know" said the Screaling. "William can't afford to let bygones be bygones, and certainly not after losses like that. He'll be pushing his local commander for results harder than ever."

"So where'll he go from here?" asked Osmund, "Build another causeway?"

The Screaling pursed his lips. "Unlikely" he said. "Those Normans died horribly, and from what I know about soldiering, he'll struggle to get men onto another causeway. No – but put yourself in his place. What would you do?"

Osmund thought a moment, and said, "Boats. I'd bring a fleet of boats and cross the swamp that way – right along where the causeway ran."

"Yes?" said the Scraeling. "What makes the Normans different from us, Osmund? Think!"

"Numbers" frowned Osmund, "and . . . oh. I see. Cavalry. And you can't put horses in boats. Yes, got it uncle."

"So what's left?" asked the Scraeling, and the young man frowned again.

"Well, he can't float; he can't swim, and he can't bloody fly! That only leaves a land approach. But we've got that covered. Ossa and his men know the safe trails, and we're guarding those."

"Yes" said the Scraeling enigmatically. "But Ossa isn't the only one who knows the trails, is he? Look, cast your mind back to when we came to the swamp after we left Reading. Who did we see in the camp then, that we never see now?"

"No" said Osmund after a moment. "You'll have to tell me, uncle. Who?"

"The monks of Ely Abbey" said the Scraeling. "When did you last see Thurstan or any of his brethren?"

"Hardly surprising, is it?" returned Osmund. "Not after Hereward took the abbey's treasure for safe keeping then let the Danes bugger off with it."

"That's one way of putting it" admitted the Scraeling. "Hereward's a fighter rather than a thinker, I do admit."

"So . . . the monks?" asked Osmund and the Scraeling spread his hands.

"Just a feeling" he answered slowly. "The longer it takes William to crush Hereward, the more severe he's likely to be on anything – or anyone – he finds here. We've already agreed that this place isn't going to be home to us for much longer. Maybe others have come to the same conclusion. Only yesterday, with the causeway coming closer and closer, we were talking about scattering into the marsh. The monks can't run. Well, they can – but their abbey can't. And they know the secret trails."

"And Hereward will be William's price for sparing the abbey?" Osmund said, and the Scraeling nodded.

"More than likely" he said, "if Hereward doesn't make his peace with William first. We've discussed that, if you recall. And if he does, or if they do, the Normans will want to make a few examples. Probably more than a few. And if anyone finds out who you are . . . Reading isn't so far away cross-country, you know."

"Osmund, I'm going to suggest to Skuli that it's time to bring up *Nordvedr*. And until that's done and she's ready, I think you, Ossa and all your clever men need to be watching the secret trails as never before. I really do."

Aldreth, the next day.

The monks walked towards the man who'd challenged them and stopped before the levelled spear.

"God's peace upon you, my son" said the taller of the two. "There's no need for the weapon."

"You let me worry about that and just stand there" said the outpost before he called "Sergeant!" over his shoulder.

"Who's this?" asked the sergeant, himself a veteran of Hastings. "And what d'they want?"

"Just two humble clerics who speak your language and have come to hear confessions. We're not important" said the monk, "and certainly not as important as the person who sent us. With a message for your officer. Your commanding officer, that is."

"Messire St Brieuc?" scoffed the sergeant, "He don't want to be wasting his time with you. Gimme the message." And he held out his hand.

"Can't" said the monk, tapping his head, "It's in here, and I've no permission to tell you what it is. Even if I thought it was a good idea – which I don't. But what I am told to tell you is – it'll be the worse for you if you don't let us through to – Messire St Brieuc, was it? My son" and he smiled.

The sergeant hesitated. The instincts of a lifetime's soldiering told him not to mess with this one. "You'll need to be searched first" he said. "Don't know who you are or what you're up to, do I?"

Both monks smiled again and the shorter raised his hand. "Of course. Bless you, my son."

Two days later.

Half an hour until dark, maybe a bit more Osmund thought. *Give it two hours after that until the start of moonrise, then Ossa's boys'll be on the job.* He knew that full darkness made the marsh too dangerous to move in, even for the men of the swamp, so he allowed himself a moment's contemplation of the dish of eel that he knew awaited him on his return after dark. Then he shrugged himself back into concentration on moving away from the stillness of the lake and silently through the long marsh grass towards the slope of the hill before him.

He was alone, performing one of the extra patrols he had promised the Scraeling he would make from the moment of their conversation onwards. *No real need for it* he thought, but he knew what lay behind the wily Breton's suggestion, and deep within himself the young man acknowledged that it was better he and Morcar pursued separate paths for as long as the swamp was home to them both.

What irritated him beyond measure about Morcar, he realised, was the earl's assumption that all would defer to him because of who he was – who he had been – Osmund corrected himself. That, in turn, led him into the sort of action for which Osmund had punished him the other night. *Funny how you can expect obedience and loyalty one minute and show none yourself,* thought the young man. *Morcar's never shown those qualities in anything I know about him – not to King Harold, or to the Bastard even; certainly not to Hereward or his men. He's just a—* and he froze at the jingle and clink of a horse's harness from beyond the crest now only five yards ahead of him.

Dropping to the ground he slid through the grass and into the shelter of a scrub-oak that clung to the top of the ridge. From there he slid up to a bush on the crown of the ridge and raised his head to look over the top from beneath the bush.

Below him, in the lee of a stand of alder and oak, stood three Norman cavalrymen, their mounts held by another off to one side. Even as he watched, the middle horse stamped and flung up its head so that the soldier holding the horses spoke soothingly to it and patted its muzzle. *Sandflies* thought Osmund absently, as he took in the fact that the Norman standing slightly in front of the group was deep in conversation with three black-robed monks.

Can't hear them thought Osmund *and no chance of getting closer. Still – don't need to. Uncle Ranulf was* — then a crushing weight hit him across the small of his back and light exploded inside his head.

In the clearing.

"No" said Leo. "My word on it, father. More importantly, the king's word on it too. There'll be no punishment – after all, what could you do against—-" He was hurled sideways as Odo jumped in front of him, the *skreek* of his blade coming from its scabbard echoing in his ears.

"Messire!" from the hilltop that had just exploded in front of them, and Odo's arm across his chest.

"Sergeant? Report! Sergeant!" from Odo and another hail from the top.

"Bandit, messire. One only. Shall I bring him down?"

"Hold your position! I'll come to you. Messire?" to Leo.

"What's all this about, Wulfstan?" demanded Leo, his own blade in his hand, but the shock on the prior's face was its own answer. "Go, Odo" he commanded. "Nothing to fear down here. Go!" and Odo set off up the hill at a run.

At the top Odo found his sergeant kneeling beside a body in the grass below a scrub-oak, and another trooper making his way across the hillside from where he too had overlooked the meeting-place below. Odo glanced round in the failing light before he knelt by the body.

"Who the hell's this then?" he asked, and the sergeant shrugged.

"Dunno messire" he answered, " 'Cept he was takin' it all in. What you and the monks was up to down below, like. I watched 'im from up the tree here, then I jumped 'im. Did I do right? Thought that's what I was here for?"

"You did right" said Odo and knelt to look at the thin trickle of blood oozing from the man's head, just above the ear. "What'd you hit him with?"

"Me fist" said the sergeant, holding up a hand encased in a battle gauntlet, "hard's I could – he's a big bugger, an' I didn't want him getting up."

"Agreed" said Odo, pulling off his own gauntlet and feeling for a pulse in the side of the neck. "He's still alive. You" to the other trooper, "get down there and bring up a hobbling line – no, two – and tell messire it's under control. Go!" and as the man hurried away, he turned back to the sergeant.

205

"Why didn't you kill him?" he demanded and the man looked uneasy.

"Thought of it, but then— well messire, then . . . I thought . . . might be as well to know what he knows, like, what them buggers in the – beg pardon – in the swamp're up to. Didn't know he wasn't part of them monks neither. I c'n top him if you like? Shall I cut 'is throat?"

"No sergeant" said Odo. "You did well, very well. Consider yourself attached to my troop from now on. I can always use someone who thinks like you do. Well done."

"Thank you messire. Thanks very much" said a relieved sergeant, flexing an aching fist.

The Isle of Refuge, that night.

"Take your time Osbert" said the Scraeling, fighting down the urge to scream at the man. "Just take your time and tell me everything. Start at the beginning now." *Of all the men in this camp*, he thought, *it has to be Osbert the Simple*. He smiled encouragingly at the man and Osbert smiled his vacant smile back.

"Well, lord, I fancied fish y'see. Hasn't had fish f'r ever so long, an' I thought t'myself, I thought, 'Osbert' I thought, 'why'n't you go an' catch one? Maybe two, 'cause 'f I gets two I c'n give one to Leofe. Y'know Leofe? Her's the widow . . . ah . . . y'know— "

Sweet Jesus thought the Scraeling, *I'll strangle him in a minute.* He smiled at Osbert. "Anyway, Osbert. Did you get your fish then?"

"Oh aye, lord. Lotsa things old Osbert can't do, but he c'n always get fish. Three, I got; a lamprey'n two perch. Gave 'em all to Leofe I did, but if y'd like one, lord . . . ?"

"No thank you Osbert. I've eaten. But what's this you told Skuli about Osmund?"

"Who?" and the Scraeling's fingers flexed involuntarily.

"Skuli" he said, slowly and patiently. "Skuli. You know, big Skuli the Norseman? You told him something about Osmund. You know Osmund, don't you?"

"Osmund?" grinned the simpleton, " 'Course I knows Osmund. Was there when he kicked that feller's arse f'r sitting in 'is seat, I was. Rare turn-up that!" he chuckled.

"Yes, that Osmund" said the Scraeling, still patiently. "Did you see Osmund today?"

"Aye. By the lake. Y'know, the lake where I got the fish? Just coming home I was – did I tell you I got three— "

"Yes, you told me that. Well done Osbert. But did you speak to Osmund?"

"Speak to him? No, lord, didn't speak to him. Dunno if he saw me" he went on, "because he was busy with some other fellas he was. Normans an' monks, y'see."

The Scraeling's mouth went dry. "Normans and monks, Osbert? Tell me about those."

Osbert chuckled. "Terrible man for fighting, that Osmund" he said. "Tooken on too many t'day though. Knocked 'im about something awful they did. Wasn't fair, though, him with's hands tied like they was. An' him havin' t'walk behind the horses too. No, wasn't fair."

The world spun about the Scraeling and he had to close his eyes. When he spoke, his voice seemed to come from far away. "He was walking behind the Norman horses?" he asked, and Osbert's simple "Aye" was like a death sentence.

Aldreth, that night.

"Doesn't say much, does he?" said the guard to his companion as they looked at an Osmund collapsed, fettered and chained to the corner-post of a forage shed.

"Might when he wakes up" suggested the other. "Blacksmith's forge's still lit, an' there's a coupla handy fire-irons there too."

But Osmund was already awake, determined to hold down the pounding waves of pain that coursed through every part of him from the beating he'd received after Odo's troopers had hustled him, semi-conscious and bound, down the hill. Then the nightmare walk back to the Norman camp behind Odo's gelding, when he'd staggered, fallen, been dragged and fought to his feet so that he'd been glad enough to collapse at the foot of the pole where they'd hurled him for the armourer to do his work. The sentries' coarse laughter receded and he opened his eyes to squint through eyelashes gummed together with blood, fighting back the urge to groan.

Slowly, and without moving his head too quickly or too far, he took in the details of his prison. The forage shed was about twelve paces by eight, he estimated, and its flimsy construction of reed screens showed how hastily it had been built. He might have pushed the whole thing over, he realised – yesterday. But that night he was constrained by his injuries and the fetters on his feet. Not to mention the stout chain, too short to allow him to rise, that was shackled back to a corner-post. And there was no eyelet that might be wrenched free, for the chain was looped round the post. No – Osmund realised that he'd be there until the post came out of the ground or he was unlocked, and the young man bit back another groan.

He fought to clear a head that had received an undue share of punishment that day, and through the mists of pain and despair he determined on two things – he would feign unconsciousness as long as possible, and after he was woken he'd conceal his knowledge of French for it was the only weapon he had. It might even work to his advantage, he told himself, because it was time something did.

The Isle of Refuge.

Osmund's taken. Osmund's taken went through the Scraeling's head like the pounding of waves on a rocky shore, and he fought despair and fear in equal measure. *Think* he told himself. *Think, you fool. You were cunning enough to send him out to the swamp to avoid Morcar – be cunning enough to get the boy out of the danger you got him into.*

He paced the ground beside the hall in his dragging, lurching gait, oblivious to the curious stares of those who had heard Osbert's story but who were deterred by the scowls of Skuli's Norsemen from approaching him. *He'll be close-guarded, almost certainly. After the carnage of the swamp, the Normans won't hold back. What would you do in his place?*

He would, the Scraeling decided, keep his mouth shut as much as he could for as long as he could. What, after all, could the Normans hope for from one as obviously young as Osmund? But there was danger in that also, for if they decided he was of no use to them they were likely to cut his throat out of hand. And the only way of heading that off was for help to arrive quickly.

Well that's all right then thought the Scraeling with self-loathing. *But how, you bloody apology for a kinsman? How? Options?* he thought. *A night raid.* No. Too well-guarded. *But Ossa's men can move through the swamp like creatures of the night.*

Yes. But what then? If Osmund's guarded, he's likely to be chained. *I'd chain anyone as big and powerful as him.* How long would it take to free him? And how many men? The Normans were there in force.

An exchange, then. They had Waleis de Sambry, and the Scraeling had taken him. But would Hereward agree? *Bugger Hereward.* If push came to shove, Skuli's vikings would deal with him and his closest. *Promising, yes . . .*

Hang on. The Normans would surely wonder what was important enough about a young man who – hopefully – hadn't opened his mouth because he had nothing to tell, to warrant exchange for a Norman soldier of rank. Wouldn't they?

No. Better not to draw attention, for the Normans to think Osmund's—

"I'm telling you, Morcar, fuck off! An' I won't tell you a third time! My chief's busy, right?" Skuli's tones broke in on the Scraeling's reverie, and he blinked his way back to the clearing.

"And I can imagine why!" crowed Morcar, turning away. Then he saw the Scraeling frowning at him and he called past Skuli, "Scraeling, I hear your young hero's fighting the Normans all by himself again. Shame he hasn't got someone to take the heat off him this time, eh? Shame he hasn't got anyone at all. Maybe all he needs is a confessor. Reckon he'll get one?" and he swaggered off laughing.

Skuli growled, stepped after him and the Scraeling called him back. "Not today, Skuli, but soon's— " and he stopped, for an idea had blossomed in his head.

Skuli looked at him. "Soon's . . . what?" he demanded.

"Mmm? Oh . . . ah . . . soon's you can, Skuli, I want you and the boys to turn this place inside out to find me something. And when you've found it, I want you to go and see Hereward. Tell him this— "

And what he said next brought a muttered "Odin's balls! You sure?" from the viking, and an emphatic "Oh yes. I'm sure" from the Scraeling.

Aldreth the next morning.

The monk lurched towards the man who'd challenged him and stopped before the levelled spear.

"God's peace upon you, my son" he said. "There's no need for the weapon."

The sentry sighed. Another dreamer. "Told you before – no. No, I didn't. Wasn't you. He was taller" he said, peering into the black hood. "Anyways. You want t'see my officer I s'pose?"

"Indeed, my son" said the monk with a smile. "If you'd be so— "

"Well, you're in luck. He's here, on rounds." He raised his voice. "Messire Mortain!"

Odo stepped from the simply-built hut fifty yards away, a bowl in his hand, and squinted into the light. "Yes?"

"One o' the monks t'see you, messire. Shall I send 'im down?"

"No, bring him. You're relieved, and there's food ready."

"There y'go" said a happy sentry. "You're good luck you are, friend."

The monk smiled again. "Happy to be of service" he said, and fell in beside the sentry to walk down to the hut with his shuffling, lurching gait. He nodded to the man who came out to take the other's place on watch.

Odo finished his bowl and walked towards them. "D'you bring a message father?" he asked, "From the abbey?"

Well, well . . . thought the monk at the question. "No, my son. But there will be one today" he replied. "It's a . . . a personal matter that brings me."

Odo's face clouded. "Oh. Well, let's hear it. I'm sure Messire St Brieuc will give it full consideration."

The monk hesitated. "It's . . . ah . . . it's a personal matter, my son. As I said."

"Father" said Odo patiently, "understand that my commander's a busy man. And you'd know how and why better than anyone. We've just lost two hundred men, and in two nights' time we're coming through the swamp, so there's to be no more cock-ups. I'm his second, and it's my job to keep the little things off his back so he can see to the big things. Once again – what d'you want?"

"Yes" said the flustered monk. "Yes, I'm sure you can help me, but I thought . . . it's about the prisoner, you see . . . a prisoner, that is . . . and I thought the commander – Messire St Brieuc . . . it is 'St Brieuc' you said, isn't it? I thought he'd be the one to see?"

Good God thought Odo, *this one's in a rare sweat. Wonder why?* "Yes, father" he said, "It's Messire St Brieuc. What's this about a prisoner?"

"He was taken yesterday" said the monk. "Tall young man, dark-haired, big across the shoulders."

"I know" said Odo. "I was there. He was spying for the swamp-men. Y'know, Hereward's boys."

"No" said the monk. "No, he wasn't. He was out wildfowling. Wildfowling and gathering plover eggs."

Odo looked at him and lifted an eyebrow. "What d'you take me for?" he asked. "I saw all he had with him. No snares, and he couldn't have been expecting to get many plover eggs – unless he was going to carry them in his pockets. Fact is, all he was carrying was a big, ugly dagger. How'd you explain that?" *What the fuck's his interest?* he asked himself.

The monk shifted uneasily. "Well, he was sent out to check the snares and collect eggs." Then, in a rush, "Look, the boy's simple, you see. Has been all his life. Took sick as a baby and nearly died. Fever. Brain fever. When he came out of it . . . well, his body grew, but his mind . . . didn't."

Odo glanced down at him. "Father, what's your interest in him? I'm not going to bother Messire St Brieuc unless I hear something better'n that."

The monk dropped his gaze, a foot came from beneath his robe and he scuffed one sandal in the dust. With his head down he said, almost inaudibly, "I'm his father."

"Of course you are" said Odo. "You're everyone's father. So what?"

"No" said the little monk. "No – ah, you don't understand. I'm really his father. That is, his mother and I . . . ah, her family lived in the swamp. They still do. And I . . . I'm their confessor. Have been these many years. And, well . . . it was long ago, and I was . . . we both were younger then; not sure if I'm making sense— "

He broke off in the face of Odo's laughter. "You dirty little bugger!" he crowed cheerfully. "If *bugger*'s the right word. Warned her about sin, did you, then showed her what not to do? Well, I never! Might take holy orders myself!"

The monk flushed crimson. "My son, I've made my peace with God over it . . ."

Thurstan doesn't know! exulted Odo. *One of his monks has been dipping his wick in secret all these years, and he doesn't know!* Aloud, he said, "How did you find out what'd happened to the boy, father?"

"Ah . . . another hunter, my son. He saw the boy taken and led away. He went to the family, and they came to me. Understandably, his mother's frantic. I . . . I undertook to try and get him back. He's harmless, you know – he really is."

"Don't know about that, father. Seems to me he's got a question or two to answer first, eh?" returned Odo as he pretended deep thought. *How can we use this randy monk and his little secret?* he asked himself. *Do we need a little squeeze where Thurstan's concerned? Well, we don't know that we don't . . . but up to Leo, I think.* "All right father. Think I can understand that, but I'll have to move it up to my commander."

"Messire St Brieuc?" asked the monk, an odd note in his voice.

"Yes. Messire St Brieuc. If that's all right with you" said Odo with heavy irony.

"Of course, my son. Of course. God bless you for your understanding" said the Scraeling, raising his hand.

The Chronicle.

*W*hen *I heard Odo's words it seemed to me for the first time in years that God had relented and come over to our side. I had found my way in, because people rarely change, and in this case one person's readiness to believe the worst of another opened a door for me. Often enough in the markets of Constantinople I'd managed to sell amber for much more than its worth by representing it as having been obtained through deception, cunning or even outright theft – "That's why it's cheap, see?" had been my line, and only rarely had it failed me.*

Yes, well. I might have presented myself as Osmund's family priest, or his confessor, or even as a representative of the abbey looking after a parishioner in trouble – and been solidly rebuffed by a soldier who cared for none of these things. But Odo's weakness for the salacious had persuaded him that he was better than the forsworn, sinful and broken reed he'd decided I was – and who suspects that which he derides? Thank God for the sanctimonious, and thank God also for those who love to judge themselves superior to others around them – for we all do, you know.

So I was in. I would be allowed to see Osmund, and I'd be amazed if I couldn't manage to pass him some instructions under the guise of blessing him in English. But another idea was nibbling away at the back of my head, and it had come from something Odo said, so I suffered his stream of ribald quips about ministering to the varied and various needs of the abbey's parishioners in what I hoped he thought was an embarrassed silence. I thought furiously as he rode and I walked along the way to Norman headquarters.

Headquarters, Aldreth field command.

Odo came from Leo's office and gestured to the Scraeling. "Messire St Brieuc will see you" he said. "He's doing you a favour – he's a busy man. We're both busy men, so I'm not staying" and he strode past, waving away the monk's thanks and forbearing to mention that, like him, Leo had concluded that the monk's secret might well be useful if their dealings with the abbey looked like turning sour.

From behind his table Leo looked up at the black-robed monk, who leaned on his staff and looked back at him with every sign of interest. "My second tells me you've an interest in our prisoner, father" he said.

"Yes, messire. In fact, I want him back" said the monk, and Leo's brows came together.

"Oh do you?" he said, aware that the monk was still looking at him oddly. "And why?"

"We're related" said the monk. "Apart from which, he's got nothing you want."

"You think so?" *This the bloke Odo described as nervous and shifty? Doesn't look or sound much like it – but Odo's hardly ever wrong.* "And just what d'you think I want?" he asked with an edge to his voice.

"I think you want Hereward, and I can give him to you" said the monk, and Leo sat up abruptly. "If I'm right, of course. Want him?"

Leo's mouth opened, then shut again while the monk looked at him, still with that odd look on his face. At last Leo found his voice. "I'm going to get Hereward anyway, you cheeky little bugger" he said, "and I don't need you to do it."

"Yes you do" said the monk, peering at him again. "You won't get him going in through the trails the monks know, not as long's your arse points

213

downwards. Why not? Because a clever little friend of mine called Ossa's got those trails covered. And a few more sorted out for the band to scatter through the swamp. And then you'll have to start again. All over again. Won't the Bastard just love that, on top of your recent butcher's bill? By the way, Waleis de Sambry is well and unhurt, and he sends greetings"

"Who are you?" Leo managed. "Who the *fuck* are you?"

"Well, I'm not a monk. Good job too, in view of your language" smiled the man who leaned still on his staff. "But we'll come to that. Don't you want to know how and why I'll give you Hereward?"

Leo scowled. "Go on then."

"Ah, you're that interested. Good. Well then, I can give you Hereward because Hereward wants to make his peace with the Conqueror. He's no hero, messire, for all they'll probably say and sing about him one day. But believe me, he isn't. He's not a driven man. He'll settle for his family lands, and peace to enjoy them. I know, because I'm well familiar with driven men."

"Really? Who?" snapped Leo, aware that this conversation was getting away from him.

"Three be enough?" The monk took a hand from the staff and raised three fingers in turn. "Harold Godwinsson. His brother, Tostig. And Hardraada. Heard of the Landwaster?"

"Of course I've heard of Hardraada. Everyone has – even you, obviously. Talk's cheap."

The monk nodded. "True, Messire St Brieuc. And if he's so well-known, you'll have heard of his secretary, the ah . . . let me see now . . . "

"The Scraeling" supplied Leo. "The man who kept his armies fed, clothed and mobile. Hardraada's chief adviser and right hand."

"Another of Odin's big, strong viking raven-feeders" nodded the monk, and Leo pounced.

"And that's all you know about Hardraada!" he snapped, springing to his feet, fists on the table. "The Scraeling was no warrior. He was a cripple!"

"He still is" returned the monk mildly, and he loosened the girdle at his waist to let the robe fall open. Leo found himself staring at a left leg that was stick-thin and so short that the big toe only just reached the ground when the man stood upright.

"Of course, usually I wear a shoe built up with a wooden foot" said the monk, "but it gets so heavy, sometimes I don't bother. Anyway" he went on, "that good enough for you? And you're being a bit harsh, by the way – I'm no axeman, but I'm no bunny either, even if I say so myself. I'm the Scraeling, Messire St Brieuc. You did ask who I was, I believe."

Leo sat down again, heavily.

"I can get you Hereward, messire" said the Scraeling. "I really can. With no further loss of life. That should appeal to someone who lost two hundred in the swamp the other day. shouldn't it?"

Leo's mind reeled. "You, who've been living in the enemy camp – you walk in here, telling my second some trumped-up story about being a renegade priest, then you claim to be Hardraada's lieutenant – next you'll be Christ himself, I shouldn't wonder! Offer me a reason why I should trust you to bring me Hereward?"

The Scraeling smiled, and straightened. "I'll offer you two if you like" he said, and his staff fell towards the table. Leo put up a hand to catch it, and when he looked back again there was a dagger gleaming under his nose.

"This's been on my forearm since I strapped it there this morning" said the Scraeling. "If I meant you any harm, messire, we'd have come to it before now." The dagger went from sight as quickly as it had appeared, and the Scraeling took his staff from Leo's nerveless hand with a word of thanks.

Leo swallowed, and his tongue felt huge. "And your second reason?" he asked, more for something to say than because he wished to know, but the reply jolted him upright.

"What's your family name, Messire St Brieuc?"

"Eh? What? My family name? Why?"

"Just a thought. If you'd be so kind – what is it?"

One of us is mad. Quite, totally, fucking mad thought Leo. *Why'm I doing this?* He heard himself say, from a hundred miles away, "De Lannion. I'm Leo de Lannion. Why, for Christ's sake?"

The Scraeling paused, light-headed at the thought of what he was about to do. "Because that's my second reason" he said. "I'm your uncle."

In a feeder creek of the Ely marsh.

"Careful, y'handless arseholes!" snapped Skuli, and Auti hid a grin. There was no careful way of bringing up a *drakkar* from where she'd lain hidden in the mud and water of a swamp, but Skuli's bark was from his love for the long and sleek form that had just broken the surface rather than for anyone's instruction. *Bet Skuli never looked after a woman like that* he thought, and grinned again.

"What're you grinning at, you clumsy piece of snot?" demanded Skuli and Auti lied brilliantly.

"Jus' happy to see the old girl again, Skuli" he said smoothly. "An' lookin' forward to feelin' the sea again, in her. Aren't you?"

Skuli grunted, mollified. "Well, watch what y're fuckin' doing anyway" he ordered, "Or we'll be patching holes 'fore we feel the sea. Heggr, Erik, rig lines bow 'n stern; rest of you, get started bailing."

"Shall I close the drain-cocks first?" asked Auti guilelessly, and Skuli flinched but recovered quickly and belligerently.

"Hasn't anyone done that?" he demanded, pop-eyed. "Odin's balls, you lot're as much use as tits on a bull! Where d'you keep ya brains, f'r . . ." He paused for breath and Auti moved in with a wink at his crony Heggr.

"Well, I would've skipper, but I'm such a clumsy piece of snot . . . thought I'd wait for the word from a real seaman. Know any?" and Heggr turned away, unable to keep back the guffaw.

"All right. All fucking right!" And Skuli swung a leg over the bulwark of his beloved *Nordvedr*. He paused, then turned back to say malevolently, "I'll close the bloody things myself, then I'll know it's done right! After you've rigged the lines, unlash the mast an' sweeps and check them over while she's being bailed. Think you can manage that?"

"No problem skipper. *We* haven't forgotten anything so far, have we Heggr? What's that? Oooohh, skipper . . . where'd you learn them nasty words!"

The Isle of Refuge, later that day.

"He's . . . he's done what?" demanded Hereward in disbelief, "What'd . . . say that again?"

"The Scraeling's gone into the Norman camp" said Skuli for the second time. "Dressed's a monk – one of them from the abbey. Found him the black robe m'self."

"Why?" asked a dazed Hereward, "What the fuck's he up to?"

"Told me to tell you that. He's sure the monks've sold us out t'the Normans, an' he thinks he c'n find out one way or the other. And besides – the Normans've got Osmund, remember. Anyway – something Osbert the Simple said when he told the Scraeling 'bout Osmund got him thinkin'. Don't ask me what, Hereward – the Scraeling's too deep for me. Soldiered with him thirty years I have, an' he still makes my head ache sometimes, he's that clever."

"Jesu, the way those Normans are about anything coming out of the swamp these days, he'd be safer pissing on a wasp's nest!" muttered Hereward, gnawing a thumbnail. "Give him any chance at all?"

"The Scraeling? Put money on him" said Skuli confidently. "Hardraada hisself used t' call him 'the most dangerous little bugger alive', an' he wasn't just talking about his cunning. I've seen him drop mailed men with arrows, knives an' throwing axes – never mind that fucking sling of his, too. Anything you can shoot, throw or launch, Hereward – an' if you've never noticed, he's got shoulders like an ox an' arms like knotted ropes. If he has t'fight his way out, I'd be sorry for the Normans trying t'stop him."

"Aye? Must say he's not my idea of a fighter, Skuli" replied Hereward, and the viking chuckled.

"That's 'cause all you see is the leg. Like most – all they see's what's wrong with him. Let me tell you, he'll come back with his dagger still in the sheath. He *enjoys* this sorta thing Hereward. Telling you – he'll talk his way in and talk his way out, an' he'll be pissed off if he has t'fight 'cause by his lights he's failed then. But lemme tell you – if he does hafta fight, the bugger he kills won't know he's dead 'til he shakes his head an' it falls off. Telling ya!"

Headquarters, Aldreth field command.

"You're . . . *what* did you . . . what the *fuck* d'you mean, you're my uncle?"

"Why not?" asked the Scraeling reasonably, "a moment ago you were prepared to believe I'd announce myself as Christ himself, I think you said. Why shouldn't I be your uncle?"

"Because . . . because you're the Scraeling. Hardraada's Scraeling. You said so!"

"Not that you believed that either!" said the Scraeling, his eyes twinkling.

"But Leo, I wasn't always Hardraada's Scraeling. I was born at St Brieuc, Brittany, and christened Ranulf Denis Chrétien Nominoe de Lannion. 'Ranulf' because I'm the first son of your grandfather Ranulf, Sieur de St Brieuc, and 'Nominoe' because his wife, Alice, is descended from the ancient kings of Brittany through Nominoe's line, and Ranulf has decreed that the Sieur's oldest son is always to carry that name. As you must know. Well, that was me. I'm the first."

"Christ's bones!" gasped Leo, staring at the other as if he were an apparition, and the Scraeling laughed.

"What, nephew, no 'Hello uncle'? Or a 'Pleased to meet you uncle?' Just 'Christ's bones'? Oh well. Family's family I suppose. Whose son are you? Let's see – Alan's? Roland's perhaps? Guinard's? Any more?"

"No. No more" muttered a white-faced Leo. "Guinard's my father."

"Now" mused the Scraeling, "Guinard'd be ... let's see ... born the same year they put me away, and that's when I was five, so he's, ah, fifty now. Yes? And who's Sieur – that'd be Alan wouldn't it?"

"No ... no – Alan's dead" returned a visibly shaken Leo. "Hunting accident – horse hit a wall, front legs, somersaulted, landed on him. The old man was still alive then. It broke his heart, my father told me – I was born the year he died. 1046."

"Not much luck with horses, our family" returned the Scraeling. "Know how I got this leg?"

Leo shook his head and the Scraeling said. "No matter. Tell you one day." A thought struck him. "Just by the way" he said, slipping into Breton, "did you know about me? Was I ever mentioned?"

Leo swallowed and reached for a wine-flask. His hand shook as he poured two cups. "No" he said in the same language. "And yes. I heard you mentioned, but no details. Just that you'd been afflicted by God, and returned to God. I had the idea you ... you were possessed, or had the falling sickness or something of the kind. And when father was ten, the vikings struck Les Trois Etoiles, and you disappeared. They said masses for your soul ... the whole thing. He said grandmother grieved terribly."

The Scraeling sniffed. "Shame the heartless old bitch hadn't grieved a bit earlier and kept me at St Brieuc after the accident they banished me for" he said, "and perhaps I'd still be there today. But if I were" he said, raising his cup to Leo, "I wouldn't be discovering my nephew now, would I?"

Leo raised his, and they sipped. "Mmm" said the Scraeling, "so brother Roland's the Sieur de St Brieuc, is he? Not that it matters – I wouldn't recognise him if he came through that door. Or perhaps I would. I saw my own face in you right away, young man. Y'see, I didn't know who 'Messire de St Brieuc' might be, but soon as I saw you . . . aye. Oh yes."

"And your aunts" he went on. "Anne, I do remember, but the twins – ah, Emma and Margaret, weren't they? I can't remember them at all because I never saw them, but we at the convent said a *Te Deum* for them when they were born. Clothilde told me why. I would've been about seven, I think." and for a moment, Leo realised, he was far away.

"And who's Clothilde?" he asked and the Scraeling came back to himself.

"Clothilde?" he said. "Tell you about her another time too, nephew. But now – have I convinced you?"

Leo closed his eyes and nodded. "Yes" he said. "You're Uncle Ranulf all right. Or you're the Devil, because you're surely not Christ!"

The Scraeling laughed and raised his cup again. "I'm glad, nephew. There's much I want to tell you. And much to ask you besides. But first things first. I'm serious about helping you end this business here in a way that'll get a smile back on the Conqueror's face. I said I can get you Hereward. In fact, I can get you Morcar too. And I'd love to. Now – two things first, another after. Can you give me the rest of your day? And can you keep that second of yours well away while we do it?"

"Yes" said Leo. "In fact, I'll do the first by doing the second. Good enough?"

"Yes my boy, very good. Just what I'd expect of the Scraeling's nephew, and no error!"

"And the other thing?"

"Your prisoner. I need to know he's safe and he'll stay that way. Would you be good enough to bar anyone but yourself from questioning him? You'll understand why when I tell you a little about him."

Leo looked at him a moment before he stepped to the door and said to the sentry, "Pass the word for messire Mortain."

In the forage shed.

"What d'you make of him?" demanded Odo as he looked down at an Osmund slumped against the pole.

"Eh?" replied the interpreter. "What d'you mean, messire?"

"His answers" replied Odo. "How's he saying what he's saying?" The man frowned. "How's he . . . I've told you what he's saying, messire" he said, and Odo fought back the urge to curse his stupidity.

"Yes, but *how's* he saying it?" he repeated. "You know, does it sound, well, believable? Look" he went on as the interpreter's face clouded, "he was caught listening in on a meeting between the boss and the top monks from the abbey. They were speaking French. If he was listening, how does he come to speak French? And if he speaks French, what do I make of the little bearded monk who told me, this very morning, that he's a simpleton who was out catching wildfowl and looking for plover eggs? Y'see what I mean? Something odd there, eh?"

So that's it thought Osmund, keeping his head down on his chest as he tried to convey a picture of woeful despair. *Good one, uncle Ranulf.* Now, what had he said that didn't fit with that? *Nothing* he realised, nothing so far because he'd claimed only that he lived in the swamp and had been about to try his luck at the lake. By chance he'd had a fishing line in his pocket, so he'd decided to make that the centre of his story.

The interpreter nodded. "Got it" he said. "Anything you can tell me that might trip him up?"

Odo considered. "Ask him again why he was out today. See if he mentions wildfowl or eggs."

The interpreter turned again to Osmund, and after a moment he said. "'Food. Getting food' messire. That's— "

Osmund broke in with perfect timing. "Wild birds and their eggs. Tell the lord I get eggs and birds. And fish!"

"Ask him where his snares were, then. And what was he going to carry everything in?"

Osmund looked his amazement at the question then took the front of his shirt in his bound hands, spoke and tugged at it. The interpreter asked another question, laughed and turned back to Odo. "His shirt, messire. He was going to take it off and put what he caught or found in it. He's simple, right enough, an' that's putting it kindly, I'd think."

Odo thought. "Ask him what he was doing up the hill, then, instead of getting food as he'd been told."

"Says he heard the bells, messire. Bells that horses carry."

"Bells? *Bells?* Bugger's got bells in his head" muttered Odo, but then one of the soldiers spoke.

"Beg pardon, messire, but I was holdin' the horses in the clearing there, and one of 'em was jumpin' about real fierce 'cause of the sandflies if y'remember. Harness was jinglin' right enough. C'd that be it?"

Odo nodded reluctantly. "Just ask him who his father is, would you?" he said to the interpreter, "and listen carefully to what he says, and how he says it."

Oh shit thought Osmund. *Can I get away with being simple?*

"Dunno, messire" came back the answer. "He don't seem to know neither, 'cause all he does is repeat 'father'."

"That right?" said Odo. "He might know more than you do, then, because I'd say that's about what I heard— "

The door swung open and a helmeted head was poked round it. "Messire? Messire St Brieuc's compliments an' he'd like you to attend him soon's you can manage it. An' to post sentries outside this door, 'cause he wants t'question this prisoner hisself."

Odo raised an eyebrow. "Right" he said.

Leo's office.

"That's how I'll get you Hereward" said the Scraeling. "Unlike any of the rest of us, he's got to live here after. So we're going to make a hero of him if everything goes as I've suggested to you."

"It's not certain, Ranulf" said Leo. "There's no hope for the men who hold the paths we're using. Asking a lot of a man to condemn his own sword-brothers isn't it?"

"Well" said the Scraeling, "Hereward'll certainly bring that up. But the men I want to hold those paths aren't his. I was thinking of nudging Morcar into that particular job – he's as vain as he's nasty, and if I can get him moving in the right direction, he'll jump in all right. And that'll make the second part of things a bit easier, because I want him where I can bag him for you."

Leo blinked. "Were you serious about that? Handing over Morcar too?"

The Scraeling looked injured. "Certainly, nephew. Surely you don't think I was just trying to impress you? Consider him yours. This is how I see it . . . " and he spoke on while Leo listened intently. At last, Leo sat back and grinned.

"Thank God you're not a heavy cavalryman, Ranulf" he said. "I'd eat my destrier to avoid facing you across a field. How'd the de Lannions get you then?"

"Blind chance" said the Scraeling blandly, "just a vintage year!"

Leo chuckled and raised his cup. "I'll drink to that, uncle. So we've got the business sorted out – or rather, you have. Now, what about the prisoner?"

"Well, I've been thinking about that as we've been talking" said the Scraeling. "And – wait for this – what I told you was correct. He *is* a relative of mine. Therefore, Leo, what follows from that?"

Leo squinted at him. "Follows? Ah . . . oh shit! He's a relative of mine too? Yes, thought so . . . go on, start at the beginning . . . "

The Chronicle.

*S*o *I did. After Odo had been pointed towards a series of tasks that would take him most of the day, I told Leo of a night in the domed city at the ends of the earth when I took a poisoned Scythian arrow in a shoulder-blade and of how Penda the Saxon varanger had not only saved my life at risk of his own but had nursed me back to life and health. Of how we had become sword-brothers as we freed Hardraada and his varanger lieutenants to put down the Scythian Guard for the imperial sisters, Theodora and Zoe, and of how the big Englishman's prowess with the axe had won him a reputation little short of fearsome in a week's street-fighting through the city of the eastern emperor.*

I told him, with rather less candour, of our meetings as ambassadors in the years after I had returned to Norway with Hardraada, and he to England to serve the sons of old Earl Godwin. I say 'with less candour' because, as I've written, Senlac had left me the only man alive who knew all there was to know about the downfall of the greatest warrior of the age, and I was content to let matters remain so.

But I did say to Leo that, but for Penda Raedwaldsson and his service to England in the matter of Hardraada's invasion in that desperate time of five years before, William would never have got off the beach where he landed.

Leo's office.

"That's a big claim, uncle" said Leo looking at me levelly, "because I was part of that and I'm telling you, old and wise men claimed it was the mightiest force ever assembled in France."

The Scraeling spread his hands. "Even so, my boy" he said, "But I saw the Norse army the English crushed. I *provisioned* the Norse army they crushed, and I know what it took to slay that monster. And – with all respect to your duke – Harold Godwinsson fought William with an army that'd marched three hundred miles to fight Hardraada and the same back again, only to lose by half an hour of daylight."

Leo tugged thoughtfully at his nose. "But this Penda" he said, "what's he to you? By blood, I mean?"

"Ah" said the Scraeling, "during my recovery, I was surprised – to say the least, Leo – to discover he spoke Breton, because hardly anyone outside Little Britain does. And I only discovered it because he asked me about my real name, which he'd heard in my ravings as that poison drained out of me. He was interested in the name 'Nominoe', who's an ancestor of his too, because his mother was a Breton of the Nominoe line who'd married a shipwrecked Englishman, Penda's father. And who insisted all her children learned Breton as well as French and Latin. So we became 'cousin' to each other on the spot. And that was good enough. We never tried to work out the exact relationship, because by the time we got out of Constantinople we were brothers for life." [7]

Leo seemed to be elsewhere. He frowned at the Scraeling. "Big chap, was he? I mean, he carried you away from that fight, you said?"

"Easily, according to the other man there" returned the Scraeling. "Oh yes, he was big all right. I used to joke about hiding behind him in battle." *Funny, that phrase didn't hurt as it once would have,* he thought. "You're not short yourself, nephew, but Penda had inches on you and shoulders I could stand on comfortably."

"That right?" asked Leo. "And – let me see – our prisoner's his son then?"

"Exactly" said the Scraeling. "Exactly. That's why I want him back. Our interests coincide, you might say. You want an end to the Fenlands strife,

---

7 *See 'The Landwaster' for the back-story of Penda and The Scraeling.*

and having that treacherous bugger Morcar would keep the peace anywhere he isn't. I want Osmund because I owe his parents. And you needn't worry about turning a rebel loose to take up where Hereward left off, because I'm going to take him out of England."

"Hmm" said Leo. "You haven't much time for Morcar, then?"

"Less than I have for a viper, Leo" said the Scraeling with some heat. "A viper's an honest enough creature, because it won't hurt you unless you threaten it, and that's fair enough. But over the last six years, as an English earl pointed out in my hearing not long ago, Morcar's sold out Tostig Godwinsson, his brother Harold and your William. All of them, because he doesn't care who he rats on. And because of him, William made Northumbria a desert. No doubt there. Morcar's a complete shit, my boy, and he fouls all he touches. No – give me the viper any day!"

"See what you mean, uncle" said Leo reflectively, "and from what I know of the trouble he's caused the king, I'd agree. But look – shall we have this young man in? I'm more than a little interested . . ."

The Chronicle.

I wasn't, of course, being strictly and completely honest with Leo, and the thought gave me a moment's pause for I liked the young man. But I was at full stretch in the matter of getting Osmund not only out of that camp but out of England also, so I put aside a conscience that had in any case taken something of a beating over the years, and got on with it.

My deception wasn't a major one, I told myself, but necessary, for the fact was that I couldn't know which secret tracks the monks of Ely would choose for their betrayal. I had to control that, and I'd do it through Ossa. I was confident that my little brown man would co-operate, for many – in fact most – of Hereward's original band were as weary of the struggle against the Normans as Hereward himself, and all of them for the very good reason that, as realistic and practical men, they could see no successful end to it.

No – the men of the Isle of Refuge wanted peace, and it was largely the refugees and blow-ins from elsewhere who were opposed to it. And chief among that group were the men of Northumbria, Morcar's men, who were as proficient in boasting as they were helpless in the swamp.

Aye, there it was. I could, I told myself, see it all and I had all I needed.

There in the swamp I had a war-leader and a war-band who were sick of a lost cause and who wanted only to resume their lives. I had a band of dangerous malcontents, equally incapable of rescuing the cause under a leader who brought ruin to all he touched. Outside the swamp I had a foeman who had every reason – including our newly-discovered relationship – to see things my way. And if I put these things together the right way, I would win clear with the young man who was my son in all but name. Aye – worth a small and inconsequential lie.

Leo's office.

He's got a good head on him thought the Scraeling in the very instant of Osmund's stumbling towards him to fall on his knees. The young man had been shoved through the door by the sergeant who had led the three-strong escort from the forage shed, and after one incredulous glance at the Scraeling, Osmund had feigned total delight in his "Father! Father, oh father!" as he rushed across the room.

"Thank you sergeant. You can fall out now."

"Messire? Beg pardon, messire, but he's . . . he's . . . ah . . . he's . . . "

"Yes sergeant, he's a big bugger. But I'm pretty sure he's harmless, and I'm not going to release his hands, so don't worry. Take your boys away for something to eat. Didn't you have the guard last night?"

" 'S right messire. Second watch it was."

"Thought so. You might like to get your heads down too, then."

"Right messire. Thank you messire. Er . . . you're sure? I mean . . . "

"Look, man, I might be getting on a bit – " Leo couldn't be more than twenty-five thought the Scraeling with amusement as he pretended to soothe an Osmund pretending to be distraught "– but I'm not so far past it that I can't look after a prisoner with his hands bound. Especially when he's as thick as a post, Messire Mortain tells me. Now – off with you before I change my mind, yes?"

"Aye messire" said the sergeant, coming to the salute, "and thank you."

The door crashed shut behind him and those inside clearly heard the sergeant's voice recede into the distance, "Now that's an officer worth saluting, is old Ironarse. Knows what's going on, thinks about his men, fucking demon in a scrap . . . "

Osmund stopped babbling as the silence inside the office lengthened, and looked up to find 'old Ironarse' regarding him sardonically and a Scraeling trying not to laugh out loud.

"Give it a rest, Osmund" said Leo in French, "I'm on to you, and besides – the way you're scrabbling at my floor, you'll probably wear a hole in it. But he's good, isn't he?" The last to the Scraeling who gave way to laughter in the end.

"The best" he said, chuckling. "Thinks as fast as he moves. By the way, I wouldn't dismiss him just because his hands are tied, either."

"If you say so," said Leo, "so we might's well untie them. At least while I've got my uncle – and his – to look after me." And so saying he rose and stooped over Osmund to work on the cords while Osmund looked from one to the other with an expression on his face that sent both men into fits of laughter.

"Now Osmund" said Leo, "That dried blood on your head bothering you? No? Good, because I'm not going to wash it off. Want you looking thoroughly miserable once I return you to the shed for further questioning, y'see. All right uncle?"

Osmund found his voice. "Uncle Ranulf, what's going on? Why's he calling you 'uncle'? And who is he?"

The Scraeling chuckled again. "Osmund, I'm happy to say that he's my nephew. Just like you. No – he's closer than you, because he's my brother's son. And once he remembers his manners and pours us a cup of wine, I'll tell you a story you'll not believe, because I'm not sure I believe it myself . . ."

The Isle of Refuge, that night.

"They're coming in, Hereward" said the Scraeling. "They're coming in tomorrow night, and they're coming in such force they'll over-run us. St Brieuc's got a lot to make up for, and if he doesn't crack us this time, he . . . well, he might's well join us, because he won't want to face the Bastard after a second failure."

"I can understand that" said the Wake. "But how're they coming? And at night? They're mad – those tracks are dangerous enough by day!"

"Thurstan and that deputy of his, I'm afraid" said the Scraeling. "They've sold us out. And if you press me, I'd say it's 'cause they're worried about what the Normans are likely to do once they fight their way onto the Isle.

So they're going to guide the Normans over the tracks." He watched anger struggle with disbelief in Hereward's face.

"Look" he said, "I moved freely about their camp. Monks can do that, y'know – I saw and heard everything, including four confessions, and it's common knowledge what's going to happen and when. And it won't be pretty, Hereward – we're one up because of what happened to the causeway" *and God help that boy of mine if the Normans ever find out what he had to do with it* "and they're pissed-off about it. So we need to think and plan as never before. And quickly, too." He held his breath. *If ever I had to trade on a reputation for cunning . . . .*

Hereward thought for long moments before he stirred. "What's the Scraeling got up his sleeve then?" he asked, and the Scraeling let out his breath in a long silent hiss. *Got you!*

"Been thinking about it all the way back" he said, "and a couple of things come to mind." He paused, for all the world a man choosing his words carefully, then said slowly, "Hereward, you may not like this but it's the best advice I can offer."

"It's time to give up. Whatever we were once going to achieve here, well, we're not now. It's too late. Maybe we could have once, but . . . but now, the Bastard's too strong. The Normans are everywhere because while we've been fucking around in our own little patches – some of us here, some up in Northumbria, some over in the west, others in Devon and that other place I can never pronounce – they've been pouring in for the land William's been offering. He's got Frenchmen from all parts, Bretons, Flemish, men from Italy even. He's never been better off for men, Hereward, and he's only going to get better. That water in the jug?"

"Ale if you like" offered the Wake, indicating a small keg and the Scraeling shook his head.

"No thanks. Cool heads and careful thinking, eh? Where was I?"

"You were telling me how far in the shit we are" supplied Hereward. "And I've got your drift. I even agree. But what do we do about it?"

"We have to – you have to – get the best terms you can, Hereward, and that's the top and the bottom of it. Normans affronted you and your family in the first place didn't they? And everything followed from that. Well, Normans can restore you to what you've lost. And I'd be amazed if the Bastard refuses, because it'd be the cheapest victory he ever won. Once he does, as their earl you can make everything right for the people of the Fenlands."

Hereward rose and began to pace, hands behind his back and his head down. After a moment he stopped, turned to where the Scraeling watched impassively and said, "Two things. First, how do we fend off this attack? Second – how do we convince Morcar and the others? I can see what there is in it for me and my folk – but there's nothing for him."

The Scraeling nodded. "That's because he had his chance of making his peace with the Bastard, and he tossed it to the winds. Just as Siward said, remember? But to answer your question – we don't fend off the attack. We let it happen. And we let Morcar's band take the brunt of it while you and your men scatter deeper into the swamp. After a decent interval, you come out and make your peace with the Bastard – sorry, with the Conqueror – right? I can arrange that too, by the way, through St Brieuc. We're both Bretons; did I mention that?" he said guilelessly, and held his breath again.

Hereward tugged at his beard. "Don't like putting it on Morcar like that" he said at length. "I can't like the man; never could. He's trouble, and I know that. Old Siward didn't tell me anything I didn't know that night. But still— he's one of the last . . . the last of old England."

The Scraeling sighed. "That's a good thought, Hereward, but you really should leave it there. First, what did 'old England' ever do for you except kick you out? Next, if Morcar's 'the last of old England', it's only because he took care to keep out of the way when its really big affairs were going on. Like Senlac for instance. And Stamford Bridge before that. Siward told us what 'old England' thinks of Morcar, and for myself, I agree. But I'll just say two things more, and then I'll leave it, right?"

He got up and poured himself some more water. "The first thing" he said, turning back, "is that if I were discussing this with Morcar, you'd be tied hand and foot and lying in that corner this minute. Ask Siward. Morcar would not only drop you in the shit if it suited him, he'd put a foot on your head to keep you there and no regrets. He still might, if he thought it would get him William's forgiveness. However, he's as thick as he's nasty and it hasn't occurred to him so far – but it probably will occur to him if he survives this attack, because anyone who does will realise that the game's well and truly up, Hereward."

The Wake nodded, convinced. "And the other thing?" he asked and the

Scraeling sighed again.

"All that said" he replied, "I know you're still not convinced, because you're not Morcar. A moment ago I said that you – *you* –" he emphasised, "would need to make the best terms you can. I didn't say *we* because I'm out of it, Hereward. Skuli and the boys have raised *Nordvedr*, and we're away. There's nothing for me now in England. Not now."

"The boy?" asked Hereward, and the Scraeling shook his head slowly. "Told you the Normans weren't in a forgiving mood, didn't I?"

"I'm sorry" said the Wake. "Was he really your nephew?"

"His father and I were close" said the Scraeling. "A long time ago, and a long way away. Anyway – when I turn my back on England, I promise you I'll take Morcar out of here. More than he deserves, mind you, but if it makes your decision easier – the only decision you've got, in my thinking – then I'll take him away. All right?"

Hereward nodded slowly, then more quickly. "All right" he said.

"That's settled then" said the Scraeling. "Good, because I think it's best if you break this to Morcar and tell him where you want him to station his men. As it happens, I can be quite clear which trails through the swamp the Normans'll be using. Not now, though – later. Let me lay it out for you . . ."

Later that day.

"We have to get to the abbey well before dark, because we don't know when the monks'll move, although it'll probably be just after twilight" said the Scraeling, and Ossa nodded. "Close enough to see them come out; not close enough for them to see us."

"And when they comes out?" asked Ossa.

"We follow them to the spot we talked about; the spot where you'll leave your men. Then we jump them, strip them, and hand over the robes to the men you've selected. The Normans will be expecting monks, remember. Then the monks – our monks – lead the Normans along the trails we want them on. Just as we agreed. When battle's joined, you and your men leave them to it and disappear to join lord Hereward at the place you know about. Good enough?"

Ossa considered a moment, then the brown face split in a smile. "Good enough, lord Ranulf. Good enough. What'll happen t'the brothers?"

"Little enough, Ossa, and certainly not what treachery deserves. They'll get cloaks in exchange for their robes – worst that'll happen is they'll have a cold night under guard. At some point they'll be tied up, and their guards'll bugger off and leave a dagger behind. By the time they get free, we'll be long gone."

"You going then, lord? You and Skuli?"

"We're going, Ossa. It's over. And it's over for you too – lord Hereward will make his peace with the king, and he'll make it for you and all of his folk. Aye, it's over."

"Lord, I'm that sorry 'bout Osmund. Word's gone round, like. Know you was close – heard him call you 'uncle' many a time. All my boys loved him too. 'S it right he was a thegn? Boys reckon they couldn't miss it? Still wasn't too proud to learn from likes of us though. An' I'll never forget him kickin' an earl's arse for us. Never!"

"Thank you Ossa" said the Scraeling, genuinely moved. "Yes, Osmund's father was a royal *hus-carl* who fell at Godwinsson's side, and there was a lot of him in his son. Osmund was a leader and a fine young man. Matter of fact" he said suddenly, his eyes dancing, "he still is. Ossa, let me tell you something that not many people know . . . " and, leaning forward, he dropped his voice.

The Chronicle.

*A*nd that's how it happened, my word on it. The sagas and folk-tales tell *of how the monks betrayed the doughty Hereward, who held his ground against overwhelming odds until he was dragged from the Isle and away through the swamp by his selfless retainers. In fact he stayed just long enough to see the defenders beset on every side, because Ossa and I had made a job of ensuring that the Northumbrians were well spread in their defensive positions. To give them their due, they fought to the end and they died bravely, but there was never any doubt that they were going to die.*

The same tales relate how the fury of the Normans was vented on the inhabitants of the Isle. That was a little more accurate, but only a little because the bulk of those who died were Morcar's men, and they died because the Normans offered neither mercy nor quarter. They'd suffered among the trackless swamps and treacherous waterways for weeks, months and years, some of them, and they took their revenge in full measure that night. Leo had flung all he could muster into the assaulting columns that, under the overall command of Odo Mortain, stormed along the paths and erupted onto the Isle of Refuge in a torrent of steel and fury.

At my secret insistence Hereward had kept Morcar hard by him where he commanded, and for the look of the thing I had insisted that Siward take his battle station there also so that, I said, the wise heads could see, confer and act as the battle demanded. I'd have been wary of such advice myself, but then I knew more than either Morcar or Siward.

However it was, though, when the first path-head onto the Isle was breached by a wedge of Normans and the shield-walls began to fall back in the torchlight towards the centre, I elbowed the one-eyed hus-carl who commanded Hereward's bodyguard.

The Isle of Refuge.

"Get the earl away, man – this fight's lost!" the Scraeling urged. "Another day!" He didn't hesitate, but took Hereward by the elbow and drew him backwards against the protests he made for form's sake.

"Come, lord" said the *hus-carl*. "I've a boat waiting at the back yonder. Come! As the Scraeling says – another day, lord!"

"I've a boat waiting too, but it's bigger than his and I'm not waiting to see who'll help me fill it!" said the Scraeling, an eye on the dozen fights going on at the path-heads. Morcar's men were giving a good account of themselves and fighting like wolves, but he gave it ten or fifteen minutes at most before the pressure from their front drove them back from the path-heads. And when that happened, the Normans would flank them, surround them, cut them up and then spill over the centre of the Isle. "Who's coming? Morcar? Siward?"

"And leave them leaderless? Thought more of you than that, Scraeling" said Siward.

"Siward, this fight's lost!" the Scraeling snapped. "Come away to where you can fight another day. Stay here, and the only thing you'll do for them is die with them."

"A man might do worse!" he returned, and the tears ran down his cheeks in the torch-light. The Scraeling cursed inwardly, and then inspiration struck.

"Siward" he said, and was it his imagination or was the clang and roar of battle a little louder? "You're an earl of England, same as Hereward. He knows, even if you don't, it's his duty to survive because humble men need someone to rally to. Aye, he knows, and he's done the right thing. Stay and die if you can't see your duty. But know, if you do, you're doing it to indulge yourself. Leading's not about doing it all yourself!" Siward flinched as the words struck him, but – aye, no doubt. The clamour of battle was louder, and then Ossa popped up by the Scraeling.

"Now or never, lord" he said.

The Scraeling turned back to the others.

"I'm away" he said. "I'll take anyone who knows where his duty lies. Anyone."

Morcar turned silently and fell in with the group forming by Ossa. *Yes!* the Scraeling thought with grim satisfaction, *that saves my having him knocked on the head* . . . Siward rammed his blade back into its scabbard, angrily wiped his eyes with the back of his hand and joined the group also.

The Scraeling fell in beside him and snapped "That's it, Ossa. Go!"

The mouth of the River Ouse, not long after.

The broad-beamed and high-sided Norman transport lay quietly to its anchor in the blackness of the night, as far inland as she had been able to get on the tide of two hours before and in the lee of a small island lying athwart the stream. Two sections of soldiery sat or lay around the broad deck, making themselves as comfortable as their mail would permit. On the command deck Osmund and Leo sat on a bench in quiet conversation.

"Fancy us being cousins. Of some degree anyway" said Leo. "Isn't that amazing?"

"It's all of that" replied Osmund, "and I'm not that sure of how I feel about it. You're a decent man, and I just can't see Normans that way. Not the men who killed my father."

"Now hang on Osmund" said Leo. "Two things, for a start. First, I'm not a bloody Norman – I'm Breton. But yes, I do fight for the Normans. That's because I'm a soldier. Youngest son of a youngest son, and the only possibility of making my way. Same as lots of others, maybe even your father – I don't know. But the second thing – your father died doing what he swore to do. No-one sneaked up on him in the night and murdered him. In fact, from what I saw, he did quite a bit of killing himself."

"He . . . he . . . what *you* saw? What . . . would you explain that?"

Leo sighed. "I didn't intend to mention this. Not yet. But . . . ah . . . as it's come up, from what I know, and from what uncle Ranulf's said, I . . . Osmund, I believe I faced your father in battle. On the ridge. At Hastings."

Osmund's response was flat and fast. "You can't have. You're still alive!"

Leo grinned, but there was no mirth in it. "Yes, and there's a reason for that. Osmund, I was his last foeman and I saw him fall. An arrow took him, but before that—"

"Messire!" An urgent and low-pitched call split the night and Leo jumped. "From the island messire – something coming down the river. Pretty sure it's the target, messire. Orders messire?"

"Pass the word to the island not to challenge. Officers, stand to" snapped Leo as he strode down the three steps to the main deck, "by word of mouth, and quietly! That lantern ready?"

"Aye messire" from the two men crouching below the bulwark. "Er . . . messire – need more lanterns f'r boarding . . . ?"

Leo chuckled. "No, Gilles, we're not boarding. In fact, if that's the ship we're expecting, it's full of the sort of people your mother frightened you with when you were little and naughty. No – just be ready to wave it when I give you the word."

Osmund felt the night move below him as battle-ready men stepped forward to the bulwarks, but then a stillness that was total fell like a cloak and he could hear the blood surge in his ears as the whole world held its breath. He blinked as a darker patch of blackness slid from the far side of the island but, at the very moment he was sure what it was, two flares of light split the gloom as the covers were yanked away from lanterns and he heard Leo snap for their lantern to be raised in reply.

"Well met!" came a familiar voice from the darkness, and as Leo gave the order to ground arms Osmund could hear the sigh of men released from tension even above the rattle of spear-butts on the wooden decking.

"May I board?" came the voice, and the black shape altered to come across the stream to nudge the transport gently while ropes flew.

"Lanterns now" said Leo, "all of them." And light sprang up along the bulwarks to show *Nordvedr*'s serpent-mouth agape and easing in at the level of the transport's bulwark. "That ladder – over with it" called Leo, and a rope-ladder coiled under the bulwark was lifted to the rail and allowed to uncoil over the side to the waiting longship.

The Scraeling scrambled over the side, turned to fling an instruction behind him and held out a hand to Leo. "All well?" asked the cavalryman as he led his guests to the command deck, and the Scraeling nodded as he shook hands with a waiting Osmund.

"Never better" he said. "One gift ready to come aboard, the other awaiting you – oh, within the month I'd say, just for the look of things. This is Ossa, by the way. He'll come to you when Hereward's ready to make his peace. In the meantime Hereward'll be spreading the word that he won't surrender to anyone but you, his conqueror. That won't do you any harm with William, will it now?"

Leo grimaced. "Might help make up for two hundred men drowned in a swamp" he said, and inclined his head. "Ossa?" he said, nodding at the little brown man. "Good of you to bring him, uncle."

"Well, that was part of it" said the Scraeling. "Ossa wanted to say god-speed to my other nephew here. We'll leave them to it and inspect your parcel, shall we?"

They returned to the maindeck as a cloak-shrouded and trussed figure was manhandled over the bulwark and dropped on the deck. "Got an armourer standing by, have you?" Leo gestured, and an armourer came forward with leg-irons swinging from one big fist. His mate flipped the figure over and sat on him, stretching to hold the fetters in position while the armourer riveted them with half a dozen blows of his hammer.

A dagger appeared in the Scraeling's hand and he sliced through the ropes that bound the heavy wool to the man on the deck. He peeled back the folds of the cloak.

"Hello again, Morcar" he said. "Someone here wants to meet you. And he's a very important man, so— what's that? Morcar, that's not polite! Ooohh, neither's that . . . oh Morcar, really! This is a real high-up, Morcar, so I'll thank you not to swear in front of him. Should think so! Where's your fucking dignity?"

Aboard Nordvedr.

"Don't worry about the Scraeling" said Skuli to Siward. "He knows what he's about. He's getting his boy back, an' he's putting Morcar where he won't do no-one no more harm at the same time."

"His boy?" frowned Siward, "Osmund? The Normans cut his throat's what I heard!"

"Ah, that" said Skuli. "Just a rumour, I reckon. Come to think of it, Morcar prob'ly started it while his arse was still hurting." He sniggered.

"Just the same" said Siward, "I can't abide Morcar and everyone knows it – but handing him over's a bit . . . bit the other way, I think."

"Siward, I dunno much 'bout England or what goes on in it" said Skuli. "A fight's a fight to me, an' with the Scraeling around there's allus plenty o'that. But even I c'n see, well, . . . it's over, Siward. The Bastard's too strong, an' if y'ask me, Hereward's doin' the right thing. Look at y'rself, man! F'm what I hear, y'r earldom's still fuckin' smoking – an' who you got to thank for it but that evil little bugger we just tossed to the Normans? Eh? Tell me y'don't know I'm speakin' the truth?"

Siward sniffed once and nodded slowly.

"Look" went on Skuli, "There'll be no more've that with Morcar in a Norman dungeon. Scraeling tells me he's sure the Bastard won't top him, 'cause that'll only make him a hero. No – he'll live down a hole f'r the rest've his life, lookin' up at the sky through a small window if he's lucky. He had it comin', Siward. He surely did. You, now – Scraeling'll put you ashore wherever an' whenever you want. Or you're welcome t'come with us."

"And where might that be?" asked Siward, and Skuli grinned.

"Dunno yet" he replied, "and none've us are bothered."

Aboard the transport.

"Well, that's it then" said the Scraeling as he took a cup of wine from the tray offered by Leo's man. "Can't keep you from things much longer, nephew" he said, but Leo waved dismissively.

"No hurry, uncle" he said. "From what you've told me, Odo's in full control upriver and Hereward's going the other way fast as he can. So I'm not needed."

The Scraeling raised his cup in acknowledgement. "Y'know Leo, the mark of a good commander – one of them anyway – is knowing when to leave things to his subordinates. Hardraada had that gift, and there wasn't one of them who couldn't have stepped into his shoes at need." *Which is exactly why I made sure they all died* he thought. "You'll go a long way. Wish I could be here to see it."

"Well you know, uncle Ranulf, that'd cause more problems than it solved" mused Leo, raising his own cup. "The way things are in your family, only one of your nephews'd smile at a time!"

Osmund chuckled briefly. "There's truth in that, cousin Leo" he said. "But here we are. Where do we go from here?"

"You're going a long way away" returned Leo, "As fast as this bunch of pirates will take you, Osmund Pendasson of Reading."

Osmund choked on his mouthful and the Scraeling goggled.

"Oh yes" said Leo, enjoying his moment, "I know who you are, because uncle Ranulf here isn't the only one who can add things up. Oh uncle, don't tell me I've caught the Scraeling flat-footed? Really? Now there's a thing!" He laughed and tapped his head.

"About a year ago" he said, "I was summoned to a meeting of area commanders. The king was there, of course, and so was Walter Giffard. Among Giffard's lieutenants was Ivo de Bois, and we shared a flask or two. Ivo and I go back a long way, because he was my first commander when I was . . . oh, about your age Osmund, or a thought younger. Anyway – we shared a drop or two, as I said, and that surprised me for a start, because the Ivo I knew didn't have much time for drink. Ivo's always modelled himself on the king, y'know, in everything. He's William's man through and through; has been all his life" he added, almost as an aside.

The Scraeling found his voice. "And . . .?"

"And" resumed Leo, "I hadn't seen him since Hastings, and there he was – married now, to a Saxon heiress. William's policy of course. And it all came out just after I congratulated him on his marriage and asked something daft, like how he found married life."

"Go on" said Osmund, and Leo nodded.

"Let me mention something before I do" said Leo. "Osmund, cousin, if there's anything in this life I'm sure of, it's that Ivo de Bois is absolutely besotted with his wife. No error, cousin, he'd do anything for her and their children short of killing the king. Thought I'd mention that. And 'their children' means *all* the family. Thought I'd mention that, too."

"Anyway, out came the story of how his stepson had defended his family honour and his father's memory. Oh yes, that came out. And of how the boy had disappeared straight afterwards. Ivo tormented himself with the question of what he could have done, because Gytha ... that's her name I think ... was tearing herself apart over it. But there was nothing he could have done. Nothing at all. Justice – yes, Norman justice – would have had to be done and, all things considered, the best course was for the boy to have disappeared. Which is what happened. And I made him see that, I think. Yes, I'm sure I did."

"So— other than a fairly common Saxon name" said the Scraeling, "what makes you think Osmund's ... "

"Oh come on, uncle!" Leo snorted. "*You* did! You told me all about your English cousin, Penda. Penda, the *hus-carl*. Penda, the axeman. Penda, who died keeping us from his king. Keeping *me* from his king, matter of fact."

He turned to Osmund. "Osmund, let's get back to what we were talking about just before Ranulf here turned up tonight. I said I didn't intend to mention it then, but ... now's the time. Here – let's get rid of this flask, shall we?"

And he told the story of the last moments of a battle on a Sussex ridge. The moments when men weary unto death from their day-long struggle put forth the last of their strength, some to save a king and others to kill him, in the failing light of an October day.

"William sent in four knights" he said, "Giffard, Eustace, Malet and Ponthieu, because Harold couldn't be allowed to live. Or the next day would see us buggered, root and branch. And I was part of the group that went in before them to clear their way through the last shield-wall so they could launch a killing charge. A wall that was held by a motley collection of Saxons led by a giant. A giant with an axe that wove and spun round his head like a child's toy."

He shuddered, his eyes far away. "But no child ever did with a toy what that man did with his" he went on, "for no-one could come near him. And it was numbers in the end. Numbers. We had the numbers and he didn't. I can't remember how often we charged, but somehow he inspired them to fling us back every time. Until our destriers got a foothold on the ridge.

237

And then it was a matter of time, and we cut it bloody close, I can tell you."

Leo raised the cup to his lips, sipped and told of how Penda's axe-stroke had taken the head from his lance; of how he had smashed the stump over his opponent's helmet in a despairing attempt to avoid what would come next, and of how it had been enough to send the killing-stroke wide and into his horse's shoulder.

"When it threw me" he said, "I was dead. Dead as anything you'd see on a butcher's block, and I knew it. But Penda held his hand. Out on his feet as he was, desperate as he was because he knew he wasn't going home, that man stayed his hand until I got up."

Into the silence, Osmund whispered, "And what then? What happened then?"

"Then? Well, I pissed myself" said Leo. "I pissed myself, right there on my feet, because I was terrified. Even from the back of a destrier, that man was a giant. On the ground, he was big as a fucking tree. Aye, uncle, you were right. You *could* have stood on his shoulders. But then . . . then he screamed and clapped a hand to his face. And I saw the arrow sticking out of his head. Clean into an eye. And when he hit the ground, I remember it shook. But that might've been Eustace's group coming up behind, because the way was clear then. I don't know – something hit me from behind and knocked me over."

"And I think Penda – your father, aye, and my cousin, I suppose – was the last axe between Godwinsson and his death." He sipped, and the others heard the cup rattle against his teeth in the silence.

The Scraeling realised he was holding his breath, and let it out in a long hiss. "What a story" he said. "*Vale*, Penda, man amongst men and the greatest of them all."

Leo grunted. "Funny you should say that, uncle" he said. "That's exactly what I said when I went back up the ridge the next morning and saw him lying there. And there's one thing more" he said, putting his cup down on the rail beside him and stepping backwards to fumble in a chest under the bulwark.

"Osmund" he said, turning with a long, cloth-wrapped bundle in his hands. "I've kept this for five years, near enough. But it's yours, cousin, because it was his, and . . . and . . . here. It's yours." He held it out to Osmund, who took it and turned to the light of a lantern.

Unwinding the cloth, the young man stared for a moment at what was revealed and then turned to the Scraeling. Across his hands he held a great axe – the terrible Saxon long-axe; the handle more than four feet long and the crescent blades a foot in length from tip to tip of each broad cutting-edge. The steel of the head and each razor-sharp edge glittered and twinkled in the lantern-light as Osmund's hands shook uncontrollably.

"My father's axe" he whispered. "My father's axe." He lowered the deadly head to the deck, swallowed and raised one hand to his eyes.

"It's your axe now, Osmund" said Leo into the silence. "Whatever you defend with it, however you use it, may it always be as nobly as your father did for his last time."

"You've . . . you've kept it well, Leo" said the Scraeling, seeing that Osmund was helpless in tears. "That was good of you."

"That weapon deserved no less" said Leo. "Nor the man who wielded it."

"The end" said Osmund shakily. "There was a . . . a knob on the end. I remember it. Father said . . . he said it helped him to lock his hands? In the cut? . . ."

"Ah" said Leo. "Uncle, any more in that flask? Yes, Osmund. There was a knob there, but . . . when I buried your father – it was the day after he died, y'see, and . . . he'd been lying where he fell all night, and nothing on earth could loosen his grip. And I wasn't going to cut him, as one of my men suggested. So I called for a saw, and I cut through the handle instead – 's why it's a bit uneven, y'see? – and your father went into his grave still with the end in his hand. No-one but you – and me, of course – has touched that weapon since I took it from his hand. I've looked at it a lot since then, and I've always thought . . . thought . . . 'When'm I going to get rid of this'?" he lied in jest, forcing the others to smile. "But you can always fit it with another handle" he said, raising his cup. "Up to you."

"No" said Osmund. "No, I won't. I'll leave it as you did. Remind me of . . . of both of you. My father and my cousin. Thank you. Thank you, Leo."

"And my thanks too, nephew" said the Scraeling. "For burying Penda. That also was good of you."

"Well, as I said" returned Leo, "the man deserved no less. The dead there – the Saxon dead – were left for the creatures of the field. Didn't agree with that, myself, 'cause wasn't as if we were moving on in a hurry.

No, they weren't buried. But Penda is, and I had my confessor speak the words over him decently. He's buried where he fell, on the ridge about five yards from where the Fighting Man flew. Took a bloody great hole, I might say." That brought a chuckle, and Leo stretched.

"You a religious man, uncle? You were once, weren't you? The convent, I mean?"

"Suppose I was" answered the Scraeling. "I was meant for the Church, yes. Once on a time. But since . . . I've seen too much, done too much, aye. And I've been kicked in the teeth once too often to be one now, I think. You?"

"Not really" said Leo. "I'm a soldier, and soldiers make their own luck, I've always thought. But all the same – I've been one of two men about to kill each other, not knowing they were related . . . and I was the lucky one. And all this time later, you turn up. You, a story from the past. And Osmund – son of the man who spared my life. And we're related – uncle, nephews and cousins – in some fashion anyway. No, I'm not religious; but I'm always going to wonder Who's will we've been part of here, eh?"

"And you think it's His will that you free me?" said Osmund.

"Don't know about that, Osmund. But it's certainly *my* will, because your father bought your life when he gave me the chance to take his in a fair fight between two warriors. And that'd be so even if we weren't cousins – but I'm glad we are."

"Anyway" and he stretched again. "Anyway, I've got a story to tell Ivo de Bois and his Lady Gytha one day. One day soon, my word on that. A story that'll help them both sleep better at nights from now on, eh?"

"Now, uncle. I've not only freed a dangerous rebel, but I've armed him too. So it's time to get him as far away as possible, before the king gets to hear about it. And, so we can all sleep at nights too – why doesn't The Scraeling go with him?"

The Scraeling spread his hands. "Where did I get nephews like you two?" he asked.

✻✻✻

Epilogue

The Dane was a big lad but there was no doubt he'd taken on a big job because the landlord had three backing him up, and none of them were small either. But what annoyed the Scraeling was the way they made a meal of the straightforward job of tossing a drunk into the street.

In fact, he thought, they'd already pushed him away from the door three or four times, catching him as he struggled to his feet and shoving him, off-balance, from one to the other with each fetching him a hefty blow to the head before sending him on. Even as he watched, a crashing punch to the side of the head stretched the Dane full-length on the floor, nicely-placed for the boot that was drawn back as the Scraeling raised his voice. "That's enough! You want to kill him, or what?"

The kicker, who happened to be the landlord, peered through the wavering light from the tapers that danced in the draughts sent in by a freezing December day, and bared gapped teeth in a smile. "An' who the fuck's this dwarf?" he sneered, "You with this turd? Oh – right! I got it – he's your bum-boy, right friend? Ain't he, boys?" he appealed to his cronies, who guffawed. "Well, dwarf? You worried you won't be slipping it to him t'night, are ya?"

"Suppose I must be" said the Scraeling into the silence, "if you say so. I try never to argue with an expert, y'see, and it's quite clear that you know more about taking it up the arse than anyone in the room. Probably anyone in the town, come to that, from the number of times you've pawed that poor bugger. Like feeling men, do you?" Skuli guffawed, but the Scraeling felt Osmund tense beside him.

"Well by Christ, you've got a mouth on you!" said the other. "What if I just shove my fist in it, smartarse?"

"There you go, giving yourself away again" said the Scraeling, relaxed and calm with arms folded one inside the other before him on the table. "I'm a smart *arse*, and you're talking about shoving bits of yourself in holes. Yes friend, I think you've got a problem there. Let's not turn our backs on *him*, eh Skuli?"

"Fuck you, I'll give you a problem all right!" snarled a thoroughly enraged landlord as the other patrons erupted in laughter and he started forward, enormous hands open to grab the cloaked figure before him. But Skuli slid smoothly to his feet in between the landlord and his quarry; his forehead jerked forward in a travel of perhaps six inches to smash into the bridge of the landlord's nose with a crack that echoed through the room and with a power that sent the man staggering backwards over an empty table.

For a moment everyone in the room froze, then with a roar one of the landlord's cronies charged at Skuli. Two steps into the charge, though, he met Osmund's shoulder driving in at waist-height hard enough to shock the breath from his body and send him backwards to the floor, where one steely forearm slammed across his throat for the second of consciousness left to him before his skull was caught between the floorboards and what felt like Thor's hammer.

The Scraeling shot to his feet like an uncoiling spring, someone screamed and Osmund looked up from the floor to see, standing over him, a man frozen in the act of swinging a three-legged stool; frozen by the throwing-knife that transfixed his forearm just above the elbow. Then two things happened very quickly; the landlord struggled to his feet spraying blood from a smashed nose, and Skuli backhanded him without so much as a glance in his direction.

Whereupon the landlord crashed backwards, just as his last henchman cast a fearful glance at the menacing tableau turning to seek him and decided that his future lay elsewhere. His first blind step towards the door took his crotch straight into a long-armed and well-aimed punch from the floor, and as he doubled up in agony the Dane staggered to his feet, seized him by the hair and slammed a knee into the man's face to send him backwards to the floor in a senseless heap.

"Allus stay on ya feet 'f ya can, Osmund" said Skuli, who hadn't moved. "Much safer, 'cause – *Fuck you, shit-for-brains! Stay there, y'hear me?? –* "

this to the landlord who had stumbled to his feet in time to be felled yet again by another backhand sweep from an arm that had all the flexibility of *Nordvedr*'s snarling stem-post.

The Dane moved forward, between the patrons frozen fast in their seats, past the man the Scraeling had nailed, past a Skuli still lecturing Osmund on his shortcomings as a tavern brawler, and crouched over the landlord.

"Fuck me" he said thickly, "Y'r nose's all over the place! Here, let me . . ."; his hand moved to the middle of the landlord's face and he twisted, hard. There was an agonised scream from the landlord, who fainted, and a now-sober Dane turned and straightened, grinning and wiping his hand on his breeches.

"Thanks friend" he said, holding out his hand to Skuli, who took it.

"No bother" said Skuli, "but all down to the boss here" he said, nodding at the Scraeling. "Watch him, though. He's dangerous." He glanced round at the other patrons, none of whom had moved, and raised his voice. "Anyone else?"

Again no-one moved, and the Scraeling stepped forward to the man who crouched, rocking and whimpering, over his arm. "Finished with my knife?" he asked. "Just ease it out – mind the edge. And if you get blood on my clothes and you're lucky, I'll kick your arse. If you get blood on my clothes and you're not lucky, I'll kick your arse *and* twist your arm. So ease it out, yes? That's it . . . fine . . . well done. But *wipe* it, you dirty bugger!"

He looked at Skuli and Osmund. "Had enough?" and they nodded. The Scraeling looked at the Dane, who was probing inside his mouth with a finger. "Want to come?"

The Dane grunted and spat out a tooth. "Might's well" he said. "Table service's gone off anyway, hasn't it?"

The Chronicle.

*T*hat brought Haakon to us. He had been a hird – or in English and Norse a hus-carl – to a Danish jarl who had died of the sweating-sickness the previous year, freeing him of his oath just at the time when, by his own admission, he had been bored anyway with Svein's lack of ambition.

"No work for a soldier" he'd said. "Nothing since Svein let the Bastard pay him t'fuck off out of England two an' a bit seasons ago. And not like to be any

more, either, seeing he's top dog in the north now. Even that weedy little prick in Norway's gone now, an' his mealy-mouthed brother's king."

That had jolted me. Magnus dead – aye, it was no surprise in itself, but for a fleeting moment the thought of what might have been flashed through my mind. Would that he'd gone earlier; say at about twelve, I thought bitterly. So Olaf was king? Olaf, whom I'd propped up after Stamford Bridge and nursed homeward from Riccall. Olaf, who wouldn't have viewed Elisabeth as a 'state asset'. Well. No point in that now.

As we made our run down the Narrow Seas and round the shoulder of Iberia – a run often enough interrupted by the need to seek refuge from the winter weather in ports, villages and even coves – I thought just as often on Haakon's appearance in a Flemish tavern in time to be both an end and a beginning for Osmund and me, for that is what he was. He closed a door on my life and opened another immediately in the guileless manner he had, and the same door was wide enough to accommodate Osmund also.

Not that I could see it at the time the first door closed, for then its closing seemed to write a finish to all that I'd held dear in life. Haakon told me, almost in passing, that my beloved Elisabeth was dead.

Portimao, Portugal, February 1072.

"How?" asked a voice that the Scraeling only just recognised as his.

"Sweating sickness" came back the big Dane. "Went through Kobenhavn quick as blink, oh, two years back. Hundreds got it; others didn't. 'Bout half who got it died of it, like my *jarl* did last year, and the court got it same's anyone else."

"And the queen?"

"She got it. Told you that." Haakon peered at the Scraeling in the dim light of the tavern. "You all right? You know her?"

"Met her. Years back. When she was married to Hardraada" and the Scraeling was glad that the tavern owner's tightfistedness had led him to delay the lighting of the tapers until later in the cold grey day.

"'S right, I'd forgotten you were mixed up with him" nodded the Dane. "Well. Sorry t'be the one who told you, an' I'm sorry for her too. She was a real lady, an' she was real good to the ordinary folk. They loved her, an' they loved the little boy too."

"The little boy? She ... and Svein ... had children then?"

"Just the one, Scraeling, and double-quick too. Old Svein don't waste time an' he did the business on his wedding night. Aye, married November and held his son up to the council July after. Little bugger couldn't wait to get into the world, could he? I know – my *jarl* was part of the household and I've walked more rounds of that fucking palace than anyone I know. Oh, I spoke to her hundreds'f times, 'cause she never passed you without a word."

"The boy died too, then?"

"Eh? Oh no. Soon's she felt ill, the queen put the boy from her. Had her chief lady – Russian woman, the name's gone, but she had an arse that would've just fitted these – " he leered, holding up his hands, " – had her take the prince away an' dared her t'bring him back before the physicians had her out of bed for a week. An' of course, she never got out of that bed again. Real sad day, that. Aye, she was a lady all right."

"How'd you know all this?" asked the Scraeling mechanically and Haakon sipped, belched, and shifted his weight to fart.

"Ooohh, that's better" he said, then winked. "One of the maids of the queen's bedchamber ... sometimes she spent a bit of time in, ah, other bedchambers. Like, mine!"

The Scraeling raised his cup in a wordless salute. "I knew Svein too. Fact is, I met him when Hardraada got fed-up trying to kill him and sent me to talk peace with him."

It was the Dane's turn to raise his cup. "Well, bugger my boots" he said. "Fancy me supping with the high an' mighty!"

"You wouldn't have known it" said the Scraeling. "There's nothing high or mighty about me, and anyone'd have taken Svein for a merchant rather than a king. But I liked him. Talked sense, no fancy airs, just wanted Hardraada to leave Denmark alone – that sort of thing. Man who'd rather pour you a cup than do you an injury."

"Bit before my time" said Haakon, and belched again. "But I c'n believe it, from what I know 'f him. He's a good father, too. Loves little Kristian."

"Who – oh, the boy" said the Scraeling. "That what they called him?"

"The queen always called him Kristian – very devout, she was, see? But he was christened, ah, lemme see ... aye, Randulfr Denis Kristian Sveinsson of the House of Estrith" said Haakon, and because he looked away at that moment to signal the potman he missed the Scraeling's stiffening in shock.

The Chronicle.

*T*here it was – the last message my Elisabeth could send me, and she couldn't have written it more plainly in letters of fire. She had had her "little de Lannion" after all, aye. Clever as she was, she knew that only one other in the world would hear the name and understand, for only two people in our world knew my full name. Leo de Lannion made a third, now, but it wasn't likely that his acquaintance would ever extend to the crown prince of Denmark.

What would I have done with that news if I'd received it in Flanders instead of Portugal? Would I have sailed for Denmark to catch a glimpse of our son? I thought not, and none of my thinking after altered that one jot. No, the past was a closed door and, for all that my son was and all that he would one day be, it was proper that it remained so.

But I made some excuse to Haakon that day and slipped away to spend a long while on my knees in offering prayer for Randulfr Denis Kristian Sveinsson of the House of Estrith. And I requested of the priest in that place that he add his prayers to mine for a young boy's future and for the soul of his mother, Elisabeth, and I supported the request with an offering that caused his jaw to drop in astonishment.

That was the door that Haakon had closed, although of course he never knew that. But as I've said, he opened another for Osmund and me, and it was this. Haakon had determined to go and seek his future in the service of the Eastern Emperor, and in the days after our meeting my thoughts had returned again and again to doing the same thing. Why not? What other was there for Osmund and me, with Scandinavia, England, and France closed to us?

Only what I'd promised him on a night in the Ely marsh. To find a world that would take 'the Scraeling and Penda's brat.' And we did.

***

Author Notes

It's tempting to speculate on just why an embattled Duke of Normandy whose Breton and French neighbours obliged a near-perpetual defence of his frontiers should take on the invasion of an offshore island such as Britain.

Principle played a part in it, and William was enough of a feudal monarch to deprecate oath-breaking. But inasmuch as the circumstances of Harold's alleged oath of homage cast no favourable light on William either[8], there seems to be need for other explanations also, and one of them surely lies in the Conqueror's notable cupidity. Put simply, he was greedy. He was also single-minded, brave, forthright and determined, and those qualities surely form the matrix for the Norman Conquest, arguably one of the moments when the world turned.

The battle of Hastings, or 'Senlac' to the Saxons, was a defining moment in all sorts of ways. In one day's fighting most of the leaders of Anglo-Saxon society vanished, leaving an administrative and political vacuum available for William to fill, but the opportunity brought challenge with it.

In the first place England was a land of well over a million people while the occupying Normans numbered no more than eight thousand initially, so that holding England by force was an unlikely solution. Next, William's continental holdings – separated from his hard-won kingdom by a stretch of water that was frequently tricky and always unpredictable – were the initial source of his power and as such they demanded his ongoing attention. Together, these problems shaped his solution.

The Saxon casualty-list at Hastings simplified things considerably. At one stroke, William inherited all English land, and from then on all land was held 'of the king', to be disposed of as, where and when he saw fit but

---

8 *Refer to 'The Landwaster' for this.*

usually in return for service of various kinds. Principally this was military service and the earliest such rewards went to those who had participated in the invasion, at the expense of the Saxons who had fought or fallen at Hastings.

Even after the post-Hastings period, however, the absolute nature of the king's control over land was underlined by the manner in which Saxon widows and daughters were forced into marriage to 'approved' Norman husbands, a practice that effectively Normanised the aristocracy as well as forcing closer union between conquerors and conquered. The revolts that such high-handed treatment inevitably produced were themselves useful in extending Norman control, for their suppression led to the landscape becoming dotted with fortifications that only grew in size, power, and complexity.

We should not wonder, then, at the speed with which English resistance collapsed. In part this was another outcome of the fearful toll of Saxon leadership taken by Hastings, because 1068 and 1069 saw the traditional English militia, or *fyrds*, of the West Country turning out under Norman leadership to repel the raids made there by the sons of Harold Godwinsson. Yet another indicator of the reality of a Norman presence supported by sound administrative, military and political structures is that, after only six years, Norman control was such that William felt able to spend more than three-quarters of his time and energies in Normandy, where they were certainly in demand.

The experiences of Gytha Pendasson and Frithuswith Aelfricsson, then, were typical of widows and heiresses in the post-Conquest period, while Garth's view of Ivo de Bois may also be seen as realistic. Controversy remains over the extent to which the activities of Hereward 'the Wake' were motivated by ideology, but the lack of any stake in pre-Conquest England for Hereward surely points to his motives as nothing more than local brigandage inspired, initially, by the wrongs done to him and his. The fact that he was eventually reconciled to William also indicates that the degree of offence his activities gave the new king of England wasn't insurmountable.

Just as the Scraeling told Osmund. . . . . . .

Chronicles of The Scraeling.

The First

The Landwaster
Russia, the Eastern Empire, Norway and England 1031–1066.

The central character and narrator of 'Chronicles of The Scraeling' is the crippled Ranulf de Lannion, whom we meet as a fifteen-year-old.

When a band of Viking pirates bursts from the sea to fall on an isolated Breton convent in 1031, they get more than the provisions and rape on which they're bent. When they leave, the leader's whim includes the ward of the convent, a crippled teenager of noble birth put aside there to prepare for the priesthood by a family ashamed of his handicap.

Alone in a totally alien world, the boy derisively nicknamed 'The Scraeling' survives by becoming indispensable to the band through putting his intellect, his learning and his organisational skills at the disposal of its ruthless leader, whom the eleventh century will come to know as Harald Hardraada. So well does he serve them throughout their mercenary adventures in Russia and Constantinople that the fearsome Hardraada himself pronounces the adult Scraeling 'the most dangerous little bugger alive.'

But Hardraada is ignorant of the truth of his own words, for beneath the mask The Scraeling harbours a secret and dark purpose – the destruction of the Viking scourge that ruined his world. He sets about it with a relentless determination that shocks even those in whom he confides, building steadily towards the 'one shot, one chance' opportunity that will, in the end, present itself to a marksmanship nursed and honed for over thirty years.

The Scraeling has a knack of either being at the centre of great events or of creating them, and his influence on the turning-points of the eleventh century is profound. At the same time, and perhaps because of his origins as one of life's underdogs, he has an empathy for women in an age that saw them merely as chattels and pawns, and the women in the stories are strong and striking characters. Even the most vulnerable of them display heroism, and that only continues through Breton nuns, high-born Byzantine ladies, Saxon heiresses and widows, and one truly memorable Russian princess.

The Second

The Scraeling
Norway and England, 1066–1072.

The story opens on the morning after the Battle of Hastings and moves between the Conqueror's struggles to consolidate his rule over post-Conquest England and a Norway where The Scraeling, now first minister to Hardraada's son and successor, Magnus, is contemplating the happy situation of becoming husband to Elisabeth of Kiev, Hardraada's ex-wife, while he steers Norway down the path of peace and co-operation with the other North European nations.

None of this happens and, his dreams dashed by political expediency, The Scraeling journeys to England to pick up the pieces of a previous life. Here, he finds a relative widowed at Hastings discovering her own suffering through political expediency in being married off to one of William's divisional commanders; which is the Conqueror's settlement policy in action.

This brings him into contact with the Norman army of occupation in general and the Fenland Rebellion of Hereward the Wake in particular. In true Scraeling style, his efforts and cunning eventually orchestrate an end to the rebellion in 1071 that results in a 'win-win' situation for everyone except himself, unfortunately, and he turns the prow of his longship towards sanctuary in Constantinople, the only bolt-hole left to him and his ward, Osmund, a refugee from Norman justice.

As with 'The Landwaster', most of the characters of the story actually lived and behaved much as suggested. The story focuses on people on both sides of the Conqueror's policy of holding England down by intermarriage rather than military might, and of what that meant in practical and everyday terms for both conquerors and conquered. To that end the people in it, and two very strong women in particular, assume pride of place over great events.

However, the Fenland Rebellion is seen against the background of the relatively short-lived English resistance to the Norman Conquest and both events represent no less than the truth, as the few historians of the immediate post-Conquest years hold it to be, about a little-explored period of English history.

The Third

The Varanger
The Eastern Empire, 1072 – 1075

Fleeing Norman retribution after the collapse of the Fenland Rebellion, The Scraeling and his group of '*the last, weary, raggy-arsed end of Hardraada's day*' take military service in a Constantinople where the ruling House of Doukas is tottering in the aftermath of the crucial battle of Manzikert and the emperor, Michael VII, would rather be a scholar.

Sick of the dirty tricks and expedience associated with high politics, The Scraeling seeks only a quiet life while he tries to advance Osmund's career in the armies of Constantinople. However, events won't leave him alone because one or two surprises from his youthful sojourn in that city with the Landwaster, Hardraada, turn up to complicate things. These surprises answer one or two of the questions that perceptive readers of 'The Landwaster' may have wondered about, and some of the answers are definitely, definitely . . . surprising.

Entering the covert service of the royal family, The Scraeling manages to foil an attempted *coup d'état* and deal with the machinations of a first minister and eunuch with aspirations beyond his station; a ruling family riven by faction, and an over-protective mother who's also Dowager Empress. All while staying one step ahead of the reader, plot-wise.

While this is going on, Osmund (who is 'The Varanger' of the title) forges on with his military career; in the process winning hearts, minds, promotion and some fairly desperate battles.

The Scraeling's disenchantment with high politics and affairs of state form the book's theme, but in the end he comes to accept the inevitability of dirty hands to the political process – particularly when philosophy and principle run up against personal emotion and intellectual detachment becomes impossible.

As the realist that The Scraeling's life and career have taught him to be, an ageing and gentler Ranulf de Lannion – *"the most dangerous little bugger alive"* remember? – looks, at last, for a contented and peaceful retirement and, with all the loose ends tied up and everyone happy, the ending of the book sees him about to embark upon it. Well, perhaps. . . .

To my readers:
Thank you for reading "The Scraeling". If you enjoyed it you may find the following excerpts from 'The Varanger' of interest also.

MJ Burr
info@cliowrite.com

The Varanger

Constantinople, 1080.

When I began the task of writing my own life story I had little idea that it would take so long. Not that it matters, because time is something I now have in abundance, even if time were not already endless where I sit, high above the ancient waterway.

No. My concern is less for my own time than that of my reader, for only the writing of my English adventure brought me to realise the length of my stay in England after The Bastard's conquest in the year of Penda's death, fourteen years ago. Not that my involvement with his new kingdom worried Willam of Normandy unduly, of course, for while there I had no part in great matters of the sort I had been accustomed to directing for Hardraada the Landwaster.

In fact, one of the greatest lessons taught me by a life passed in both high and low stations is that the aspirations of ordinary folk are held to be of little account when set against the desires and ambitions of their rulers. As example, just as Elisabeth was lost to me to satisfy the ambitions of one king, so was Gytha Raedwaldsson lost to her son Osmund and to the memory of her husband, Penda, to satisfy the ambitions of another. Aye, bitterness comes easily to those bereaved at a whim.

However, and as I have written elsewhere, it is true that what does not kill us makes us strong. I have known much adversity in my life and, while I do not seek to boast of that, I must acknowledge how it made me fit to play what part I have in great matters. As I have also written elsewhere, my sojourn among Hardraada's pagans that began with the night of fire and ruin ended a lifetime later in my triumph over him and all his kind as I brought the world of the viking crashing down. And again, from the ashes of my life in Norway came the joy I soon after discovered in England, in seeing how my cousin and sword-brother Penda lived again in his son Osmund, and during our long flight down the north wind to Constantinople I discovered that my union with golden Elisabeth had given me a son as precious as his mother.

It shows the truth of the story I once heard in a tavern in Nidaros when I rode high in Hardraada's favour, and if you, my reader, find it surprising that a minister of the crown would frequent such a place, let me say now that any too proud to do so is dangerously ignorant of that pulse of the common man which ought surely to be the first concern of government.

However. The story concerned a bird of the north who enjoyed to the full the last days of an uncommon long summer, even after his fellows began their flight to the south for the winter. Seeing no reason to cut short his pleasure, the bird dallied long past the normal time of departure until the cold winds persuaded him to take to the air.

There, though, he quickly discovered that flying alone was taxing and the strong, cold winds soon sapped his strength so that, one day, he fell from the sky and into a farmyard. As he lay, completely spent, on the ground a kindly horse wandered over to him and sniffed at him gently before releasing a stream of warm, liquid manure over him. Warmed by the life-giving gift, the bird regained his feet and began to celebrate his good fortune by singing loudly. Loudly enough to attract the attention of the farm cat, who pounced from the corner of a building and made a meal of him.

And the moral of the story, I heard the teller say, was threefold. First, it's always later than you think and things are always worse than you think. Second, not everyone who shits on you means you harm. Third, when you've had a lucky escape, sometimes it pays to accept the lesson with humility, and reflect on what it can teach you, rather than boasting of it.

Adversity, then, can teach us much. By the time Nordvedr's dragon-prow first snarled into the warm waters of the Eastern Empire I had made up my mind that, bereft of my love and our son, the only duty I had in this world was to my cousin's son and his advancement in the emperor's service. Nothing else would touch me; nothing else would move me. In a world where every man put himself first, I would put Osmund first in all things.

To that end, then, and mindful of the bird, I took care to keep my head down and my mouth shut.

But the cat pounced, anyway.

Welcome back, Scraeling—

So how's Constantinople thirty years after the Landwaster? . . . . .

They hadn't, he said, had a real emperor since Zoe the Macedonian, bless her memory. But then, she'd been kin to Basil the Bulgar-Slayer. Not that they'd mean anything to me, of course.

I nodded, trying to look as if I'd never heard of either, but in my mind I saw the beautiful, doll-like figure with the ice-cold eyes in a face of stone as she told Hardraada and me how we might kill her husband nearly forty years before. Aye, Zoe was a real emperor by anyone's standards.

Zoe . . . Maniakes . . . John the Eunuch . . . Isaac Comnenos . . . and Kia. Black-eyed Kia, my first woman, and a skilled, practised and enthusiastic harlot she was too. Did I want to return to all that?

"Look" Hardraada had once said to me in speaking of the City and the people who ruled it, "for a dozen years you lived among the most devious, cunning, two-faced, scheming and evil buggers that your God or mine ever put on the face of the earth."

It seemed that little had changed.

Well, there's politics . . .

"I'm offering you the position of being the power behind the imperial throne, Ranulf. Will you be the emperor's Scraeling, as you were Hardraada's Scraeling?"

"Not in a hundred years" he said. "Or a thousand. I did that for two kings of Norway, and turned down the king of Denmark. Why? Because politics, government, kingship , to settle our – call it what you like – is the same dirty game the world over, and I want no further part of it or in it."

Leading to mayhem . . .

"Haakon!" he screamed, and from beside him came "Here!"

"Get them out! Out! All who can stand!" And Osmund raised his voice in the song of the ravens. It was picked up instantly, on either side, and in a dozen heartbeats the line of axemen had ploughed forward to reach and pass the survivors of Nampites' Varangers, and there they held for long moments as the Valach recoiled before the fury of the axes and the chanting giants who wielded them, until a ten-yard gap opened and *Come on, Haakon, come on!* dinned in his brain while he tried to swallow and couldn't . . .

Of various sorts . . .

Osmund wrinkled his brows. "Ah . . . Sinope wasn't it? We were going there to stop the Turks capturing it? Yes?"

"Yes" said the Scraeling. "And Sinope's a city."

"And cities've got walls" said Haakon slowly. "Right?"

"Right" prompted the Scraeling. "So . . ?"

"So if y're going to capture a city with walls, aye, y'need a siege train. That what they're called?"

"They are" said the Scraeling, "and I'd put my best bit of amber on a siege machine being brought up here about now. One'll do, I think, to settle us."

"Freya's shiny nipples" said Skuli reflectively, "that's cunning. One of them'll piss in our porridge-pot all right. . ."

And any amount of dirty work at the crossroads . . .

The great book lay open on the table, but the eunuch had seen all he wanted to see of it. There it was – the final piece of the puzzle, buried in the *History of the Reign of Empress Zoe, called the Macedonian*. They were all there, but most of all, the one designated secretary, Ranulf de Lannion.

The eunuch had identified his quarry, and he raised the onyx goblet higher so that the big whorl in its side struck fire from the sun. "Bright little bastard, aren't you?" he asked aloud but he wasn't addressing the goblet. He opened his hand and the goblet shattered on the tiled floor. "Not now you aren't. That's how quickly bright little bastards can take a fall."

. . . . end of sample.